UZMA ASLAM KHAN grew up in Karachi, Pakistan. She is the author of one previous novel, *The Story of Noble Rot*. She has taught English language and literature in the US, Morocco and Pakistan, and now lives in Lahore with her husband, author David Maine. *Trespassing* has been published around the world and been translated into several languages.

From the reviews of *Trespassing*

'Against a solidly researched background of Pakistan's turbulent political climate in the 1980s and 1990s, Khan creates a story of cultural and ethnic conflict in spare and elegant prose that resonates beyond its immediate setting'   *Observer*

'A tender book, distinguished by subtle descriptions of nature. It is a celebration of the importance of perception, inquisitiveness about the smaller details of life, but Khan does not shy away from the bigger picture. Writing intelligently, she explores colonialism, identity and belief, without presuming to offer any conclusions or solutions. Khan works with questions; hints and queries replace absolutes'   *New Statesman*

'A narrative as intricately patterned and vivid as lengths of top-quality silk ... This image of doomed love and a violent society is original, emotional and inevitably sad'
                    Sunday Telegraph

'Uzma Aslam Khan gives us a Karachi of heat, humidity and perpetual noise ... The book moves skilfully between private agonies and the big dirty politics of the region ... Khan's picture of her home town is detailed, generous and committed'
                    Time Out

By the same author

The Story of Noble Rot

TRESPASSING

Uzma Aslam Khan

HARPER PERENNIAL

Harper Perennial
An imprint of HarperCollins*Publishers*
77–85 Fulham Palace Road
Hammersmith
London W6 8JB

www.harpercollins.co.uk/harperperennial

This edition published by Harper Perennial 2004

1

First published by Flamingo 2003

A catalogue record for this book is
available from the British Library

ISBN 0 00 715278 7

Set in Sabon by Palimpsest Book Production Limited,
Polmont, Stirlingshire

Printed and bound in Great Britain by
Clays Ltd, St Ives plc

Contents

v

DIA

SALAAMAT

DAANISH

DIA

Part Two

SALAAMAT

ANU

DIA

DAANISH

SALAAMAT

RIFFAT

DIA

for Dave

'To look is an act of choice.'

JOHN BERGER

TRESPASSING

PROLOGUE

Death

The fishing boats dock before the dawn, while the turtle digs her nest. She watches with one eye seaward, the other on the many huts dotting the shore. The nearest is just thirty feet away. She burrows fiercely, kicking up telltale showers of sand, recalling how much safer it had been when the coastline belonged to the fishermen. Now the boats sail in like giant moths, and though she wonders at their catch, it is for the visitors from the city, hidden in their huts, that her brow has creased beyond her age.

She is ready. The first egg plops softly in the hollow beneath her womb, and the rest follow, unstoppable now. The fishing nets glisten in the moonlight with small fry. How long before she dips into the waters again?

A boy, not yet fifteen, lights a K2 and leans back into the ridge of a dune. Long locks tumble over his shoulders and flare in the wind. Between puffs, he kisses the end of the cigarette, so content is he. The turtle watches him watch her when most defenseless. But she knows him; all the turtles do.

I

Her eggs are smooth and oval, like a naked woman's shoulders. The boy caresses his cheek, wanting really to caress the eggs, wanting really to caress the shoulders.

His locks billow and his mood is suddenly ruffled by thoughts of his father and uncles, who did not go out tonight. They say the foreign trawlers have stolen their sea. They trespass. Fish once abundant close to shore are now disappearing even in the deep. And the fishermen's boats cannot go out that far, even for the fish still left to catch. An uncle tried. It was he who was eaten. His family mourns the brave man's drowning, and his father's decision to break with tradition. They will move to the city. The boy will go first. But he is afraid, as afraid as the turtle is, of the men in the huts.

He pulls on his cigarette and wonders at the turtle. She meets his gaze with the soothing, crackly wisdom of his grandmother. He shuts his eyes and drifts into soft sleep.

Then he jolts awake: voices. Glancing quickly at the reptile, he sees her still giving birth. But dawn is tinged with foreboding. The shadow of a man stretches upon the dune beside him and creeps forward. The boy ducks. Squinting toward the huts, he sees a woman, naked below the knees, waiting. The intruder walks into view, stumbles and farts. He will not even rob the turtle gently. The boy bristles with anger, wondering what to do. He decides quickly. If the man takes a single egg, he will take the woman.

A shaggy arm crooks toward the nest, and waits, ripe fingers nearly scraping the reptile's orifice for a gift. The boy dashes. The woman screams. Others emerge from the hut's interior. The intruder hurtles back. The egg drops safely into the sand a fraction of a second after he is gone.

Their first kick dislodges a knee. Long hair is a hindrance, he thinks, as they use it to drag him over the line of rocks circling the hut's porch. *If I live I'll never wear it below the chin again.* There is salt in his mouth. Salt and gravel. His blood and his teeth. He swoons, but instead of their blows,

2

he hears shells split. Thud! Crack! The men are pelting him with the eggs.

A moan rises from the pit of his groin, up to an empty cavity below his chest, shrugging its way higher, out of his nose, his ears, and mouth. He vomits oyster-white albumen and curdled vitellus, bloodied placenta, and something green. Liver?

Though blind with pain, it is he alone who sees the mound of the mother meandering silently back home.

Part One

DIA

I

Detour

MAY 1992

Dia sat in the mulberry tree her father had sheltered in the night before his death. A large man, he'd been limber too. Squatting had come easy. The crowd below had included journalists, neighbors and police. They'd asked if it were true: was he getting death threats?

Her father weighed ninety kilos and hunkered like a gentle ape, shuffling about in the foliage, appraising his audience with two small brown eyes that flashed like rockets. Every few minutes, he mustered up enough nerve to shake some berries. When they struck a particularly distasteful newsman or auntie, he slapped a knee with glee. Then he wept unabashedly.

The tree had been planted the day Dia was born. Her father had said the sweet, dainty, purplish-red fruit was like his precious daughter when she slid howling into the world. So when he tossed the berries at the throng, Dia, watching from inside the house, knew he was calling her. But her mother insisted she stay inside.

'He's gone mad,' she whispered, clutching Dia. 'I shouldn't have told him.'

Told him what? Dia wondered.

Today, up in the tree, a book of fables pressed heavily in her lap. The weight was partly psychological. She should have been studying. She'd failed an exam and ought to be preparing for the retake. Instead she flipped through the book's pages, where lay miscellaneous clippings about history and bugs. She found a page ripped from a Gymkhana library book and read it aloud:

'Silk was discovered in China more than four thousand years ago, purely by accident. For many months Emperor Huang-ti had noticed the mulberry bushes in his luscious garden steadily losing their leaves. His bride, Hsi-Ling-Shih, was asked to investigate. She noticed little insects crawling about the bushes, and found several small, white pellets. Taking a pellet with her to the palace, with nothing but instinct she ventured on the best place to put it: in a tub of boiling water. Almost at once, a mesh of curious fine thread separated itself from the soft ball. The Empress gently pulled the thread. It was half a mile long. She wove it into a royal robe for her husband, the first silk item in history. Since then, sericulture has remained a woman's job, in particular, an empress'.'

Dia tucked the stolen page back into her book. The best episodes from history were of discovery. She liked to slow the clock at the moment before the Empress thought to drop the cocoon into the water – just before she metamorphosed into a pioneer. What had moved her not to simply crush the little menaces, as most people disposed of pests today? How relaxed and curious her intellect had been, and how liberally she'd been rewarded!

The setting fired Dia's imagination too. It would be an arbor at the top of a hillock, with plenty of sunlight, a long stone table, basins, and attendants ready with towels and disinfectants. When they'd made a circle around the Empress, Dia commanded the minute hand to shift. The Empress dropped a cocoon into the water.

It shriveled and expelled its last breath: a tangle of filament the Empress hastened to twist around her arm like candy-floss on a stick. The attendants gawked. Their mistress was sweating. The wind was soft. The sun snagged in the strand, a blinding prism growing on the arm of the Empress, as if she spun sunlight. When the sun went down she'd cooked all the cocoons from the imperial garden. Miles of thread hung in coils around both her arms. The attendants dabbed at her brow and helped her down the hill, back to the palace. The Emperor called for her all night. But she couldn't sleep beside him with arms encased so. The maids burned oil lamps, dias, and she sat up alone, occasionally looking out at the moon and down at the mulberry trees, making a robe for her husband that by morning would reflect the rays of the sun, and by next evening, the moon.

Dia smiled contentedly. Now she'd play What If, and retell the story.

If, for instance, the Empress Hsi-Ling-Shih had suspected how her discovery would shape the destiny of others, would she instead have tossed away the threads, never to speak of them again? If she'd known that a thousand years later, several dozen Persians would pay with their lives for trying to smuggle silkworms out of China, would she have made that robe? If she hadn't, perhaps one of the many innocent daughters of those murdered men might have one day stood the chance of discovering something else.

Would the Empress have squashed the caterpillars if she'd known what would happen twenty-five hundred years after her find? If so, the Sicilians who'd been trying to make silk from spider webs wouldn't have kidnapped and tortured

their neighbors, the Greek weavers, to elicit their knowledge. Instead, the Greek weavers might have lived to a
ripe old age, and one of them would perhaps have borne a
great-great-grandchild capable of unraveling . . . the mystery
of Dia's father's death?

Or, what if the Empress had seen even further into the
future? Seven hundred years after the agony of the Greeks,
history repeated itself. Now it was the Bengali and Benarsi
weavers who suffered. If she'd known how the British would
chop off the nimble thumbs that made a resham so fine it
could slip through an ear-hole, perhaps the Empress would
have trampled over the maggots. Then the subjugated nation's
exchequer would not have been exhausted importing third-
rate British silk.

If all that wouldn't have stopped her, then would the death
of Dia's father?

Dia stopped the clock and reconstructed the scene.

His mangled body drifted down the Indus, past one coastal
village after another. The villagers had seen too much destruction to care about yet another corpse. They stood with sticks
pressed into the muddy banks and stared in silence. Finally,
after four days, word reached a coroner. Mr Mansoor's
bullet-ridden remains were heaved out of the river like sodden
fruit and the village psychic swore that for five hundred
rupees she could *wring* him back to life. She demanded
one toenail, a dot of his saliva, another dot of his sweat
and one of his seed. At the latter a few onlookers snickered. Dia recognized two reporters from the night her father
was up in the tree. She lunged for them, but was gently
ushered aside by the cook Inam Gul. But she'd already
seen the only part of her father left uncovered: his bloated
feet, themselves a blue and branching river. Inam Gul tried
to cover her ears but she heard the rumors: his kidneys
had been shot through with electric currents, his thumbs
snapped, arms sliced, and he'd been made to walk on spikes

and broken glass. Because of his weight, the barbed bed had cut through bone.

If four thousand years ago the Empress had never discovered silk, where would Dia be now?

The elders tried to teach her that Fate could be postponed – maybe by a year or several hundred, by his naughty sister Chance – but not altered. How one's destiny unfurled was not to be second-guessed. Perhaps it would take a longer story, with unexpected players, but eventually, it followed the course that it was meant to take.

Eventually. The timing nagged. Who could tell actual time from postponed time? If all detours lead to a predetermined outcome, it hardly mattered, then, if one was early or late, if a meeting was held today or tomorrow, if a letter was couriered or the stamps pocketed. People talked of how the country was in a state of transition. Soon the dust would settle, and miraculously, the violence in Sindh that had claimed her father, among others, would vanish. But they couldn't say when, how, or who would bring about the course that was ordained. In fact, they liked to add, come to think of it, the dust hadn't settled anywhere – even the industrialized West had problems. In fact, it had *never* settled. What else had history shown? The river always flowed into the sea. Which branch entered first was irrelevant. Leave tomorrow, they advised, in God's hands.

Only her mother believed otherwise. She said the elders wanted to saturate the world in indifference, to wrap a bandage around it that would hold back all the things that could move the country forward. It was all a ploy to keep things working in their own favor. Take marriage, for instance. They wanted it to remain a union that suited them, not the couple. She told Dia the worst thing she could do was listen to that, and perhaps was the only mother in the country to repeatedly warn her to marry only out of love, not obligation.

*　*　*

With the book in hand, Dia made her way swiftly down the tree.

The garden exploded with the twittering of tufted bulbuls and squawking mynas. Jamun and fig trees were in bloom. She turned down a path that led to the pergola beyond which her family had taken tea every evening, barring rain. With one brother in London, and the other in love and computers, now only she and her mother were left to keep the tradition.

The thought of visiting the silkworm farm tomorrow lifted Dia's spirits. The caterpillars had begun spinning their cocoons. Though they were notoriously private when conducting their artistry, in previous years she'd learned an art of her own: stillness. She could freeze even in a room with humidity of over seventy per cent, with sweat dripping from her brows, and binoculars swiftly fogging up. She'd watch tomorrow.

But then Dia remembered a promise to a friend. Opening the kitchen door she stopped in mid-stride and cursed, 'Damn that Nini! Why am I so nice?'

The cook looked up. He hadn't covered the chapaatis to keep them warm. Dia scowled, wrapping the bread herself, while the cook pretended not to notice. 'Why am I so nice?' she repeated for his benefit.

Inam Gul shook his head in agreement, adding, 'Mahshallah, you are so very nice.' He was toothless, benevolent, and instantly forgiven.

'That stupid Nissrine wants me to accompany her to a Quran Khwani tomorrow. She's going just to look at the dead man's son. Says he's supposed to be good-looking and is studying in America. Can you imagine how shameless she's become?'

He commiserated, 'You're too nice.' A dribble of yogurt hung on his chin.

'Wipe your chin or Hassan will get angry – first you let his chapaatis get cold, then you finish all the yogurt.'

The cook licked away the evidence. 'I had just a teaspoon.'

His arthritic fingers stuck a point in the air, indicating the size of the spoon.

'That's the second lie you've told today. Since one was for me, I'll tell one for you too.'

Grinning, he opened the refrigerator and began scooping up the last of the elixir.

Dia continued, 'I'll go for exactly one hour. If Nini wants to stay longer, she's on her own. I can't believe it! If she has no respect for herself, at least she should respect the dead. What's she going to do, pick him up, with his father still warm in the grave?'

When the plastic yogurt pouch was empty, the cook chucked it in the wastebasket, hiding it deep among the waste. 'The dead will be watching.'

'Maybe you could send her away when she comes to get me. You know, say I've got diarrhea or something. She wouldn't want me embarrassing her by running to the toilet every few minutes.' The cook enjoyed that. 'Or maybe I should embarrass her?' He enjoyed that even more. His fingers caressed the air as he tried to picture it. Dia was inspired. 'Yes, that's what I should do. But how? What should I do? Help me think of something to mess up her plan.'

The cook licked his lips and thought seriously for a while. He scratched the white wisps of hair that puffed up around his head like down and hesitated, mumbling again, 'The dead will be watching.'

'Tomorrow, I promise, a lot more yogurt,' Dia urged.

He whispered the scheme in her ear.

DAANISH

I

Toward Karachi

At the time the cook plotted against him, Daanish awoke some thirty thousand feet above the Atlantic. Once sleep receded, he returned to his earlier occupation of churning over the same conundrum as Dia: the passage of time. Neither would ever know they churned simultaneously. He didn't know her. He could hardly say he knew himself, strung as he was atop a plump canopy of clouds that glittered red and gold, the sinking sun bobbing along beside. Below, hidden from view, tossed the ocean once before traversed, in the opposite direction. That had been three years ago.

Twenty-one hours earlier, he'd been boarding the Peter Pan bus from Amherst to New York City. Liam had seen him off. He'd said, 'Going home's jarring enough for me and mine's just a few hours away.'

Liam was not given to gloom and Daanish wished he'd bid a more reassuring goodbye. 'You sound like the angel of fucking death.'

This elicited an equine grin. 'I mean: going home means

facing you've changed. Listen to yourself. You never swore before coming here.'

'I did. You just didn't understand.' Daanish nudged him fondly and saluted farewell.

'Write if you can. Don't be a stranger.' Liam stepped back as Daanish mounted the bus. 'And,' he caught Daanish's eye, 'I'm really sorry, man.'

On the ride to Port Authority Liam's counsel wove in and out of the dogwood branches lining the interstate, the square suburban yards dotted with plastic bunnies and dwarves, the stores with names like Al Bum's and Pet Smart, the clockwork efficiency with which passengers embarked and disembarked. Don't be a stranger, said the disheveled porter who shuffled after him on to the frenzy of 42nd Street. Don't be a stranger, frowned the driver of the taxi Daanish flagged down halfway to Grand Central. Don't be a stranger, repeated the manhole covers bouncing under the weight of the fastest cars Daanish had ever seen: Mustang, Viper, BMW, Lexus. And when he finally reached his terminal at Kennedy Airport, the rows of angry travelers turned to him and gestured, Don't be a stranger. The flight is twelve hours delayed!

Khurram, the passenger assigned the seat next to his, returned from the toilet. He reeked of in-flight cologne and other treats. 'Luckily, not too bad,' he exclaimed, beaming. He was referring to their prior discussion of whether, nearly seven hours into the flight, the toilets would be tolerable. Normally, within the first hour, they became open gutters in the sky. The toilet vomited chunks of brown, yellow and red, with the flush serving only to chop up the chunks. Reams of toilet paper poured out of the waste disposal and twisted across the cabinets as if the passenger who sat on the toilet seat had suddenly discovered graffiti. Used diapers filled the sink. However, those who braved this torture could always be assured a generous supply of cologne.

'I think it's Givenchy,' Khurram continued happily, patting the fragrance deeper into his round cheeks.

He must have poured an entire bottle on himself, thought Daanish, feeling his chest contract. 'You mean you think it *was* Givenchy.'

In the aisle seat sat Khurram's small, self-contained mother, with feet neatly tucked under her kurta. The son, easily twice her girth, leaned across Daanish and pointed at the sun bleeding scarlet over the world. 'So beautiful,' he shook his head approvingly. 'You getting best view.'

Was this a hint? Should he offer to swap? And be wedged between a bursting rumen and piercing female eyes? Not a chance. He looked out the window and said, 'Somewhere in the world, the sun is just waking up.'

Khurram leaned further and raised a hand as if to exclaim, Wah! Just imagine!

Daanish was thinking that there were some people who rode the subway all day simply because they had nowhere to get off. He was beginning to enjoy the length of his journey. He was afraid of landing.

Had his father ever felt this way on one of his numerous voyages around the world? Had he dreaded returning to his wife and son? Did travel do that? Daanish couldn't say. He'd become a traveler only three years ago and then been grounded: classes, work-study, papers, girlfriends. Now he was jolted again. In eleven hours, he could have all that he'd left behind. No, not all. Not his father.

Down in Karachi, at this moment, was the Qul. Perhaps his father's spirit dwelled among the scarlet clouds, and would drift through this very plane. The inch-long plane bang in the middle of the Atlantic floating in the screen of the satellite monitor. Daanish was inside it too. He could wave to himself. He did.

Khurram looked up and grinned genially. He was happily consumed by a slew of fancy gadgets purchased in the land left behind: a discman, hand-held Nintendo, mobile phone, talking calculator. He warmly demonstrated the marvels of each invention. The talking calculator in particular amused him, so Daanish punched numbers and a deep voice announced them legato for all those too moronic to know any better: one-thou-sand-nine-hun-dred-and-nine-ty-two mi-nus one-thou-sand-nine-hun-dred-and-eigh-ty-nine e-quals three.

'Well,' smiled Daanish, 'I'm glad someone else can verify how many years I've been away.'

He was offered the discman and pocket disc album. Most of the CDs were country, a few pop, and one rap. He pictured Khurram first in cowboy gear, then gyrating with Madonna, then dissing mother-fuckers. He laughed. *Don't be a stranger.* Well, Khurram in costume was no stranger than American yuppies chanting Hare Krishna, or smacking the sitar like a percussion instrument. No stranger than Becky inviting him to a party because he made her look ethnic. 'My friends think it's about time an exotic face entered our circle,' she'd casually explained. No stranger than Heather and her girlfriends dancing around corn crops to beckon the earth-god, 'just like the American Indians did'. She was an atheist, she equated his religion with fanaticism, she could not explain the origins of the name of her home state, Massachusetts, but she really understood those Indians.

'Your choice?' he enquired of the Ice-T record.

'Oh no, my niece's. She said it is very good and I would like.' As a second thought, he added, 'My mother and I were visiting Bhai Jaan in Amreeka. He has a business. Very successful.'

'What business?' asked Daanish. But Khurram, lost in his toys, didn't answer.

The satellite monitor showed Daanish in a bean-pod gliding over the Bay of Biscay. He looked out the window but it was too dark so his full-grown self had to believe the miniature self.

His father had flown over this very shore nine years ago,

to attend a medical conference in Nantes, France. He'd spent his last hour there doing what he always did on a visit to any coast: combing the beach for Daanish's shell-collection. He'd not found much: a few painted tops, limpets and winkles. The real treasures came later, on his trips to the warmer Pacific. Some of those beauties were strung around Daanish's neck. He twirled them in a habitual gesture Nancy likened to a woman playing with her hair. The larger shells he'd left in Karachi. In about ten more hours, he could see them again. This filled him with more joy than the prospect of uniting with anything else at home, even Anu. Then it terrified him. He'd hold his shells in a house that no longer held his father and where he'd hold his mother for the first time since she'd become a widow. He feared she'd cling.

He tugged at the necklace. Khurram's mother, with a face as crumpled as a used paper bag, leaned across Khurram exclaiming that the shells made beautiful music. Daanish unclasped the necklace and offered it for her inspection. The woman's thin, serrated lips sucked and pouted while she fingered the shells as if they were prayer beads.

When she paused at a tusk-like one Daanish told her a story about a diver who'd been paralyzed by the sting of a glory-of-the-seas cone, shaped just like the orange cone she was rubbing. Seventy feet beneath the surface of the sea, he'd hovered in total darkness, knowing he could never kick his way back up to life. When the body was found the oxygen tank was completely empty. Daanish tried to imagine the terror of hanging in a frigid dark sea without air. As if watching myself diminish, he thought. As if the dying could actually see their fate: it could shrink into a two-inch cone in their hands. He shuddered, wondering what his father had seen in his last hour.

The woman was nodding sagely. Her fingers wrapped around each piece, the grooves of her flesh searching new grooves to slide along.

He offered her names. 'That one that looks cracked my father found in Japan. It's a slit shell. Those two dainty pink ones are precious wentletraps. They used to be so rare the Chinese would make counterfeits from rice paste and sell them for a fortune. But now the counterfeits have become rare.' Daanish had been given both the real and the false. He asked the woman to tell them apart.

She smiled but wouldn't play along. Daanish's names and histories mattered little to her. It was enough that the shells felt good and made beautiful music. After rubbing each one, she returned the necklace and abruptly asked, 'What do you do in Amreeka?'

'I study.'

'Are you going to be a doctor or engineer?'

'Um. I don't know.'

Her shrewd eyes darted across his face. Then she turned away, back to her silent place. Occasionally, she looked around the plane and boldly examined the others as if chairing a secret inquisition.

It would have served no purpose telling her he wanted to be a journalist. She'd question the profitability of his choice. He'd been questioning this himself. Like Pakistan, the US was not the place to study fair and free reporting. In the former, he risked having his bones broken. In the latter, his spirit.

But journalism intrigued him for the opposite reason his other passion, shell-collecting, did. One kept him in tune with his surroundings while the other demanded dissonance. One was beautiful on the outside while the other insisted he probe into the poisonous interior, like a diver. He'd tried to explain this to a father who'd grown increasingly unhappy with the choice. In one of their last discussions, Daanish retorted that the profession was in his blood.

His soft-spoken, introverted grandfather had been the co-founder of one of the first Muslim newspapers in India. The paper had played a major role in advocating the cause of the

Pakistan Movement, and been praised by the Quaid-i-Azam himself. Daanish was taught early that in British India, when it came to the written word, Muslims lagged far behind the Hindus and other communities. Prior to the 1930s, they didn't own even one daily newspaper. His grandfather had helped establish the first. As its maxim, it quoted a member of the All-India Muslim League: *To fight political battles without a newspaper is like going to war without weapons.* The paper sharpened its weapons. The British responded by banning it, imprisoning Daanish's grandfather, and leaving the rest to the Muslims themselves: the co-founder was shot dead by a fellow-Muslim in his office.

After Pakistan's birth, his grandfather was released and the family moved to the new homeland. But ten years later, for reproaching the country's first military coup, he was again imprisoned.

Decades later, in his last letter to him, Daanish's father wrote, 'Do you want to throw away the opportunity to educate yourself in the West by returning to the poverty of my roots? You will fight Americans, only to find you also have to fight your own people. This is not what your grandfather languished in jail for. He once warned me, "Only the blind replay history." Think.'

Daanish hadn't answered him. He hadn't explained that when it came to a Muslim press, it wasn't just the subcontinent that was impoverished. He had only to dig into the reporting on the Gulf War to know it was won with weapons that exploded not just on land but on paper. Yet few fought back.

Next to him, Khurram snored. His Nintendo showed a score of 312. The discman was turned off. Daanish considered borrowing it, maybe listening to Ice-T. *Freedom of Speech . . . Just Watch What You Say.* When he'd first heard those words he knew they must reach Professor Wayne. So he included them in a term paper. Wayne slashed out the citation in thick red lines and added *no pop references*. Daanish argued that the coverage on the war was at least as pop as a rap song. Later, foolishly, he wrote about it to his father. The doctor advised him to change to medicine or risk a life of regret.

They were entering Germany, journeying through a tunnel of shifting darkness, now black, now thin sepia. Frankfurt in twenty minutes. The ladies and gentlemen of the bean-pod were requested to kindly fasten their seatbelts and extinguish cigarettes.

'We're landing,' Daanish's companion awoke and beamed.

'Sleep well?' asked Daanish.

'Oh yes, I always do.'

The bean-pod slanted downward. Daanish's stomach lurched. The lights of Frankfurt danced outside his window. Mini-wheels grazed the runway. Lilliputian engines slowed, and then there was another announcement. Only those ladies and gentlemen holding American, Canadian, or European pass-ports could disembark for the duration of the stopover. Those naughty others might escape, so they must stay on board.

For the first time during the flight, Khurram appeared crestfallen. He was not naughty, wouldn't they believe him? No, explained Daanish. Khurram's mother looked away. She needed no explaining.

And then the bean-pod did a funny thing. It swung to face the direction from which it had just come. It nosed upward. It increased altitude. It sped back across the Atlantic at such speed the hair of the naughty passengers blew this way and that. The sky turned from sepia to gold. The sun bobbed alongside again. On arrival, the passengers brushed their hair into place, collected bags, and stumbled out on to a sunny college campus. Daanish consulted his watch: 4.35. He was late for work.

2

High Volume

'You're late,' barked Kurt, manager of Fully Food. He had a football-shaped head on a boxer's body gone soft, like Lee J. Cobb in *Twelve Angry Men*. To him his workers were Fully Fools.

'Hey Kurt,' Daanish muttered. 'I got held up.' He swiftly brushed by before Kurt could get started. 'Held up? This is a high-volume job.'

Daanish hung up his jacket, bound the knee-length apron, adjusted his cap, and entered the dish room. The kitchen reeked of sweat, bleach, stale greens, ranch dressing thrown in vinaigrette, cheese dumped in orange juice. Wang from China and Nancy from Puerto Rico said hi when he took his place at the sink but no one else bothered.

He started hosing down a copper pot that reached halfway down his thighs. Particles of ravioli sprayed his eyes and lips. The fare tonight was pasta and meatballs, mince pie, mashed potatoes and gravy, pan pizza, and the usual salad bar. Daanish learned each day's menu not to prep his palate

27

but to prep his muscles and olfactory nerves. Starch and gravy were the meanest to clean. The crust of that pan pizza would be a bitch. He chuckled at how readily he'd picked up such phrases, though barely two months had passed since his arrival. Turning off the hose, he started scraping off the glutinous residue of Reddi-Mash from the pot's interior with a knife. The smell made his stomach weep. He'd skip dinner again.

His mind replayed the day's events: woke at seven after a bad night (his roommate came home drunk at three in the morning again, and with his usual timely expertise, proceeded to vomit once inside the door); breakfast (tea and an English muffin) alone as usual; Wayne's class at nine; bio at eleven; lab at two. After work he'd go for a swim and march straight to Becky's. His family kept calling to ask, 'So, how is it?' What did they expect? What did he expect?

Nancy passed behind him with a stack of plates. She nearly slipped on the sodden floor but caught herself in time. '*Pendejo*,' she hissed. Then to Daanish, 'Better wear those rubber gloves, pretty boy, or your woman won't have you.'

He gave her a mischievous grin. 'She will.' Still, he briefly examined his bare hands. Steam and bleach were turning them to flakes of goose meat. Nancy slapped the gloves beside him. He slipped them on.

When the student diners finished their meal they piled the trays on a conveyor belt that rolled inside to Wang and Youssef. Wang, square-framed and sticky, emptied the contents of each plate into a massive trash can, whipping thick colors inside it. Youssef, a sleek Senegalese, scoured the silverware and glasses. Nancy piled the plates and carried them to Amrita from Nepal, who soaped and rinsed them. Ron, an African-American, loaded dollies. Vlade, Romanian, did too.

Daanish hadn't told Anu that his scholarship entailed spending twenty-five hours a week under Kurt. Let her think he was asked to do nothing but bend over books, to become a man of letters. Why confess he bent over sinks, scouring away letters – of alphabet soup? In Karachi, he'd only entered the kitchen to be fed. Becky teased that mommy spoiled him. She could talk. She sat outside in the dining hall, worrying about her waistline while daddy paid the bills.

Once, over the phone, Daanish had told his father about the job. The doctor had little to say. He'd given him advice once and only once on the drive to the Karachi airport, when seeing Daanish off. His warm smoker's voice asked his son to remember it. Then he added, 'Hold your head up high. Life is yours to build. One day you'll look back and laugh at the spaghetti in your hair.'

Daanish battled with the pizza tin. His back was to the others but he heard Ron swear. Turning, he saw Youssef struggle with several glasses drenched in blue cheese dressing dribbled generously with strawberry sauce and strewn with granola. In one of the glasses a napkin shaped like a wafer carried a message from the other side of the belt: *Eat me.*

'Sick mother-fuckers,' said Ron, sealing the trash and slinging it over his shoulder.

Kurt hovered over Amrita, his favorite prey. She was slow with the washing, especially when attempting not to be, but never missed a crumb. Kurt rested knobby knuckles on his hips and thundered: 'How did *I* get this far? By *working*. You think everybody gets the chance to work, Anna? You know how many people bang on our doors begging for this? This is a high-volume job. You're lucky to have it.'

She bit her lip and dropped a plate.

'Would you believe it!' He threw his hands up. Amrita gathered the broken pieces but instead of disposing of them in the bin reserved for shattered ware, she quickly thrust them in the recycle bin. 'Would you believe it!' he repeated. 'Is it any wonder they call it the developing world?' He followed her from the wrong bin to the right one, insisting the first hadn't been cleaned out properly. Then he trailed her back to the dishes. 'A high-volume job, Anita,' he continued. 'How do you think we built this country?'

Ron stopped wheeling a dolly of Mayo-Whip and glowered. Nancy gave Daanish a look that said: Kill Kurt and I'll love you for ever. Everyone else merely chugged along. Like machines, thought Daanish, wanting badly to touch Nancy.

Kurt continued, 'We didn't do it by standing around, that's for sure. You can keep hoping the work will go away the way they do back where you come from, but it'll only *pile up*.'

When he finally left the dish room, Nancy said to Amrita: 'Don't worry girl, he couldn't find his dick with two hands and a map.'

Daanish wanted to console her too but didn't know how. Instead, when Vlade wheeled silently by, he was suddenly reminded of bullock carts on the streets of Karachi. The soulful Masood Rana resounded in his ear: *Tanga walla khair mang da*. The cart-driver asks for contentment.

At 9.45 he removed his Fully Food gear, picked up his jacket and stepped out into the crisp mid-October air. He ought to go home, shower, and work on a paper. Instead, he walked up the hill to Becky Floe's house.

They'd met just over a month ago at the gym. He was lurching out of the swimming pool and on to the sopping tiles when he saw her lime-colored swimsuit and tadpole-like toes inches from his chest. The nails were painted pink to match her freckled flesh. She was broad, heavy-bosomed, about five foot six, and proclaimed: 'You're so graceful, Day-nish.' His chlorine-blazed eyes blinked. He'd never seen her before, but she even knew his name. He'd forgive her inability to say it. For the first time in his life, he'd been sought.

She held his hand as he walked her home. The weather had become suddenly warm – Indian Summer she called it. Her potato-colored hair dripped onto an aquamarine T-shirt that read *Choice*. He wondered if that was the name of a band.

She wanted to know all about where he was from. Was it just like India? He wasn't sure why she needed this reference because she'd never been there either. She'd left her country just once, last year, for a month in Mexico. When he described his food she said it sounded, 'Just like in Mexico.' So did the climate, the traffic and beggars. The people, the passion, the politics. The music, corruption and drugs. That month, she explained, had been priceless. It made her understand all that was authentic.

'So, did you grow up in, like, a palace or something?'

'Oh no,' he laughed, 'my father's a doctor.'

She eyed him quizzically, as if unable to believe the Third World had doctors. The look quickly turned to disbelief when their conversation progressed to his job at Fully Food. 'You're a doctor's son but you need financial aid?' In the sunlight, her unshaven legs changed from blonde to strawberry.

'Well, yes.' Realizing she wouldn't be convinced till he quoted figures, he clarified, 'In Pakistan, on average a physician earns about ten dollars an hour. While this is extremely high compared to the national average, it's not enough to send a child to America on, is it?' In the following years he would come to repeat these figures numerous times. He'd say, with far more exasperation than the first time, 'Not everyone who's brown or black is either dirt poor or filthy rich. There are in-betweens.'

Becky continued to look uncertain. Then she kissed him lightly on the cheek and sent him back down the hill.

He'd never expected to be pursued by an American woman. Walking to his room he wondered if he had been, might have been, would be again, or should he forget it?

Two days later, she invited him into her room. It was littered with books like *The Woman Warrior*, *Sexuality and American Literature*, and *Intercourse*.

While she talked, he kept wondering if this was a date. If so, what should he be doing? All his previous encounters with women had been hasty squeezes in Karachi, inside jammed cars while a designated watchman kept an eye out for the police, who had a radar for unmarried couples. So his interactions with women were feverish and clumsy. He'd never talked to a single one he'd kissed and barely even seen what he'd touched.

Becky abruptly ended her chatter and said, 'You know, you dream too much. You've got to take hold of your life, grab it by the neck and let it know who's boss. They haven't learned that in Mexico.'

He didn't doubt that she'd grabbed her life by the neck. And he did concede that back at home, daydreaming was a favorite pastime. 'It can be soothing. Life takes its course, and you become a spectator. Sometimes you really have no other choice.'

'You *always* have a choice.' She began stomping noisily about the room, doing he wasn't sure what. Today she wore a pink T-shirt that said *Take Action*. Her hair was wet again, from swimming. It dripped on to her shirt so the top halves of the letters were darker, as if taking action. She started drying her hair. 'You have a choice about every step you take, and if you're ever doubtful, you should choose to do something about it.' The hair dryer droned as she waved it about.

'Sometimes,' he shouted over the dryer, 'you're faced with obstacles that are bigger than you. When there's no electricity and you can't turn on the water pump, and it's a hundred and ten degrees, what choice have you but to sit and let the sweat pour off?'

Grrr, went the dryer, *woosh*, *wap*, *ee*. She appeared not to have heard. In an instant, she was done with drying and shining a mirror.

In their ensuing encounters, Daanish never saw Becky idle. Even while peeing, she crammed her senses with the numerous glossy hair and make-up magazines stacked under her toilet sink. He found the collection odd for a Women's Studies major, remarking also that it was not displayed with the books on feminism. But he thought it wise to keep these observations to himself. In general, he let her talk, waiting eagerly for the day their kisses would culminate in more. He was nineteen. These days especially, his virginity was making him feel ninety.

Perhaps it would happen today.

He knocked on her door. He could hear furniture screech. She shouted, 'Who's it?'

Daanish tried hard to infuse desirability into one small word: 'Me!'

Nothing for several seconds. Then at last: 'Can you come back?'

3

Choice

JANUARY 1990

Back meant more than two months later, for the New Year's party where she wanted to appear with someone ethnic. But when college resumed, Becky never opened the door again. So two weeks into Winter Term, he crawled into another.

It was 4.30 in the afternoon, twilight, when he trudged up the hill again, this time to Penny's dorm. Temperatures had plummeted to sub-zero. Daanish had never known such cold. His winter boots had cost him nearly all his savings from the first term, and he grew anxious. Would the glue dry? The stitching tear? Leather thin? Shoes were notoriously short-lived in Karachi. Here they seemed to wear well. This cheered him, even though he couldn't stop shivering, despite the thermal vest and leggings, the doctor's black turtleneck from his London years, two wool sweaters and a down jacket. The jacket he'd purchased only yesterday with the birthday check his parents had sent. He pulled it closer to his chin and felt their presence.

He stepped where the snow was solid, not merely to save

his shoes from leather-munching slush-demons, but also for the sound of snow crunching under his boots. Good, sturdy boots. Around him, icicles hung off branches, changing to russet gold in the setting sun. Two crystals suddenly rose upward and grew in size. One sported a handsome cap. They flew into a large dogwood that slouched over the gym where he and Becky had first met, and began to whistle.

It was the high-pitched call that made him realize he'd been looking at a pair of cardinals, and not a flurry of possessed hail. The birds considered him, breasts forward, the male's crest erect, the female singing again. Daanish paused. His father would have enjoyed this – the frost, the birdcall in the starkness. Back at home, he was probably in his study, smoking Dunhills. Daanish sank lower into the doctor's woolens. Beneath all the layers, a string of seashells pressed into his flesh.

He'd skipped lunch again – it was hard for him to eat at Fully Food even on his days off. His stomach rumbled. If he'd had an extra five dollars, he'd have walked straight into town and ordered one of those delectable melts he'd seen his roommate eat.

Passing the house where Becky lived, he casually glanced in its direction, hoping she'd see him walking to another building. It was on one of his many hikes up to Becky's that he'd bumped into Penny last fall. She was, in her own words, a poetess, dancer, and nurturer. Not as trim as Becky but in her own way, just as spry, and though she too favored authenticity, it was secondary to circularity. Actually, she clarified, authentic was the offspring of circular. Or was it the other way around? It didn't really matter, since it all came back to The Beginning. She liked her own explanation so well it became a poem. In fact, it always *had been* a poem, she was just the medium. Like Becky, she too believed in taking action, but, she cautioned, always listen to your body first.

Fine advice, Daanish had mused several weeks ago, when

she led him to a forest of birch and maple, stripped from the waist down, and jumped into a pile of golden leaves. At last! He undressed, nearly screamed when the chill hit him, and rushed in after her. They rolled on the thick mattress of fallen leaves, Daanish trembling and ecstatic. But why was it taking so long to find her?

'You're a virgin!' she giggled as he plunged into her belly for the fifth time. He thrust up her Amazonian thighs, poked the crack of her buttocks, and went full circle (just as Penny knew one always went), back to her belly. She was both irritated and amused, and at last said, 'We've got to stop. This is beginning to hurt.'

He was mortified. She sat up, fingered his penis till it grew stiff again, and encouraged him to listen to his body.

'What does it say?' she whispered.

His eyes nearly fell out of their sockets. *What do you think it says?* he wanted to shout, the color in his cheeks horribly like the sanguine leaves beneath them. He was harder than the trees smirking around him, and began to despair. He was going to climax in her hand.

'Let it happen,' she encouraged. 'Don't hold back.' She prepared to lie down with him again but it was too late. His semen sprayed her knees. The forest shook with mirth, dropping yet more leaves.

The color rose again to his cheeks as he trudged up the hill, remembering that day. Disturbingly vivid about it all was the sound of their bodies on the mattress of leaves. It was not like crushing paper, nor like rubbing two starched shirts. Not quite like a voile dupatta trailing on grass, but maybe closer to a child's rattle or iron shavings sliding at the bottom of a can. It was a sound that lowered Daanish to the sinking depths of shame. Every walk he took that fall brought the memory back stronger, and when a chipmunk bounced or bird hopped in the blanket of leaves that covered the campus, he heard the chorus of the laughing trees.

Fortunately, snow covered the campus now. And Penny had very kindly decided to downplay the event – thank God it hadn't been Becky. He was successful at last in the early morning after their first night together. Perhaps he'd been too sleepy to panic, and had instead, as Penny advised, listened to his body.

She was waiting for him in a flowing pastel skirt and coarse purple sweater. Her thick legs were wrapped in mauve tights. She warmed his lips with her own. Her room smelled of lilacs and cooked fruit, a result of the candles burning on the windowsill. On the bed and loveseat were piles of pillows. The ceiling was covered in a deep purple sheet on which she'd drawn her galaxy: crescent and circular moons, and stars. In a corner sat a covered dish. Daanish eyed it hungrily. She lifted the cloth: cheesecake with two pencil candles.

'I'm starving,' he drooled.

'How long are you going to reject dorm food?'

'As long as the sight of it makes me puke.'

'Then you have to come up with something else, Day-nish you poor thing, or you'll get sick.' She kissed his nose and lit the candles. 'Happy Birthday!'

'Thanks, Penny.' He blew the candles out and waited impatiently for a slice of cake. He wolfed in silence, suddenly depressed. She was the only one in this college of three thousand who knew he turned twenty today. She ruffled his hair while he ate. She was giving, kind, and yet he could think of nothing at all to say to her. He sat on Penny's bed, under Penny's galaxy, in Penny's candlelight. If she snuffed it all out, where would he go?

4

Toward Anu

MAY 1992

Daanish sat down with a thump. He'd made it back to his seat just as the Fasten Your Seat Belt sign lit up. The water acquired from a pleasant stewardess for himself and Khurram spilled over them both. But as usual, his companion was delighted. His eyes danced, 'Now we are having fun.' Though water had fallen on her too, in the aisle seat Khurram's mother stayed rolled up in a deep sleep.

Khurram said, 'You don't talk very much. You are like my mother, but not my father. I got his tongue. And when he jabbered on, she did just that.' He pointed to the blanketed bundle. Only a shriveled nose and closed eyelids poked out. He slapped his chubby, Levi'd thighs and laughed heartily. 'Now I am insisting you tell me what is going on in your brilliant mind. I know you are like my brother in Amreeka. Always thinking. Never enjoying life. One day you will be so successful, and by the grace of Allah, support your jolly younger brother!'

Daanish laughed. 'I have no brothers.'

'Ah! That is first thing you are telling me.' He looked at his watch. 'It is taking fourteen hours.'

'I'm glad I'm not the only one keeping meticulous track of the time.'

Khurram rubbed his hands. 'No brothers? Your poor parents. Sisters?'

'No. Only cousins. And too many.'

He swiveled around to better face Daanish, and his stomach torqued under the seatbelt. 'How can you say that? There can never be too many.'

Daanish didn't have the heart to tell him that as of three days ago, he didn't even have a father.

The ride was markedly smoother now, and the seatbelt sign switched off. Khurram returned to Nintendo. After a while he said, 'We'll be in Lahore soon. Then Karachi, at last. Who is to picking you up?'

My father, thought Daanish, his absence hitting him.

They touched Karachi four hours later.

'We're here!' Khurram unfastened his seatbelt. There was a bustle of activity: bangles ringing, babies screaming, the overhead storage compartments snapping open and banging shut, briefcases and shopping bags bludgeoning bottoms. Passengers were preparing to dismount before the plane had even halted. The withered voice of a stewardess asked them not to, but then she and the crackling radio together gave up.

Finally the door opened and Daanish followed the others down to the runway. The sky was a light gray haze and the leaden heat immediately stifling. Not a star shone through. He adjusted his watch to local time: 3.30 a.m.

'The car is waiting,' said Khurram, when they'd made it through the tangle of immigration, baggage and customs.

'Which car? I haven't seen my family yet.'

'Oh ho, don't you remember? You are the forgetful type! How did you manage alone in Amreeka for three years?'

'Khurram, it's been great, but I should stay where my chacha can see me.'

'You really don't remember calling from my mobile when we landed in Lahore? Are you sick?' They were wheeling two carts each, though only one suitcase was Daanish's.

Daanish frowned, 'Remember what?'

'*Arre paagal*,' Khurram's cart tipped. He wrestled with a suitcase bursting at the seams. The lights were too dim to know if anything was lost, so he pawed around the gravel. 'I told you your house is so close to mine, and since we have a driver, what is the point of disturbing your poor chacha? The flight is delaying already. We called him, and even talking to your mother. Everyone finally agreed. Nobody likes driving alone in the middle of the night these days. *Kooch to yaad ho ga?*' Khurram's old mother zipped ahead with purpose. All those leg curls on the plane seemed to have rejuvenated her thoroughly.

Daanish was speechless. He had absolutely no recollection of the phone call. He wanted to know if he'd spoken to Anu or if Khurram had, and how she'd sounded. But he couldn't shock Khurram any further. He followed him, feeling suddenly that *he* was the bumbling child and Khurram the adult.

The parking lot was strewn with men idly wandering about and yawning. The drawstrings of their shalwars dangled like goat-tails. They smoked, hawked, and watched families re-unite. Two little children ran up to Khurram and boldly squeezed his midriff. 'Khurram Bhai! Khurram Bhai!' they squealed. The girl had stick-like legs that skipped under a golden dress, while arms bedecked in bangles and fingers finely tipped in magenta nail polish waved excitedly. The boy climbed into Khurram's arms and was attaching a balloon to one fat ear, when all at once there appeared half a dozen others. Each began vying for Khurram while his mother, with whom he'd barely conversed during the entire flight, zealously orchestrated the grabbing and pinching.

Daanish stood apart, eyeing the baggage, wondering how

they'd all fit into one car – or were there several? His attention was suddenly caught by another man obviously affiliated with the party, but like himself, not quite a part of it. He was a striking presence: dark, with cheekbones women would extract teeth for; coal-black, oiled ringlets that brushed a prominent chin; eyes an odd, bluish opal; soldierly stature; shoulders straight and solid, with curves decipherable enough through a thin kameez in the dim light. He seemed aware of cutting an impressive figure and turned his head, allowing Daanish a view of his haughty, chiseled profile. Daanish raised an amused brow.

The cluster began to move. Daanish followed. Khurram introduced him to the others. The men and children hugged and kissed him too, the boy offering to tie his ear to another one of his balloons. The handsome man pulled Khurram's cart. Daanish decided he was the driver.

'We are dropping him first,' Khurram pointed to Daanish. 'He lives on our street.'

'Is that so?' an uncle smiled while the others nodded amiably.

'Yes,' Daanish replied. 'Thanks for squeezing me in.'

Khurram was now the star of the show and Daanish swore he'd even begun to look different. Gone was the chubby boy with toys. He walked erect, thrusting his belly forward like a beacon. He described with great authority his knightly escapades at supermarkets where he could, blindfolded, name every variety of cheese-spread and crackers just by taste. He spoke of bank machines that spit money by touching buttons impossibly convoluted. And all the while, he punctuated his stories with orders to the driver – 'Be careful with that suitcase, it has tins.'

There was only one car, a metallic-green Honda Civic. 'Where's mine?' Khurram demanded of the driver.

'Your brother-in-law took the Land Cruiser today,' explained an uncle.

While Khurram cursed the missing relative, the driver began loading the trunk. Khurram sat in front with a child on each knee and two duffel bags at his feet. The others piled at the back with the remaining luggage. When the handbrake was down, an aunt put a bag on top of it.

The balloon hovering above Khurram burst with a bang and the boy started howling. The little girl clapped her lady-like hands. 'Cry-baby!'

'Come to me,' said the boy's mother, admonishing the girl. Everyone shifted and craned while the boy attempted to soar like Superman to the back. For this cleverness he was awarded with ching-um and forecasts of future prowess. He settled happily in his mother's lap, his head propped against a bag his father held. The bag slowly drifted into Daanish, already balancing three others, and with a spine being rhythmically sawed by the doorjamb. The little girl wondered if she'd been dealt the short shrift and began to weep. She was promptly told to be quiet.

They were on Drigh Road. A thin light pierced the haze and the sky turned smoky purple. To the south, Daanish could see service lanes ripped out. He'd heard about this. It was part of the Prime Minister's development scheme: yellow taxis, a new highway, and a computerized telephone system with seven digits instead of six. But the new lines hadn't been implemented. The roads lay clawed and abandoned like old meat. Once the city awoke, pedestrians would scoop the dirt in their shoes and kick it into the sooty air, to resettle on the next passer-by.

When he'd lived here, he'd rarely been one of those pedestrians. Karachiites walked out of necessity, not for pleasure. Till now, he'd simply accepted this. Beauty and hygiene were to be locked indoors, adding to their value. No one bothered with public space. As if to illustrate, the little boy, tired of the ching-um wrapper, bounced over the bags on Daanish, unrolled the window and tossed the paper out.

DAANISH

He then proceeded to empty his pockets on to the street – more wrappers, a Chili Chips packet, and fistfuls of pencil shavings.

No one noticed. The family was filling in the absentees about local events. Since the start of the year, more than three thousand kidnappings were reported and now at least as many Rangers prowled the city. 'They stop anyone,' said the mother to whom the boy, now bored with littering, had returned. 'Shireen told me they were blocked by these horrible Ranger men, but her driver very cleverly kept driving. Anything could have happened.' She shook her head.

'Never stop for them,' agreed her husband.

'There's been a curfew in Nazimabad,' she added.

Another man piped, 'Dacoits are now attacking everyone. Not just the rich. Just this month they raided a fishermen's village. I can't imagine what they took, there are hardly even any fish left!'

'Oof,' said a young woman, 'the price of fish! Don't even talk about it.' She promptly gave Khurram's mother minute details of the quality, size and price of the seafood in the market. The other woman interrupted with her own wisdom.

Amongst the men, another discussion was rapidly rising in crescendo. Khurram was declaring, 'This street is the longest in Karachi and that is a *fact*.' Daanish wasn't sure how they went from Rangers to road lengths, but he was once more struck by Khurram's newfound confidence. Even his speech was clearer.

Suddenly, just about every street in Karachi became the longest. 'No,' said one man. 'It is M.A. Jinnah Road.'

Another shook his head, 'Abdullah Haroon Road – the longest in all of Pakistan.'

'Nishtar Road,' said the first, suddenly changing his mind.

'How long?' challenged Khurram. 'Give me *facts*.'

'Oh what does it matter how long? As long as Karachi!'

The discussion would take place altogether differently in the

43

States, thought Daanish. There, first a printed page had to be found. This established objectivity. Then an opponent located another printed page defending *his* position. The result was that debates took place only in writing, while in person, people seldom argued. As the written debate was limited by the availability of material, more original points of view were less likely to be favored. He learned this the hard way, in Wayne's class.

Here people frequently argued with each other; usually everyone spoke at the same time, and hardly anyone could sustain interest in the debate for very long. The men had ceased disputing the status of the road's length. Conversation progressed to its original name – was it Shara-e-Faisal or Nursery Road? Khurram insisted it had always been Airport Road while another swore on Highway Road. Then it changed to the distance from one point to another, the time it took to reach one point from another, the likelihood of traffic between the points, the time of day traffic was heaviest, the importance of the time of day in gauging the traffic, the overall increase in traffic, the necessity of cars, the necessity of two cars, and the overall decrease in time, especially time to spend with your friends and family doing just this: chit-chatting. They laughed heartily, agreeing on basically one thing, that the purpose of the match was not to win or lose but to exchange the maximum number of words, for words carried sentiments like messenger doves.

Daanish's mind wandered no less than the talk around him, only his had a center: his father.

When the doctor had driven him down this stretch three years ago, he'd spoken of himself as a youth newly returned from England, newly titled a doctor. He'd pointed to the dense smog choking the city and frowned. 'It was a different country then. Barely twenty years old – roughly your age. Cleaner, and full of promise. Then we got ourselves into a war and were cut in half. What have we done?'

44

Daanish had felt bleak currents swirling around them, and wished the doctor would offer a more savory parting speech. Suddenly, he'd stretched his arm and patted Daanish's knee. 'But it's reassuring to know that you will be a finer mold of me. You will go away and learn how to come back better than I did.'

Daanish shuddered. It was not how he wanted to remember him. He preferred the way his father had been at the cove. Daanish held the picture an instant, and then willed himself there.

The cove was a deliciously isolated respite several kilometers outside the city. Though silt and human waste had destroyed most reefs off Karachi's shore, just around the bend of the inlet was a small forest of coral where the doctor took Daanish snorkeling.

The first shell Daanish ever came to know was a purple sea snail. It was a one-inch drifter, floating on the surface of the sea, traveling more extensively than most anything alive – or dead. The doctor rolled in the waves on his back, his stomach dipping in and out of the water like a whale's hump, his hairy navel a small blue pool. Daanish slunk in after him, peering at the shell bobbing like a cork in the curves of a soft tide. His father explained that if disturbed, the mollusk oozed a purple color that the ancient Egyptians had used as a dye. Daanish plucked it out. While his fingers curled around the fragile violet husk, the animal ducked inside. The eight-year-old Daanish tried to understand where it had been, and how much time had lapsed between the Pharaohs, and him.

Later, they scrambled over the boulders that hugged the cove at each end, and walked the length of the beach, his father poking and prodding the shells swept at his feet. He found an empty sea snail and handed it to Daanish. It would come to rest around his neck.

*   *   *

He touched it now, back in Khurram's car.

His house would be swarming with family. They'd have flown in from London, Islamabad and Lahore. He could picture his aunts wiping tears with dupattas, picking rosary beads, reciting from the Quran in a weeping chorus. The doctor had cared nothing for such rituals, yet Daanish knew Anu would want them. He could see her teary, kohl-smeared cheeks. He could feel her pulling him, through Drigh Road, past Gol Masjid, down Sunset Boulevard. She was calling for him to make up for her loss.

He looked up at the haze, yearning for yet more interludes.

5

Recess

APRIL 1990

It was spring break. Most of the students had gone home for Easter. The campus, devoid of human life, was ceremonious: the lawns burgeoned with bluets, buttercups and black-eyed susans; the trees with chickadees, titmice, and the plaintive phoebe. Daanish spent his time walking and listening, absorbing the grounds in a way he'd never done before.

He wandered off into a far corner, down a long, narrow path flanked by two straight rows of enormous oak and cedar trees. Behind one rank of trees rose a short wall stretching all the way from the start of the path to the far end. It was the only boundary wall of the campus. Daanish inhaled deeply, delighted to be walking on land that needed only one demarcation. There wasn't a single house, school, university, park or office in Karachi that was free of four encircling walls, though the US Consulate there had the tallest four walls of all.

He soon approached a rectangular, sunken garden, nestled thickly in the trees. Egg-smooth pebbles littered the circumference of the hollow. Wild thyme sprang from between the pebbles. The patch had been planted with tricolor pansies, bluebells, and cowslips.

Daanish stepped down and stretched beside the flowers. He saw faces in the gnarly old trees. Some uprooted and changed places with one another. Bluebells rang. Cowslips sneezed and a shower of gold dusted his cheek. Up in the sky, white clouds drifted. No haze, no smog. No potholes, beggars, burning litter, kidnappings or dismissed governments. Such beauty in a country that consumed thirty per cent of the world's energy, emitted a quarter of its carbon dioxide, had the highest military expenditure in the world, and committed fifty years of nuclear accidents, due to which the oceans teemed with plutonium, uranium, and God alone knew what other poisons. It had even toyed with conducting nuclear tests on the moon.

The plump sparkling clouds whispered: We're dumping it on *them*, on *them*.

It was bloody seductive.

Blossoms fell in his hair. He yawned and felt like Alice, tumbling from one chasm into another. Would he too wake up in the safety of his own? His eyelids began to flicker. An oval nuthatch scrambled down and around the length of a bole. He spun with it. The nuthatch became a smooth, round medallion of pure gold. It bobbed on the end of a chain. On the other end of the chain was a key. The key was in a car's ignition. The doctor drove the car. The medallion swayed like the hands of a clock gone haywire, backwards and forwards, turning minutes into seconds. Inscribed on its one side was the word Shifa. Healing. Underneath, the doctor's name: Shafqat. Affection. His own father had presented it to him when he returned from England. On the medallion's other side was the Pakistani flag. Daanish belonged to that flag. He'd come back to it, the doctor declared, better than he had himself. The key-chain bobbed when he said it.

And it danced down the tree, tapping uproariously as it

went. The grass was fluorescent and a touch moist. He ran his fingers through it and the pores of his skin opened as he welcomed each sensation. A barn owl swooped across his vision. The moon began to rise. He slept soundly till dawn.

6

Arrival

MAY 1992

Her fair skin set off a head of dark, crinkly hair. She held
him close, thanking Allah for bringing him home safely. Had
the scene occurred under a street light in his college town,
passers-by would be faintly embarrassed, if not repulsed. He
thought if she said, 'Thank you *Jesus* for returning him to
me,' instead of 'Thank you *Allah* . . .' people would smile or
snicker but not think her a fanatic.

He shut his eyes. Never before had he stood in this house
plagued by how others might see him. He tried to clear his
head, to instead enjoy Anu's welcoming arms, flabbier now
than when he last embraced them, three years ago.

Khurram and his family waved goodbye. The handsome
driver's eyes pierced his own, turning a hint green. 'You are
my friend now,' Khurram called out. 'Anything more I can
do for you, I am just down the street.'

'Such a nice boy,' said Anu as the car drove away.

Lurking behind her, Daanish now saw, was the shadow of
his father's eight sisters. It grew closer, a single mass with

sixteen tentacles, pawing and probing like Siamese-octopi. He was being welcomed just like Khurram had been at the airport, but he did not desire it.

One arm caught his throat. 'You poor poor child! How your father loved you!'

Another tugged his hair, fighting with the first, 'How exhausted you must be! Come into the kitchen with me . . .'

A third whipped his cheek and cried, 'You look sicker than our own! Were you in Amreeka or Afreeka?'

A fourth spun him from the waist, 'You're just like *he* was at your age!'

A fifth yanked his shirt-tail, 'Who did you miss the most?'

A sixth, 'Me!'

Seven, 'His father, ehmak.'

And eight, 'Look how his jealous mother keeps him all to herself!'

It was true. While they jerked and pinched her only child and hurled insults her way, Anu still held him, and now they were all entangled, resulting in a chorus of loud protests from small bodies in the arms of each aunt, small bodies with wills and suckers of their own. He fell headfirst into their lair.

'Ay haay,' shoved Anu. 'Let the boy sit down at least.'

She gripped what little she could find of Daanish's arm, disentangled it from the others, and with determined possessiveness, led him into the kitchen. The others followed like a school of squid. 'Sit down, bete.'

Scowling at his aunts in black and the babies in their arms, Daanish pulled a chair up next to Anu. She emptied several plastic food containers into metal pots then lit the burners of the stove. His aunts continued making observations, their children still shrieked, but at least no one touched him.

'I'm really not hungry Anu, just tired,' he protested weakly. 'You haven't even told me how you are.' She never shared. Just fussed.

'What is there to tell? Allah has returned my son to me safely, even if He chose to take my husband.'

Her back was to him but he knew she was crying. Softly – tears never interfered with her work – but steadily.

How differently his father would have received him. In place of his mother's flurry, a thick veil of smoke would infuse the air as he sucked one Dunhill after another. He'd ask what it was like there. Daanish would only select details that would tickle him: the ghostly reflection of an opossum on clear summer nights; pink-haired waitresses with pierced noses (the doctor would guffaw at this perversion of his most favored female accessory, the nose-pin); having a wisdom tooth extracted to lite music: 'Every time you go away, you take a piece of me with you'; children delightfully camou-flaged for Halloween. Anu never absorbed curiosities.

She was saying, 'I wanted so much to come to the airport but who would drive? Your one chacha has the flu and I didn't want to trouble the other again. He went twice to the airport already but the flight kept getting delayed. We didn't know – none of the airline people answered the phone. You must be so exhausted.' She stopped abruptly. Tears stained her face. 'How do you like the new table? I got it soon after you left. Your father never even noticed. You can have one just like it when you settle down.'

He frowned. Settle down?

'Your father took too long to shed his restlessness. That's why you had him for barely twenty-two years. If you do it earlier your family can see more of you. To settle down is to do the world a favor.'

'Oh Anu.'

The doctor would call this *her* logic. He'd say it the way he said *her* blood. It was the subject of most of their fights, he having migrated from Hyderabad, she from Amritsar. She traced her ancestry hundreds of years back to the Caucasus. Hence her pristine white skin, which, to her dismay, Daanish hadn't inherited (though she consoled herself that darkness hardly mattered as much in a boy). The doctor said it was pathetic how people grasped at anything to prove they carried foreign blood. And since the foreigners – from the Central Asians to the Macedonians, Arabs and Turks – were conquerors, it was the half-teaspoon of conqueror's blood that made people like Anu gloat over their pedigree. 'Everyone here has a master-subjugator complex. No one takes pride in being a son or daughter of *this* soil,' he snapped at her once, scooping up a mound of earth from the yard and throwing it back impatiently.

One week later, he was gone again, traveling across the seas, bringing back shells for Daanish.

Anu arranged several steaming dishes before him. Their rich cardamom and ghee scent on this early morning, after Daanish had traveled some seven thousand miles and been sleepless for nearly as many hours, gave him a headache of astounding symmetry. Commencing at the forehead, it cleaved his skull evenly in two, like a coconut shell. It was as if the two halves were trying to find the one-in-a-million combination that could fit them together again. He gazed in agony, first at the dishes, then his mother, then at a baby cousin who'd escaped from his mother, and raced toward him on all fours.

'I'm tired,' Daanish muttered again.

'Boti!' the child squealed. The mother, delighted by her young one's forwardness, hurried to the table. Resting her wide hips on a cushioned chair that went *pish!* she proceeded to feed her child one of the dishes Daanish's mother had set before him.

'You're tired because you're *hungry*,' Anu stressed, scowling at her sister-in-law.

Daanish's other aunts drifted toward the food. Some of them sat, others stood, all picked at the various curries, kebabs, and tikkas for Daanish. They fed their children generously, but never offered a word of praise. In the doctor's presence, Daanish's aunts had never so blatantly used Anu. The doctor had died without ever knowing his sisters. He'd died without knowing Daanish. He'd died. Slowly, and with a soft, defeated eye, Daanish began to eat. Anu dried her eyes, smiling gratefully.

When a faint yellow light washed the kitchen, he rose at last. The sun was rising. He gave his mother a tight hug. 'I'm falling over with fatigue. Everything was delicious.'

She kissed and blessed him copiously. 'Sleep well, jaan. There is all day tomorrow to answer me.'

7

The Order of Things

Mounting the staircase Daanish scratched his head, wondering what the question was. He threw back the door to his room.

The interior was unrecognizable. Once a warm, moody beige, the walls were now a clinical white. So were the built-in bookshelves that replaced the rickety ones on which his father had placed books for him to read.

The doctor had never presented a gift in wrapping paper with a card. He left it where he believed it belonged. This often meant the discovery wasn't made for days, even weeks. It was in response to this 'game' that Daanish developed a keen memory that gradually evolved into an urgent need for systematic tidiness that Becky termed 'anal retentive'. By memorizing the exact position of every object in the house, including every book, Daanish could identify a new one. If he could see it, even if, as a child, he was too short to reach it, his father let him have it.

Anu knew nothing of this. When the doctor presented

her with gifts that popped up in plant pots, spice jars, lipstick tubes (a meter of resham so fine it fit in the finger-sized cylinder perfectly, so when Anu twirled it, out sprang the cloth, softly on her cheek, exactly as the doctor had envisioned), parandas and petticoats, Anu first gasped, then placed the surprise in a more suitable spot. She never strove to discover the impulse behind what she called her husband's unsettled ways. But Daanish went along with his every fancy to the point where the father's imagination became the son's order. Anu, by changing the color of the walls and replacing the bookshelf, closet, floor lamp, even the bed, had changed for ever the order of things. Without knowing it, she'd eliminated the doctor's presence from Daanish's room. The one at college was more his own.

He dropped onto the new bed on which the lovely guipure bedcover Anu had made him years before was now a starched white sheet. When had she made the changes? Not after the death, that was barely four days ago. It would have been a breach of decorum. The family expected her to mourn, not pack or decorate. Then when? Why didn't his father stop her if she'd done it during his lifetime?

His temples throbbed. The headache had lost its symmetry. He probed around his neck for knots.

Perhaps his father had never entered Daanish's room while he was away. Perhaps it made him sad to be in it without him.

The new bed was no longer under the window, where he'd spent so many nights gazing up at the stars. It lay beside the new closet, and the landscape outside was mostly invisible. He saw only a patch of sky and an antenna from the roof of a house piercing it. The house was one of the four to have gone up in his absence. Barely ten inches from his window was the skeleton of yet another one.

He lay down, shoes still dangling on his feet. This mattress was soft; the old one had been firm. Every time he switched position, the springs bounced. Finally, he lay on his back, arms stretched to still the movement.

He could hear his aunts puttering downstairs, covering the floors with sheets, piling siparahs on side-tables. Soon pages would rustle and the recitation would commence. He didn't want to be a part of it; it wasn't a part of his father. He had to find a way of braving the ensuing weeks.

It was seven o'clock in the morning. Were his father here the alarm clock would sound the BBC chime. A crow perched on the windowsill. It was large and gray-hooded. Our crows are bigger than American crows, he thought, eyelids drooping. They're the only things we have that are bigger.

ANU

I

Guipure Dreams

Four days earlier, she'd sat on his bed, fingers tracing the weave of the guipure bedcover sewn at the cove.

Once Daanish's father had shown him life beneath the sea, it was hard for the child to surface again. Now, it was essential that all the images of his submarine life be removed from his room. Then he might return.

She folded the bedcover into a small square, then spread a new cloth from the market in its place. Then she began emptying his cupboards, removing all his shells and shell boxes. Along the way, she paused to marvel at the careful system with which he organized the pieces. Labels drawn in purple ink recorded where each had been found and when. Sometimes he'd even noted particulars about the shell's life or collector's value. The best ones were in the left drawer because, he'd explained, left-handed shells were a rarity. He had only four in his entire collection of nearly three hundred.

She picked up a box the doctor had brought back from a trip to the Philippines. It was the only gift he'd ever placed directly in his son's hands. He'd been too excited to wait for Daanish to find it. The child had stared into his father's eyes, exactly like his own, and both pairs of hands had trembled. The box was of finely chiseled, green soapstone but the child had only partially registered its beauty. He'd pulled back the gold seahorse clasp and beamed, stupefied and delirious, at the chambered nautilus inside. That was what the doctor had called it. He'd said it was left-handed and that he'd never even heard of anyone finding a leftie nautilus. But there it was, perfectly intact. The doctor had dabbed it with mineral oil to preserve the pearly coat.

Anu examined the spiraling beauty. It shimmered on the cream-colored cushion in the box, alive even in death. Underneath was the note, written in the smart, controlled hand-writing of Daanish the thirteen-year-old: *December '83, on Aba's return from the Pacific. Called chambered nautilus because it has many rooms inside. Aba says its brain is very developed, it has three hearts, and its blood is blue. He knows because he's a doctor. It's 180 million years old, as old as a dinosaur. What a find!*

Also on the cushion was a close relative of the nautilus, an argonaut. Anu clearly remembered the day Daanish had found it at the cove.

She tucked the slip of paper back into the box and put it on top of the pile in her arms. From downstairs, the doctor called. He was dying, and there were things he wanted to get off his chest first. She'd heard enough already. Once, perhaps, she would have heard it all. But gone were the days when she would have worn his confessions like a string around her neck. She put the heap of boxes down on the floor. Then she lay on the new bed and spread the guipure lace around her, remembering the cove.

It was shaped like the round neck of a kameez, some forty feet across. The right shoulder was a cluster of enormous rocks, the first of which Daanish called the shoulder-boulder. When he and his father swam, Anu hoisted herself upon it. Around her spilled yarns of the guipure lace she turned into tablecloths, curtains, and more.

She began the bedcover on a chilly early morning in November as Daanish waded into the sea, shivering. The water was cold and composed. She'd tested it while they cleaned their snorkels. An aquamarine shawl enveloped her shoulders. She'd worn her hair long in those days, and left it loose, though it would take hours to disentangle later. The doctor liked it that way. He'd drape it over her shoulder, then gaze at her profile from the water. He preferred her left side, the one that wore the ruby nose-pin he'd given, not given but hidden, at the bottom of a perfume bottle. When it was noticed, she'd not known what to do: empty the bottle and risk splashing drops of the expensive scent, or wait till it had finished? She ended up pouring Chanel into a jar, retrieving the ruby, then pouring it back, spilling his money all over her dressing table and sneezing uncontrollably.

The shoulder-boulder was naturally pitted to seat her. The doctor hollered for her to come in with him, but she flatly refused to wear a bathing suit. He taunted her modesty because he knew she'd never give it up. If she were the changing type, he would not have married her.

The bedcover in her lap was taking a surprising turn. Patterns unplanned emerged and she obliged by seeing them through. When Daanish kicked around the boulder, heading for the deeper sea, he waved. She waved back. What would he see? For a moment, it pained that she'd never know. But this was nothing new. Her husband often left for voyages to the bigger ocean, where she'd seen islands peppering the globe in his study, and young girls dressed in flowers peppering his photos. He was always irritable upon his return. Once she asked Daanish to ask him why. The son reported cheerfully, 'He says I'll understand when I grow up, something about falling into the trap of comparison.' But she always felt his frustration had something to do with the photos.

One day, he'd send her son to one of those dots on the globe. She prayed for him to return untransformed. Like her, he should not be the changing type.

The sun caught in the heavy lace like anchovy. This year the monsoons had poured into autumn. A river, normally dry by now, still ran along the east end of the beach. Plovers, herons, and even a pair of mighty spoonbills bathed in the waters. The birds she could see. The fish beneath the surface she could not. A mischievous desire suddenly overtook her: before the doctor returned, she wanted the spoonbills to fly away. She knew he'd never seen them before. She could impress him for having noticed and identified them. But she alone would have been the witness. Anu covered her mouth, slyly giggling.

After half an hour, she folded up the lace, tucked it under an arm, and hopped down onto the powdery sand. There was no one about. For the time being, this cupular cove and everything it held – the river, cave, rocks, powdery sand, and pristine isolation – were all hers.

She padded toward the left shoulder of the cove, where a line of jagged rocks gradually grew taller, and sheerer. At the base of the incline the sea and wind had etched a cave that could be entered at low tide. The doctor liked to have his tea there. Turning up her shalwar till it pressed her calves – she'd never have rolled that high for him – Anu minced across the slippery stone toward the cave's mouth. The sea cooled her ankles. If she tripped and fell into the gravelly seabed, though it would hurt, later that night she'd notice her soles had been scrubbed pink. Now, seaweed caught in the hem of her shalwar. Lemon-colored fish scrambled between her legs, like she was their marker. What did her son and husband see? It must be something like this. Then why didn't they just stay here?

She ducked into the cave, twelve feet deep, its height very slightly less than hers. She could feel the cold stone press down on her head like the foot of a giant. The light inside was eel-gray. When the sea lapped the cave's sides the giant above her bellowed.

At the far end, the doctor had arranged slabs of flat rock. On one she began arranging pakoras and quartering fruit. In her estimate, they'd arrive within five minutes. Waiting, she spread the guipure bedcover around her again, carefully avoiding the wet floor. Whatever she'd lost in childbearing floriferousness when her ovaries were removed, she made up in that luscious fabric for her son. It rippled around her like a second sea. As before, the design came unexpectedly. Only she could see beneath it. Let them use snorkels and masks; she had eyes.

At precisely the time anticipated, Daanish's voice was heard. Her cheeks glowed with the warmth reserved for him. But then she heard his father's booming laugh. For a fleeting second, her brow furrowed. This was her time, her place. Then, just as rapidly, her irritation drained away. The world was normal again. Her family was safe. They were hungry. She was their marker. It was time to be theirs.

Over tea, Daanish examined the bedcover. He insisted the figures were sea urchins, fan coral, jellyfish, and sea snakes. Names his father had taught him. Names his father would never share with her. 'Just like you'd been there too, Anu,' Daanish said. He was so innocent. But there was a new light in his eye. Something forming. A dream or ambition. When it blossomed, he would lose his innocence, and she would lose him.

The doctor asked where her shawl was. She looked about in distress. He laughed, saying it had blown off just as they rounded the boulder, and from the water he'd seen the sun filter straight through her kurta, so she might as well have worn a two-piece and jumped into the sea to get good and wet.

'Please,' she tsked, 'not in front of him.' Daanish was digging for shells at the cave's entrance, listening. Smirking, almost. Growing older by the minute.

The doctor held the lace up to her face and grinned, 'You might as well have worn this.'

Again she yearned, like a shooting pain, to be alone in her world with her dreams.

And again, when it passed, normalcy.

Fourteen years had gone by. Downstairs, the doctor writhed in bed. He was still calling. Once she would have gone to him, believing it would lead him back to her – to the way he'd been when Daanish was born. She would have sat quietly beside him, listened, and consoled. It would have been part of the patient waiting. But she had stopped waiting. She had realized that to wait is to watch yourself grow old. Her future rested not with her husband but with her son.

She rose from his bed, clasping the boxes and the guipure bedcover. It flowed all the way down to her feet like a net with which to get her boy back.

2

Argonaut

Hours after the doctor stopped calling, Anu found him in a cold heap on the floor.

At the hospital, she sat outside Intensive Care while his family arrived, weeping. The nurses would not allow her inside. What did they know about intensive care?

'Why didn't you call us?' the sisters charged, as if she had eight different sets of hands with which to dial the phone. She'd made one call, and that to her brother, which was how the doctor made it here at all. The sisters hugged her, piling on accusations, demanding to be comforted. 'Why didn't you bring him earlier?' another insisted. 'How long had Bhai been unconscious?'

Anu went through the motions: she'd been upstairs cleaning, how could she have known? She'd heard nothing. One minute he was watching Hindi films, the next he was on the floor. Who can say what the future holds? The Almighty decides.

Privately, she prayed the Almighty would decide in her

favor, forgiving her for ignoring her husband's last call, and for lying about it now.

The walls of the corridor were pasted with gray fingerprints and red paan stains. Two feet away, a man was hawking in a toilet. She could hear the unbuckling of a belt, the pants fall, shit drop. The air was pungent and stale. Not a window in sight.

Before they shut the door on her, she'd seen the sheets on his bed were stained before he even lay down. Clumps of hair and dust tumbled on the floor like weed. The ceiling fan rattled loud enough to wake the dead – but not the comatose. The nurses had long, black nails. She looked with horror at the unpacked needles and gloves. Bottles of antiseptic lay uncovered.

Anu walked down the corridor. The lights went out. A generator came on. She braced herself for a long wait. To wait is to watch yourself grow old. Earlier today, she'd told herself this. Now here she was, no longer waiting for the doctor to adore her, but waiting, instead, for him to merely live.

Still, there was no harm in remembering those first few weeks after Daanish's birth, when he'd cherished her.

The delivery had been arduous and she returned from the hospital too weak to cook. Her husband advised complete bed rest. He refused hired help, taking extended leave from the clinic to nurse and feed her himself.

The fare was one month-long meal for he knew only two dishes: khichri and mutton korma. He even thought to prepare the meals in their bedroom, carrying the materials to her dressing table, where, for the first and last time in his life, he allowed her to watch over him. He said it was this opportunity to supervise and not the bed rest that would revive her.

She smiled indulgently at his disorder, as Daanish lay tight in her arms. So complete was the baby's need that she was washed clean of any desire to direct the doctor. She choked down the coarsely chopped, slippery globs of onion that littered the gravy, the rubbery meat, and glutinous rice that was saltier than the sea. She knew the reasons for all three: he should let the onions char; the butcher was cheating him; when he washed and sifted the lentils and rice, he cleaned with such vigor he removed most of the good grains too, but then forgot to adjust the spices and reduce the cooking time. At times, she worried for the child: how did the milk taste and would it affect his temperament? But the doctor was so earnest in his care his mistakes made him more endearing to her than he'd ever been, or ever would be again. It was while he sifted the lentils that she loved him most. Something in the way he churned the grains with a metal spoon as they soaked, for not long enough, in a large plastic bowl. The chink of wet seed against steel. The snaking drift of liquid as it ebbed and trailed after the spoon. The black specks that surfaced. Him flicking them out, clumsily taking shiny golden ones too. She understood him then, for as a girl, she'd done the same. It was sharing, with him, and the baby, each differently but at once, that eventually revived her, though neither father nor son would ever know.

Many times thereafter, she recalled the happiness of those bed-ridden days. At first, the memory brought intense, private hope, for the fulfillment of which she was determined to wait. But gradually, it filled her with something else. Hope obstructed the passage of the strength she needed to accept the direction her life was taking. She had to make room instead for endurance and God's will. At what point in her life did this process begin?

Strolling down the grubby halls of the hospital, she paused at one of the dust-opaque windows and smelled smoke. Outside, somebody burned litter. She stood, wondering whether to return to her in-laws or breathe the noxious fumes. She decided to stay here awhile.

If she tried, it was possible to put a date to the day hope left her. In effect, three dates – on the first, almost leaving; then burning brighter than ever before; and at last extinguishing entirely.

The first was during a grand luncheon at an old British-established club. Seated around a table at the center of the dining room were ten intellectuals and their highly clipped, coifed and choreographed spouses. While all the other wives were shown a menu, the doctor ordered for her. It was a western dish she'd had once before and disliked. He knew this. She said nothing.

The club was frozen in time. On the walls hung portraits of Winston Churchill. The billiard room forbade entry to ladies and dogs. Waiters were called 'bera' from the British word bearer. They wore the same starched white turban, shirt and trousers as they had under the colonizers. Some of the uniforms were so stained and tattered the doctor would say that one day a delegation of nostalgic British historians would snatch and turn them into antiques in one of their museums. The waiters would never get a penny *and* they'd be naked.

Six years had passed since the nation's first polls, which had coincided with the year of Daanish's birth. The election results had not been honored. The country had lapsed into a civil war and lost half its territory and population. One of the men present at the lunch was a third generation Iranian who still mourned the loss of his tea plantation. He lit a cigar and reminisced.

Anu looked around the table, remarking the pedigree of each. Some had two drops Persian, others half a drop Turk. There was one who claimed his ancestors had sprung from Alexander the Great, and another had roughly one teaspoon Arab. But none had descended from Mahmud of Ghazni, as she had. She bore the stamp of the tribe with pride: the clear, fair complexion and the bloom on her cheeks.

She was momentarily taken aback when the Iranian began bemoaning the very activity that consumed her, and one which the doctor often resented her for. The cigar-puffing gentleman said, 'We will always be divided. We'll always be Punjabi, Pathan, Pukhtoon, Muhajir, Sindhi, or what have you. But we will never be united. The Quaid's dream is slipping from our fingers. Our children won't even know he had a dream. They won't know why they're here. They will be rootless.' He peeled open a napkin and arranged it over a heavy heart.

'It's your weak morale that will tear us apart, Ghulam,' said another, a Hyderabadi with dark, pockmarked cheeks. 'You mustn't let your sons see you this way.'

'But Ghulam is right,' said a third, from UP. 'Things are only getting worse. At least once we had a great university in Aligarh. Now what is there? Will we be forced to send our children away from us?'

'We have nothing to fear,' declared a Punjabi. 'Islam unites us.'

'That's exactly what the Prime Minister wants us to believe,' cautioned the doctor. 'Why else is he suddenly supporting the Islamic groups? Why else are all the liberals in exile or in jail?' He pointed to the waiter circling them with a tray of drinks and demanded, 'Is this to be my last public beer?' While the waiter poured, an argument erupted.

Amongst the women, the topic ranged from births to beauty parlors to who had been seen at the last grand luncheon where exactly the same three subjects were discussed with equal zeal.

'You should try Nicky's instead of Moon Palace, darling,' said the Hyderabadi wife to the Iranian wife. 'She gets the curls just right.' Looking disdainfully at Anu, who wore her hair in a frizzy bun, she sniffed, 'That is, if you want to stay in touch with things.'

'Mah Beauty Parlor is far superior,' said the wife of the Punjabi. She was from Bangalore, and in the past, had confessed her husband couldn't stand her for it. She was pregnant with their third child. 'I had my hair set there just yesterday. And you won't believe who was having hers done beside me!' She looked around expectantly. 'Barbara!' While gasps and exclamations issued, the woman continued, 'And I found out that her grandmother was my grandmother's neighbor's khala's mother-in-law's best friend's sister!' More gasps and exclamations.

The wife from Delhi, whose husband had taken the doctor's warning to heart and was on his third beer, piped, 'I believe it's her daughter who recently had twins.' She was not a popular woman. In her absence, the others declared she always overdid it. Anu had to concede they had a point. Today her hair had taken coils to new limits.

But Anu remained silent. Wanting in names to drop, she was fundamentally awkward in high society. She had not been born into it. Nor had the doctor for that matter, nor many of those present, but somehow she alone showed it. She was twenty-three, married at sixteen, educated only till class nine, clever enough to understand English but could speak it with an accent that was hateful to her in English-speaking company. Besides, she would only ever have one child. Soon after Daanish's birth, her ovaries had had to be removed. It seemed that in her presence, the women always took particular pleasure in repeating the names of those who'd better proven their reproductive worth. But they would never have the pink bloom on her cheeks that her pure blood gifted her.

Across the table, the increasingly incensed doctor was saying, 'What is the point of banning horse racing? I tell you, people will continue to do as they please but under the table. The Prime Minister is sowing the seeds of corruption with one hand and buying off Islamists with the other.'

'We're heading for another military coup,' sighed the Iranian. 'Another US-backed martial regime.'

The meal arrived. Hers was placed before her: stuffed shellfish. She disliked eating fish. She preferred them drifting between her ankles, at the mouth of the cave. They were silver and gold then, but cooked they simply stank.

'Don't use the fork,' the doctor leaned across and whispered.

What was she to do, eat with her fingers, *here*? She flushed. Some of the others heard and laughed – at her.

'The spoon,' he urged.

She glanced nervously around the table, and her worst fears were realized: all eyes rested on her plate. She broke the cheese crust with the end of a spoon. It was surprisingly cold. Scooping up a small morsel she began nibbling miserably. Then she noticed something like a bullet where the fish's belly must have been. She did not want any more.

The doctor boomed loudly, 'Don't you like it?' Laughter.

'Not hungry,' she muttered.

'Just two more bites,' he urged.

She picked up the spoon again and probed around the bullet. There was another one. And another. Her face would explode with the blood rushing into it. Giving her husband a last, desperate look, she plucked out the first lump with her fingers. Seven more rose with it. The crowd gasped: she held a string of gray pearls.

He helped her wipe them, then fell into a lengthy description of the rarity and size of Tahitian pearls. 'I'm afraid the meal is uncooked,' he said more to them than her. 'I couldn't possibly have had them bake it!' Uproar. Applause. Her hands and clothes a sticky mess, smelling putrid. Her insides as hard and lifeless as the gems. He couldn't afford this. She'd tried to tell him as much each time he gave her gifts. So now he performed in public.

'How *eccentric*!' a sophisticated wife shrieked, eyeing the doctor with a mixture of fascination and horror.

'How *lucky*,' the one who overdid it whooped.

And the one who met the film star at the parlor declared, 'What an entertaining husband he must be!'

As their enthusiasm grew, she understood they expected her to wear the necklace. She left for the toilet, returning with the polished stones around her neck. Even when dessert arrived no one noticed she had not eaten a thing, though her neck was the object of the ladies' minute, chilling study, and the doctor of their coquetry and awe.

But then the following morning, optimism returned.

The six-year-old Daanish was in the television lounge with the doctor. She worked in the kitchen, preparing a picnic for the cove. Woozy with the heat, she decided to carry the small tub of lentils she was washing to the breezy lounge. On the television appeared a dusty old white man. His fingers and face were chafed beyond any others she'd seen in his race. Nor did his voice carry the smooth, metallic timbre typical of goras. Most amazing of all was what he did with his hands: exactly what she did! He dipped a crewel-like pan into a river, brought up sand, and sifted – but for what?

'Gold,' the doctor explained to Daanish. 'He's content to live a life waiting for the odd nugget to fill his cup. Though he's spent over half a century doing it, he's still as poor as the dirt that hides his fortune. Some men won't give up.'

Well! thought Anu, her fingers pausing in the yellow-tinted water. She studied the prospector's sturdy, startling blue eyes and ropy physique. She followed the cracked gray mouth as it spewed strange, chewy sounds. Her fingers idled pensively. She smiled. For a brief, exciting moment she connected with a man. Not the one stretched across most of the couch (who'd still not noticed her bunched at the end) but the one from a different world. The one who understood that it was the spirit with which she waited that made the effort worthwhile. That commitment itself was reward.

A commercial break. A cheerful Anu packed the lunch and tea. The prospector was a sign of better things to come.

It was time to go to the beach. On the way out, the doctor asked her to wear the pearls. Her face fell. The shame of yesterday threatened to rekindle. Should she ignore him? Deciding against it, Anu hurriedly clasped the string around her neck.

At the cove, the doctor and Daanish cleaned their masks, adjusted their snorkels and were gone. She settled in the cave with her lace, working today on a tablecloth. Once again, she wondered what they would see. Closing her eyes, she tried to imagine it. But something was wrong. Her sewing was uninspired. The cave, instead of being the respite she'd known it to be, felt alien. The giant's foot pressed even closer to her head. She knew what it was. She was feeling the weight of the pearls. They circled her collarbone like lead pellets, each to her what it must have been to the crustacean itself: a blemish, a pustulate growth. Sand in her rediscovered joy. Cysts on her ovaries. She tried focusing on the salt blowing on her lips that was always strangely healing, and on the guipure in her hands, but neither offered any comfort. She thought of the prospector with hands like hers, always sifting, searching. But even he eluded her now. She put away the cloth and began laying out the sandwiches.

Daanish returned, shivering, shrieking, 'The water's getting cold!' She warmed him with a towel. At the mouth of the cave, the doctor dried himself in the sun. Daanish joined him.

'Come and drink your milk,' she summoned Daanish. To the doctor, she announced the tea.

He stayed outside. So did Daanish, who began lifting stones, peering into tide pools, digging.

'You don't want sand to dirty your milk, do you?' she called.

He looked at his father, awaiting his direction. The man gazed moodily away.

She repeated, 'The tea will get cold.'

For a moment, nothing. Then an impatient, 'Can't you see I'm not ready yet?'

She waited.

In amongst the neritic clutter around the doctor's hairy legs the boy declared he'd found a prize. He presented it to his father, who held it up. From inside the cave Anu could see the shell was thin and petal-shaped. The sun filtered right through. It shimmered like a translucent slice of skin.

'A paper nautilus,' said the doctor. 'Aristotle called it an argonaut. I'm uncertain why. Perhaps it had something to do with Jason and the Golden Fleece. Do you know the story?'

Of course not, thought Anu. When it came to questions, the doctor heavily favored the rhetorical kind. Daanish blinked at him lovingly. The child had buried himself in the sand. A hint of his red swimming trunks poked through. He'd washed the nautilus clean with the water in his pail. It glistened like a ribbed eggshell. He took it back from his father gingerly, as if afraid it would slip from his fingers like sea foam. 'No,' he whispered, afraid his breath might blow it all away.

'The Argo was the name of the ship that carried Jason. Those who went with him were called Argonauts – sailors of the Argo.'

Explain, explain. That's what the doctor loved to do. But only she knew the things he could not explain.

'And if you look at it this way,' he plucked it again from his son, who licked his sandy lips nervously, 'with the narrow end down, then, it looks like a billowing sail, doesn't it?' Daanish winked, trying hard to see it. 'The animal that makes it is an octopus. Riding along with it in her arms she must look like a sailor. What do you say?'

Daanish clapped his hands with delight. 'Yes! She'd have her own boat!'

The doctor laughed, thumping him lightly on the back.

In the cave, Anu poured out the tea. The pearls around her neck were cold and ravishing. Tears, as large as each stone, welled in her eyes.

He continued explaining. 'Strictly speaking, this is not a shell. It's a nest made by the octopus, and it's at this tapering end that she pockets the eggs and carries the whole thing with her – a purse, cradle and ship all in one.'

'What happens when the babies are born?' Daanish asked, his eyes wide with anticipation.

'Good question. When the thousand little baby argonauts hatch, she rejects the cradle, so children like you can have them. It's a miracle, isn't it, that something as flimsy as this can survive the thrust of the sea and surface unharmed?'

The child nodded fervently. Behind her tears, Anu's guipure blurred into spray.

'Argonaut,' the doctor continued, 'was also the name of those Americans who went West in search of gold. That fellow we saw on TV just this morning could be a descendant.'

Ah, thought Anu, here he was again: the prospector. He'd appeared like a sign to give her hope, but how naïve she'd been! Well then, she would no longer count on signs. If she continued waiting for the doctor, she'd be left behind both him and Daanish.

When they got home later that evening, she took off the necklace and left it carelessly in the hall. He carried it to her saying she did not appreciate the shape of his love. He was suddenly and inexplicably enraged. 'It may not appear as you want to see it,' he shouted, 'but if you weren't so blind, you'd see it exists!'

Curiously placid, she wondered where. In the trips to the South Seas and places she couldn't even name?

Where? In his study? Anyone could become an expert just by reading. But she didn't need a single page to tell her why he never discussed anything he read with her. It would thin his expertise. It would fatten hers. It would mean that she too could explain things to Daanish.

Where was his love? In all those high-society parties he dragged her to, just to embarrass her?

In the food he never liked?

The conversation he never made?

Her lineage? His want of it?

Or in her only child, whom she knew even then would be sent far away, for, pah! *education.*

Coolly, she fingered the pearls strangling his strong, healer's fingers and brushed his large pink nails with her own. 'Give it to the one who sees where. Tell her I send my love. I'm sure she'll understand the shape of it.'

His mouth opened in momentary shock, snapped shut, and then he was off on an unconvincing tirade. He stumbled and once even stuttered, not having had the chance to look up counter-arguments in a book.

She turned, delighted with the audacity she'd never known herself capable of. She was riding the roiling sea, a panner of gold, a sailor with eight long silvery arms and a purse with Daanish kicking inside.

She had learned how to swim.

Anu walked back to Intensive Care. Still no news. The doctor's brothers too had arrived. His sisters continued to sob and exchange stories from their childhood, all of which proved how they knew him better than she did – the woman he'd wedded, by their own arrangement, twenty-three years ago. She shed no tears. She pictured her son bending over his books in America, his thick brows slightly furrowed, turning page after page, getting excellent marks on every test. He was so bright. He must have put on weight in that land of plenty. She'd memorized every photograph he'd sent, but he'd been clad in so many layers it was impossible to detect any changes.

He looked just as sweet and loving as ever. He was going to
be a great man.

Suddenly there was a frenzy. Nurses were in and out of
the room. She asked why and demanded to see her husband
but they brushed by her. She peeped inside the door but was
swiftly ushered back. She saw him briefly on the bed beneath
a forest of tubes: silver hair, ashen cheeks, thin, wrinkled
eyelids. He'd been unconscious now for over nine hours.

'What did you see?' demanded his sisters. 'We should
know.'

Perhaps she'd been too harsh that day. She saw the pearls in
his fingers. He'd not even looked at her for the following two
excruciating weeks, till at last she'd begged for his forgiveness.
That was the last time, sixteen years ago, that she'd ever
answered him back. Earlier today, when he called her, she'd
simply run away. Now she was left alone with the tortuous
guilt of watching him die. No, she wasn't even allowed to
watch. Sitting down heavily beside his sisters, she held her
head in her hands.

Another nurse stepped out, followed by Dr Reza, a distinguished colleague of the doctor's. Dr Reza was exhausted
and did not have to say anything. The sisters began to howl.
So he had died, as he had lived: outside her presence, in
another place.

She shut her eyes, resolving to grow no older waiting for
Daanish to return.

3

Girls

MAY 1992

It was almost noon and the house had filled with mourners. Daanish had still not awoken. It was time to take a break from the Quran reading. Anu brought out tea and sweets. Several stylish wives were present. Many of them, she knew, could not read the Quran. She watched their lips move, feigning recitation, and wondered if the doctor saw it too. She still felt his presence in the house, absurdly, more even than when he was alive. He had probably watched while she finished re-furnishing Daanish's room. Had probably frowned when she took away all the books he'd given him, right down to the shelves on which they rested. Would he come down from his new other place to stop her? She believed if God disapproved of her actions, He would tell her. But the doctor was rather powerless now.

All he could do was watch her next move.

While the mourners refreshed themselves with tea, she climbed up to Daanish's bedroom. He slept, as always, on his stomach. A white sheet covered him from the waist down. His suitcase remained unlocked but on the new white rug she'd thrown next to the new bed lay the few things unpacked from his carry-on: dental floss, a razor, socks, underwear, a novel, a ballpoint pen. The bag was unzipped. She snooped around inside it. Another book; the doctor's Kodak camera that he'd passed on to Daanish; a lovely eggshell and lacquer box the doctor had brought back from his last trip; an envelope. On the new bedside table lay Daanish's shell necklace. Anu fingered all his things, trying to understand what they meant to him. With some – the necklace, camera, lacquer box – she knew already. But not the books and envelope. She read the covers: Edward Said, Kurt Vonnegut. She'd not heard of either. Anu mouthed each name several times, softly. The Said had been heavily marked.

She opened the lacquer box. A label in block letters read, *BIVALVES*. There were a dozen different brightly colored shells, some smooth, others furrowed. Daanish's note was dated June '89 – two months before he'd left. *Sheer muscle power. By snapping its two valves, a scallop, for instance, can swim many dozen feet per bite. At the cove one day, Aba first told me about giant clams. 'Four feet long!' he said. 'They live right here, in our very own ocean.'*

Anu quietly shut the box.

Next she examined the envelope. It contained letters from the doctor and herself and a stack of photographs. She glanced at Daanish: he neither snored nor stirred. The boy would probably not wake up till evening. Settling on the rug, she began looking through the pictures.

The first few were of Daanish and a very handsome boy with golden hair in a beautiful garden. In some pictures the garden was covered in snow. In others it was ablaze with color. She smiled at her son lolling on the grass, frowned that in one he seemed to be smoking, and panicked when in yet another he appeared to be in a tall tree, balancing the way he always had on a bicycle: standing, and with hands in the air. But always, though dark, he was so good-looking: tall, with his father's wide amber eyes and his suddenly boyish disposition.

Resisting the urge to wake him up with an embrace, Anu continued on. There was the golden boy with a pretty girl. Then there were girls with no boys. Then there were girls with Daanish.

Anu backtracked.

There was a girl leaning against a tree. Red and yellow leaves scattered all around her. Against the strong colors of her surroundings, she looked especially pale, glassy almost, like a fish. A white fish with hints of yellow on its gills, poised before an orange brocade. Her head was slightly tilted to the left so her right eye seemed larger than the other. It looked directly at the camera, a bluish-green eye.

Anu skipped to a picture with the same girl and Daanish. They were seated around a table, at some party it seemed. Daanish held the girl's waist with one hand and a drink with the other.

She stared hard at the picture, and neither an eyelid nor a finger moved. Only her mind worked. She backtracked to a picture of another girl. This one was almost his height and had stringy brown hair. She seemed to be dancing in a field of corn and was not as shapely as the other one. Anu skipped ahead: there was Daanish and another tall girl in a dark room with candles all around, and tinsel stars hanging from above. She sat in his lap.

By the time Anu had sifted through all the photographs, she counted six different girls in close physical contact with her son. She thought hard. And came to a conclusion: at least there wasn't only one. He was distracted, but probably not yet committed. His bride would just have to handle that. After all, she had.

Anu collected the photographs, camera and lacquer box. She contemplated the shell necklace but softening, left it on the table. With the three items in hand, she returned downstairs.

As lunchtime approached, the mourners began to leave. Soon she was left alone to feed the doctor's sisters. They began complaining that no fresh food had been cooked that day. Her son had come back just that morning, what did they expect? She left them grumbling in the kitchen. In her bedroom she regarded the objects fished from Daanish's life in his faraway world. She did two things. First, she telephoned Nissrine's mother to say Nissrine should hasten her arrival at the readings. Second, she returned the lacquer box to Daanish's room, but with some unexpected debris inside.

4

Shameful Behavior

The following day, Anu wept proudly as Daanish came downstairs to meet the several dozen friends and relatives waiting to grieve with him. He embraced them all, quietly accepting their condolences, winning the approval of the stylish women who continued appraising him as he walked on. Nodding to each other they proclaimed, 'A spitting image of the doctor.' Since he'd left for America, these women had ceased snarling at her. Many had sons who'd not received a full scholarship, certainly not to any college as well-known as the one he attended. They knew this. It was the one aspect of her son's going away that Anu enjoyed.

The men sat apart. Daanish snaked toward them, passing the girl Nissrine, her mother, and a friend of Nissrine's called Dia. She was pleased to see Nissrine did not make eye contact with her son, but dismayed that the other girl examined him quite boldly. Even Pakistani girls were like that these days.

Anu watched as his bare feet padded over the white sheets. His toes had grown even hairier than before. He picked up a

siparah, and settled down to read. His body began to sway
with the rhythm of the recitation. Occasionally, he looked
up and gestured reverently at a new arrival. Frequently, he
caught her gaze and smiled ever so sweetly.

She knew he was not fluent in his reading of the Quran,
and the three years away would certainly not have helped.
She had wanted him to continue studying with a maulvi but
the doctor had disallowed it after the boy turned twelve.

Now she watched as Daanish seemed visibly relieved when
arriving at a familiar passage. She could feel it roll over his
tongue smoothly like a jingle. At other times, his facial muscles
tightened. It was the same with many of the women, including,
to her dismay, Nissrine. She seemed quite hopeless really, her
accent still British, her Urdu pathetic. But the family was
a good one. There were rumors that her father's business
was dwindling but instead of returning to London, where
it had thrived, the family was staying in Pakistan for the
girls. Of this, surely the doctor would approve. He was
probably chuckling as Nissrine struggled over a prayer for
him. And what did he think of Anu arranging the meeting so
soon after his death? Would he be surprised? Tickled? Was
it eccentric enough for his pleasure or was that pleasure only
to be instigated by him?

About one thing he would not approve: Nissrine was a
distant relative of Anu's, ensuring that Anu's blood, not his,
would continue. Her grandchildren would have the same fresh
mountain glow on their brow as she did, not his swarthy,
sea-faring pallor. And there was nothing he could do about
it. Except observe.

Nissrine sat quietly with a pale peach dupatta covering her
head. The color became her fine, white complexion, almond
eyes, and rosebud mouth. She kept her head lowered. Surely
Daanish would take to her. She was not blonde like that other
one in the pictures, but she was graceful and demure. Every
man wanted to come home to that.

The recitation was punctuated by women pulling their hair and crying, 'Hai, hai.' One she barely even knew now clutched her, kneading Anu's head into a massive bosom. Anu choked, trying both to free her windpipe and straighten her neck.

But then something saved her. A scream. A *real* scream. The keening ceased abruptly. The wrestler released her. She surfaced again, gasping, adjusting her eyes to the light in the room, painfully bright after the darkness of the woman's embrace. Tidying her hair she noticed most eyes rested on the lady-like Nissrine, who was shifting discreetly with an arched back. There were murmurs and nudges. Then, slowly, eyes still on the girl, the recitation continued and the wailing started again. Anu quickly moved five feet from the wrestler.

But there was another scream, louder this time.

It did come from Nissrine.

Anu gaped in astonishment as the girl reached frantically for the back of her kameez, pulling it away from her skin as if the cloth were on fire. Her peach dupatta lay bunched on the shrouded floor. Beside her, Nissrine's friend flushed and her mother shook Nissrine admonishingly. 'Stop it!' she hissed.

But Nissrine kept coiling like a cat with a tick on its hip. All the other women in the room began objecting. They pulled on earlobes, muttering, 'Toba toba.' It was a terrible omen. Anu swooned, wondering if this was the doctor's doing. Was he trying to interfere with her plans?

'Stop it!' Nissrine's mother commanded again.

Dia whispered something that sounded like, 'It's only a cat's paw.'

Daanish and several other men entered the room. Two uncles, determined to enforce order, began pushing into the circle surrounding the two girls. But the women barricaded them. 'Go back,' they shouted. 'We know how to handle this.' An argument erupted between the aunts and their husbands.

Dia was now holding Nissrine's hand and seemed to say, 'Catch a petal.' With her other hand, she pointed at three plump white strings close to the wall. Other eyes settled confusedly on the objects.

'What's going on?' an uncle demanded.

'What's wrong with those two girls?' another pitched in.

The women tried again to send the men away. Daanish, Anu saw, was staring at Nissrine's friend. His lips disclosed a hint of a smile as he inched closer to the circle. Anu rushed in after him.

Dia's nose was flushed with excitement. Her blue dupatta had fallen off her shoulders. She kept looking toward the writhing objects on the floor, shaking Nissrine and saying, 'Stupid, they're only caterpillars. Silkworms.' Then she looked around her, stuttering to Nissrine's mother, 'I'm so sorry. Sorry. Really, very sorry.'

Daanish was moving in closer. Someone stopped him. *'Ay haay, hato na!* It's not right for you to be here.'

'I know what's right for me,' he answered firmly, causing both girls to look in his direction. When she saw him, Nissrine started weeping.

'Oh Nini, let's just go,' Dia said. They collected their bags and prepared to leave, hastily bidding Anu farewell. Nissrine was sobbing loudly now, Dia apologizing, Nissrine's mother enraged and incoherent.

'Shameful,' Anu muttered to Nissrine's mother.

'Please,' she replied. The rest of her speech ignited in a ball of fire on each cheek.

Daanish picked up the larvae. 'What should I do with them?' he called out to Dia.

At the door, she turned around. Her eyes were large and russet, with dark flints of defiance burning at the center. 'Find out yourself!' Then her face crumpled. 'We didn't mean this. And we're really sorry about your father.' She hurried away.

Anu bolted the door behind her.

DIA

I

More Apologies

'Look. I said I was sorry.' Dia leaned into the wall of the dining room, popping mulberries with one hand, holding the phone with the other. The cook was in the next room, watching cricket. No, watching ads. Dia tilted her head and saw the TV: two women were waiting to be interviewed for an airhostess's job. Cut to the next scene. The one who got it revealed her secret to the loser: a tube of skin-whitening cream. Now she could fly!

Nini's voice on the receiver was weak from crying. Dia chewed nervously. They'd been on the phone an hour, but her friend had unwavering stamina.

It hadn't gone the way she'd expected at all. The caterpillars were meant to tweak Nini, not cause such a scene. At the thought of the widow, Dia's stomach ached. She listened to Nini and it ached even more.

The two had put themselves in many ludicrous situations before, often without the other one's consent, but it had never caused such a rift. She wondered if this was what happened to women on the verge of twenty.

Desperate, Dia popped three spongy berries at once. She exhaled loudly. The hair framing her forehead fluttered. 'Listen, Nini. Let's not make the mistake of falling out because of a man. How many times have we seen that, huhn? And yes, it was rather extravagant of me to put not just one but *three* dozing silkworms down your kameez but you have to admit you only started screaming when I told you what they were. But forget that now. Just say what you want me to do. I said I was sorry. I've said it a thousand times. And I mean it.'

'How did you come up with such a hideous prank, Dia? You know I hate bugs.' Nissrine blew her nose loudly.

'*Elephant*,' Dia hissed under her breath. Out loud she said, 'Yes, I know you hate them. And Inam Gul knows too. When you won't be my partner in crime, he's always there for me.'

'Tell him from me: Grow up.'

Dia popped another berry. It was the sweetest of the lot. She chewed loudly, secretly rather proud of the cook for coming through with yet another wicked plot. If Nini had blown it out of proportion, it wasn't his fault.

In the other room, a milk commercial was in progress, featuring a heavily made-up woman only too delighted to have her day interrupted by a slew of visitors. This way, she got to make them tea!

'You don't understand.' Nini blew her nose again.

'*What* don't I understand? What? You keep saying that but you won't bloody-well explain *what*.'

The whimpering subsided into stifled chokes. Finally, Nini cleared her throat and said in a cool, decisive tone: 'That boy's mother sent a proposal for me.'

There was silence. Then: 'God.'

'Don't have a heart attack for me.'

Dia shook her head. *Then for who else?*

'My mother asked me. I thought about it. And I decided, well, why not?'

Dia spat the pink fruity mass out and screamed, 'Why not? *Why not?* Is that all you can say? Nini, who are you?'

Nissrine clicked her tongue. 'I knew I'd get a lecture from you. That's why I kept it to myself.' She sighed and her voice softened. 'I want more from life, Dia. I'm sick of being stuck in this house doing what I've always done. I want something different.'

'Oh, Nini. Is any change better than none? What makes you think marrying a stranger will give you the kind you need?'

'Don't worry,' she answered bitterly. 'After what happened yesterday, his mother will probably rescind.'

'I would never have gone if I'd known.'

'I know. That's another reason I didn't tell you. I wanted you to see him, Dia. I wanted us to gossip. I knew we wouldn't if you knew.' She added dreamily, 'Even after our marriage. If . . .' Her voice trailed.

Dia paced, disgusted. Nini needed to be shaken back into her old skin. But it was as Nini said: now that Dia knew her intentions, she'd no idea what to do. Walk around Nini gingerly? How? They'd never been cautious around each other, ever.

Nini waited. Dia decided to use the strategy that had brought them together in the first place, when their math teacher paired them up to solve a sum, advising: 'When in doubt, count your fingers.'

'Let's talk about the pros and cons, Nini,' Dia spoke gently. 'First the cons. One, you don't know the boy. Two, his father's just died. Three, he's an only child. Four, he's an only child and an only son. Five, he lives in America. Summary: he's all his mother has, so she'll be even more possessive of him than the usual mother-in-law. He's having a blast far from her in America, probably living it up with women there, while a teeny tiny voice in his brain nags him of his duties to his Ami jaan and country. So, when he's had his fun, to pacify his guilt, he'll be ultra-protective of Ami jaan (who'll symbolize the nation), and ultra-conservative with his wife (who'll symbolize his authority in the nation). But mind you,' her voice had risen uncontrollably. This was no good but she couldn't help herself. 'He'll want to keep his American self alive too, just for fun. We all need good times, right? Now the pros.' She paused. 'You tell me the pros, Nini.'

The answer was sharp: 'Have you ever used your delightful powers of analysis to find out why you're so arrogant? *You* haven't met him either, Dia, so your assumptions are just as unfounded as mine. Yes, many men are like that. But maybe, just maybe, he's different. After all, you seem to think *you're* different. Face it Dia, you need a man in your life too, and you won't ever know if the one you pick is better than the one I do.'

Dia was stunned. It was not simply the hateful tone that stung like a physical blow. It was the knowledge that so many women fell into just this trap: arguing, or just plain fretting, about men. On the other hand, there was an unspoken agreement between men: Woman was not a topic worth mentioning, unless she aroused them sexually. But Man was a topic women devoured from every angle. Dia was certain this was the most obvious yet neglected reason for their disparate positions in society: time. Women spent it on men; men spent it on men.

And now here she was, spending close to two hours today, and several hours yesterday, cogitating emptily about one of them. Didn't Nini see how silly this was? How typical? How dangerous?

She longed to stop the clock right here. 'Please let's not fight. You do what you want. I'm just sorry about yesterday.'

Nini waited. But Dia had nothing to add.

Outside, Pakistan took a wicket and Inam Gul stamped his feet. The screen cut to the milk ad again. The woman carried out the tea from the kitchen looking refreshed and jolly. The reason for her bouncing spirits was that she got to use the milk! The guests consumed the tea in record time. The camera focused on her husband who said, 'Begum, chai?' So she scurried back to the kitchen in ankle-wrenching stilettos, her gold bangles ringing with jubilation.

Dia thought: Nini should have auditioned for the role.

Then she ached with remorse again.

After a long pause, which Dia was terrified of breaking, Nini spoke. 'You asked before if there was something you could do. Well, I've been thinking. If his mother decides not to revoke her proposal, well, your support still matters to me. So, will you be here when he visits with his mother? You're still my sister, Dia. Still.'

Dia smacked her forehead in dismay. 'Of course.'

In a tremulous whisper, Nini cooed, 'My mother needs me to acquiesce. You're lucky your mother doesn't depend on you to give her life meaning.' She hung up.

Receiver still in hand, Dia muttered, 'Let's hope your daughter is lucky like me.'

Moving to the front of the house, Dia bitterly wondered how many parents had shrunk their daughters' worlds to fill their own. She stooped for her sandals, eager for the oasis that was her farm. While struggling with the buckle, she glanced up at the wall. The face that greeted her was her father's. It was framed in ornate gold that was as false as the portrait. His painted jowls did not jiggle, his lordly mustache was reduced to a blanched apple peel, and his eyes seemed to have stepped into the wrong room, where a film about his life was in progress. The reel had gotten stuck right when he was being kidnapped so he'd no choice but to see the moment over and over again. His life was in the painter's hands and every time she stood here, Dia wished to submit the painter to the same torture.

She hadn't told anyone, not Nini, nor the cook, that the Quran Khwani yesterday had brought back painful memories. For forty days after her own father's death, she'd sat like a statue in this house, and learned something valuable:

some mourners came to grieve, others to collect gory details. Still others arrived to clutch the frozen Dia and shower her with pity, and yet more helplessness. '*Allah malik hay.* God decides.' That was the message they'd pounded into her. *You've no control over events. So why bother making anything of your life, little lady?*

Yesterday, when she'd apologized to the widow and her son, she'd meant it.

The cook, who'd been snubbed by his favorite of the three children ever since she returned home yesterday, shuffled woefully toward her. 'Have you forgiven me yet, my child?' He stood below the portrait.

'Oh, Inam Gul, it wasn't your fault.'

He stroked her head. 'Then come, let's watch TV.'

'The mood's gone.'

His nose tried to smell the air. 'What does Nissrine Bibi say?'

'Have you been eavesdropping again?'

'No!' He stared in horror.

'Then how did you know who I was talking to?' She watched happily while his lips curved around toothless gums. He seemed to miss his teeth most when cornered. 'Don't worry. I have very few secrets. But I'll tell you Nini's.' The cook's eyes popped with anticipation. 'She wants to marry that boy she took me to see yesterday.'

'Oh ho, what a clever girl!' His head bobbed loosely from side to side.

'She's a fool, Inam Gul, don't you forget it.' He changed his expression likewise. 'I'm going to the farm now, to forget about people for a while. If anyone calls for me, tell them I'm in my cocoon and won't come out for weeks.'

'Toba toba.' He tugged his earlobes, but knew better than to argue with Dia.

2

Numbers

For most of the drive, the land was stripped and parched, dotted with occasional bands of drooping mesquite. The route led straight to the mighty Indus, about 100km east. Riverbeds ought to teem with life, thought Dia, each time she passed through here. Especially a riverbed as old as this. But except for a kingfisher poised regally on a wire, hinting at the proximity to water, there was no evidence of the fabled grandeur of the Indus. Only books and old men like Inam Gul told of princesses like Sassi, dwelling in the glorious lakhy bagh on the banks of the river, surrounded by music, fountains and burnished horses.

Dia herself hadn't traveled all the way to the river for years. Now its banks teemed not with Sassi's pavilions, but with some of the nation's deadliest gangs.

She rode between two armed escorts. Both had greasy pockmarked skin, filthy fingernails and wasp waists. They handled their Kalashnikovs the way nearly all of the city's convoys did – muzzle pointing not up but back, at the following vehicle. Sometimes, one of the two would give his shoulder a rest and lay the weapon on his lap, with the muzzle at her. In the last five years she often wondered which was the greater risk – going with or without them. She was never permitted to know. It was believed her father had been kidnapped on this stretch.

Three rumors spread after the murder. One: it involved the synthetic dye company that had lost its contract. Two: it involved the cocoon importers who'd lost theirs. Three: the killers were fools to target the man and not his wife.

The sericulture project had been entirely Riffat Mansoor's. It was she who introduced a silk line in their textile mill, and she who questioned the wisdom of importing the seeds when silkworms could be bred at home. The climate suited the growth of mulberries, the food of the insect, and she owned a large plot of land near Thatta on which to cultivate the trees.

Dia's childhood was spent shuttling from farm to factory, the one an enchanted semi-tropical paradise, the other a whirl-wind of equally enchanting activity. At the mill, she'd walk wide-eyed around the workshops where thread was woven into sheets of shimmering white cloth, dyed in cauldrons of bubbling color, and painted into breathtaking designs. Back at the farm, she danced between the trees, gay with her own version of things. The irrigation canals were the boiling cauldrons. The twigs her reel. She unraveled her cotton dress into a skein of thread, and twisted these over the reel, till a pattern spread. She dipped it in the canal, and tossed it up to dry. It billowed down softly, a puff of her breath. She wore the breath around the farm, and everyone swore they'd never seen a finer silk.

It had taken her mother's vigor to make the project work but eventually, after several false starts, fifteen acres of mul-berry trees successfully yielded the sixty tons of leaves required to feed the one and a half million silkworms needed to produce roughly nine hundred pounds of raw silk. Riffat's fully self-sufficient side business gave the mill, already successful in cotton, an added allure. Throughout Karachi, women swore only by Mansoor Mills.

Dia was ten years old by the time her mother's project was a nationally conceded achievement. Her fellow-schoolgirls regarded her as queerly as men and women regarded her mother. Nissrine told Dia that people snickered about Riffat's appetite being as voracious as the caterpillars she bred – only it wasn't leafy greens she was after. Her husband may have given her free reign of his business, but could he satisfy her at home, in the bedroom, when she came out of *her* cocoon?

Dia shut her eyes and leaned back in the car seat, simmering at the gossip.

But when she recalled her parents together, the picture was no consolation. They spoke to each other only about work or children. Dia had never seen Riffat glow or throw back her head and laugh her beautiful, silvery laugh around her husband. The two never touched. They barely even argued. They were business partners, not lovers. Yet, her father wanted Dia to read him stories full of promises of eternal love, of Sassi waiting on the banks of the Indus for her lover's ship to roll in. Stories of earthly tragedy, but with attainment in the afterlife.

Dia opened her eyes again with a start when she realized her slouching position pressed her further into the guards. She sat up. Her back was beginning to ache, as it always did by this time in the drive. They hadn't even gone halfway. The land outside was still thirsty and desolate. Not even a kingfisher in sight. She smelled the sweat of the guards. They could probably smell hers. She tried not to wonder if this aroused them.

Whatever transpired between them, her parents became the topic of even more gossip when Riffat decided to discard chemical dyes. They were expensive, hazardous, and not even colorfast. Though organic dying was a method none of the other factories relied on, it had once flourished in the subcontinent. There was evidence enough to support this. Three-thousand-year-old madder-dyed cloth and indigo vats had been excavated in Moenjodaro, barely 300km north of where Dia rode in the car now. The technique seemed right outside Riffat's doorstep, and had been for centuries. Could it really be lost?

She discovered most colors could be obtained from plants easily grown here. She also learned which part of each plant needed to be harvested, how long this took, and what color it would give. Turmeric and myrobalan produced yellow; henna, madder, and pomegranate red; indigo blue; tamarind and onion black; chikoo brown. So she reserved the remaining five acres of the farmland for cultivating the crops.

Within two years, they yielded consistently and the contract with the dye company was annulled. They began receiving angry telephone calls.

Riffat grew tense. Her temper ran high. The family ceased piling into their Toyota Corolla for weekends at the farm. Her parents went from rarely speaking, to frequently fighting. And still the phone kept ringing. And more customers pledged loyalty to the mill.

On the night before his death, her father climbed up the mulberry tree planted when she was born. Why? Was it to turn back the clock and have her that small in his arms again, back before the threatening phone calls and gossip about his wife?

Dia had huddled indoors, petted by the cook, while her brothers argued with the crowd outside and her mother, for the first time in her life, stood frozen with shock. Her husband cowered in the foliage like a child, while the world laughed. But then at some point in the middle of the night, he must have climbed down and left the house before anyone awoke. He was never seen alive again.

The cook maintained that the answer to her father's death lay in nothing as obvious as an angry minister with shares in a severed company. According to Inam Gul, Dia's father was simply unlucky. He was in the way. The province was seething with free-flowing anger. Probably, the killers had known absolutely nothing about him. He was a random target, or a victim of crossfire. There were hundreds of such deaths in Sindh that year. There was no reason for it besides the will of Allah. The same will that had made killers out of some and gentle, caring folk like her father out of others.

But Dia could not accept that the death had been mere fluke – a simple detour. It pained to think that if it hadn't been his battered and bruised body, it would have been someone else's. This meant that even when alive, he'd been nothing but a mere number. And so was she. And Nini and Inam Gul. Everybody.

3

Life at the Farm

A quartet of armed guards paced the farm's exterior. The boundary wall extended into five rungs of barbed wire. The iron gate was topped by a plethora of slender spikes pointing up at the grayish-yellow sky. Inside the gate sat two more guards, but unlike her private escorts and the sentinels outside, these two were draped in soussi lungis from the mill. The cloth was dyed indigo and mint and shimmered like cock feathers in the sun. Together, they formed a friendly duo: they were two of Inam Gul's three sons.

Their bare arms and torsos glistened with sweat and the lungis wrapped them so tightly she could see the contours of their very different body types. On Shan, boyish and slight, the cloth rippled around the curves of a small tight bottom. But on Hamid, it hugged a pair of bulky thighs. She noted also his solid, wrestler-like gut. He would have been very handy with a pair of oars on a stormy night at sea.

The cook and his family had come into Dia's household two years before her father left it. They'd moved to Thatta from their village, driven out by the trawlers that invaded the local fishermen's zone. Mr Mansoor had seen Inam Gul's family outside the tombs of Makli Hill, close to the farm, and offered them work here.

As Dia entered the grounds, the two sons lowered their Kalashnikovs to let her through. 'How is everything?' she piped, relieved to stretch her legs and be in congenial company again.

'We'll have to see,' said Hamid. 'Sumbul says there are fewer good cocoons than last year.'

'And that was worse than the year before,' Dia sighed.

The yield of leaves had peaked at sixty tons when she was a child. But in the last three years, due to the increasing water shortage, this had begun to drop startlingly. A reduced diet meant larvae either never reached the cocoon-stage, or that the cocoons were thin-shelled, too small, or pierced, resulting in poor quality threads.

The water channels tinkled melodically, reminding Dia, with each drop, how much depended on them. In the stifling, pre-monsoon heat of May she fanned her face with a corner of her dupatta and hoped the year would be a wet one.

Leaving the guards, she took her time strolling between the rows of mulberry trees, carefully planted eighteen feet apart. Ahead of her fluttered a pair of black swallowtail butterflies. They chased each other, landed on a twig, and mated, tail to tail, resembling a single creature with two heads and four wings. The male must have overpowered her with his scent, she mused. In moths, it was the female that produced the aphrodisiac. It could be so powerful that immediately upon her emergence from a cocoon, if a male hovered nearby, she'd lure him. She'd have sex at birth. Dia had tried many times to witness this, but in all her trips to the farm, never succeeded. This season, she was determined to.

She crossed over to the shed. From the outside, it resembled a greenhouse: low-lying and flat-roofed. Adjacent to it was a two-room shack. From here came Sumbul, Inam Gul's tall, languid daughter and the farm's most valued worker. A lilac kameez offset her smooth, nut-brown skin, and she looked like a jacaranda tree in bloom. Approaching Dia Sumbul swayed, carrying a baby on her hip and a clipboard in her right hand.

'Salaam Baji,' Sumbul greeted her.

'Waalai-kum-asalaam.'

'How is Aba?'

'Oh fine,' answered Dia. 'Mischievous as ever. He sends his love. How's your husband? Is everything okay at home?'

Sumbul smiled, tugging the braid that had slipped over her shoulder. It was so long and thick she'd twisted it in a U-turn. 'His mother's gone back to our village for a few weeks. Things are better. But,' she looked away, 'I think a fifth is on the way.'

Dia sucked in her breath; Sumbul was only her age. 'And you still don't want Ama to give you pills?'

'What if he finds out?'

'Keep them here, at the farm. He'll never know.'

Sumbul sighed, adjusting the baby to her other side. 'No, Baji.'

Dia shook her head but said nothing; the choice was Sumbul's.

Together they entered the shed.

The interior was hot and humid, fanned with a continuous stream of fresh air. It was divided into four sections. The first, empty during this season, would soon hold the eggs laid by the current batch. In the second room was a long table with trays of wriggling larvae feeding on finely chopped mulberry leaves. Dia walked past the trays, greeting the women who tended the maggots. As in the days of the Chinese Empress, now too silkworms were bred by women. With the exception of the gardeners and the security guards, the farm was entirely run by them, which was why they were allowed to work at all.

When they first started, the sight of the larvae had made the workers squirm. Touching had been out of the question. But now the insects were handled as mechanically as braids and babies; sliding a handful down the shirt of any farm worker would never produce the effect it had on Nini. Despite herself, Dia smiled.

Sumbul, guessing the reason correctly, asked how the plan had worked.

'Well, unfortunately Nini overreacted. She has marriage on the brain.'

'Marriage?' Sumbul adjusted the baby again. 'Well it's no surprise, is it? Nissrine is so beautiful!'

'Is it her beauty that's made her change? She doesn't even know the boy she's after.'

'Most women don't,' replied Sumbul. 'Inshallah, she can make it work.'

But why should she? Dia wanted to scream. Why should Nini accept the limits that others so maliciously placed upon her? Why was it up to her to make it work, with a man who was a complete unknown, no less? Not wanting yet another argument with a woman she liked, Dia again said nothing.

They walked down the length of the table. The larvae were white and blind; their only activity was eating. But having been bred for so many centuries, they'd all but forgotten how to eat. The women had to chop up their food in tiny slivers and change the supply nine times daily or the fussy creatures would starve. If in their wilder days, they required no hygiene, now the perforated paper beneath them had to be scrupulously cleaned, or this too would elicit a hunger strike.

Toward the end of the table were caterpillars that had molted a fourth and final time. It always happened this way, thought Dia. An insect's life was so measurable, and yet so mysterious. Perhaps the paradox was the allure. As diligently as she studied them, there would always be details – like the changes inside a cocoon or the moths mating at birth – which escaped her.

She studied the sheets stacked on the clipboard. On top was the tally for this year. The news was not good. Fewer caterpillars had lived through the fourth molt than ever before. Watching them slither on a bed of leaves, she made believe they talked to one another. They whispered: Let us vow never to spin our fine threads for these wretched humans again!

Sumbul's baby woke. He writhed and rubbed his eyes with tiny fists, threatening to holler. Sumbul swiftly opened her kameez and offered him a breast.

Dia said, 'Don't you half expect the silkworms to form a guerilla alliance and revolt? People have always depended on animals for food and clothing, and then, four thousand years ago, along came a Chinese empress who made insects our property too. Maybe mutiny is the real reason output is down.'

Sumbul laughed. 'You have such silly ideas, Dia Baji. I can only imagine what you and my father must say to each other all day!' Her baby was falling asleep in mid-suckle. He loosened his grip on her swollen nipple and a string of milk ran down his chin. She mopped it clean with her shirt, which she then buttoned up.

Dia felt she was looking at Nini, just a few years from now. Too few years.

Sumbul continued, 'My grandmother always believed my father was the misfit in the family. He was never a very good fisherman. I think he's much happier at your house than he ever was at sea.'

'But he still misses the village,' answered Dia. 'He talks about it often. He especially worries about the eldest, Salaamat.'

'Strange that you should mention him. He visited me just this morning.'

'Oh? How is he? And when will he visit his father?'

'I can only tell you he's happy. Look what he gave me!' Sumbul smiled as she dug out two hundred rupees from somewhere in her bosom. 'His employers are good to him and he's good to me. Their son just returned from Amreeka. You'll never believe it: he was on the same flight as that boy whose father's Quran Khwani you went to. The boy Nissrine wants! He sat beside him the whole time. Salaamat picked them up at the airport and even dropped the boy home.'

'Oh!' Dia exclaimed. 'Maybe your brother can find out more about this American boy through his employer's son, eh? If it's bad news, I'll pass it on to Nini. If it's good, we won't tell her.'

Sumbul chuckled. They left the larvae and hovered outside the third section of the shed. Entrance here was strictly forbidden. Inside lay the silkworms that had begun to turn yellow, indicating they were ready to start weaving their cocoons and hole up as pupae for two weeks. It was a delicate stage. A silkworm wanted absolute privacy as it spun. The slightest interference could result in a faulty cocoon or even in death. Over the years, Dia alone had witnessed the process, for she'd perfected the art of absolute stillness. As a result, her mother allowed her inside. But Sumbul, especially Sumbul with a baby, would have to wait outside.

Dia took a pair of binoculars from a drawer, positioned them over her eyes, and crept inside.

On the tables, thousands of caterpillars were in various stages of spinning. Each had transformed from the drunken, lifeless chunk on perforated paper to an agile ballerina leaning forward on its tail. Everywhere she looked, each nosed the air like a wand and out passed silk. It was more like a scene from a fable, in Sassi's lakhy bagh perhaps, than something that truly happened. That it happened here, in her mother's farm, in the middle of the scorched Indus plain, amid the chaos of Sindh, made all her ethical quandaries regarding the breeding of another life form to suit human interests vanish. Standing in a room with eight thousand tiny creatures, witnessing them perform a dance that few humans even knew occurred; this was life. They sashayed to the left and swiveled to the right. They bobbed and undulated, dotting the air in figure-eights. They worked ceaselessly for three days and nights, with material entirely of their own, and with nothing to orchestrate them besides their own internal clock. Each, a perfectly self-contained unit of life. When Dia watched one spin, she came closer to understanding the will of God than at any other time.

By courtesy of another stolen page from a library book, she'd discovered that the ancient Egyptians had believed the dead could see butterflies and moths. Her thoughts always returned to her father when she stood here. He was here too. And he could see inside the cocoons. He witnessed each pupa grow, knew when its head began to turn and point toward the little opening at one end. He saw the creature kick and curl, preparing for the fourth and final stage of its life.

After fifteen minutes, she slid outside. Sumbul and the baby still waited.

Once the cocoons were spun, most were taken to the factory. There the moths were destroyed, or they consumed the silk thread as they ate their way out. To extract the thread, the cocoon was boiled in water, just as the Empress Hsi-Ling-Shih had inadvertently done four thousand years ago.

It was in the last part of the shed that those pupae selected for breeding were stored. Dia found this aspect of the breeding process unsettling. The cocoons moved. They were never found in the same corner where they'd been left. Nor had she ever actually seen the movement. It made her shudder to think the sleeping pupae could not only produce enough force to shift, but seemed to know when they were alone. Even more disturbing was the red liquid that oozed out from the shells. She knew what it was: waste stored in the pupa's abdomen.

But in texture and color it resembled menstrual fluid. As the pupae bled, the stench was overpowering.

Dia walked with Sumbul toward a woman with the last of the moths from the previous batch. The moths were bred to be flightless. They were stark white and wore a fierce expression, enhanced by feathery feelers that arched like indignant eyebrows.

The helper reported that this particular moth had produced about three hundred eggs, which had hatched into the youngest caterpillars in the front room. She was being taken outside, to die. Sumbul stroked her feelers. The moth twitched and glowered with protruding chocolate-brown eyes.

'What a life,' Sumbul mused. 'Larvae for four weeks, pupae for two, moths for another two. It's over so fast.'

'Yet the silk they weave lasts for centuries,' answered Dia.

'While other creatures leave nothing at all behind.' Planting a light kiss on her baby's head, Sumbul added, 'Except children.'

4

Choice

A strike was announced by the MQM the following day. Since the political party's leader had exiled himself to London, he had urged his followers to accelerate their campaign of civil unrest and this was the eighth or ninth strike that year. Some of the shops around Dia's house remained open but in the northern reaches of the city, a curfew-like situation set in: the shutters stayed down; streets were deserted; buses were burned. It was disastrous for both the farm and the mill: the workers would not be able to leave their homes. But as always, Riffat left the house immaculately dressed, determined to put in her hours.

Dia had already missed more than a month's worth of classes this year because of the strikes. Since no one ever answered the phone, there was no anticipating the college's closure. She lacked her mother's stolid defiance. Racked with uncertainty, she performed every ritual – from washing and dressing to a hurried breakfast – as if it weren't really happening. In the car, she sat in limbo, haunted by what the city said: God decides.

Today the college gates were open.

Nini awaited her inside. Even in their bland uniform, a poorly-fitting kurta the color of cat vomit, Nini moved with the grace and stature of a swan. Her oval face was smooth and chiseled, her lashes thick enough to rustle. It was a miracle really, thought Dia, that Nini had withstood pressure to marry this long. Proposals for her had been flowing in torrents since the day she turned fifteen. But then they'd stopped abruptly when news of her father's declining business broke out. Dia wondered how much Nini's eagerness to marry now stemmed from a fear that it was her last chance.

They kissed once on the cheek and Dia swung an arm into hers. 'We have Pak Studies first period. Let's skip it.'

'Fine,' said Nini. 'You've got crumbs in your mustache.' She brushed them off.

They crossed the hockey field. On one side loomed the classroom building, also the color of cat vomit. Every morning, students assembled there while the college principal tried to talk to all five hundred of them without a microphone. Most of the women either skipped the assembly or stood around discussing last night's TV drama, the various joras made that week, shaadis attended, and who was seen with whom. The principal, a handsome woman in her fifties, was best loved for her saris. When Dia and Nini joined the women, those in the front row had passed their verdict. It was trickling down to the middle rows and eventually to the back, where they stood. Today's sari was a blazing orange French chiffon with yellow swirls. Very bold. Very bubbly.

The assembly over, the two friends ambled to the far side of the field, passing the stone benches that studded its length. These were claimed immediately after assembly by those who'd passed the verdict on the day's sari. They wouldn't get up again till 2.00 p.m., when the college closed. The benches glittered with nail polish, lipstick, hair curlers, thread, wax, combs and clips. The college offered courses in beauty care without even having to hire staff.

Around the corner from the cafeteria was a walkway leading to a Catholic school that Dia and Nini had attended. Students from the two institutes were not meant to intermingle, but the policy was laxly implemented. As children, they'd sneaked over to the college and spied on the women that to them were all beautiful and wise, ruling over themselves like queens, while the schoolgirls were mere nun-toys. They'd grow up to be stolid commandos, just like the women! But now, it was the reverse. College women visited the school with longing, envying the girls that believed in them.

Hibiscus and jasmine bushes bordered the path. Behind these towered trees planted when the grounds were first laid out, in the early 1800s. The pebbled tracks between the trees offered Nini and Dia more space to wander in than all the city itself. Here they were unhampered by the eyes and hands of men, or the women of the white benches. The grove was clean and quiet, and there wasn't an armed guard in sight. This was not to say there weren't any – both the college and the school had sentinels at their respective and enormous front gates. But here it was easy to forget they were there.

It had been three days since they'd last met, at the Quran Khwani, and two since their telephone conversation. Dia didn't know how to start on the topic of the boy.

'What did you do yesterday?' attempted Nini.

'I went to the farm. Then I read. Alone and to Inam Gul.'

'How's it going, your studying for the retake?'

'It's going nowhere. The books are so stupid.'

'I'm sorry,' Nini muttered.

Nini, as always, had passed all the tests. She'd always been a gifted student. She did what she had to do – memorize and spew like a parrot – keeping her independent views on what she spat to herself. Nor was she, unlike Dia, at all bothered by the cheating that went on during the exams. She'd shrug and say, 'God watches us. That should be enough.' In her English accent it sounded funny: God wolches es.

They'd been friends since the day a teacher brought the terrified child to Dia's class. Nini chewed her nails when asked to read out loud because her accent provoked giggles. Dia soon learned that Nini had been taught none of the customs her family, recently migrated from England, suddenly demanded she uphold. Nor could Dia, who wasn't expected to do the same, help. Alone, Nini determined to learn what was desired of her. She visited relatives regularly; picked up key Urdu phrases and used them on cue; learned to cook; excelled in school; groomed immaculately; behaved with modesty. She embodied two conflicting worldviews, modern and traditional. Like the fabled Hansel (or had it really been Gretel?), the young Nini had the presence of mind to mark her way back to a home she'd never been encouraged to know.

And now she wanted to leave it.

And leave it the traditional way.

She'd never bring shame to her family. They'd made what they set out to make.

Dia looked at her. 'Explain it again. I've tried, but just don't understand.'

'You don't *want* to, that's the problem.' Nini spun around. 'You have fixed notions. Mind blocks. You think you know my future?'

Dia croaked, 'I've never known what's going to happen. If you don't know that, you haven't known me.' She took a deep breath. 'What if marrying this stranger makes your life worse? Then where will you be?'

'Don't be such a pessimist. What if it gets better?'

'But that's a gamble. Think of all the women who've gambled and lost.' She began to recite their names. She was on the ninth – Sana, who'd married an engineer in America, and left her home and family only to find the groom had another wife, and two children besides – when Nini cut her off with a laugh. It was a hard, world-weary laugh. Dia wondered who the greater cynic really was.

She had her answer when Nini said, 'You and I know nothing about freedom, Dia. Look at us. Always stuck behind walls and in cars. If we step out, what is there? If it's not physical danger, it's gossip. *Did you see Tasleem's daughter Nissrine, romping around so boldly on her own?* How many times have I been warned never to provoke that? My parents' image is my headache. You call that freedom? Come on!'

'My point,' Dia insisted, 'is that you'll have the same headache *plus* many others.'

'You haven't mentioned the ones whose marriages work,' countered Nini. 'Some women have more flexibility around their husbands than their fathers. Look at your mother. She blossomed after marrying a man she didn't know and has been an inspiration to so many other women. Karachi's becoming a city of entrepreneurial mothers. They get what they want. They just have to give in first. It's simple mechanics.'

Dia turned away. Yes, her mother had thrived, and yet her warning echoed in the grove. *Marry out of love. Not obligation.* Dia pictured her parents sauntering between the trees. Strangers, not friends. 'If that's as good as you think it can get, it'll never get any better. We're more than simple mechanics. It's okay to aim higher, or have dreams.'

'And where do dreams get us?' Nini shook her head. 'I worry about you. If you're not careful you'll end up lonely, like . . .'

'Oh please,' Dia cut her off. 'Like Ama? She used to be our role model, remember?' How conveniently Nini used Riffat when it suited her and condemned Riffat when it didn't. That was just how the public treated her mother – as a useful name to drop. Nini was as two-faced as the rest of them.

They sat in silence on the ground, facing a bed of periwinkles. Behind the flowers rose the school wall, its top a heap of glass shards. Nini took Dia's hand. 'You know I love your mother.'

Dia looked at her tennis shoes, then Nini's. Several months ago, on a whim, they'd sat exactly like this in her garden, under the mulberry tree, feet together, shalwars pulled up high above the knees, and spray-painted the shoes. With eyes clamped shut, they pressed and heard the colors wheeze out. Laughing, they agreed not to open their eyes till the job was done. Dia felt the cold chemicals settling around the canvas on her feet. She favored circles while Nini went for zigzags. Now, feet together, Dia saw how the pattern still fit exactly. Every purple swerve begun on one foot ended on the other. A golden slant rising on Nini's right small toe descended on Dia's left small toe.

Dia inhaled deeply. 'What makes you so eager now? When you got proposals before you weren't keen.'

'Why now?' Nini repeated and shrugged. 'Time.'

'Time?'

'There are things that simply happen when they should.' Her tendril-like fingers clasped Dia's shorter ones. 'I felt it when we left England. It was time for it, somehow. And now it's time for another move. There are moments when you ought to let yourself be carried away.'

Dia snorted. 'You sound fifty. Next time let's spray-paint our hair. I'll do yours white, and you can do mine, I don't know,' she threw up her hands. 'Orange!'

Nini let go Dia's hand. 'I'm doing my best to be sympathetic. You aren't trying at all.'

'You're barely twenty, Nini!' Dia said aghast. 'You've got *loads* of time.'

Nini glowered. 'After the disaster at the Quran Khwani, his mother's probably changed her mind. In case she *hasn't* – God knows I *would* – we're only talking about an engagement now. The marriage will come after his graduation, when he's got a job.'

Should she bother to ask the obvious? Why not? 'Since he's going to be the breadwinner, shouldn't you be sure he has a job? And a pretty good one?'

'His father was a great doctor. The son's likely to follow in his footsteps,' Nini replied adamantly.

'Do you even know what he's studying?'

'Well,' she twirled her hair. 'He's supposed to be very bright. After all, he got a scholarship to study in America. I'm sure he'll be hugely successful.' She gazed absently at the wall, as though it were a crystal ball.

Dia felt vaguely nauseated. 'So the answer is you don't know?'

Nini glowered again.

'Talk about dreaming,' Dia hissed.

A bell rang. It came from the direction of the college. The first period had ended. 'I suppose we ought to go,' said Dia.

But neither moved.

At last Nini stood up. 'Since your twenty questions are up, I suppose we should.'

'Eighteen,' countered Dia, still sitting.

'What now?'

'If his mother rescinds, or if for some other reason the engagement doesn't materialize, and if you feel *it's time*, does that mean you'll simply agree to the next proposal?'

'I wondered why you hadn't asked that one yet. The answer is: if it's as good as this one, yes.'

'So it's entirely chance – this man or that. X or Y. Random?'

'That's twenty. And yes, dear Dia, chance has a lot to do with it. If I fell in love, chance would have a hand. If I marry at thirty, chance will have a hand. If I have triplets, guess what: chance. I don't see why this offends you.'

'Some things you can control,' Dia snapped back. 'I suppose by "good" you mean his name and his American education?'

'That's twenty-one,' said Nini, sealing her lips.

'And this is twenty-two: How much of your faith in chance has to do with your father's slumping business?'

Nini's mouth twitched. It was her turn to look away.

Dia wanted to be the one to take her hand now. She wanted to say, You're beautiful, desirable, and will have many chances yet. Good chances. But she couldn't. Nini had given herself over to desperation and Dia hated her for it. Brushing her uniform she rose, and began walking back toward the path that linked the school with the college.

SALAAMAT

I

Sea Space

MARCH 1984

After the assault, his left ear transmitted sound like a cowry pressed to a normal ear and slowly withdrawn: the world had become the echo of a fading sea. At rare moments, when aroused by fury or desire, the pitch rose to an ominous roll of a drum, as if the ear cavity had filled with water again, just as it had the day the fourteen-year-old was battered by the egg-thief, and tossed into the chipped slate waves. At such times the pain was so severe the young boy embarked on a mystic quest to contain the thundering turbulence within him like a dam he swore to never let a soul unlock, not even the girls from the city he was soon to scope.

Days were busy. He helped at a teahouse run by his grand-mother, a place exclusively for women. When he first began, soon after his grandmother found him bashed and beaten, rocking in the sea, he'd been the oldest male to ever set foot in the ramshackle hut. Initially, customers complained. But the proprietor argued her grandson was neither emotionally nor physically fit for either the city or the sea, to which a few stubborn fishermen still set out every evening, competing in vain with the trawlers that had stolen their sea space. Besides, she pleaded, the boy was deaf. He could not spoil the luxurious privacy of their female sanctuary. Reluctantly at first, the clients conceded. It was hard to argue with a woman who served good tea.

Within a few months, the boy's mysterious silence, his calm, and most of all, the ease with which he did women's work – scouring pots, refiring hookahs, weaving fish-baskets – endeared him to them. Some even enjoyed flirting with a youth who was neither man nor boy. They poured their secrets into him.

At night, after the women returned to their homes, he helped his grandmother clean the tavern. Then he walked along the beach alone. The lights of the huge trawlers blinked, warning him away. But he'd stay, picturing their immense conical nets at the bottom of the sea, swallowing what his father's net should, and shouldn't.

He remembered clearly the face of the man who had lunged for the turtle's egg, two years ago. He saw himself again as on that night, a child with long black ringlets, smoking a K2, watching the reptile shovel her nest. He saw the shadow on the dune, the woman in only a flimsy tunic waiting for the prize her man had promised. He shut his eyes against the pain surging in his eardrum, but still went on remembering.

He is running. The man is a hulk of a rogue, at least six foot four, soon joined by others. Together, they overtake him. His locks are ropes with which to drag him out to sea. The salt burns his eyes as he rocks, back and forth, back and forth. He keeps his stinging eyes glued to the rising sun, a stargazer writhing in a net. And just when it seems the sea will swallow him, he touches a giant marbled shell. It carries him over watery hills till his path is smooth. He presses his cheeks into the turtle's hump of a home, going where she goes.

*　　*　　*

On the beach, calm descended. The flickering lights of the trawlers anchored too close to shore no longer infuriated him. The drums died. His ear once more registered sound like a cowry. In the two years since the attack, he'd learned the secret of overcoming the torture of memory: focus on one beautiful thing.

His head held high, Salaamat gently kicked the phosphorescence around his feet. Then he walked back to his house, one of the many quarters in the maze of crumbling walls that comprised the villages of the coast of Sindh. Packs of stray dogs rolled in the sand in front of the compound. They panted. Curiously, he could hear that. Sometimes he could hear much more than that.

He passed his grandmother and the other elderly women stationed in front of the complex. They were the sentinels of the village. His grandmother had been sitting here the night he'd nearly drowned. She'd seen his body loll in the waves and called for help. She sat here long into each night and then again at dawn, pitching her thoughts out to sea as her sons had once pitched their nets. But no one could trawl in her waters. She beckoned him to her.

He settled near a tailless black dog with bald patches. It scratched its chin against his heel. The old woman pulled on her hookah. He could hear this too. The urn was of glass, shaped like a large water drop, with bands of colored thread twisted around the middle. He watched the smoke rise and swirl around the water in the urn. He heard the low gurgle, and the high-pitched suck as the smoke traveled up the long slender pipe, then flew out in two sinewy ribbons from his grandmother's nose. She passed the hookah to the woman on her far side. Then, slowly, she took a long sip of her famous tea. He alone knew the reason for its fame: liquor. She brewed her own. The row of elderly women was almost intoxicated. Almost. They never crossed that line. Only their husbands did. It was one reason the women kept the teahouse for themselves.

'It is time for you to go now,' said the old woman.

He looked up, surprised. Two years ago, his father had wanted him to try his luck in the city, but she'd insisted he stay, arguing he hadn't regained his strength since the assault. She'd forbidden the subject to be broached again. But now she opened it herself.

'Go? But where?'

'Where else,' she replied flatly. Her voice was husky, and as always, uncompromising. 'There is little left for you in this village. The fish are gone. Your spiritless father lies in the darkness of his room, willing the current to turn back to the days of his forefathers. It will not. Those ships are here to stay.' She spat, and sucked on the hookah again.

The dog beside Salaamat rolled on its side, revealing five swollen teats. He thought angrily of his father, who mourned uselessly at home, while his mother labored at a shrimp-peeling factory set up by the foreigners. He looked at the gaudy hulks anchored nearby. She worked for *them*. She swallowed her outrage and gave her life to the enemy. They gave back five rupees for every kilo of stolen shrimp she cleaned.

The secrets of the women who met in the teahouse rang in the ear that only he and his grandmother knew was not entirely deaf. Some of those women were here now. Like him, they did not want to go inside. Their stories sprayed and splattered at his feet like the hissing surf. There was Farya, whose cotton nets were lost to the nylon needs of the trawlers. She sought comfort in jeering at Shireen, who sold her body to feed her husband's heroin needs. And there was his poor mother, whose punctured, obnoxious hands his father pushed away. It was Naila who gloated over that, right in his ear.

'You will go to the city and gradually, the rest will follow.'

Then she looked at him. 'Beware the strangers. Hold them at arm's length. Good luck, my son.'

He glanced up at the moon, textured like a turtle's egg, like the one he'd tried to save. He'd watched turtle hatchlings long enough to know their first journey to the sea was made all alone, purely by instinct. Their mother would depart when all her eggs were laid and never return. The fishermen said only one in a hundred hatchlings survived the perils that awaited them, and if the survivor were female, years later, she'd return to her birthplace, to lay her own eggs. He pulled a wet curl away from his eyes and wondered what happened to the males.

2

Look, But With Love

APRIL–JUNE 1984

He learned new words fast. Sand was replaced by granite, mud with cement, fish with scraps of rubbery mutton, and that too on good days. He smelled no salt in the air, only smoke and gases that made his chest burn. The moon was dimmed by lights a thousand times brighter than those the trawlers had burned. The brightest were for weddings: little colored bulbs strung from trees and rooftops. An entire house could light up like a private galaxy. Women did not sit outside homes, wedding or not, smoking. At first, he barely saw any at all. And there were ways to cross the rivers of asphalt without being hit by wheels.

For days after entering the city Salaamat sat on roadsides watching, stunned by the variety of wheels. On the beach, he'd seen weekend visitors ride down the shoreline on motorcycles, but he'd never known how many kinds of vehicles there could be. Now here they were, whizzing by him, vehicles each with names he longed to know. At a paan and tea stall (the tea was wretched but he learned to drink it) that hired him, he asked regulars to teach him. While painting the paan leaves with betel juice, he timidly repeated: Nissan, Honda, Suzuki, Toyota. It helped him forget how differently those around him spoke. Here he was not merely half-deaf but half-dumb. Avoiding speech, he quietly studied how the car models changed depending on the year, and formed opinions on which color best suited each style.

But what he loved most were the buses. He accidentally said so one day. The customers laughed, sucking on supari. 'Every man dreams of having a car and you dream of buses!'

He explained his tastes to no one.

The buses were decorated as lavishly as boats for the annual fair at his village. They were boats that rocked on a solid sea. He studied the designs, drank the rich colors, memorized the names of the shops that made them, all in Qaddafi Town. He learned this was near the eastern outskirts of the city and as soon as he'd saved enough money, Salaamat hopped on to one such bus.

The interior was pink and gold, and in each corner was a different picture: fish dancing; storks wading; a lofty crown; parrots with girlish eyes, preening. The tranquility of each scene contrasted with the activities of the commuters, who spat paan juice everywhere, extinguished cigarettes on fish fins, blew their noses on crown jewels. The sea salt he'd been unable to smell since coming here ate into the paint and left the interior crusted with rust. The bus shook with its load; five men hung from each of its doors and many more stood on the fenders, thumping the bus when it was time to jump off. Salaamat kept asking the conductor for Qaddafi Town. Finally, the man grabbed his kurta cuff and pushed him out.

Knees wobbling, Salaamat entered the first bus workshop he passed. It was called: Handsome Body Maker.

Seven buses were parked inside, in various stages of construction. A large man stepped out of an office, gruffly asking what he wanted.

'I . . . I want work,' Salaamat replied.

The man turned toward the office, shouting something incomprehensible. Two others appeared. The mighty one, who was Handsome, opened his palm and shook it rudely under Salaamat's chin. 'Wah! We should thank the Almighty the foreigner has come to us!'

Only one of the others, bald as an egg, laughed. Touching Salaamat's locks he said in a high-pitched voice, 'A pretty boy like you should have no problem finding work.' He turned to Handsome, adding, 'You are Handsome but he is Pretty.'

'But he's so dark,' protested the rose-cheeked Handsome between chuckles.

'It'll rub off!' said the bald man.

The third man was the smallest. He had a thin mustache and heavily oiled hair, and as yet had not cracked a smile. He squinted, 'Where are you from?'

Salaamat tossed his head proudly and named his village.

'A machera!' the skinny man sneered. 'No wonder he's black.'

'There are no fish here, meri jaan,' said the bald man, wagging a finger. 'Of course, if you're clever, you can catch other things.'

Salaamat cleared his throat. 'I'm clever and can learn a new trade. I ask only for food and lodging and will work as many hours as you need me to.'

The men looked at each other. Handsome said, 'For an ajnabi, you speak confidently.'

The bald man again fondled Salaamat's locks. 'Keep him. He speaks well.'

Handsome smacked his back and declared, 'Then, Chikna, I'll let you decide what to do with him.'

The skinny man interjected. 'We can't allow an ajnabi in here.'

'Since when have you owned this place?' Handsome retorted.

The skinny man said nothing, but Salaamat understood his gaze. This was the one to watch.

There were four doors behind the buses. Toward these Chikna now led him. Pointing to the small bundle in Salaamat's hand, he asked, 'Is that all you have?'

Salaamat nodded, looking closely for the first time at the seven buses. He stared, trying to understand their progression from one stage to the next. The first was just a skeleton – a brown mass of metal plates with four wheels. But the last was a glinting gem.

'That's called a chassis,' Chikna pointed to the first. 'The bus owner gives us that and we do the rest.' After a pause, he added, 'How old are you?'

'About seventeen.'

Chikna shrugged. 'I've been working here since I was seven. Maybe it's too late for you.' He pushed open a door to a storeroom. The floor was strewn with painted strips of steel, chains, wires, paint cans, stickers, hubs, brushes, lights, a pile of crowns and lopsided, childlike sculptures of eagles and airplanes. 'You can sleep here.'

Salaamat dropped his bundle inside.

'There's a toilet at back,' Chikna continued. 'Our families live in there,' he pointed two doors down. 'You can eat with us, but we've had our lunch. Can you wait for dinner?'

Salaamat nodded. He hadn't eaten but wasn't going to say so.

Outside, more workers were arriving. 'What can I do now?' asked Salaamat.

'Today, just watch. Tomorrow you'll start with me.' He walked away.

Salaamat shut the store's door and moved toward the buses. He wound his way around each, coming finally to the last. He then stood and took in every detail.

The exterior was painted a glittering magenta. Along the sides were nailed the strips of metal with garish floral patterns that he'd seen in the storeroom. The bottom edge of the bus was ringed around with chains ending in hearts. Wings figured elaborately everywhere: there were flying horses painted near the headlights and a sculpture of an eagle with a foot-long wingspan attached to the fender. The top wore a sort of palanquin, a bed of intricately worked metal, with the front decked in one of the airplane structures also in the store. The plane looked like a ship's figurehead. Attached to one wing was a national flag, while on the other a sign read: PIA. Whoever painted the bus had not simply wanted it driven but sailed, and not simply sailed but flown.

But the best awaited him at the back. Here was the most beautiful woman Salaamat had ever seen. She had eyes the size of his palm, a sensuous nose, and plum-like lips half hidden behind a flimsy cloth held in a henna-dipped hand. On her right side was written, Look. On her left, But With Love. She did exactly that to him.

Salaamat was spellbound. The harder he stared the more certain he felt that she blinked, then blinked again. Her lips twitched in a smile she attempted to restrain, but failing that, she covered more of her face with the transparent dupatta.

'Ah, I see you've met Rani,' said a voice. Salaamat forced himself away from the picture. It was Chikna. 'She's a naughty one, I'd be careful. And don't let Hero see you get too close. He's very jealous.'

'Hero?'

'Him,' Chikna pointed to the skinny man who was painting two buses down. 'You two already started on the wrong foot. And now Rani seems to find you as pretty as I do.' He tilted his head and raised a brow saucily.

'What does Hero do here?' asked Salaamat.

'He's our painter. He made Rani. He loves everything he does. He's in love with himself.' Chikna tweaked Rani's cheek roughly.

Salaamat had to stop himself from fighting him, for he

could hear Rani wince. 'I want to make a bus just like this one,' he blurted. 'I want to learn to make all these things. Including her.' Rani hid behind her cloth and Chikna threw his bald head back and laughed.

3

The Ajnabi

For the next several months, daily, Salaamat was told to go back home. Everything about him – his looks, accent, language, carriage – was mocked and shredded by the thirty or so workers who poured their lives out on bus art. All of them belonged to one of two groups. The Punjabis, like Handsome and his family, did most of the metal work. And the Pathans, like Hero, handled the painting. Salaamat alone belonged to a third group. He became the ajnabi. The alien.

Perhaps Chikna told Hero what Salaamat had confessed his first day: that he wanted to paint as well as him. Since the very next day till the end of Salaamat's first year, Hero would never let Salaamat near him while he worked. If he came too close, Hero would wrinkle his nose, 'Where's this rotten smell coming from? Oh! It's the fish.' And then he and the other Pathans would frantically wave the imagined odor away.

Though he kept his left ear to them, it was hardly a friend: it carried enough taunts to make the drums roll and the dam threaten to break. How dare they call *him* the outsider when it was *his* people who were the original inhabitants of Karachi? All around him – the buses, streets, shops, migrants from other provinces, and now, refugees from Afghanistan – all were mere appendages to a place that for centuries had thrived as a tranquil fishing village. But now those villages were pushed to the periphery, and the native populations forced to work under outsiders who claimed the city belonged to them. In a sense, his employment here was no less shameful than his mother's at the shrimp factory; they both worked for those who displaced them. Perhaps hers was less shameful – he'd still not earned a paisa from his labor. He fumed, banging strips of chamak pati into twisted shapes, peeling off stickers from Japan, putting the lot together on the body of the glowing buses. And then he stepped back and admired what he'd done. The old technique of overcoming rage returned to him.

He focused on one beautiful thing.

In the evenings, when the workers had left and Handsome scratched his ballooning stomach and gossiped with his younger brother Chikna, Salaamat's technique began to evolve. He no longer let the giant turtle take him across smooth seas to a safer place. He now grasped Rani. Not in any ocean, but right there, in the dark and littered storeroom that was his sleeping cell.

He cleared a fourth of the space to stretch in, and over the weeks, his encounters with Rani grew increasingly fierce. At first he only lay with her in his arms, gently nibbling her full lips. Then he began rubbing her tunic. Then he got impatient. So did she. One day Rani brushed up against him and moaned, 'Hurry!' He clicked his tongue, clutched her two henna-doused hands roughly in one of his own and smacked them. Then he pushed the small, pearl button at the top of her kurta out of the buttonhole with his tongue and teeth. At the third pearl he sank in her cleavage, pecking at her soft breasts while she yelped. He tightened his grasp of her hands and pushed her neck back to bare more flesh. Her breasts were enormous and smooth. He lifted each with the back of his free hand so it grew even rounder. Then he yanked each nipple with his teeth and tongue the way he had the pearl buttons. She screamed. Feverishly, he threw off her shalwar. When she struggled, before parting her legs, he squeezed her neck. That silenced her. From now on, this was how it had to be.

The next morning, he rushed out the room to check on the seventh bus. His greatest fear was its completion. The bus still needed some touching up – the owner wanted the interior throbbing with heart-shaped lights, and these had still to be made. Salaamat dreaded the day the hearts went up. Though he was swiftly learning to work with steel almost as well as any Punjabi, he'd still never held a brush. He was still very, very far away from replacing Rani when she left.

But she stayed with him, the only thing in the world that was his.

During meals with Handsome's family, Salaamat listened quietly to the chatter. Above them lurked a portrait of the General, Handsome's hero. Handsome told of his two nephews who were being trained to fight the Soviets in Afghanistan. He looked up at the portrait and blessed the General. Then he blessed Amreeka for training and arming the freedom fighters, thundering, 'We are Amreeka's best allies, and they are ours. With their help, we are coming closer to saving Islam.' Shoveling hunks of meat in his enormous mouth, he spoke next of the many anti-Soviet rallies organized by the religious parties to whom Amreeka was giving aid.

During the day, Handsome's family kept apart from the Pathans and vice versa. What little Salaamat managed to hear of the latter's chatter was no different from Handsome's. In fact, Hero and his friends had more than two nephews between them joining the war. They seemed to know dozens of boys up in the mountains, boys much younger than Salaamat, who were learning to load and use weapons he couldn't even imagine. It was a community of young Heroes. Why wouldn't Handsome be pleased with that?

He soon had an answer: thousands of war refugees were pouring into Peshawar daily, pushing some of the local residents south to Karachi. Of these, too many were in the bus-body-making business. If this continued, the Pathans would drive the Punjabis out. Those who'd pushed villagers like Salaamat to the edge fiercely resented being pushed out too.

At night, before taking Rani, Salaamat constructed a comical scenario in his mind.

Hundreds of men were packed into a small space like his sleeping cell. The door kept opening and yet more were shoved in. Soon there wasn't an inch to stand in, so colossal men like Handsome stepped on scrawny ones like Hero. The scrawny men stumbled into the back wall and pressed into it, trying desperately to find a little gap. But there was none. Eventually, even the Handsomes got mashed against the wall like mosquitoes.

It was not unlike what happened on buses every day. Sooner or later, everyone had to fall off. Who cared who fell first? If he fell with Rani, it wouldn't be so bad. He never had enough of pressing into her anyway.

One evening at dinner Chikna left the room in a state of nervousness, and returned in a state of increased nervousness. 'It's the Authorities,' he panted.

Handsome frowned, 'That's twice this month.' He pushed his plate away and marched outside, Chikna in tow.

Three of them waited, equipped with batons and a list of grievances – nonpayment of taxes, unregistered documents, expired licenses, a distaste of bus ornaments. Ornamentation, they argued, was a traffic hazard. How could the driver see when the bus was a distraction?

'But it's a distraction from the *outside*,' Salaamat, still in the room, heard Handsome explain.

The Senior Authority raised his baton menacingly. 'How can he see out the rear-view mirror when he has that,' he smashed a crown off the fender of a bus, 'staring at him?'

Salaamat stepped outside. The Authority had attacked Rani's bus. A part of him was relieved: the more damage the bus suffered, the longer she'd stay. But another part was outraged. How dare this man threaten her?

As the Senior Authority advanced toward the rear, Rani covered herself entirely. He tapped the cloth away with his stick and leered. Before he could catch himself, Salaamat blurted, 'The crown would not have been staring at him through the rear-view mirror.'

'Oh is that right?' The man spun around. 'Would you like to show me what he would have been looking at?' The two other Authorities, absorbed in smashing more fenders, joined their boss.

The boss swung his baton. Before Salaamat could pull away, it cut across his arm. He buckled. A second man struck his knee. A third, his stomach. 'Who are you to answer us?' they hissed. 'You're just an ajnabi.'

Salaamat's head began to whirl. He saw three pairs of glistening boots. One pair aimed for his groin. 'We'll show you your place.'

None of the other workers moved. None, not even Chikna, had spoken. They'd given him what he'd asked: food and lodging. The rest was up to him. Ghee burned his nose as he began to vomit.

Nearly three years ago, the first kick had also struck his knee. Then too he'd vomited. He heard the wind in his hair from that night, hair since trimmed. But though short now, his locks were still reins to steer him with. The Authorities yanked them as they punched.

There had been the sound of waves. His grandmother's watchfulness. Soft, soft sand. And then the turtle's shell. He reached out. Rani was beside him, mopping his forehead with cool fingers, invisible to all but him.

Just before losing consciousness he saw Handsome peel several hundred rupees from a thick wad of notes in his pocket.

Three days later, after tossing in delirium on the hard floor of his littered room, he stumbled outside to find Rani gone.

4

In the Picture

MAY 1985

He had Fridays off. He spent them roaming the city, on foot
and by bus. He made sure to travel on a different one each
time, and in his head kept meticulous track of their various
designs. Before his first year at Handsome's was up, he'd
sat in over a hundred inner-city buses. But he never saw
Rani again.

It was on a sweltering day in May, on a bus with a two-foot
PIA plane model on its roof and a driver who skated down
a runway only he appeared to see, that Salaamat met his
youngest brother, Shan.

'You're here!' he said, surprised at his own happiness. The
boy had been twelve when they'd last met. Now his voice was
beginning to crack and on his upper lip hovered a wisp of fuzz.
'You look well.'

Shan barely knew him. 'Yes,' he shrugged.

'Are you alone?' Salaamat pressed on.

The bus screeched and swerved. Salaamat's head bumped
the canopy of a green waterfall.

'No. Aba has come. So have Sumbul and Hamid, Chachoo and his family.'

'Where are they?'

'In Thatta. But we're about to move here, in the city. Aba's been hired at a rich man's house. His name is Mr Mansoor. He's very important.' Shan straightened his shoulders proudly.

The bus stopped, then started again. Shan hadn't mentioned their mother.

Salaamat looked at his brother, lean and dark like himself. Like her. He saw her fingers, pink and crinkled like the shrimp she peeled, rejected by a husband who lived off them. He whispered, 'And Ama?'

'She died.'

In the jammed bus still more commuters were piling in. They shook like a tin of nails. When Salaamat spoke his teeth rattled. He cursed the driver for mimicking a pilot. Then he cursed Shan. 'Bastard! When? Why wasn't I told?'

Shan stepped back. 'A few months after you left,' he cried. 'Dadi said there was no point calling you. She said you had to keep working.'

'That wench! Just because she saved my life once, doesn't mean she owns it.'

Shan moved further away.

Salaamat's ear began to ache. He'd only distanced his brother even more. But what did it matter? From the day his grandmother told him to leave, his family had forgotten him. Except perhaps his mother, and his sister Sumbul. They'd cried when he left. Yes, they'd have thought of him. He took a deep breath. Except for his pounding ear, everything went deathly still.

After a long pause, he asked more gently, 'Is Sumbul well?'

'Yes.' And then: 'She often speaks of you.'

Salaamat could not resist a smile. 'What were you doing in Thatta?'

'We were guarding the tombs of Makli Hill.' He lunged into an elderly man, then straightened up again. 'Chachoo and his family are still there, but we're going to the rich man's house. This is my stop.'

Salaamat hopped out with him. He loosened his shoulders. They were always sore now since his thrashing by the Authorities. But the men never had the chance to beat him again. He'd learned to quickly duck into his den whenever they came.

Shan caught another bus, and a third, and finally, in the late afternoon, they reached a neighborhood unlike any other Salaamat had frequented on previous Fridays. Streets were wide and tree-lined. Shops had tinted glass and words scrawled in beautiful, swirling script. Houses were like forts, with massive gates and towering walls topped in barbed wire partially concealed behind ropes of ivy. The air was cleaner. But one thing remained the same: boys played cricket in the street.

It was into a street with a game in progress that Shan now turned. The bowler had the definite advantage, for the lane was at a sharp incline and he stood at the top, while the batsman hunkered below, braving the speed of the descending toss. 'Out!' came a voice from the top of the hill. A girl's voice. The wicket, three frail wooden pins, soared into the air.

'That was just the wind!' complained the batsman. 'Anything would send this stupid wicket flying.'

Salaamat squinted, but the bowler was in shadow. The umpire, a man nearly as wide as Handsome but not as tall, raised a finger and declared, 'Out!' From up the hill the invisible bowler hooted.

'That's favoritism!' screamed the batsman. The umpire rolled on the balls of his feet and grinned at the bowler skipping into the sunlight, down toward him.

The bowler *was* a girl. Well, more than just a girl. Her yellow kameez was both thin enough and tight enough to reveal two small but shapely breasts, and an equally shapely behind. The umpire embraced her, 'Shabash, beti!'

Her smooth, nut-brown cheeks were flushed and sweaty, her shoulder-length hair a delicious mess. 'Aba,' she laughed, 'that's three for ten runs at the end of just three overs.'

The lone fielder picked his nose. 'This is so damn boring,' he announced.

'Yes,' said the batsman. 'Boring and only for cheats.' He threw down his bat and stormed inside a gate with wrought-iron waves rising from the top. The fielder dug into his other nostril.

Shan gathered the three pins and walked up to the umpire.

It was the girl who took the pins from him. She smiled. 'Thank you.'

Shan chewed his lips timidly. He addressed the father, 'I've brought some things, Mansoor Sahib.'

Mansoor Sahib looked at Salaamat. 'And this is?'

'Oh,' said Shan vaguely. 'My eldest brother. But,' he quickly added, 'he won't be staying here.'

Salaamat held his head up high. The sahib seemed to be waiting for his greeting but Salaamat said nothing.

All four entered the gate. They walked up a long, swirling driveway shaded with jamun and peepul trees. A sweet smell infiltrated his nose. Yellow wings fluttered across his vision. Up ahead and to his right, in an enormous mulberry tree, sat a pair of blossom-headed parakeets, nibbling at each other's beaks. Finally, they reached a mass of round rocks, from which toppled a miniature waterfall. Salaamat sucked in his breath. This was exactly the kind of picture painted on the ceilings and corners of almost every bus he'd seen or worked on. No, it was better. The picture stretched on, till they came at last to a clearing bordered by laburnum trees.

In the center sat a woman at a glass table. 'Just in time,' she looked up. Her gaunt face was framed with short hair arranged in a copious swoop to the side. Salaamat thought even Shan prettier.

'I won, Ama,' said the girl.

'I know,' the mother laughed. 'I saw Hassan storm away.'

'He always loses,' the girl rejoiced.

Her father sat down. 'Maybe you should let him win from time to time.'

'Don't you dare!' her mother intercepted. 'What he needs is a wife who can bowl better than him.' She and her husband exchanged glances, while the girl, still standing, watched keenly, her wide eyes darting from face to face, her smile fading.

Then the woman turned to Shan. With a curious, bemused air, she asked of Salaamat, 'And this is?'

'My brother.' Shan reddened again.

Standing with both legs apart and hands behind his back, Salaamat still said nothing.

'Perhaps he's in the army,' Mr Mansoor offered. 'Everybody seems to be these days. Should we eat?'

DAANISH

I

The Gag Order

SEPTEMBER 1990

It was a fair question, thought Daanish. Does the United States want a war? But he was learning which questions could not be asked.

Wayne leaned back into a swivel chair. A sign in his office read: *Trust your choices. Everything is possible.* There was an identical one in the classroom where he lectured. Tilting his chin he regarded Daanish from down the length of a thin nose. 'I merely suggested you explore different avenues. Good journalism is snappy and digestible. You're an amateur. Your writing style is ponderous and, well, pretty emotional.'

Daanish studied the page he'd written in the journal students were required to keep. Each week, class discussion revolved around the most popular subject, with tips on how to gather more information and how to beef up its selling points with eyewitness-type phrases and expressions. 'Interviewing witnesses,' Wayne loved to say, 'is key. Make your audience be them. Make 'em gasp, make 'em drool.' The last class discussion was on the removal of various vitamins from store shelves. The mass media reported that the decision had resulted in more protest letters to the government than on any other issue in history. In class, students voiced their outrage on the infringement of the public's right to choose their product. Small groups compared the various articles on the 'crisis', and a consensus was drawn on which report best served the interests of the oppressed people. Some articles interviewed those who no longer had access to their favorite vitamin. It made readers gasp. It made them drool. It made the students want to write like that.

The week before, the topic had been a certain museum's refusal to exhibit nudes. 'Censorship,' Wayne had said, 'is our worst enemy. Let's not forget that it's almost the two-hundredth anniversary of the First Amendment to the Constitution, the right to free speech. Today we'll examine the many ways the media has asserted it. But first,' he raised a finger and his voice began to fill the auditorium impressively. His lower lip plunged into the upper in a passionate pucker. He bounced. 'Remember that as guardians of the press, as those who'll go forward into the world with four years of meticulous training, as those who'll be eyewitnesses of the vast turbulence around us, it's our role to speak the objective truth to those who stay behind and depend on us!'

It had been six weeks since Iraq invaded Kuwait. Not one class discussion had addressed the attack, let alone its reporting. No one mentioned the international sanctions against Iraq or the freezing of its assets. Without oil exports, the nation was unable to import food. Daanish had found nothing in the US media about the effects of those sanctions nor about the peace settlements he knew, through the international press, were ongoing. Americans had been told little besides the fact that 40,000 US troops had been sent to Saudi Arabia. They'd been told the deployment was defensive, even though it was as large as the one in Vietnam.

Daanish spent hours in the library, searching and delving

through the less influential American and foreign papers. What he found led to the writing of the following entry in his journal:

After eight years of fighting Iran, Iraq needed to rebuild its economy. It needed oil money. However, the day after the Iran-Iraq cease-fire, Kuwait began increasing oil production, in violation of OPEC rules. Oil prices were cut in half. By the following year, Kuwait was producing more than two million barrels of oil per day, much more than its OPEC quota. To make things worse, it began extracting this oil from an oilfield on the disputed Iraq-Kuwait border, a border created by the British. It did this with US approval. After all, the US supplied the technology. Some lesser-known newspapers, at great personal risk, are reporting that during the Iran-Iraq war, Kuwait was actually drilling the oil on Iraq's side of the border. Since Kuwait was one of the biggest Iraqi creditors during the war (an amount exceeding thirty billion dollars), this could mean it loaned Iraq its own product! Now, after the war, it has been demanding the debt be paid, while simultaneously increasing production.

These are events not mentioned in the more popular newspapers and magazines, but in light of Iraq's invasion, I believe they ought to be. All angles of the situation ought to be examined, all parties ought to be included in the debate and the debate ought to be made available to the public. But why is the public not being told what the UN, US, Iraq, Kuwait and other relevant Middle Eastern nations are discussing? Does the US have other plans?

Perhaps. We need to also examine how the American government dealt with Iraq during the Iran-Iraq crisis, when it was taken off the 'terrorist' list. Compare this with what happened immediately after the cease-fire. Practically overnight, it was again declared a threat in a document with a name worth noting, War Plan 1002–90. Why the about-face? It was the same Iraq, the one that had been funded and armed by the US during the war. Mirroring the government's shift, the US media also began to portray Iraq differently. It was no longer an ally. It had become the enemy.

The American public has been told that the 40,000 US troops currently stationed in the Saudi desert are there to protect Saudi Arabia from the 120,000 Iraqi troops moving into it from Kuwait. Why haven't we been shown these Iraqi troops?

A good student of journalism should not accept statements as true till hard evidence is available, particularly not on the brink of war. So an in-depth discussion of the circumstances leading into Iraq's invasion of Kuwait must be had. We should read the smaller publications that dare to exercise their right under the First Amendment. These might be the ones that are better – as you yourself have said – 'guardians of the truth'.

'This is a perfectly reasonable entry,' mumbled Daanish, looking up from the journal. In red ink, Wayne had written, *A weak analysis. Choose another topic. Explore other avenues.* 'What do you mean by exploring other avenues? That's what I've done. No one else in class has touched the topic, though it's a lot more important than vitamins.'

Daanish was pleased with himself for remaining calm. Though he wrote boldly in his journal, he rarely found the courage to confront Wayne in person. So far, he was doing well.

'Look,' said Wayne, shutting the journal abruptly. He leaned forward, fixing him with icy blue eyes. Daanish forced himself to glower back. 'I can understand how upsetting this must be for you. Miles from home, nostalgic perhaps. Lonely. You've done well to get this far. I'm proud of you. Really, I am. It's good to take pride in your own.'

Daanish was aghast. 'Pride in my own?'

'Well, you being an Arab and all, these events . . .'

'I'm not an Arab,' Daanish retorted, before his lips snapped shut. Not this, he thought. Wayne had never accused other students of being swayed because of their backgrounds. But Daanish's had become a weapon to silence him with, though Wayne couldn't even get the details right. He opened his mouth before knowing how to say this, and, with the same scorn that he heard in Wayne's voice, said, 'Arabs comprise less than thirty per cent of Muslims.' But this was not his most important point. He sat quietly, listening to his heart race.

Then: 'I'm a student of journalism. My journal has nothing to do with my religion.' The next sentence hung on the tip of his tongue: Have I ever questioned *your* skills based on *your* faith? He swallowed it.

Wayne leaned back into the swivel chair again. He looked at his watch. 'Well,' he shrugged, 'your role as a budding journalist is to understand that all media persons deal in facts, not opinions. Fact: Saddam invaded Kuwait. We cannot change that by asking why. You're free to speculate,' he rotated his arms in a magnanimous gesture, 'but your speculations are not news. Your opinions have no place on the front page.'

This time Daanish did not pause. 'But that's *all* that's *on* the front page! What do you call this?' He pointed to a page in his thick stack of articles. 'Headline: *More Than a Madman*. Are you telling me that's a fact? And what about him being called a Hitler? They're actually trying to prove that he's some reincarnation of him! Did they learn to report in such a *factual* fashion in college?'

Wayne smacked his fleshy thighs, making to stand up. 'You're going to get nowhere by siding with Saddam, young man.'

'I am not siding with him.' He was shivering. It wasn't cold. 'It's a sign of my professional commitment that you're unable to detect my true feelings for the man.' He paused, determined to let that sink in. His head was pounding now. He'd never stood up to a teacher before. Vaguely, he worried that he was pushing himself off a cliff.

'I'm asking if the media is presenting us with facts or, or

mere labels. Something easy to latch on to so that if there is a war – and would it go through all this trouble if it didn't know the administration intended one? – there'll be too much hatred against the "enemy" to question its destruction.' Yes, he had definitely pushed himself off. His organs swished under his skin. Still he kept on. 'Who is really being brainwashed? The irony is that the top of this article begins with a photograph of school children in front of a photograph of Saddam and the caption reads: *From birth, Iraqis are taught to obey their supreme leader's every command.* The caption could easily read: From birth, Americans are taught to obey their ruling troika: the White House, Pentagon and the Media.' He sat back, shocked at himself.

Wayne marched toward the door. He waited for Daanish to do the same. 'I did say you were likely to get emotional. Uh! Uh!' He held his hand up in a restraining motion. 'Just listen. I'll tell you what, you mull over it. The vitamin story may seem mundane to you, but perhaps there's a lesson here. You're only a sophomore.'

Now Daanish's courage did fail him. His voice sank to the bottom of his pants. He bit on his belt. His words were not in his throat, they were in his hands, but as he rolled off the cliff, he let them go.

Another professor passed by the open door.

'How's it going?' Wayne cheerfully greeted her.

They walked away, leaving Daanish in the corridor. He could hear them discuss the venue for the next board meeting.

2

Revisions

JUNE 1992

Daanish stood at the window. His head was leaden with yet another night of intermittent sleep. Every morning since his return to Karachi, he'd given up the fight for rest soon after dawn, when the builders arrived next door. He watched now as a bare-footed, bare-chested old man climbed a bamboo ladder, balancing a cement bucket on his feeble head. His hair was dry and bleached, like sugar-cane husk. Between the first two toes of his right foot he carried a trowel. The bucket on his head, and two more in his hands, wavered. With the heel and toes of his free foot, he pressed the sides of the ladder till it steadied. In this way he arrived at the top rung.

The old man handed over the buckets to a younger worker hunkered on the roof. Wiping his face with a wrinkled cloth, he then lit a cigarette, savoring it as though he was the one indoors, standing aimlessly at the window like Daanish.

The sky was a peach-gray pierced by dish antennas, sooty rooftops, telephone wires. There were hardly any trees.

Beyond, but invisible to Daanish, was the sea. Like him, it lapped different shores. On this one, the old man was born on the wrong side of the belt. Here, Daanish could scribble slander on a napkin and hurl it his way. Here, he never had to scrub pots the size of church bells, or clench his jaw in the presence of Kurt or Wayne. If he wanted, he could step outside and lord it over anyone. Simply by crossing an ocean, his place in the universe changed.

The laborer tossed away his cigarette. A figure walked toward him. It was Khurram's driver, carrying an aluminum pot. He'd seen him at some point every morning, when Khurram's family did not need him. As on the day he'd driven him home from the airport, Daanish was struck by his good looks.

After the girl in the blue dupatta left the caterpillars, Daanish had asked his uncles what they were but the men brusquely recommended destruction. 'Forget about that rude incident,' his chacha had advised.

He couldn't. So he decided to slip outside with the three fat slugs and ask the construction workers. They passed on the inquiry till it reached the driver, who knew immediately.

'How?' Daanish asked, holding the larvae in his palm.

'My sister works on a farm where they're bred,' the man answered. His face was forever expressionless, as if it had simply been jammed.

'What do you know about them?' Daanish pushed.

The man moved to Daanish's other side and asked him to repeat the question. Then he replied, 'Feed them a lot. When they've spun their cocoons, if you want the thread, boil them.'

'That's a bit extreme,' Daanish mused. 'What do they eat?'

'Leaves. There's a large mulberry tree in the empty plot at the end of the street. They'll eat lettuce but they prefer the leaves of that tree, especially if chopped.'

The builders were pleased to take time off and chat with the boy from Amreeka. Though Daanish was pleased to get away from the mourners, he soon tired of being asked for a visa.

'You should see how I'm treated at their Consulate! I'm nothing to them! I can't help you!'

They hadn't believed him.

Daanish turned away from the window and looked in one of the drawers where his shells had been. They were gone now. His temper began to rise. For the millionth time, he opened the door of the new closet and rummaged through the pile of clothes Anu had stacked. His beautiful shell boxes had been stored in the old closet. They too were gone. He slammed the door shut.

Anu was the only one who could have gone through his things. Yet she denied it. He shook his head: the doctor would *never* have invaded his privacy. It had to be her. Why? And it seemed she was still at it: his books and the envelope full of photographs were also gone. So was his bloody camera!

This was not how he remembered her. She'd changed. He did not want her to. She ought to be steady, like the boulder she sat on while he and his father went exploring. They'd been a piece, like a vase of cut glass, with her the light from the back and his father the glowing foreground. With the front gone, she was strangely like a gaping well. He was afraid of peering in too far.

She'd not even told him what 'question' she'd posed the morning of his arrival. 'There is plenty of time to answer me,' she'd said, but then the next evening, knew nothing about it. He cursed again.

Shedding his clothes, he stood before the full-length mirror. The light-brown eyes that answered back were his father's. After hearing of their likeness for years, he saw it clearly now. He was exactly his height. The weight he'd acquired this year at college, when the plastic flavors of Fully Food finally stopped nauseating him, was beginning to settle around his midriff in a soft, barely noticeable belt of flesh, probably exactly as it had begun to do on the doctor when he was twenty-two. His legs were still sleek and sinewy. Swimmer's legs. Going by the doctor, they'd always be Daanish's best feature.

Becky had admired them the day they first met, when he walked her home from the gym. Thinking of her made him remember the missing photographs again. He'd liked the one of Pamela leaning against an oak tree. The ground was strewn with autumn leaves reminding him of their tryst in the sunken garden where Daanish loved to roam. Only, there was none of the humiliation of that time with Penny. By the time he'd met Pamela, Daanish knew better than to poke a stomach or buttock like a blind mole. The photograph was taken just before she sat on the bed of leaves and began to slowly undo her blouse. It was a three-quarter view, so her right bluish-green eye appeared larger than the left. Above it, a thin eyebrow was raised, giving Pamela her characteristic expression: Oh yeah?

Damn! Where was it? For the next half-hour, he searched every corner of the rearranged, freshly painted room. His eye fell on the lacquer box, one of the few items not missing from the duffel bag. But this too had been touched. He'd never before seen the photograph inside it. What on earth was it doing there?

His head began to throb. He got into the shower. Because there'd been no electricity since yesterday, the water pump hadn't been switched on. The tank was almost dry and the pressure so low only two holes of the showerhead released a few drops. Still soapy, Daanish returned to his room and stood naked on the new white rug. He looked up at the ceiling fan wishing for the telltale whine that sounded when it spun. But the loadshedding continued.

Soon his sweat blended with the soap and he was covered in a thin coat of slime. He left a trail of gray footprints on the rug. This pleased him. As the rug's color muddied, his head began to clear. Toweling himself dry, he listened to Anu making preparations for the Quran Khwani downstairs. It was just after eight. The mourners would start arriving around nine. There were fewer now that three weeks had passed since his father's death but there were still more than he wanted to meet. He combed his hair and braced himself for another day of being the Amreekan orphan.

But he didn't go downstairs. Instead, he returned to the drawer. He kept the three cocoons there now. Exactly as the driver said, the insects had spun their homes. Though he was disappointed to have missed the weaving process, the downy balls entertained him in their own way. They moved. First he'd left them on a pile of newspapers on his desk. When he returned, they'd jumped into a walnut bowl that held his pens. By the following day, they'd hopped onto the desk, far away from the newspaper. No matter where he put them, they wanted to be somewhere else. At last he found a place they found acceptable: inside a dark, dry corner of the drawer. According to the driver, if Daanish wanted the threads he'd have to cook them next week.

Kneeling for a closer look, he whispered, *cocoon*. It had a calming sound. Soft like sleep, like nestling. He fit into it somehow. 'What should I do with you?' he asked. 'You're so different from my beautiful shells. They can't live without water, you can't live within it.'

He thought of the gazelle-eyed girl in the blue dupatta. If she returned, he wanted to be the first to talk to her. He wanted to tell her he'd followed her advice and found out what she'd left. He wanted also to look more closely at that smooth, caramel face with the gracefully tapering chin. But he'd not seen her again. Did he even remember her correctly? Hell, he needed a picture of her too.

It was the hope of finding the girl that finally forced Daanish downstairs.

3

There, of course!

A swift glance revealed the girl was not there. He kissed his mother good morning and picked up a siparah, heading for the adjoining room, where the men sat.

The room looked on to a small garden fringed with hibiscus bushes. The grass was beginning to scorch in patches. His street badly wanted water. Two lanes away lived a minister, so no loadshedding ever plagued that street. Some of the mourners were discussing this when he joined them. They fanned themselves with newspapers and Daanish knew that in amongst the prayers for his dead father were prayers for bijly, and a brand new lot of politicians.

Along the opposite wall sat three of Daanish's uncles. They came and sat beside him, too hot to read, keener on conversation. His chacha turned to him. 'All his life Shafqat Bhai knew you would make him proud. Everything he did, every hour of toil, was for you.'

Another uncle chipped in, 'Our children in Amreeka do very well. There, of course, they have all the opportunity to shine. And they do! Look at Daanishwar!' He thumped Daanish heartily on the back. 'Come, you've told us nothing of your experiences there. All good things must be shared.'

The other men nodded with gusto.

When Daanish remained noncommittal, an older cousin nudged him. 'I hear it's very quiet and peaceful over there. Not like here, with army troops muscling their way into our neighborhoods.'

Immediately his phoopa interrupted, 'Things are a lot better since the army operation. I know. I drive through Nazimabad every day, unlike you in your elite street. I see how many fewer buses and trucks are being burned. It's because of the troops!'

'Yes,' said his chacha. 'But we have to question their tactics. They're rounding up anyone from the Muhajir areas and beating them regardless. This is only going to fuel the MQM's anger.'

There was a general murmur of consent, in which Daanish's phoopa remained aloof. After a pause, he looked up. 'It's the Punjabis who are being made to pay. We're going to be driven out. I'm thinking of taking my family back to Lahore.'

'Rubbish,' said another. 'It's the Muhajirs. How many of us are in prominent positions? The quota system must end.'

'You all control Karachi!' came the bellowing response.

The chacha was quick to intercede. 'One thing we can all agree on: those Sindhi separatists are imbeciles.' Everyone nodded. The chacha continued, 'Now, what is the point of getting into this discussion here? My poor brother would not have wanted it.' He padded toward the center of the room, where sweets and savories lay in large clay platters. He began passing them around. Next he poured out warm Pepsi, explaining, 'Without water for tea, it's the best we can do.' Daanish's stomach turned; it was barely ten in the morning.

His chacha turned to him again. 'Today, it's Daanish who will talk!'

Just a hop across the ocean, thought Daanish.

'You'll be a better mold of me,' the doctor had said. The test had begun.

'But what do you want to know?' Daanish asked.

'All that you've seen these three years!' they replied.

He shrugged. 'In many ways things are really different, but in others, they're not.'

'Tell us what's different,' said his phoopa. 'We don't care about the rest.'

'Yes,' said another man Daanish did not recognize. 'We don't want same same.'

'Well,' Daanish shifted. 'It's hard to explain.'

The men waited.

'Here we have many restrictions but few rules, there it's the opposite. There are few restrictions but many rules.'

The men exchanged glances. It was a poor beginning. Before he could start again someone asked, 'Are there plenty of jobs available?'

'Well,' Daanish cleared his throat. 'Actually, since the Gulf War there's been a bit of a recession.'

The room was silent and the silence grew. Someone shook his head, 'That war was a crime.'

Everyone nodded and a general moroseness took over. His chacha said, 'What did those poor Iraqis ever do to them? I tell you, oil is a curse. Look at Iran. Look at Libya.'

Another nodded, 'And look at the Saudis. Look how low they stoop.'

Daanish's phoopa scowled, 'Are you insulting the holy land?'

'No,' he replied, 'I'm insulting the beggars who live in it.'

The phoopa declared, 'They are our brothers.'

'They are closer brothers of the Iraqis they let the Americans bomb.'

'Urdu speaker,' he retorted.

Someone began to recount how he took a different route

to work every day for fear of being kidnapped. 'The situation has gotten so bad,' he said emphatically.

'But there have been fewer kidnappings since the army operation,' Daanish's phoopa insisted.

'There's going to be a civil war!' announced another unknown.

'There's going to be nothing besides more rumor and your hysteria!'

Daanish's chacha again began serving sweets.

Daanish looked around in despair. He must quickly tell the men of his other, better life. He'd have to reconstruct it the way he'd tried to reconstruct this one for an exotica-starved Becky. He'd failed her; he was probably going to fail his uncles too.

While he wondered what to say, the dispute continued. For some reason, a man was thumping his chest and booming, 'I am a thinker.'

'Ask those that built this country!' his opponent snapped. 'We are the ones who really toil for Pakistan!'

'Please, please,' Daanish's chacha sighed. 'Think of my brother.'

A taut silence again descended. More Pepsi was served. More eyes turned desperately to the ceiling fan. Not a thread of an air current blew past them. The room began to smell of feet, armpits, fermenting sugar.

Then, again, 'Someone needs to topple this government.'

'In our country,' said an elderly man thus far silent, 'Prime Ministers do nothing but play musical chairs.'

'*Han, han.* As soon as the people stop cheering, another one sits down!'

There was laughter, and jokes as to which one of the two still circulating had the bigger bottom.

The old man tugged his long white beard and declared, 'Definitely he does, but *she* has two. Three if you count her husband's favorite horse!'

Applause. The air lightened. Perhaps the pressure was off Daanish now. But no, when the laughter subsided, his chacha hooked him. 'It doesn't happen there, does it? There, the President always completes his term.'

There was a general chorus of, 'There, of course!'

Daanish breathed deeply. He must contribute positively this time. 'Another great thing is that there, people stand in lines.'

'There, of course!'

He was getting in the spirit: 'The bijly seldom goes.'

All eyes gazed beckoningly at the stubborn ceiling fan. 'There, of course!'

Daanish shut his eyes. 'The air is clean and crisp. In the winter, the snow gives gently under your boots, in autumn the colors are like the softest firelight, and in spring . . .'

He was back in the sunken garden. He could smell the dew as he lay on the grass. Pollen dusted the air. He wasn't even sure what he said next, just that everyone agreed, and that another presence had crept beside him. It had eyes like his, a plump midriff, and legs strong and lean. It listened, transfixed, as Daanish confessed to missing his walks in the cedar forest. So it went with him, laughing in a wonderful, grizzly way, happy to be out in the world instead of locked in the inward, tail-biting frenzy of the mourners. It said, 'My son, you will be a better mold of me.'

And then the room fell silent. Slowly, the men began reading again. Daanish realized he was scrunched in his chacha's embrace and that his face was wet.

4

Every Thirty Seconds

When the war broke, television showed planes dropping missiles with absolute precision. At the same time, the print media disclosed that the Pentagon had rules for war coverage. In his journal, Daanish insisted these rules amounted to deleting the war entirely. Absolutely no gore was shown. There were no wounded soldiers on either side, no schools in flame, no detonated sewage systems, no Iraqi civilians – the American public would not see even one, dead, dying or alive. There were no war hospitals, no interviews with patients receiving any medication, no broken oil pipelines, no blown-up dams inundating thousands of square miles. None of that happened. The war was surgical and pure. There was no suffering. And Wayne continued deleting Daanish's journal entries.

In the TV lounge of Daanish's dorm, only a handful of students followed even the sterilized news. One day he looked inside it on his way to Fully Food. The lounge was dark and warm with plush pink sofas. Pizzas speckled the carpet. Coke stained it. There was a rustling as fingers probed paper bags for popcorn. The seventy-two-inch screen featured an aerial sortie. Ready – aim – fire. The projectile cruised in a velvety sky. It could have been fired from the starship *Enterprise*. Any minute now, the spacecraft would save the world from ugly green aliens.

A student, donning a T-shirt that said *Food Not Bombs*, yawned and said he'd had enough. He then emptied his popcorn down the shirt of the woman beside him. She laughed, hollering at the missile, 'That's what you get for oppressing your women, suckers.'

Days later, Daanish skipped all his classes, and skipped Fully Food.

Hunkering in a corner of the library, he started taking notes from a few small American publications that defied the Pentagon's gag order. One disclosed the use of weapons employed during the Vietnam War but since declared illegal by the UN and the US. It quoted a CIA agent saying the fuel-air explosives, used to clear out dense jungles in Vietnam, made no sense in the flat desert of the Middle East, and yet the bombs were being used on frontline Iraqi troops. About napalm, a US Marine officer admitted it had been used, just as in Vietnam, against both troops and civilians. So were cluster bombs. Another lamented that on television, one general called the air strikes 'a party'.

Daanish noted all this in his journal, growing increasingly motivated. Here were a few courageous reporters. Surely it would be interesting to compare these reports with others?

He moved on to the popular press, struck by its sloppiness, its glaring inconsistencies. One magazine wrote that Iraq's military was invincible but then bragged that the government could and would contain it. Another said officials persevered to avoid Iraqi civilian casualties, then quoted a general saying the number of civilians killed did not interest him. It was as if the reports were censored but not proofread.

*　　*　　*

Hours later, Daanish stepped outside. Walking aimlessly through the college grounds, he gradually made his way downtown, his neck sinking deep into the collar of his jacket. The wind had picked up during the afternoon. The darkness, at barely five o'clock, had set like cooling lacquer. He passed cafés piled with students and checked his pockets – not even two dollars left from his last paycheck, and the next would be cut. Stopping at a window, he looked inside. A woman carried a glossy black mug of steaming hot chocolate Daanish could almost smell. He pulled away.

The streets were still aglow with Christmas lights. Wreaths and colored balls hung from eaves. Ferns brightened almost every shop window. From one store blew the soft refrain of children singing carols. Ahead of him, beneath an orange street light, a group of friends met and exchanged tales of New Year's parties. Becky hadn't needed him to be her ethnic escort this time.

He passed a few shops with war stickers. One touted a cruise missile and read: *This One's For You, Saddam*. Another showed a warhead detonating. It said: *Say Hello to Allah*.

Around him the air was cold and gay, verging on euphoric. He wanted something hot. He walked back to the café. He'd spend his last dollar after all.

But at the doorway, a heavyset man blocked his entrance. 'We're closing,' he said. Daanish cast a quick look inside. No one seemed in a hurry to leave. Walking back down the street, he glanced around. The friends who'd met under the street light were entering the café.

In the following days, other Muslim students began relating similar incidents. One said someone had scribbled *Go home, Towelhead* on his door. He'd never worn a towel on his head, or a turban either. Graffiti was painted across the brick wall of a warehouse: *Save America, Kill an Arab*. A mosque was attacked, as was a Lebanese restaurant. And in the media, in place of war coverage, articles condemning Islam gained prominence. All the while, bombs dropped on Iraq every thirty seconds.

On average, it took Daanish twenty minutes to read each article. On average, the air raids killed twenty-five hundred Iraqis daily. Approximately thirty would lose their lives by the time he'd finished reading how much *they* hate *us*.

5

Khurram's Counsel

JUNE 1992

The girl did not return. Not the next day, nor the following week. Daanish, pacing over the graying rug, was growing desperate for a way to fly out the wrought-iron grills of his bedroom window. He resolved to meet absolutely no more mourners.

Below, Khurram's driver arrived with a pot of tea. Daanish called out to him.

The workers continued hauling and laying cement or else paused with the old man for tea.

'Hey!' Daanish called again, louder.

A young man balanced on top of the foundation wall a few feet lower than Daanish's window, looked up. He nudged his chin questioningly. Daanish pointed to the driver. The man pointed too. Daanish nodded. 'Call him.'

'Did you talk to the President about my visa?' asked the man.

'What?'

'The visa!'

'Call *him*,' Daanish again pointed to the driver.

The worker settled into a crouch. His toes curled around the unleveled edge of the wall. He began picking specks of dry mortar off his feet, preparing to sit under the window all day.

'All right,' Daanish hissed. 'I'll work on it. Now *call him*.'

The man hopped down, returning with the driver. The latter looked up, composed as always.

'I'm going to give you a note for Khurram. Please wait,' said Daanish.

The other man offered, 'He's deaf.'

'What?'

The man muttered something and spat.

'What do you mean he's deaf?' asked Daanish. 'I've spoken to him before.'

'You've talked in his right ear. Like this he's deaf.'

'Well,' Daanish felt his temper rise. 'Can *you* tell him, in his right ear, please, what I just said?'

'When will I get the visa?'

'Shit,' growled Daanish. He stamped to his desk, not his desk — a small, blanched, wimpy thing Anu called a desk — and scribbled a note to Khurram: *Can I borrow your car for the day? If you're free, join me? I want to go to the beach. My mother would be less likely to object if I didn't go alone, especially if you came to get me. Soon I hope, Daanish.* He stuffed it in an envelope that he folded into a plane. He tossed this between the diamonds of the grill, down to the driver, who, happily, still waited. Unhappily, so did the other. It was he who caught the plane.

'Have you talked into his right ear?' Daanish asked dryly.

He nodded and passed the driver the paper. The driver walked to Khurram's house.

'And?' said the man.

Daanish slammed the window shut.

He sat on his bed, waiting. Then he sprang up nervously,

itching for something to do. At last he moved to the drawer with the cocoons. 'I've decided to boil you, after all,' he announced. 'But only one. Which will it be?' He stared at the trio of wooly pellets, picturing a thick white ribbon curled inside of each. While elbowing their way to shape, he was sure the creatures twitched their antennae, watching him.

Also in the closet was the lacquer box, with the photograph he'd not put in himself. Staring up at him was his young father, so young his hairline showed no sign of receding. His shoulders were bunched against the clouds. A maroon scarf lay stylishly over one shoulder. His jacket and trousers, though, were the same frayed ones he'd worn till his last winter. In the background rose a brown tower. The streets were swept, paved, orderly. His mouth was wide open in the hearty, leonine laugh Daanish heard in his dreams. A woman held his hand. Not his mother. She was spry, short-haired, boyish. Her brown skin was smooth and flushed, as if she'd been jogging. She too appeared cold and delighted.

What was the picture doing here?

What did Anu want, anyway?

He put the box away irritably.

An hour later, there was a loud knock. Daanish stumbled to unlock the door.

Khurram bustled inside. 'Arre, you send message then go to sleep. It is nice for to see you again.' He hugged him fervently.

Daanish hung limply in Khurram's arms. He smiled. 'Just give me five minutes.'

Once ready, he locked the door and led Khurram hurriedly out the kitchen, avoiding the relatives who called after him.

But Anu caught up with them. 'You haven't read a word today,' she protested. 'And I haven't seen you all morning. I was so worried. I didn't know if I should disturb . . .'

'Anu please. Khurram's waiting.'

Khurram smiled without any apparent haste.

'Why don't you read too?' Anu suggested.

Khurram opened his mouth but Daanish pushed him out the door. 'He can't.' And then, pleading, 'I've hardly left the house since coming back, Anu. Everyone needs to breathe.'

'But where are you going?' She frowned. 'Why can't you breathe in here?'

He left without answering.

They drove through neighborhoods like his own that had, till just a few decades ago, lurked under the sea. Sweeping boulevards had cropped up with designer boutiques, video shops and ice-cream parlors. He said, 'Here too, all people want to do is shop and eat.'

'What else is there?' asked Khurram. More somberly, he added, 'I was thinking about visiting many times but didn't want to disturb. Salaamat told me about your father's death.' He pointed at the driver.

'Oh, is that his name?' In the rear-view mirror, Daanish caught a glimpse of the jutting cheekbones, and the elusive, opalescent eyes. 'How does he know?'

'Well, all the neighbors knowing. I'm so sorry. Your father must have been very young.'

'At heart, yes,' mumbled Daanish.

'And you the only child.' Khurram shook his head. 'There's being a lot of responsibility on your shoulders.' He pinched Daanish's shoulders as if to squeeze some of it off.

'I suppose so.'

'You must be very busy,' Khurram persisted.

'Actually, no. There's not much for me to do. The legal end's been taken care of by my uncles, the domestic routine's in my mother's hands and I'm really just a, just a . . . I don't even know. Proof of a better life? Evidence that my father lives on? Anu gets hysterical every time I leave the house. She knows every new case of kidnapping, murder, robbery, you name it. I think keeping track of national tragedy helps her cope with her own.' Words he'd been biting back forced their way out haphazardly now. 'I haven't talked this much since our flight together. My school friends are all in the States. I wish there were an internship or some other job I could do, but there isn't, not in anything that interests me at least.'

'Well,' Khurram again thumped him. 'You are having me.' He continued trying to console him, all the way to the cove.

Once there Daanish thought: I have this.

He had wondered if he could stand being here without his father. Now he had the answer. His footsteps were light as he clambered swiftly over the needle-like rocks on the western shoulder of the inlet, too elated to notice any cuts. Salaamat too crossed the mound with graceful ease; Khurram alone complained.

Daanish threw his head back. Anu had refurbished his room and taken away his things but she could not touch this.

The gray, shirty sea spilled with a hiss up the slope of sand toward him. The water was too rough for swimming, he had to settle for simply walking. Washed ashore were the ocellate cowries, blue mussels and pen shells that greeted him every time he made this walk. He upturned many of the pen shells. All were empty or crushed.

'The live ones are buried,' Salaamat said. His locks flapped around his sharp jaw like birds around a spire of granite.

'I'm not interested in the meat,' answered Daanish. 'I just like the shells. I used to collect them.' He spoke in Salaamat's left ear and anyway, the wind swept his words away.

The driver continued, 'They attach themselves to underground stones with golden thread. In the old days, people wove cloth with the thread.' It was the most he'd ever volunteered on his own. Just as unexpectedly, he wound his words back up, turned and walked calf-deep in the water, straight as a sheet of iron even when the current pulled. The dusky blue horizon cut him in two, just at the hips.

Daanish returned to combing the shore. There were some

of the less common shells – sand bonnets, spiral babylons, a mitre just like the one around his neck. There was even a shattered tiger cowry. He'd had a perfect specimen of each in his collection. Anger toward Anu began to rise again.

Khurram caught up with him, panting, clutching a mobile phone. One toe bled. 'I don't know why we come here. We passed many nicer places on the way, with people and food stalls.' He looked around him. 'There's nothing here.'

'Nothing here!' Daanish laughed. 'Look around! What more do you want?'

Khurram winced when the surf hit his cut. He sighed. 'Where to sit?'

Daanish pointed to a cluster of boulders at the opposite end. 'My mother always sat there.'

'No shade, yaar,' he moaned.

'There's a cave in there,' Daanish indicated the sheer rocks they'd just descended. 'But the tide's too high,' he added. They walked toward the boulder he'd called the shoulder-boulder as a child. Daanish remembered Anu sitting there, fitting in the knurl perfectly, her little figure balancing like a top as she sewed. The doctor and he would dig around the rock's base, finding little more than the husks of the chiton that clung to the boulder's surface.

Khurram tied a handkerchief around his head and moved inland, where the sand was plush and powdery. He began to cheer up a little, telling Daanish all he'd done since returning from the visit to his brother. Most of it involved looking after his father's business.

'What kind of business?' Daanish asked.

'Oh,' Khurram examined his toe. 'Business.'

'What *kind* of business?'

'He imports things.' Khurram stuffed his phone in a pocket.

'Can you be any vaguer?' Daanish rolled his eyes. 'What things?'

Khurram adjusted his handkerchief and paused. He looked

ridiculous: a round head wrapped in a square of cloth, paunch jutting over a belt, trouser cuffs dragging a ratty line of rope.

'What things?' Daanish repeated.

Khurram smiled mysteriously. 'Metal things.'

'That explode?' Daanish ventured.

Khurram reflected. 'No. Well, sort of yes. Mostly they lock.'

'Oh. So your father imports from China – padlocks?'

'No, from the US and Europe. But yes, you could be calling them padlocks.'

'You're being very enigmatic today.'

'I am not knowing big words like that,' Khurram replied.

They reached the shoulder-boulder. It was taken. Salaamat had stationed himself there, gazing out at the sea as Anu had done. She'd watch him wear his fins and clean his mask, an aquamarine shawl around her shoulders, lace on her lap. The shawl had blinked at him like a lighthouse as he swam away.

Khurram settled on a small rock that tilted into the base of the shoulder-boulder, offering partial shade. He shifted, adjusting himself so he could both be out of the sun and stay balanced on the rock's bowed crown. Salaamat continued to stare ahead. Daanish squatted in the sand, studying a tide pool between the boulder and Khurram's rock. There were sea cucumbers and a sprinkle of black sea urchins. He'd pointed these out often to Anu, who'd never seen his underwater world. At such times it was the doctor who sat apart. Rarely, if ever, did the family enjoy a three-way conversation. Daanish didn't know when it happened but at some point in his life he'd been asked, non-verbally, to choose between them. He frowned, swirling the tide pool with a stick, gently poking a winkle. The animal immediately scurried back into its fist of bone.

Daanish looked up at Khurram and suddenly blurted, 'I'm

only twenty-two but I believe my mother's already thinking about marriage.'

Khurram's face lit up. 'How interesting!'

'She keeps dropping hints about settling down, whatever that means, and a few days ago I heard her discussing "the girl" with my aunts. I came into the kitchen and Anu was saying, "I still think she's right for him despite what happened." I never got to know who she was, or what happened, before my chachi started coughing wildly.'

Khurram slapped his knee. 'It's sounding like marriage all right!'

'It's absurd. My father would have vetoed her plans immediately.'

Khurram shrugged. 'Maybe you'll like her.'

'Have you ever noticed how women here walk?'

Khurram grinned. 'That's usually what I'm looking at.'

'Sweeping dupattas,' Daanish began to mimic the cumbersome cloth with his arms, dramatizing as he continued, 'kurtas catching in chairs, shalwar cuffs slipping over stilettos, hair in saalan, saalan in nails. And let's not even talk about hairspray!'

Khurram laughed while Daanish took mincing steps around the rock, tripping, puffing out an imaginary coif, spraying it. 'Yaar,' said Khurram, 'I *love* it when they do such things! It's so,' he smacked his lips, 'so tasty!'

'Mind you,' said Daanish, 'I learned American women spend just as much time in the toilet.'

Khurram covered his mouth with pudgy fingers and giggled. 'How many did you know?'

Daanish waved his hand dismissingly. Then he looked up at Salaamat. 'I wonder what he's thinking?'

'You can say anything in front of him. He's deaf.'

The man had not moved a muscle. He still stared blankly ahead, his curls jostling each other gaily.

Daanish continued, 'I knew *many*. And they *all* groomed.

173

They just did it differently. And when they get older, here they plot weddings, there they buy hormone replacement aids! Shit. I come back here to find my father dead and mother scheming.'

It was the first time Daanish had used the word *dead*. It whirled around his head, leaving him momentarily stunned.

Then he saw death everywhere.

It whistled in the crevices of the steep, serrated rocks, crashed on the surf, screamed in the current, crawled behind Salaamat's vacant stare. It scattered around him as bone: on the cord around his neck, on the rock, on Salaamat's sculpted face. Bone underground, yielding yarns of golden thread. Bone in the ocean, vomited somewhere far, for someone just like the doctor to find and bring home to a son, in a case of bone.

Crouching in the sand, he buried his head between the bones of his knees, and was transported back to an evening with Anu.

They sat in the kitchen, waiting for the doctor. Earlier that morning, his father had returned from a conference in East Asia. Daanish sat at the table, wanting to run up to his room and touch the beautiful gift the doctor had brought him: a chambered nautilus, coiling in a counterclockwise curve. It was the first and only gift his father had given him directly. He was too proud of the find to risk it going unnoticed. Daanish wanted to hold it in his palm, gaze at the iridescent whorl, picture the animal that had once lived inside the many rooms of mother-of-pearl. He wanted to follow it through each chamber with a feathery gill of light, and watch how each was sealed off as the creature grew into the next one. He wanted to know why this particular specimen had grown in a different way, twirling sinistrally instead of like its right-handed siblings. What did its relatives – like the wandering, leggy argonaut – have to say about it? And he wanted to ask what it was like, being a member of a family that was over two hundred million years old. How did today's animals compare with the mighty dinosaurs?

As Daanish ruminated, the food got cold. He didn't know why, but every time his father returned from a voyage, the food just sat. Anu would reheat it twice, maybe even three times. Then she'd say to him, as she did that day, 'You should eat. You have to get to sleep.' And she'd watch her son in the silence of the kitchen, occasionally muttering about their dwindling bank account and the loan on the house that was still pending, even though the house looked like it had existed when the dinosaurs did.

She was peeling him an apple when at last the doctor appeared. Without a word, he sniffed the chicken karhai, eggplant and daal. He took one bite.

'Is it cold?' she asked.

He pushed the plate away. She repeated her question. He slammed the table with his fist. 'That's all you ever have to say: Is it cold? Do you want more? Are you well? Is it good enough? Woman, why can't you ever make conversation?'

She stared at him. Daanish, feeling he chewed too loudly, tried to swallow an apple quarter whole.

Earlier, he knew, Anu had asked the doctor how the trip went. She hadn't been complaining. She'd just asked. He hadn't answered. As long as he remembered, it was the doctor who never made conversation with *her*. He yearned, suddenly, for her to say so. But she looked away. He yearned then to hold and comfort her. But would that be deceiving *him*? He stared at the man whose large amber eyes flickered with rage. It was as if the hair in each thick brow waited to be plucked and dunked in the cauldron behind his eyes. This wasn't the same man who took him to the cove.

Daanish swallowed a second apple quarter whole – Anu had begun paring another. He didn't even want to be in the cove today. He wanted only to be with the nautilus. No, to be the nautilus. With ninety arms to swim away, and twenty cabins to roam.

Slowly, Anu rose, returned with a clean plate, and placed the newly pared apple gently by the doctor's rejected main course.

'This is driving me mad,' he bellowed, storming out.

Daanish heaved a sigh of relief. He could stop eating the apple now. 'What's driving him mad?' he asked Anu.

She said, more to the apple peels and congealing saalan than to him, 'The fact that he has not come back.' She began listlessly putting away the food. He watched her, small and plump, with a ruby stud like a bloodstain on her nose.

He ran upstairs. The doctor was there, waiting, the nautilus in his giant hands. 'Did I tell you its brain is highly developed? Scientists say it has evolved to the complexity of a mammal's.'

Daanish looked up from his knees.

Khurram smiled awkwardly. 'I thought you'd gone away.'

'That's what happened to my father,' Daanish mumbled. And then, louder: 'My mother needs me.'

Khurram nodded. 'You are all she has now. Go with whatever she wants. What will it costing you? You'll make her happy, and seeing her happy will make you happy. With your responsibilities taken care of, you can for to go back to Amreeka with no guilt.'

'But what about the girl? I don't even know her.'

'She will go where you are going, when you are ready. And there will be plenty of time to know her,' he winked.

Daanish frowned. 'That's ridiculous.'

'Why? So many people are doing it that way. They are happy, aren't they? Look, your saying yes will make the girl's family happy too.' He waved his arms. 'Everyone will be happy!'

'I wish I could be like you.' Daanish gave him a quizzical look. 'So merry and shameless.'

Khurram stood up. 'Stop thinking. It will be working out. Let's have cold drink.'

On the way to the car Khurram continued chirping, pausing only when they had to cross the ragged rocks again. The more Daanish listened, the greater became his uncertainty, and the more he was charmed by Khurram's clear-cut thinking. Maybe Khurram wasn't a simpleton, after all.

'Where will it be?' he asked Daanish. 'Mr Burger or Sheraton?'

Daanish let Khurram decide.

6

The Rainbow Parade

From the clouds, it looked as if a forest of yellow butterflies starting off on some mammoth migration had suddenly lost its bearings. The creatures flew into each other, pirouetted and fell, reversed direction, landed in heaps, or else on straw, bark and brick. And when they broke free, Daanish drifted with them.

He saw rows of gray bungalows with families on their porches. The star-spangled banner flapped on shingle rooftops. More butterflies flew by, most still yellow, though a few were pastel pink or blue. They peeped through the slots of the porch floor-planks. Others splayed on the grass beneath. Still others wound between the fingers of the happy waving families on streets named after Columbus and Cortes.

Daanish flew, covering towns in seconds, like a camera scan for Hollywood or ABC News.

A familiar figure stalled outside a flower shop on Bartholomew Boulevard. Daanish hovered in the sky, intrigued. Below was himself, sauntering past a Hallmark gift shop.

The shop's windows too were strewn with butterflies. They bore words that said, *We Kicked Ass*; *Our Colors Don't Run*; *Everybody Party*.

'It's the biggest parade in history,' said the shopkeeper as he held the door for an old lady in a dress splashed with sunflowers.

She nodded, clasping a little brown bag with greeting cards and colored bows in one hand, and a terrier with a yellow butterfly between its ears in the other. 'Makes you proud, doesn't it? Our boys did so well.'

'Uh-huh,' said the shopkeeper. 'Have a nice day, dear.'

Daanish saw himself striding over to Liam's Rambler. Was that the expression he always wore? His brow was creased, jaw clenched, back stiff, gait undecided. He hopped impatiently on the pavement. He kicked the post from which Colonel Sanders watched him with a yellow butterfly on his elfin beard. He glanced at the flower shop, then back at the car, then down another street. He was asking himself: Why should I wait for that bastard? He was reasoning: Because he's not a bastard.

Seconds later, Liam came out of the flower shop, his forelock and grin partially concealed behind a large cluster of pink zinnias and yellow irises. He twirled them proudly for Daanish's inspection. 'I always get irises for Iris, though zinnias are her faves.'

Daanish scowled, 'You could have done us a favor by choosing a different color at least. All this glorification in yellow is sickening enough.'

'There's glorification in every color,' retorted Liam. 'The ribbons are yellow but the ticker tape's a rainbow. Does that mean I can't get my girlfriend flowers?'

'The war's destroyed hundreds of thousands of people. Your media calls it a work of art, and your people wave pompoms.' He pointed to the ribbons and the tape. 'Doesn't it enrage you?'

In response, Liam tossed his head. His forelock fell back over his eyes like a curtain.

Daanish nodded. 'I'm so happy for you. Bravo. You didn't lose like in Vietnam. You'll never lose again.'

Liam climbed into the car and unlocked the passenger door. Daanish got in. Liam said, 'Iris is giving her first public recital today. That's the only reason I'm celebrating.'

Daanish's heart raced. Since the war began, he and Liam had said nothing about it to each other. It was as if, by staying silent, Liam was telling him: I'm not a part of it. And Daanish's silence replied: I'm afraid to know you. Really know you.

But now, he had to know.

'You're not celebrating the war, Liam, but you're not exactly worked up about it either. You said nothing when your country began the air strikes, nothing when all the propaganda glittered from your television . . .'

'Will you drop the bit about *your*? This isn't *my* war. I didn't start it. Hold these a minute, would you?' Liam handed Daanish the bouquet so he could wear his seatbelt.

'I'm not your fucking vase,' Daanish answered. 'I'm trying to talk to you. I can't believe how bloody smug you are.'

Liam arranged the flowers carefully on the backseat. 'You don't wanna go you can get out now.'

Daanish gaped at him. Not this – not Liam too. Liam and Wayne were different. He took a deep breath.

If he got out of the car, he knew Liam's anger would pass sooner than his. By the time Liam arrived at the recital, he'd have found his loveable, demented, equine grin. For him, nothing would change. He'd think of Daanish with a slow shake of his head. Perhaps his lips would tremble a little. He might even be hurt. But he'd never give a thought to the things Daanish desperately needed him to think about.

Behind the wheel, the olive pupils of Liam's milky-green eyes darkened. His lips really did tremble, though just barely.

Dammit, thought Daanish. *He's* hurt. About which *I'm* to feel guilty. How did Liam manage to make willful ignorance look like innocence? How did he make Daanish look like the villain? Perhaps this was the greatest power of a superpower.

Up in the sky, Daanish took one last glance at Bartholomew Boulevard. There was Liam, blissful, beautiful and wronged. Daanish flew away, aware that he was about to say, 'Let's forget this then.' He would go to the recital.

Now he skimmed rather than hovered above ground. The world blurred. When next it cleared, he was standing at the foot of his parents' bed, listening to their alarm clock with the BBC chime.

It was seven o'clock, time for the doctor to wake up. Anu was in the kitchen. Daanish waited patiently, the ambergris candles discovered – his father had hidden them in an airline sick bag, amongst his dirty linen. Daanish had lit them. They smelled like khas, like grass beginning to smoke. His father had given him a clue: whale vomit. He'd found them. He was giggling. At last the doctor stretched awake. 'Ah, Daanishwar! My clever boy.' His chest hair was damp with sweat. Daanish buried his face in it, carefully holding the candles up. The clock rang again: four bells ascending, four descending. 'My clever boy,' his father repeated. Daanish breathed deeply the perfume wafting around them.

But before he could hold the scent, it vanished. An air current sent him flying forward again. It dropped him in the fourth row of an auditorium. The room had him awestruck. The chairs were cushioned. Desks never rattled. Wall-to-wall carpeting. Controlled temperature. Acoustics so crisp he could hear nails scrape denim when the student in the first row scratched. The plush blue carpet was like a woolen blanket, freshly laundered with Squeeze for extra softness, coating the atmosphere in a pleasant hum. In Karachi, his school had seating on one level. Tall students were asked to sit at the back, where the teacher was invisible. By age fourteen, Daanish, the tallest boy in the school, could only keep up with lectures by sharing the notes of short boys.

But this room was heaven! He could see everything! The front wall had a poster with writing in gold:

Trust in your choices
Everything is possible

Wayne marched in front of the sign. He pointed to it. He told his students to always reach for the truth. He clenched his fist, declaring, 'Courage *does* pay!'

Daanish was off again. In dizzying succession he saw: himself in the sunken garden, looking up at a barn owl in a cedar tree. The bird spun its phantom head, 'Hoot!'

He saw: maple syrup dripping onto a plate of pancakes at the 24-hour Pancake House. The plate was Becky's. Daanish watched her eat. He couldn't afford his own. She wasn't offering.

He saw: the smooth gold medallion of the key-chain his grandfather had given his father when he became a doctor. On one side was a Pakistani flag, its crescent a neat, sure smile. The little globe swayed back and forth, back and forth, flipping minutes into seconds, seconds into hours. Maple syrup hung on the edge of the porcelain white lip of a jug. It grew to the size of the medallion but would not fall on the soft cakes below. Suspended on the jug's lip, it waited for Daanish's next paycheck. When this was cashed, the sweet blob dropped plumb on to the tip of Daanish's tongue. He had all the time in the world to savor it. He chewed while watching Heather and her friends dance topless in the cornfields, mimicking American Indians. They chanted, 'I can feel the spirits of the gods. I am one with my body. They are one with my body. The crop will grow.'

The drop lingered, an amber tablet he rolled over two pale pink nipples, down the slope of her breasts, up the small mound of her torso, and down again, to the whiskers of her damp vagina. The scent of maple mingled with her equally heady odor, and then with a third more pungent smell, coming from the corner of his room in Karachi.

7

The Find

Daanish awoke in the middle of the night feeling he'd ridden a hurricane. He lay in bed, groaning. Ever since his return, his days had become a sequence of disjointed pictures. Now the pictures haunted his sleep too. It was as if the long flight back had never ended. He hadn't landed. He was trapped, oscillating between time and space. He couldn't stop. He could only do one thing: remember. His short life flickered before his eyes almost as if it were coming to an end, for surely, this is what the dying did. Before his father breathed his last breath, hadn't he too remembered the ambergris perfume with which his son had once woken him?

As in his sleep, Daanish now noticed the biting stench in his room. He sat up. It came from the drawer. He walked toward it, blinking at the three cocoons bunched inside.

'Which will it be?' he asked again. They were half the size of his thumb and somehow resisted being separated. Two oozed a reddish liquid that stank of wood polish. He plucked the clean one. Carrying it downstairs, he passed Anu's bedroom. Thankfully, she was asleep.

So as not to wake her, he softly shut the kitchen door behind him. Then he threw open a window, filled a pot with water and left it to boil.

Looking around, he remembered something. In the cupboard, Anu used to keep a cluster of terracotta lanterns. He opened it: yes, they were still there. He smiled. Filling one dainty, palm-shaped dia with oil, he put it on the windowsill and lit the wick. The flame wavered, casting shadows around him.

The water came to a boil. Daanish poured it into a shallow basin. The light danced on the water's surface, arching its neck in steam. He dropped the cocoon inside.

Swiftly, the soft mass began to separate into threads. He caught hold of one very carefully with the tine of a fork and began twirling this strange spaghetti made of the finest hair. He found, to his astonishment, that he could keep twisting. The cocoon, now bobbing in the basin as a brown and shriveled nut, was wrapped in a single endless strand. He pulled and turned the fork, then pulled and turned again. It was like unwrapping a gift.

Afraid the fork would snap the strand prematurely, Daanish slipped the bundle off it and began winding the thread around his arm. He sweated profusely and his muscles ached. He dabbed his brow with the sleeve of his free arm.

Just when he felt his arm would drop, it stopped. A breeze blew out the lantern. A thin dawn pierced the kitchen. In the basin, the boiled cocoon was stripped bare. He'd retrieved the entire length of the yarn. It was as long as an artery, and as fine as a cut. He carried it gingerly upstairs.

DIA

I

Metamorphosis

Adjacent to the shed that housed the silkworms stood a shack with two rooms and a telephone. On days when it got too late for the long ride back into the city, Dia and her mother spent the night here. The shack was stocked with basic aids – towels, pots and pans, dry food, a tube of Macleans toothpaste – and even some of Dia's storybooks. Water was collected in a bucket from the main outside, showers taken in the protective arms of mulberries.

When her father was alive, her parents had slept in one room, the children in the other. They'd cooked simple meals on a single burner, and at night, rolled out frayed quilts on the floor. The children's excitement was augmented by their proximity to one of the world's biggest graveyards, Makli Hill, just half a kilometer away. Once the parents were asleep, ghosts would rise and begin their lumbering trek down to the farm. Then Dia and her brothers took turns daring each other to step out in a darkness that was inconceivable in the city, even during loadshedding. This one had cold fingers, trailing hair, ancient venom.

She suffered terrible bouts of anxiety days before her night to be dared. When it came, her evil brothers gloated: 'Take a cold shower, outside, *now*!'

Tiptoeing into the pit of blackness, she filled the bucket, shed her clothes, and stood as vulnerable as the day she came howling furiously into the world, like a purplish-red mulberry. Or so her father put it. It was comforting to know he slept soundly inside. She cast frequent glances at the door, into which she could dart if anything tried to grab her.

There were no shortcuts. She had to wet her hair, lather it with shampoo, rinse, soap herself from ear to toe, rinse again. And the entire time, she felt the wings of bats, the eyes of kings dead hundreds of years, and the screeching of those still alive.

Perhaps her terror of water had started then, years before her father's drowning.

Perhaps she was dreaming of the drowning because it happened five years ago to the day.

She was bathing in utter darkness, when all around appeared a hundred geese. They bred gold cocoons. The cocoons began to unravel. Out jumped a hundred blue and battered feet. They were her father's feet, her father who'd been wrung back to life, and they danced a bloody dance, quacking like rubber ducks. The blackness began to ooze. It condensed into bullets. The bullets scattered like beads, only they weren't bullets or beads but her father's small, shining eyes. Eyes that must have cried at the end. Plucked eyes, following the words in her storybooks as she read to him. And then the blackness ceased oozing and scattering. It began to pour. It was the river, and it was time to haul his body out of it.

She screamed.

'Shh! Dia, it's me. Shh! It's all right.'

She sat up on the floor of the shack, keening. A woman

smoothed her hair. She'd have liked it to be Nini. It wasn't. It was Sumbul, the cook's daughter. She let herself be rocked. Gradually, the nightmare flew away. And then there was nothing but a breeze, and Sumbul's maternal embrace.

Dia took a deep breath and laughed weakly. 'Your fifth child is on the way. You have a lifetime of comforting ahead of you.'

'Silly girl,' cooed Sumbul.

'Thank you,' said Dia, gently pulling away. 'I'm better now.'

'I was just coming to wake you. I think it might be time.'

Dia frowned, disoriented. And then she remembered why she'd stayed the night at the shack.

Last afternoon, she'd been making the rounds through the section of the shed where a few select pupae were kept. These would eat their way out to enter the fourth and final stage of their life as mature imagoes. Their eggs would begin the cycle again. She'd been wondering which cocoon from this batch would yield the first imago when, peering closely, she found two that had already begun to open. At last, after years of trying to witness the birth of silk moths, Dia felt she might have a chance. She hurriedly called Sumbul. Together, they watched as the telltale liquid began to drip. Perhaps within the next twelve hours, the metamorphosis would be complete.

Dia had called her mother at home to say she was finally going to watch the process entirely. But Riffat was concerned about security – Dia had never spent the night alone at the farm. Dia pleaded she wouldn't be alone. Sumbul's mother-in-law was away, so she could share the overnight vigil. Four guards, including Sumbul's two brothers Shan and Hamid, patrolled the grounds. And half a kilometer away, the cook's brother patrolled the graves of Makli Hill. Her mother reluctantly consented.

Dia lay on the floor and Sumbul repeated, 'I think it might be time.'

Dia looked at the clock. It was 5.30 in the morning. Sumbul had stayed awake longer than she. 'Show me.'

Leaving Sumbul's baby asleep on the couch, they slipped into the shed. At first it was eerily hushed inside. But the further they crept, the more sounds began to reach them: leaves rustling under the writhing caterpillars, the drone of ventilators, and in the distance, buses on the highway – going north, north to the river in her dream. She shuddered. When they reached the two cocoons, Dia's mood lifted completely. 'Look!' she whispered.

The shells had split. Two tiny heads each with two brown antennae and two stubby palps poked out. They were nibbling the husks, a sound like grasshoppers crunching leaves, or roaches in a paper bag.

And then someone tapped Dia's shoulder from behind.

She swung around, yelping. It was Shan, grinning, his Kalashnikov pointing at her. He lowered it. 'I was just joking!'

Sumbul slapped him. 'How dare you frighten us!'

Shan pouted, rubbing an injured cheek. 'I just came to tell you the phone's been ringing in the shack,' he whined.

'Well, answer it then,' Sumbul and Dia snapped together.

'The door's locked. It's that automatic kind, remember?' He waved his gun, and, half-whimpering, half-threatening, declared, 'Next time I won't be joking.' Pivoting on his bare heels, he stomped off, his soussi lungi billowing about his legs like a petticoat.

Dia returned to the moths. They'd retreated into their holes. She sighed. 'Who could be calling at this hour?'

'Maybe it's your mother,' said Sumbul. 'Perhaps I should go.'

'Yes,' Dia agreed. 'You must be sleepy anyway. I'll wait

here. Who knows when they'll come out again.' She gazed at the half-bitten cocoons beseechingly.

Sumbul took the keys and left.

Dia sat alone in a chair, waiting. If the larvae were private about spinning their cocoons, the pupae were neurotic. They seemed able to detect her even when she sat motionless, even through the shells of their cocoons, and kept their transformation defiantly to themselves. Dia wagged a finger: *I'm going to watch you this time*.

The smell was rancid. She held her nose. Out loud, she said, 'Aphrodisiac. Dizzy Ak.' The word came from Aphrodite, the goddess of love. Aphrodite tucked her charm into a girdle many other goddesses tried to steal but no, it was hers to keep. She was born with it. So were female moths. A male moth could smell the female from miles away and when he found her, it was called *assembling*.

'Dizzy. Dizzy. Ak. Ak.' Dia fumed at the cocoons.

With butterflies it was the other way around. The male carried the scent, and the females assembled around him. When he chose one, he dusted her with another type of pheromone, an anti-aphrodisiac. This way, after he was done with her, she'd never be desirable to other males.

Obviously to silk moths, people were anti-aphrodisiacs. She sighed, her thoughts continuing to roam. How much better it would be if these were the kinds of things her college taught. Her retake was on Monday. At least the college had shut for the summer holidays now so she didn't have to tolerate those crammed and dingy classrooms.

She yawned. It was almost six-thirty. The moths made no appearance. Her body ached. But she wasn't going to give up now. She was going to witness the birth of those stubborn beasts waiting for her to fall asleep.

Perhaps she'd be the first to ever see it. Next time, she should bring a camera. Maybe she could drop out of college and start photographing the mysterious life of bugs on her farm . . . she yawned again. Seven o'clock. She scowled. *Just pretend I'm not here, won't you?* Her shoulders felt like sacks of dirt rested on them. Her throat was dry. It hurt. If only she could have a glass of ice-cold water. And a quick nap on something soft.

No! She shook herself awake.

Seven-thirty. Eight. The workers would be trickling in . . .

And then Sumbul, looking greatly revived and well nourished, was standing beside her. 'Nissrine's on the phone.'

'What?' mumbled Dia.

'Your friend Nissrine is on the phone. It was she who called earlier. She says she must talk to you.'

Dia blinked skeptically. 'You're joking. First Shan and now you. It runs in the family.'

'I told her you were watching the cocoons and wouldn't want to be disturbed. But she sounded quite frantic. She's waiting,' Sumbul added.

'I don't believe this.' Dia stood up. 'If that Nini spoils this for me . . .' She shuffled out, about to keel over with exhaustion.

'I'll keep watch,' Sumbul assured her.

Dia entered the shack feeling stiff as a breadstick. She picked up the receiver. 'Hello?'

'Hi!' Nini shrieked.

Dia moved the receiver an inch away from her ear.

'Where've you been? I tried calling as early as I could but no one answered. I called the house last night. Your mother told me . . .'

'Nini,' Dia interrupted, sitting down on the bed so she wouldn't fall. 'I'm really very busy right now. Is this important?'

'Important!' Nini hollered. 'Of course it's important. Like I was saying, I tried calling last night. Your mother told me you were staying here. Then my sister just wouldn't get off the phone. I was so mad . . .'

There were some people, thought Dia, who shouldn't be allowed ownership of a telephone. Nini was one of them. In person she was calm, even gracious. She'd been a little uptight since the Quran Khwani, it was true, but she wasn't shrill or pushy by any standard. Yet the telephone transformed her. She stopped hearing herself.

'Nini,' Dia sighed. 'I really have to go. Okay? Bye . . .'

'You fool!' Nini bellowed. 'I'm trying to tell you a date's been fixed.'

'A date?'

'I thought you'd be brimming with joy,' she added provocatively.

Silence.

'Fine. You said you'd be with me when the boy and his mother visited. So I remembered you. You're invited for tea on Tuesday. I picked the day with you in mind. Since your retake is on Monday, I thought you'd be free.' She paused, letting the full weight of her news sink in. Then, 'If you do care to come, try to dress respectably, would you?' She slammed the receiver down.

Dia stared at the plastic apparatus in her hand.

She put it back down.

So the doctor's son had agreed.

Nini was going to let herself be displayed.

Dia would be a silent witness to the humiliation of her best friend.

She had lost her then.

She lay back on the bed, staring at the ceiling fan she'd been too tired to think of switching on. It had three screws on each of its three blades. What if the whole thing fell on her, now?

She might see her father again.

Some of the black smears on the telephone might be his fingerprints.

She could see herself in the fan's shiny center. Small and flat.

She wanted badly to curl up in her father's arms and have him switch the light off.

And then she willed it. He also switched the fan on. It was cool and she drifted into a deep and comfortable sleep.

At one o'clock in the afternoon Dia walked back into the shed, now bustling with activity. Workers chopped leaves, cleaned trays, recorded numbers. She absently greeted them all, forcing her way into the room where she knew bad news awaited. Sumbul was not there. The two moths were. Each faced her head-on. They'd won. She folded her arms. *If Nini had not called, I would have . . .*

Sumbul entered the room with Sana, an expert moth-handler, and Dia's mother.

'Hello, darling,' Riffat kissed her. 'Sleep well?' She stood with a clipboard in her hands, looking, as always, impeccable in a sleeveless tunic with purple embroidery down the seams, over a purple shalwar bleeding into violet. Her chin-length curls were soft and lush and her face glowed. No one would guess she was past fifty.

Normally Dia enjoyed bumping into her mother unexpectedly like this. But today she turned instead to Sumbul. 'What did I miss?'

Sumbul looked pleased and guilty.

Sana carefully lifted the female and carried her into the next room.

'She'll be the first mother of the next batch,' announced Riffat, jotting down notes.

'No!' said Dia.

Sumbul nodded. 'I saw them chew their way out and then immediately, their tails pinned together. They stayed that way for three hours! They only pried loose about ten minutes ago,' she added, and then covered her mouth quickly with her hands. 'I shouldn't have said that! Now you'll just feel worse.'

Dia stared at the remaining male. 'After keeping me waiting all that time, couldn't *you* have waited?'

Sumbul and Riffat smirked, exchanging glances. 'They never do.'

2

Not Clear At All

They left the safe environment of the farm, crossed the troubled province in an armed escort vehicle, and within two hours arrived securely home. Although the tension linking these points had killed her father, it barely grazed Dia or Riffat. Sometimes Dia wondered if this immunity was really a privilege. Didn't all shelters fracture one day? And if so, shouldn't the signs be more visible?

The two walked up the winding driveway. At the fountain, they turned into the arbor, and Dia decided her uneasiness was nothing more than the disappointment of missing the birth of the moths. And of course, her disappointment with Nini. She tried to push her friend out of her thoughts. 'I smell pakoras.'

'Mm,' said Riffat. 'I love it when Inam Gul spoils us.'

They ducked under the trellis of jade vine, and the path widened to a ring of laburnum trees. In the center stood a glass-top table glittering in the evening sun like a pink topaz, arranged with hot refreshments and a tall jug of chilled almond juice. The cook was obviously in a good mood today; tea varied in complexity depending on his whim. At his best, he served an assortment of sweetmeats and savories in Riffat's finest dishware, adopting the debonair style he claimed had been his trademark in younger days. (When you were a fisherman? Dia would ask, but he'd ignore her.) At other times he'd barely remember to make tea at all, and complain if reminded.

Now he held out a chair and napkin for each. 'Tea is on its way,' he announced, marching back into the kitchen.

'You never know when it'll hit him,' laughed Riffat, pouring juice for Dia.

While she sipped it, Dia found she could not banish Nini from her thoughts. On Tuesday, Nini would go on display. The same Nini who'd so carelessly dismissed Dia's mother: *Where do dreams get us? If you're not careful, you'll end up lonely, like . . .*

Not only had Nini spoiled Dia's chance to see the moths, but she forced Dia to hear again the remarks others aimed at Riffat.

When her husband died, Riffat's in-laws had taken over management of the factory, but she hadn't let them take over her farm. She hadn't listened when they said she needed to spend more time with the newly orphaned children. She hadn't changed her routine. Her brother-in-law, whether out of kindness or malice, urged the family to let her be. 'She will have fans but no friends,' he declared. He'd been right. That was the price a proud woman had to pay.

Dia alone looked close enough to see the signs of wear: sometimes, when Riffat's ulcers made her wince, she forgot to color the gray roots of her curls or conceal the bags under her eyes. And sometimes, her efficacy revealed cracks – instead of studying her notes on farm productivity, like Dia, she was seen gazing dreamily at butterflies and clouds.

But she recovered quickly, so to others she was the same

fashionable Riffat who undertook any endeavor by first looking beyond it, then setting about getting firmly there. When she walked down the street, men and women ogled, but not because they wanted to caress her. They wanted to stop her. They were unwilling to accept that every obstacle made her chin rise higher.

In contrast, Dia was easily benumbed. She did not know what would happen on Tuesday. Nor was she able to decide what ought to happen – should the boy hate Nini? Should she produce another prank? How was she to get Nini back?

Riffat would have a plan, and unlike Dia's disastrous one at the Quran Khwani, hers would not leak. How she wished for her mother's strong nerves and sense of purpose, intimidating as it was!

They were different even to look at, sharing no features except the hooked nose. Dia was short with straight hair and light brown eyes; her mother was tall and wore her hair in a short, curly crop. Instead of Riffat's strong jaw and high cheekbones, Dia's face was oval and her cheek soft. When Dia walked down the street, even though most considered her too dark to be pretty, men always tried to touch her. At such times she wished her mother had rubbed some of her stoniness on to her.

But, thought Dia, the best thing about her mother was that she never tried to make Dia more like herself.

Inam Gul served the tea.

'Thank God there was no strike today,' said Riffat. 'Or we'd still be at the farm.' Conversation turned to the family. Dia's lovesick brother Hassan was unable to snap out of it. The girl was obviously not interested. What should they do?

'Send him to the Arctic,' offered Dia, burying herself in ghee.

'He may as well already be there,' Riffat sighed. 'I hope Amir visits this winter. Maybe Hassan needs a man-to-man talk.'

'So what does Amir have to do with it?'

'Come on now.' She plucked a samosa.

Dia looked up. 'The doctor said no.'

'Well, don't tell him then.'

When the forbidden food was consumed, Riffat spoke of one of her sisters, who visited from Islamabad the day Dia had been adorning Nini's back with silkworms. 'I've been meaning to ask where you went. We rushed back from the mill and Erum was so disappointed to find you gone. Inam Gul said Nissrine picked you up. But you haven't said a thing about it?'

Dia mumbled, 'Yes. She took me somewhere.'

'That awful?'

'Don't ask.' Dia's appetite began to diminish. 'Well, all right. Nini wanted me to attend a Quran Khwani.'

'A Quran Khwani? Who died?'

'The father of a boy her mother wants her to marry.'

'No!' Riffat gasped. 'So young. Barely twenty, poor child.'

'You'd think,' Dia fumed, '*she*, of all people, wouldn't settle for being "a poor child". She has options. She could refuse. But can't you just see her ten years from now? Cranky kids, husband away, long-suffering eyes. I'll hate her then, Ama. I'll hate her because she'll be just another woman pretending she had no choice.' Dia stopped. At last, she had voiced her worst fear out loud: *I'll hate her.*

'She could refuse,' Riffat pondered. 'But at what cost?'

'At *any* cost.'

'Calm down, darling. You're young. You've no idea how hostile society gets if you challenge it.'

'I've some idea – through you.'

A fleeting sorrow shot through Riffat's eyes, but faded quickly. 'True again, though that's still not enough of an idea. For your sake, I hope it never is. Anyway,' she added with a smile, 'I'm always on your side, whatever you choose. And whatever others say about it.'

Sipping the rest of her tea, Riffat continued, 'Imagine Nissrine's life if she resists. Waking up every morning to an icy household. Eating leftovers alone. Sly gossip forever in her ears. And that's just the silent hate. What about all the guilt from her mother? "I've lost face all because of you." Or, "Is this my reward for all the sacrifices we made?" Or, "Your father's health is failing." Or, "He's leaving me just because of you . . ." To whom would the girl turn?'

Dia turned away, uncomfortable with where the conversation was heading. It was the first time Riffat had alluded to her own difficulties. She did it as though she told someone else's story, as though this was for Nini. It wasn't. It was for Dia. She was trying to tell her that she too would have to think about these things.

Her mother kept on. 'And if it's not Nini's mother who'll say those things, it'll be someone else. And the older she gets, the more voices will chip in . . .'

Dia shut her eyes, hoping to shut out Riffat's story. If Riffat had been coerced into marrying Dia's large and delightful father, she didn't want to know. If they'd little between them, she wouldn't hear it. The man was dead now. It wasn't fair.

'. . . She'd have no one to turn to.'

'Stop saying that,' Dia blurted. 'She'd have me, wouldn't she?'

'No, Dia. She'd need to look elsewhere. Some day, so will you.'

'Pah!' She could think of nothing more convincing to say.

'I'm not saying you'll become Nini. I'm saying she's not you – and she's not going to be either. For her, giving in may not only be easier but also more fulfilling. She may not think of it as giving in. Right now, you're not in a position to judge. Yes,' she added, 'years from now, if she expects pity for her decision, maybe.'

Dia studied her intently. But Riffat's face gave away nothing.

Wisps of salmon-pink brushed through the cloud cover as the sun set. The sky resounded with the call for Maghrib prayer. The muezzin had a thin, plaintive voice and when he sang, Dia felt the day close around her. It was as if the call asked what the day had brought. The same errors? Yes, exactly the same. Even so, God hadn't lost hope entirely. There would be tomorrow, though one day tomorrow would run out. He would not keep spinning for ever.

It was the call that made Dia want to go to Him the most.

Inam Gul scurried into the bower with a mosquito coil. 'More tea?' he enquired.

'No, thank you, Inam Gul. Everything was delicious. But our philosophical Dia dwells on matters your delicacies can't appease – and she'll infect us too if we're not careful.'

Dia scowled at her mother and Inam Gul shook his head, safely commiserating with both. Then he piled the dishes and vanished into the swiftly descending darkness.

The twilight erupted with activity. Cats crossed paths and hissed; a chameleon's eyes glittered like black ice; a car honked for the gate to be opened. When darkness fell, the car rumbled into its hole, and all was momentarily still.

Dia surprised herself by being the one to reopen the discussion. 'You've always told me not to blindly go with things. That too many people let others decide their future, and it's as if individual apathy has snowballed into a national one. If all Ninis go the same way, all their offspring will too, and nothing around us will ever change.'

She was doubly surprised when Riffat did not answer. And then she worried. Her mother was rarely at a loss for words.

At last Riffat replied, 'Well, as I said, it may not just be pressure that's pushing Nini. She may not be moving blindly, even if she is following tradition. It may work for her, if not immediately, maybe one day . . .'

Dia leaned forward. 'You never used to believe in the one-day theory. You always said not to wait for miracles, but to live in the present.'

Riffat sighed. 'I know, Dia. It's just that, who knows, maybe Nini will find love, and the dear girl can be happy. That's all. Love lurks in unexpected places.' Her voice trailed.

Dia rolled her eyes. Her mother was in such a peculiar mood today. 'Ninety per cent of women do this. You can hardly call it *unexpected*.'

'Why not? Some of them, at least, do fall into love. And here I always thought you were a romantic, curling up in the arms of enchanted trees, lost in thousand-year-old stories. Don't you believe anything is possible? Some women say they find love after marriage.'

Again Dia shifted uncomfortably. *Did you?* She couldn't bring herself to ask. But she did know, as Nini too had recently pointed out, that it was the wife and not the single girl who grew into the plucky woman that revolutionized the production of silk in the country. Something about the arrangement had obviously worked for her. But was that all it was then – a settlement? Business partners, not lovers. Strangers, not friends.

Hardly a star lit the overcast sky. The cap of a crescent moon protruded from a pillow of clouds, then it too was masked.

Suddenly Riffat piped, 'What's the boy's name anyway?'

Smoke from the mosquito coil snaked between their knees. Dia rose to place it further away from them. 'Oh, some Daanishwar. Daanishwar Shafqat, I think Nini said.'

She'd barely returned to her seat when Riffat abruptly sat up. 'Shafqat? Are you sure? Any idea what his father did?' The voice had risen and was noticeably tight.

Dia folded her legs thoughtfully. 'Nini said he'd been a well-respected doctor, although, like her family, this one's run into some financial trouble. She gave me all the "important" details: the doctor's father had been a modest, gentlemanly civil servant and brave journalist. Slogged to educate his son and all. The doctor left a widow and just one child . . .' She stopped. Was that her mother wheezing? 'What's the matter, Ama? Wait, let me turn on the lights.'

'No!' Riffat shrieked. 'No. Sit down.'

'Wh . . . ?'

'How dare you go there without my permission!' she snapped.

'But . . .'

'Be quiet! Not one word.' She began pacing between the boles of the trees.

What had provoked this? Dia knew better than to pose the question now. Riffat rarely lost her temper, at home or at work. She tried to remember the last time it had happened. Was it when Hassan came home drunk one day, armed with a whisky bottle, and threatened to crack Dia's head with it? Or when the eldest, Amir, offered one of Riffat's rings to his Scottish girlfriend – now his wife? No, even then she'd not been in such a rage.

Breathing heavily, at last Riffat said, 'I'll say this once and once only. You're not to blame, you didn't know. But now you do. Take care never to step in that house again. Clear?'

What didn't she know? What did she know now? Under her breath, Dia mumbled, 'It's not clear at all.'

A distracted Riffat returned to her dark corner and adjusted herself in the chair.

Dia gazed up at the sky, watching the wind stir the clouds that fragmented the moon. Then she glared at her mother. Her mother who always had a plan. She would know what should happen next. Dia didn't.

3

Inam Gul For Ever

The next day, when Riffat had left for the mill, Inam Gul followed Dia around the house, devising ways of discovering what had happened the previous evening.

'You have to know everything, don't you?' She clicked her tongue.

'But what do you mean?' He sucked in his lips.

'I'm sure you heard it all.'

'Heard what?'

'I'll tell you something. That American boy and his mother are going to Nini's house in two days. She wants me there.'

He clapped his hands. 'No!'

'This is no cause for celebration, you know.'

He shook his head. 'No, no. No cause at all.'

She watched him.

He watched her.

'Go on,' she said, smiling a little at last. 'Ask away.'

He steered her gently from the dining room into the TV

lounge. He fluffed up the pillows on the couch. He clasped the remote control.

'Oh no you don't.' She snatched it.

He again sucked on his gums.

'You've gone through all those films a dozen times already.' She pointed at the stack of videos in the cabinet. 'They have to be returned, you know.'

'Maybe we can watch the old one with Reena Roy again? Just once.'

'Then I'm not staying.'

He gazed longingly at the blank screen. Then his face lit up. 'In two days? What will you wear?'

'Nini also cares about that,' she said peevishly. '*I'm* not the one on display, you know.'

He nodded soothingly, then snatched the remote control quickly from her fingers and pressed *power*.

'How childish you are.'

Together they watched a brightly-attired young woman sitting on her haunches, pink and blue bangles up to her elbows. Hair fell pleasingly into her eyes as she dipped those festive arms into a tub of suds, scrubbing a shirt collar as if her life depended on it. Apparently it did. In marched a large, mustachioed man with another shirt in his hands. He tossed it in her face and bellowed, 'You can't even make one thing shine!' And just then, a packet of the perfect detergent fell into those soapy, bangle-ringing arms. The woman was so ecstatic Dia wondered if that ugly man had actually, finally, died. Maybe it was her first orgasm.

She leaned over Inam Gul and pressed the power button.

He sulked, but she could see the amusement in his eyes. 'When is your friend getting married?'

'Well she's not getting married yet,' Dia insisted. But her voice dropped. 'Although it does seem she's getting closer.'

'What can we do?'

'Tell me a story or something.' She looked away. 'Distract

me from Nini and the fact that I ought to be studying for tomorrow.'

He patted her head, confessing softly, 'I heard.'

'I don't know why she got so angry,' Dia burst out. 'She wouldn't say. Why doesn't she want me to go there? It wasn't like her at all. And what'll I do without Nini?'

He muttered and cooed. 'Calm down, beti.'

Dia tried.

She looked at Inam Gul, so old and frail, his shriveled bones clear beneath the thin muslin shirt. He'd comforted her numerous times in the seven years he'd worked here. 'Inam Gul for ever,' she used to whimper. Now she just thought it.

She liked his calling her 'daughter'. He meant it. Maybe she helped him dwell less on his lost son, Salaamat, whom she occasionally saw at the farm. If he saw her too, he greeted her kindly. The only other person Salaamat spoke to that way was his sister Sumbul. Maybe he always remembered Dia as the girl who beat her brothers at cricket. She laughed at this.

'There,' said Inam Gul. 'You're better now.'

'No,' said Dia. 'Now I'm embarrassed.'

'Embarrassed? In front of me?'

She took a deep breath. 'I've been told two conflicting things. Nini insists I be with her on Tuesday. Ama wants me never to see that boy and his mother again. What should I do?'

'Don't worry,' said Inam Gul. 'There is no conflict. Your mother says to *never step in that house again*. The meeting is at Nini's house.'

She tilted her head. 'Sometimes I wonder: are you a befuddled old man or secret service agent? Is there anything you don't know?'

He shook his head.

'Well, you're absolutely right. No one shall be betrayed.'

'That's my daughter,' he patted her again, gazing once more

at the screen. Slyly, he pushed the VCR button and began rewinding the tape.

When the video played Inam Gul snapped his fingers as Reena Roy bounced before her love.

'Romance is just a spectator sport,' mumbled Dia, remembering the conversation with her mother yesterday. *Love lurks in unexpected places*. Yes, in fantasy. In her storybooks and in Inam Gul's videos. She said to him, 'You marry your daughter off and watch other women prance about on television.'

He looked up and pouted. Then he turned up the volume.

4

Examination

There were two grilled windows. The shadows of the bars fell on the linoleum floor and a shaft of light lit a tiny space in the center. There were only two ceiling fans. Dia was under neither. The room was meant to seat twenty-five. Forty examinees were packed into it as Head Supervisor listlessly passed out exams.

To Dia's left sat a very tiny woman with a desk covered in books. She offered Dia, with great warmth, any one of them. It was not an open-book exam.

To her right, another woman began peeling scraps of paper out from inside her bra. 'I thought there'd at least be *some* monitoring,' she told Dia, peeved at all the trouble she'd taken to make subtle her deceit.

Dia had still not looked at the exam. Foolishly, she was waiting for the official, 'All right now girls, you may turn over your papers and begin.' But Head Supervisor was off in the shadows, sniffing out her tombstone. Dia saw: *Economics*. She read the first question. *How many units of x* . . . The words began to swim.

Behind the woman whose bosom was steadily shrinking, another began unwinding a bandage around her arm. Others conferred with sneaker soles and the palms of their hands. The tiny woman to her left was getting tired of consulting books. She snatched Dia's paper. Realizing it was blank she tossed it back with a look that made Dia feel filthy. It reminded her of the detergent ad. She hadn't been scrubbing hard enough.

Everything she'd studied in preparation for the test entirely left her. Her thoughts turned to Nini. What was she doing at this very moment – going through her wardrobe? Planning a menu for tomorrow's tea? Practicing how to carry the tray for her prospective mother-in-law?

She shook herself back to the paper. *Long liquidation . . . basis points . . . short-term frustrations and difficulties . . .* What made the letters shimmy like that?

Before the exam, there'd been rumors that Lubna, daughter of a minister rumored to be one of the prime smugglers of Afghan heroin, would pay someone to do her test for her. This someone was not even meant to take the retake, but here she was, beside Lubna. And she was doing her test. Lubna filed her nails, yawned, painted her nails green. Head Supervisor skated by.

There were other stand-ins. Not all got a fee. Gulnaz had threatened hers in the following way: Huma, who'd scored highest in all her exams, had been seen slipping out of the college grounds with a boy. Gulnaz's mother's friend's sister's husband was Huma's father's friend's sister's brother-in-law's friend. Gulnaz had only to say the word, and the ball would roll straight into Huma's father's lap. Huma sat beside Gulnaz. She did her test.

Dia took to seeing how many smaller words could be made from Economics. Nose. Moon. Come.

How could she face the widow again? She remembered her from the Quran Khwani: a soft, dumpy woman with long frizzy hair. Oh, Nini was cruel.

Forty-five minutes remained.

Lubna could have simply bribed her teacher instead of the stand-in but obviously didn't care for shortcuts. Maybe she'd inherited her father's sense of adventure. Now her green nail polish was being mopped off for a brown one.

Why on earth was she dwelling on Lubna?

She stared down again. But the invisible line that connected the words to her eyes and on to her brain had snapped. Briefly, she worried that this was a permanent thing.

She shifted in her seat, growing increasingly irritated with herself. There were fifteen minutes left. She glanced at the woman with the scraps in her bra and burst out laughing. Her matronly bosom was now barely a curve, and ribbony chits oozed out of her kurta like birthday streamers.

She thought: the American boy might undress Nini. What if she hated his touch? What if he had bad breath? What if he drooled? What if he hurt her? What if she hurt for the rest of her life?

What if she didn't hurt, but loved it?

What if Dia was going completely mad?

Head Supervisor consulted her watch and, with what sounded like a last breath, declared that time was up. It hardly mattered: those who wanted to keep writing did.

Dia had written three words: Nose. Moon. Come.

Miserably ashamed, she handed over the test without even her name.

At the college gate, she walked past her car and driver and on to the street. The driver followed her. 'I don't need an escort. I'm sick of escorts!' She whisked by, then turned back guiltily. He was only doing his job. His job was to drive her to college then drive her back. Drive her to the farm with two armed guards then back. Drive her to Nini's, her relatives, the bazaar, mill, and back. His job was to confine her in a safe and mobile haven, between safe and immobile havens. His job was to keep her off the street, where men leered, sometimes pinched, and sometimes did worse. She heard Nini's voice: *Look at us. Always stuck behind walls and in cars. If we step out, what is there?*

'I'll be back soon,' she told him. 'You needn't follow me.'

As she threaded her way through traffic, every pair of eyes followed her. She kept her gaze forward, noting none of the crumbling, gothic balconies lined with laundry, the chipped sandstone gargoyles, the lattice screens – all that she'd seen many times from a car. Now she had no protection, no shell, and she felt too naked to look around. The more she was watched, the more she watched only herself. Under her shalwar, her legs were too skinny, too hairy, and why on earth hadn't she bothered to moisturize them? The dry patches made her skin gray. The stretch marks on her hips were white scabs in the middle of the gray. Her belly button too was hairy. Her breasts shapeless. Face lackluster. Hair straggly.

There were no other women walking down the street. That much was registered. Also a kissing sound. Grins. Eyes that gorged. Shoulders pushing into hers. A finger lingering on her buttocks.

She kept on walking, a zombie like Head Supervisor.

She turned into a narrow lane where a gutter had leaked. It smelled of old cabbage. Should she plunge deeper into the alley, where there were fewer onlookers and more shops, or stay on the main road with more space to run? Deciding on the first, she skipped over a puddle. Now she was less exposed but more trapped. She took another turn. The lane opened somewhat. A young boy sat outside a doorway, shaving a circle of wood on his knees. He scraped the surface and the fragment slid free, curling at the end. It fell to a ground littered with wood pellicles, plastic bags, tissues, heaps of rotten food.

At a paan shop she bought herself a paan with mounds of sweetened coconut, and chewed contentedly. An odd thing happened. When she ceased moving and hung around a building, fewer men stared and those that did looked away sooner. Their eyes penetrated more deeply when she was a body in motion than at rest. Being here was partly allowed. Getting here without cover was not.

Advancing once more, again she felt the stares. Then she got in line to buy a kilo of yogurt for Inam Gul, and every man made way for her to progress to the front. The shopkeeper took her five rupees and smiled endearingly. If she'd been walking, how would he have dealt with her?

The purchase in hand, she passed a row of steaming cauldrons stirred by young men periodically adding color. Cloth of every shade hung from hooks. There were women here now, leaving their cars and entering the maze of cloth and dye shops. They were welcome, as was she. And in the shoe shops, perfumeries, and flower stands. But when she crossed the street and moved on, boundaries were immediately drawn again. The chatter dropped, air tightened, eyes narrowed.

She kept meticulous track of the quickest way back to the car. Knowing its place and that it was ready to shield her all the way back to a beautiful house, despite the riots, strikes, and toppling governments, was what saved her from panic. No matter where she strayed, the thread linking her back home was there.

Or was it?

What had happened to her father?

Had he trespassed?

Did he think, when he left the house after that night in the tree, that he was safe behind the steering wheel, that as long as he knew the miles between him and his home, and the way to get there, he was linked? Was that his mistake? Was she repeating it?

What if this was a detour and she never found her way back?

Why weren't questions like these in her exam?

Trying to keep her gaze forward she again saw her naked self walking. There was the pale flatness of her stomach. The bottom with the ugly stretch marks. The scarred knees.

Up ahead, someone blocked her path. When she brushed by him, his crotch rubbed into that jiggling bottom. She felt him, thin and stiff, and gasped, walking faster, kicking over a block of wood mounted with shoe polish. The car was down the street, first right, first right again.

5

Assembling

It would have been easier if Nini had called her early. That way, Dia wouldn't be sitting stiffly in the drawing room with the guests, waiting for Nini's grand entrance. She could be lingering with her in the bedroom, postponing this.

When she'd called earlier in the day to suggest meeting before five o'clock, Nini had briskly disagreed. 'In fact,' she'd said, 'they'll probably show up late so make it five-thirty.' It was her most overt attempt at distancing Dia from her.

Then why did she want her here at all? Dia sulked, sitting with arms crossed on a love seat in the three-bedroom apartment Nini shared with her sisters, parents, and ailing grandfather. The drawing room looked out on the carports of other units in the apartment complex. A child was riding his tricycle, pedaling like a demon, while a maid kept watch. Dogs barked, and in the distance, a couple crossed the street. She lost sight of them but knew they were headed for the embankment, from where they could watch the ocean tear up the rocks at their feet.

On the couch sat the boy and his mother. He called her Anu but she and Nini were to say Annam Aunty. On seeing Dia her shock was visible, and Nini's mother, Tasleem, had been less than pleased. Dia would have to show them she'd not brought any pranks this time. Once again she quietly cursed Nini.

The boy twiddled his thumbs and looked out of the window too. Tasleem engaged Annam in a discussion of the lovely sea breeze they got every evening at about this time.

'People ask me, "Don't you miss having a garden?" I tell them, "Not at all! Who wants to waste money on a gardener? And we have a garden, a great big one. It gives us this lovely breeze. We don't even need an air conditioner!"'

Dia blushed for Nini. Maybe she was prudent in taking her time about the entrance. Tasleem had already begun defending her slouching fiscal status. The family had had to sell their five-bedroom house and move here, a fact Annam was probably aware of. To make up for lacking an air conditioner, Tasleem's hair had been set at Palpitations (she let this information slide in when the lovely breeze came a bit too close), and was dressed in a designer shalwar kameez, worth in the range of two to three thousand rupees. Around her neck were three gold strings and on her left arm clinked six slim gold bangles. She waved this arm a lot while speaking.

Annam seemed unperturbed by Nini's modest home and offered no explanation for her shabby appearance: she wore gold, yes, but her outfit was of nylon and her sandals torn. And her son was in jeans and a T-shirt. But then, boys always wore what they wanted.

Dia had submitted to Nini's wishes. She'd dressed as her mother would have, in the latest style: long, loose kameez over a shalwar that flared like a lampshade at her ankles. It was unspeakably stupid. Her hair was brushed; there was even a semblance of a parting. But she refused any make-up. When Riffat asked where she was going Dia had had to lie after all: 'A birthday party.' She'd kissed her goodbye before Riffat could ask whose. In the car her stomach pounded with fists again. Few mothers would let their daughters go wherever they wanted. Riffat did, and in return Dia was betraying her. But, Dia reasoned irritably, her mother should have explained herself.

Nini's two sisters sat politely on cushions on the carpet, whispering to each other. Her father was absent.

Of the six in the room, she and the boy were the only ones without anyone to talk to. She wished he'd stop the thumb-twiddling. And then, though she'd vowed not to, Dia scrutinized him.

He was tall and though slender, his T-shirt gave away a slight paunch. He was about her complexion, much darker than Nini, and very hairy: his arms and eyebrows would make useful breeding grounds for vermin. Hair short, puffy. Not silky like Nini's, a delight to run fingers through. Lips chapped and frequently licked. Nose – more breeding grounds no doubt. He looked impatient, indifferent. He hadn't made one attempt to engage what could be his in-laws in conversation. Tasleem kept trying.

'You're a gifted student, your mother tells me?'

'Um.'

'You're doing so well in your studies, mahshallah.'

Annam interceded. 'He's very modest.' She blessed him.

Nini's sisters giggled.

Annam: 'He's very interested in the news. Just like his father.'

Tasleem: 'May Allah rest him in peace.'

Nini's sisters shifted.

The boy twiddled his thumbs.

The mothers smiled awkwardly. If it weren't for that lovely sea breeze, they'd all choke.

Tasleem decided to give the boy a rest. Conversation now veered to all her contacts. 'You do know them? The owners of

Sheraton? Just yesterday I was invited to lunch at their house.'
Her list went on.

At last, Nini entered.

She skimmed into the room like a swan, eyes down, feathers
preened into a smooth bun (courtesy of Palpitations). Involun-
tarily, Dia looked away. She'd rather never have known her
than witness Nini metamorphose into a tea-tray-wielding, lash-
batting, one-foot-perfectly-before-the-other-walking nineteen-
year-old who seemed thoroughly committed to clinching first
prize in the Miss World Proposal Pageant. Had Daanish's
mother attended other events? How many girls had she
appraised? Suddenly, Dia was caught between despising Nini
and feeling so vehemently loyal that she couldn't bear to see
her lose. No one could outshine Nini.

She set the tray down on a side-table. Then, carefully
avoiding Daanish's end of the couch, approached his mother.
'Asalaam-o-alaikum, Annam Aunty,' she smiled.

'Waalai-kum-asalaam, beti,' Annam smiled back, patting
Nini's head.

She did not even glance at the boy.

Her sisters giggled.

She wore a long-sleeved pale pink silk outfit from Riffat's
mill. The silver-embroidered dupatta was modestly draped
across her chest. The same shade of pink highlighted her
eyelids, lips, toenails and fingernails. Dia blushed again for
her friend: if it weren't for Nini's innate poise, she'd resemble
a gumdrop.

As she moved back toward the tray, Annam too studied
her closely. Everyone did – except the boy. She arranged
four quarter plates with napkins and forks, offered the first
to Annam, second to her mother, third to Daanish (still no
eye contact), and fourth to Dia.

'Thanks,' said Dia. 'And hi.'

'You're welcome,' Nini purred. 'Nice to see you.'

'She loves to bake,' said Tasleem to Annam. 'Though she

eats so little herself. It's always, "Eat, Ama," or "Have more, Aba." She's such a joy to us.'

Nini began serving the items on the tray: a chocolate cake, rus malai, kebabs, chicken sandwiches, halwa. As she bent over Annam, her dupatta slipped from her shoulders and into the cake.

The boy smiled to himself.

Her sisters giggled.

Nini quickly set the tray down and went to wash the chocolate off.

Tasleem cleared her throat. 'The halwa is from that new bakery you must have heard about. The owner is my sister-in-law's niece. Her husband is the president of UBL. You must try it.' She placed a hefty spoonful on Annam's plate. 'And you Daanish? Seema, get up and serve him,' she snapped at one of the giggling sisters.

But Daanish rose and helped himself to each item on the tray.

'He's very considerate,' piped Annam. 'Even at home, he always wants to get things himself. He never troubles his mother.' She sighed. She blessed him.

Daanish sat on the end of the couch next to Dia's sofa. There was now a gaping space between him and his mother. Conversation between the mothers ceased. Dia flushed.

'I've been meaning to tell you something,' he said to her.

She blinked. *What are you doing?*

'I fed the caterpillars. You told me to find out what they eat. I did.' His face grew animated, and she heard the American lilt in his voice. It was warm, amicable. He took a large bite of a sandwich.

She stared, stupefied. *Get back next to your mother.*

'It was thoroughly fascinating. They spun cocoons. I'd never paid any attention to insects, you know? Unless, of course, it was to crush them.' He grinned, then started on the cake. 'Great snacks.'

Dia's forehead prickled. The sides of her neck burned. She thought she'd faint. Why had Nini begged her to come? She glanced quickly at Tasleem. The daggers there pierced her chest. She didn't dare look at Annam.

Nini's sisters giggled.

Tasleem cleared her throat again. 'Tell us more about Amreeka, Daanish.'

He hadn't told them anything about Amreeka. *Ask him something intelligent, for heaven's sake. Get him away from me.*

Annam smiled at her son. It looked like she was biting tacks. 'Tasleem Aunty is talking to you, jaan.'

He shrugged. 'Everybody's asked me that question. Actually, to be perfectly honest, I'm quite sick of it.' He smiled, not insincerely, but without any of the warmth with which he'd spoken to Dia.

Annam smiled apologetically. 'He's still a bit shaken, you know.'

The boy considered, then decided to let the comment go.

Tasleem: 'He seems to like the cake. Seema, get up and serve him.'

Daanish still had half a slice left. When Seema offered him a second there was no space on the plate to pile it. She giggled, quickly putting the cake down on the table and running back to her sister.

'Oh you silly child!' cried Tasleem.

'I'm still working on this,' said Daanish, his mouth full.

But Tasleem rose and put the second slice on the rus malai and Daanish puffed his cheeks in exasperation.

The sisters giggled.

Tasleem turned to Annam. 'What do we do with girls these days? Our mothers never had to train us. We just learned.'

'That's exactly what I see,' Annam commiserated.

'This is interesting,' said Daanish to Dia. 'Cocoa mixed with rus malai.'

The sisters doubled over.

Tasleem: 'Stop it you two!'

Daanish to Dia: 'So where was I? Mulberry leaves, eh? I like puzzles.'

The mothers fell silent again.

With one hand, a nervous Dia fanned herself. Then she stopped abruptly, feeling guiltier than ever. Fanning is what the lovely breeze was meant to do.

Nini re-entered. Her dupatta was damp at one edge. Swiftly, she took in the seating change and cut Dia a peppery look.

But then she quickly composed herself. 'Annam Aunty, you must have more.' She lifted the tray again.

The sisters doubled over again.

Nini eyed them sternly, deftly making sure her dupatta, now pinned to her shoulders, had kept its place. It had. She scowled at her sisters.

Tasleem: 'One more sound from you two and you can leave.'

At last, the young girls lowered their heads in shame.

Tasleem to Annam: 'I thought it would be good for them to see how it is, you know, for when their time comes.' She stared at them hard, adding, 'But obviously that won't be for a long, long time.'

They looked about to cry. Dia could have hugged them for diverting attention from her. Or rather, from the attention lavished on her from the center of the women's attention.

Tasleem tried again. 'Well, will you tell us what you missed most in the three years you were away? It must have been so hard at first.'

Please answer her. And then, before she knew what she was doing, Dia whispered it. 'Please answer her.'

The boy looked her full in the face. His eyes were large, amber-hued, beautiful. The irises dilated.

Please.

He swiveled so his knees pointed toward the center of the

room again. He smiled at Tasleem. 'Well, I sure missed the food. This is all delicious.'

Instant rejuvenation. Annam practically leaped with joy. 'His appetite is mahshallah very healthy. I was worried the first week. He wouldn't eat a thing. But then,' she sighed, 'time takes care of everything.'

'It must be so hard for a mother, not being able to cook for her son,' Tasleem added. 'How you must have worried about his diet when he left. But then, there, of course, everything is so fresh and wholesome. Most of our children gain weight.' She then proceeded to relate all the stories of thriving Pakistani children in America. Wajiha's son at Stanford. Munoo's at MIT. Goldy's somewhere in, where was it . . . Texas?

The only seat available for Nini was between Daanish and Annam. Dia rose to offer her the sofa seat.

'Keep sitting,' Nini snapped, deciding on the carpet beside her sisters. Dia sat down, shuddering: Nini sounded just like her mother.

'I think it was Wajiha's son who scored the highest on his SATs. He was in the first percentile!'

Annam: 'What are SATs?'

Tasleem, laughing, 'Oh come on now, surely you know! Daanish must have taken them too. And he must have done very well, isn't that right, Daanish?'

Daanish: 'I must have.'

Annam insisted, 'What are SATs? Did the doctor know?'

'Of course, Anu. No one gets into college without taking them.'

'Then it's a medical exam? Your blood tests were very healthy.'

Tasleem hollered. 'That's a good one!'

Nini smiled. Her sisters shifted, unsure if they could giggle.

Daanish put his plate down and his arm around Annam.

'They are Math and English tests. I don't know about Wajiha's son but Anu's scored fifteen-sixty.'

Annam looked pleased, though still confused.

Tasleem collected herself. 'Of course! Have more cake.'

'I'm full.' He turned to Dia again.

No! Especially not now! You want them to kill me?

But this time the boy could not read her thoughts, and she was too terrified to voice them. He said, 'Two of the cocoons even hatched, if that's the right word. I saw the whole thing.'

Now Nini too was listening. Dia could tell by the way she held her head – the taut profile, the pursed lips. Perhaps she ought to stand up and excuse herself. Go to the bathroom and let Nini follow. Then she could explain she hadn't done a thing. He was the one prattling on. Maybe Nini would find a way to sneak her out of the house, and the meeting could proceed the way it was meant to have from the beginning. No detours.

And then she realized what he'd said. 'You *saw* it?'

'I knew I could get a reaction out of you,' he laughed. 'Yes. Saturday morning. It was cool. First this thin dark liquid started oozing, disgustingly smelly. I had them in a drawer and the wood discolored, like the fluid was acid. But it seemed to soften the cocoons. Slowly, the moths ate their way out. I couldn't believe it! They were cream-colored and spread their brittle wings, as if to dry.'

This time Dia was only vaguely aware of the fresh daggers plunging her throat. She was entranced. She'd never known anyone – not Nini, not Inam Gul, not even Sumbul – so intent on observing what most people considered trivial. The minor details, the small discoveries. These had always been hers alone to love. Others filed them away as distractions, nuisances. But for her, they were life. For him too? By the looks of it, yes. He was delighted, as if he'd gained simply by noticing. As if by sharing a fleeting moment with two, tiny unsung beasts, his world had opened.

And he was damn lucky. She'd spent years trying to see what he'd managed the first time, and she still hadn't succeeded. Saturday morning – that would be around the same time she'd been watching the pair at the farm. And then Nini had called to invite her here, and she'd missed it. If Nini hadn't called, she wouldn't have missed it. If she hadn't missed it, she wouldn't be here, knowing what she knew of Daanish.

'What time did they finally come out?' she asked.

'Just after ten. I checked my watch. And you know what else? The tips of their swollen abdomens locked together. They didn't appreciate my watching.'

'So did the ones at the farm!'

'What?'

'Doesn't matter,' she laughed. 'I didn't see it, anyway. But you did. Go on.'

'They stayed that way for hours . . .'

She leaned forward. What a *crazy* thing to feel her heart race like this. Was it his smell? Crisp, delectable. Mannish. He was like a butterfly, sprung from Aphrodite's girdle, and all the females were assembling around him.

'More cake,' insisted Tasleem.

Nini too stood up and Annam was saying something.

Even the sisters were prancing around, teacups in hand. They were helping Nini serve the tea, which she'd obviously got up to brew at some point. There was milk and sugar, and something fell.

But Dia and Daanish gazed at each other, alone in the joy of what he'd seen.

Part Two

SALAAMAT

I

Here

JULY 1992

Salaamat stood with them outside the cave.

Daanish rolled his jeans up to his knees, saying, 'At low tide, we'd eat in there when I was a kid.' The jeans were drenched and kept sliding down to his ankles.

Dia peered inside. 'It's claustrophobic.'

The water raced down the cave's length, crashing into the far wall, submerging the smooth rock where, Daanish told Dia, Anu would spread their tea. 'Years ago, I found a silvery shell here. An argonaut's nest. Then my parents fought over a pearl necklace. Anu was always irritable whenever he got her anything expensive. Later, she'd cry to me: "The roof still leaks and the twelve-year-old car keeps breaking down, but he keeps throwing away any money we have left. Don't count on an inheritance." She meant: *I'm counting on you.*' He sighed and took Dia's hand.

They strolled along the shore, leaving Salaamat alone by the cave. He lit a cigarette, remembering the ad for it. Two men scaled a mountain, just like he and Fatah had done their

231

last day together. He liked to imagine it was him in the red jacket and Fatah in the blue.

Salaamat started walking too, soon catching up with them. The wind ruffled her hair and dealt with their words similarly: tangling and tossing them up and back, at him. Teasing, stinging. He was the subject of their conversation.

'There was no other way, Dia,' Daanish was saying. 'I had to ask Khurram for his car and driver or Anu would have asked too many questions.'

'You could have only asked for the car. We could have driven here.'

'Yes, but Khurram had to take his own car. This is his father's. He's terrified of getting it scratched. I don't blame him for not trusting me that much.'

'But it's embarrassing that he's in on us. I've known the family so long. What do you suppose he's thinking?'

Hadn't they realized how close he was? Perhaps not – he always moved with great stealth. It was how he'd escaped the camp. It was why he was still alive.

'Don't worry,' Daanish touched her cheek tenderly, 'maybe I can find a way to take our own car. Except it keeps breaking down.'

They fell silent. Salaamat had to re-light his cigarette. Of course in the ad, even on top of the Himalayas, the wind couldn't touch it.

Dia's apricot shalwar was soaked through and when the tide pulled in, Salaamat could see the backs of her legs. And her buttocks. She'd been only twelve when he'd first seen her, a gleeful bowler in her father's arms. And now here she was, giving herself to another man, her clothes transparent, her honor more reckless than the breeze. But then chastity did not run in their blood.

Daanish took something out of his pocket that Salaamat couldn't see.

'I've been keeping this to show you,' Daanish said. 'It's

what I got when I boiled the cocoon. Your hair's a thousand times more jumbled than this, and I love that about you.' He proceeded to tell her how he'd twisted it while puzzling over the length.

'A thousand meters,' she smiled. 'And all a single piece. You wound it around your arm, just like I always imagined the Chinese Empress must have done. Funny, but I was thinking of her the day I first heard of you.'

'And with what warm feelings did you think of me?'

'If I remember correctly, I said: *shit!*'

Salaamat exhaled peevishly. He was sick of it, sick of being a witness, sick of being dragged into worlds that were not his. He was chaperoning the lovers because the Amreekan boy had to pretend he was with Khurram. Why was this his problem?

Still, he kept listening.

Dia said, 'After I cursed you I cursed poor Nini.'

'Don't, Dia. It's taken so many phone calls to get you to see me. Don't spoil it.' He put his arm around her waist.

Salaamat licked his lips. An unwanted pleasure pressed the pit of his stomach, sweeping down to his groin. He imagined his own hand in the dip above Dia's wet behind. It would slide down and squeeze her wanton spheres. The way she walked in the waves, swaying, almost tripping . . . With every step that succulent bottom screamed for him.

She said, 'Was I always meant to be here with you today, Daanish, or is this a diversion? If we never meet again, will I be back on track?'

'What do you mean?'

'Sometimes I play this game. I go back in time and imagine how different things would be if one tiny incident hadn't occurred. If, for instance, Nini hadn't brought me to your father's Quran Khwani, I wouldn't be here. I wouldn't have slid the silkworms down her shirt, you wouldn't have fed them, and we might never have spoken at her house. Perhaps you'd be here instead with Nini. And what would come of that? What's to come of this?'

Daanish released her. 'I'm not drawn to her, you know. I agreed to the tea just for my mother.'

'And would you consider marrying her just for your mother? Can you spend a lifetime with someone simply because you're expected to?'

'Most of this country does,' he answered shortly.

'That's exactly what she says. Perhaps you ought to marry her.'

Salaamat exhaled again. Their first row. It was touching.

Daanish said, 'Look, I know this is weird for you. It's even pretty weird for me. But you're not making it easier by asking impossible questions. You told me yourself: Nini's been distancing herself from you. Maybe it's time you did the same. And just for the record, I could never marry a woman with a mother like hers.'

She said nothing but took his hand again, then giggled. 'I like your accent. No, *accents*. A combination of sounds.'

They paused and Daanish began filling her free hand with shells. 'The last time I was here, Salaamat told me these pen shells used to be harvested for the thread they spun. He said cloth could be made from it. Marine silk – whoever heard of it?'

'Well, he'd know.' She used a half of the iridescent shell as a plate for the smaller ones. Then she looked back and noticed him. Pointing quickly to a boulder ahead of them, she muttered, 'Let's go there.'

'Good idea,' Daanish agreed cheerfully.

An uninvited Salaamat followed.

She climbed up, settling in the same incline as Salaamat the day Daanish had come here with Khurram. Then too Salaamat had been the silent witness.

The wind was in Dia's face. She greeted it with eyes shut. Daanish slid beside her. Salaamat stood next to the boulder.

The two men stared first at each other and then at Dia, both resisting the urge to plant a quick kiss.

She was not pretty. Her nose was long and bent, body too lean, brows thick and unsculpted, and skin, this close up, scarred. She had a deep gash above her right brow, and another mark – the scar of a particularly unsavory pimple – just above a fairly standard mouth. She even had faint whiskers. Yet, Salaamat's groin began to ache again.

Dia asked, 'What are you looking at?'

Daanish replied, 'Guess.'

'Well, if it's me, I don't see what you see.'

'Do you like me?'

She laughed. 'What?'

'Do you like me?'

'Would I be here if I didn't?'

'Say it then.'

She laughed again, whispering something to which Daanish replied, 'So what? Anyway, he's deaf.'

'According to his sister, only when he wants to be.'

'Forget him, okay? Say it.'

'I like you.'

'What?' he shouted. 'Did anyone hear anything?' He called down to Salaamat, 'Did you hear anything?'

'Stop it,' she protested.

'Then say it again, louder.'

'I won't if you make a scene.'

Daanish waved his arms, threw back his head. 'It's just us, Dia. Us and a heavy gray sky on a day in July, at three in the afternoon, with not a sound in the air but the waves thrashing against this rock, where we sit, alone at last. For the first time in ages, I'm in the present. I'm not waiting for some plane to pick me up and drop me somewhere else. I'm here. And it's beautiful. Later tonight, you'll lie in your bed and ask: "What if I'd said it louder, as Daanish wanted me to? And what if I'd kissed him, as he wanted me to and as I

also wanted? How much sweeter the day might have been."'
He breathed in her ear, 'Then kiss me.'

She did.

Well, thought Salaamat, perhaps the Amreekan had learned
something in Amreeka after all.

She'd said: he's only deaf *when he wants to be*. Salaamat
smiled. People were deaf and blind and dumb exactly when
it suited them.

He could tell them that. He could share what he'd heard
said all those years ago in the tomb of a governor dead six
hundred years. A tomb strung with an old fisherman's net
to keep bat shit off the painted floor. He could spoil their
moment. No, he could tell them their moment was already
spoiled.

Or he could keep sitting, watching the clouds form, wondering how long it would take them to reach his old village,
many kilometers down the coast. He'd never been back. But
he knew those foreign trawlers had been issued legal licenses
now. Nearly everyone from his village had left.

Summer used to be the season for repairing nets. It used to
be when women sat on the dunes outside the crumbling walls
of their homes, drinking tea, layers of cotton mesh sprawled
on the sand. He'd sit with them, with thoughts of poachers
quietly at bay. The talk was of rain. Slowly, the women
hummed the Sur Saarang, the melody that invoked rain:

> *Robes of rain God displays*
> *And with each drop He plays,*
> *He plays.*

Salaamat and the other children would watch the women
darn the nets, imagining they sewed God's rainy robes, waiting for the drops to fall so they could play with Him.

Now he sat at the foot of the boulder, watching this other
world tumble and crash around him. He rubbed the shells Dia

had left nearby. He was a silent witness. He'd keep her secret but he'd also keep his own. She'd never know how he'd drawn her on his first and last bus. Or that he'd thought of her in Hero's shop. Or that she had every reason to hate him.

He walked down to the shoreline again, the same that stretched all the way out to his village. There was a new game the boys were playing the year he'd left. They'd dare each other to swim out to the trawlers, even in the rainy season, and touch the anchor line. Then they'd wave to the band of boys on the beach. But if any boy swam out now and looked back, there would hardly be anyone awaiting his return. Boys were learning to be ajnabis younger every year.

2

The Bus

His second year at Handsome's, Hero left, and many of the Pathans followed. Salaamat presumed they'd joined one of the all-Pathan bus-body workshops sprouting all around. Or perhaps some had gone north to the border, and Amreeka was training them to be freedom fighters. Whatever the reason, the result was that he took over much of the paint work, though still not the most prestigious work of all: painting pictures. His job was piling putty on every hinge and joint of each bus. When this dried, he covered it with four layers of a mixture of limestone powder, mineral oil and gray tincture. Then he spray-painted from nose to tail, usually magenta, green or blue, sticking scraps of newspaper along the way. Later, he'd peel off the paper and spray the gaps a different shade. The fumes were toxic. His eyes grew bloodshot and nausea became part of the routine.

Most of the newspapers were in English. He tried to read the headlines and ads later in his room. He recognized the letters from the backs of cars, and repeated the sounds of z in Mazda, o in Toyota. He fingered the words and enjoyed their weight on his tongue. He could string sounds without meaning, the way for years he'd listened without speaking: *Seven Years Into Soviet Invasion, Refugees Keep Pouring In. Hair Loss, What Hair Loss? MQM Calls For Strike. Nice Girls Don't Shave. More Buses Set Ablaze. US Increases Aid To Iraq. Women Protest Hudood Laws. Jamaat-i-Islami Calls For Anti-Soviet Rally.*

Afterwards, he practiced painting on the used scraps of wood that littered his cell, doing what Hero had done: sketching in chalk then daubing over with oils. Wanting somehow to depict the chronology of his life, he brushed four strokes and filled the shape green. A boat. He gave it a flag. Next was the gray-blue sea carrying large white fish with gills like pockets. And blind fish with razor teeth. And deaf ones blowing bubbles only they could hear. On shore were the dunes for nestling with Rani, for baring her round, egg-shaped shoulders. He drew turtles too.

The next day, he again lived in noxious vapor, waiting patiently for Handsome to tell him he could have the glistening metallic body of the bus he covered red and green yesterday as his own private canvas today.

It happened at last, before his third year.

It was a sixty-two-seater with a monkey seat in rear and bow. Electricians had nearly completed wiring up the fifty-three lights inside to the horn that sang when pressed. As the bus trumpeted, the lights dazzled. The owner, an enormous Punjabi with a mustache rivaling an eagle's wingspan, had said: 'Make it a disco bus. Make it from the heart. When it passes, everyone should know my glory. Otherwise, I want my money back.' He slapped five lakhs cash into Handsome's hand.

Salaamat was helping a child cut a sheet of steel with a pair of enormous tin snips when Chikna approached him. 'Ajnabi, your lucky day has come.'

Salaamat held the steel between the snips while the child beat the blunt blades with a hammer. At last, they bit into the metal and a small rectangle fell apart. 'Why?' he asked.

'Why?' Chikna laughed. 'See that bus?' He pointed to the one bursting with activity. 'Handsome's going to let you paint it.'

Salaamat looked up. Workers were measuring leopard-skin plastic for the seats. 'Of course I'm going to paint it,' he shrugged. 'That's what I do now.'

Chikna flicked the hair at Salaamat's jaw repudiatingly. 'I mean really paint it. There's no one else. All the others are leaving. So he's picked you. If the owner's unhappy, you're fired. If he's happy, you get paid.'

Salaamat watched him walk away.

At last.

The child hammered the dust. His hands and face were covered in grease and his clothes stank. He asked, 'What will you make?'

Salaamat stared at the iron body. He wanted a hand in every stage of its shaping. He wanted himself shown, all over Karachi. In motion, with horn blaring and lights pulsing and at ease, for admiring fingers to touch. The name would be Handsome's but the story would be his.

In the following days he began on the undercoating. While it dried, he helped those who'd taken over the metal work. He cut steel strips into floral shapes to be nailed along the flanks when the spray-painting was complete. He sawed into the bus's gut to make the luggage-boot and nailed iron sheets over the wooden planks of the floor.

Sometimes, he caught fragments of the workers' chatter. The Soviets were receding but Karachi broiled. Some of the Punjabi workers too felt they should leave, now not to the border to defend the neighboring country, but to the Punjab, to defend their families from the stockpile of ammunition the battle was leaving behind. These were swiftly gaining popularity in Karachi – the city that swarmed with immigrants. It was coming full-circle, Salaamat smirked as he listened to the gossip: those who'd pushed the local people of Karachi to the edge were themselves running from each other. Everyone was falling off the bus. Literally.

The bus-body-making business was one of the worst hit by the riots that began last year when a Muhajir student was run over by a Pathan bus driver. Members of her community insisted it was deliberate, and yet another way they were being exploited. They torched buses, smashed workshops, killed workers, learned to maneuver Soviet and American weapons. As the trouble spread, few remembered the college girl who'd triggered the mayhem by crossing the street at the wrong time on the wrong day.

Salaamat did. While the men gossiped and he worked on the bus, he saw her: books in hand, a blue dupatta sliding down the shoulders of a white uniform. Spectacles and a long braid. No, no glasses. White shoes. With right foot first, she left one side of the street but before reaching the other, she'd make history. If only she'd waited less than a minute. Forty seconds. Maybe even thirty. Had she screamed? Had she seen what the city would become at the moment the front fender smashed into her hips and threw her high into the smog-filled sky? If only she'd taken a different route. If only there had been a sign on her side of the road: Trespassers will be executed.

'Is it only luck that's made us successful?' one of the workers was saying. 'Absolutely not. They call *us* foreigners. And what are they? Hindustani, that's what.'

'They should have stayed there,' another one spat, 'in that heathen land.'

'Pakistan would prosper if it weren't for them,' a third declared.

'Oh ajnabi,' they called out. 'What do you say? The chaos is good for you. When has a Punjabi ever let a Sindhi paint a rich man's bus?'

As always, Salaamat ignored them.

He cut the newspaper in fish shapes and stuck them on. Next, he mixed the blue and red Diko cans to get a different shade. The spray gun frothed a rich jamun color. Handsome grunted his approval. It would be the city's first purple bus.

Days later, when he peeled the paper off, he painted the fish yellow and added glitter to their fins. The children stood around appraising the sparkle. He slapped them if they touched. He nailed ornate bands of steel around the enormous girth, like a belt, then around the rear- and head-lights. He helped build and weld every possible frill: chains to dangle from the bottom, and three large sculptures: a huge turtle on the front fender ('That's not a turtle!' the others laughed. 'It's a giant ant!'); a steel dhow with two triangular sails for the metal frame of the roof ('And that's a giant moth!'); an eagle for the back fender. His only worry was the Authorities. It had been three weeks since they last came to collect decoration tax. But they would not be the ones to trouble him.

When the bus was ready for the pictures, Salaamat started at the back. He shaped a younger, more tousled Rani. She still had the enticing sheer dupatta over her head and across her chest, but while one henna-painted hand held the cloth over her beckoning lips, the other, emerging from somewhere behind her neck, aimed a heart-shaped cricket ball at him. Around her was a forest of towering trees. A petal fell on her breast. It was yellow and the ball red. He made the red bleed. Her cheeks were flushed and sweating, as if they'd recently tumbled together.

On one corner of the front he painted another scene from his first visit to Dia's house: the thick carpet of grass, parrots, a gondola drooping with blue-green tendrils. On the other, he made her farm: the lush foliage of mulberries on which had assembled moths, which he gave more pigment than real silk moths.

The bus's interior he lavished with boats decked in flags, as during the annual mela at his village. Dogs lolled on sand dunes or chased baby turtles scrambling out to sea; women loitered outside the thatched-roof teahouse; and, at the back, exactly where his Rani was painted on the outside, he made a pair of old hands holding a hookah.

Around the palanquin-like iron scaffold atop the roof, where the dhow sculpture was welded, he stuck pieces of colored tape. On the tape he scrawled *Allah* and *Muhammad* in flouncing letters in black ink, or copied snippets from the children's section of the English newspaper: *Neighborly love is the best love; Never judge a book by its cover; Don't count your chickens before they hatch*. Finally, down both its sides, in bold gold he printed: *Handsome Body Maker, Qaddafi Town, Karachi*.

When the rich owner came to collect the bus, Salaamat grinned. The mustachioed man liked it. Now his purple vessel would parade the hidden life of a native in the city of ajnabis.

3

Blue

MARCH 1987

The Friday after was the first he ventured into town with a pocket full of money. Handsome had given him a delighted thump on the back and two thousand rupees, promising the next bus would be his too. Salaamat determined to spend his first income on gifts – for himself, and for his sister Sumbul.

He discovered his bus's route ended at Orangi Town, on the northwestern tip of the city. He'd never been that far before. According to Sumbul, this was where Riffat Mansoor's weavers lived. She said cloth bought directly from one of their looms cost a fifth of what Riffat sold it for. He'd go there. He'd surprise Sumbul with the finest silk her fingers had ever touched. She, who fed the filthy grub but never got to enjoy the results – a bright, sheer mesh would sit beautifully on her shoulders.

Inside the bus Salaamat was shoved into the aft of one of his boats. Two of the tinted windows were already cracked and the disco lights only added to the suffocating heat. In all his Fridays, he'd never traveled with so many commuters. Was it because of the beauty of his bus? Was everyone admiring it? He wanted to believe this, except there was scarcely any room to twist around and absorb the finer details, let alone think of the hands that made them. All anyone wanted in here was air. All anyone got was the stench of hair oil, farts and feet.

Someone complained, 'Karachi has only two seasons – dry and damp.'

'In two months moisture will bloat you like a buffalo and you'll wish for this,' another replied.

'Still, March is the limit.'

Salaamat couldn't see out the greasy glass, so he asked where they were.

'I think we're near the Stadium. That's my stop.'

'No, you missed your stop.'

Salaamat interrupted them again. 'How much longer till Orangi Town?'

Everyone enjoyed that. '*Hours*. Besides, what do you want to go there for? It's more dangerous than Landhi. Shops have closed. There've been too many killings.'

Salaamat frowned. If they were really near the Stadium he wasn't even halfway there yet, and already he'd been riding the bus over an hour. The thin ribbon of air that crept around his ear was an offshoot of the scorching loo that blew in from the desert, sapping every last drop of him. He licked his lips, his throat as brambly as a bed of cactus. He wondered how much longer he could bear this.

Half an hour later, he had to hop off. Without asking where he was, Salaamat headed straight for a drinks-stand. Somewhat rejuvenated, he looked around him: an unknown, congested commercial district. He began to walk. Within minutes, his throat again screamed for a balm of ice. He could return to the drinks-stand. He could spend the entire day and all his cash on heavenly bubbles, then return to his cell in the evening. But in his pockets the crisp notes whispered something else. His first income: he must spend it well. In the distance was a maze of brightly-lit lanes. Rubbing the bills between thumb and forefinger, he went there.

One passage housed bangle stalls, another led into the shoe district, a third to souvenir stands selling perfume, leather merchandise, cloth. An increasingly dizzy Salaamat turned blindly into bend after bend. Bodies rubbed into him. Rancid breath hit his face. Swallowing back the 7-up rising in his throat, he collapsed on the first stool in his way.

When his head cleared and he looked up, Hero was staring at him from across the narrow alley. The man was surrounded by blue glass: vases with voluptuous bowls and long, slender necks; frosted glasses, both thick and fine; jugs with chatoyant handles. Salaamat was transfixed as one handle changed from green to purple. Hero started combing his hair, gazing at his milky reflection in a viscous blue plate. He said, 'I thought something stank.'

There were two child helpers, both fair-skinned with wheat-colored hair. One sat on a frayed rug while the other picked up articles and dusted them. Aside from glassware, there were goods of veined blue and cream marble, rugs, coins, and jewelry.

'So this is where you've been all this time,' said Salaamat.

Hero patted his hair into place and slipped the comb into his shirt pocket. Still looking in the glass he said, 'I take it you're still slaving for that fat Punjabi.'

'I'm earning now,' Salaamat retorted proudly.

Hero's lips curled in a sneer. 'You are, are you? How much?'

'Two thousand rupees,' he blurted, regretting it instantly.

Hero threw his head back and laughed. 'Then,' he held his arms out magnanimously, 'I invite you to step into my shop and urge you to spend the money well.'

Despite himself, Salaamat was tempted. The tiny stall was a pocket of solace, of a dazzling blue solace. He stepped inside. Beside him, the older child polished a pair of lapis lazuli earrings set in silver. Dozens of peacock feathers were nailed to the carpets hanging on the far wall, while against it lay slabs of aquamarine crystals. He touched a string of beads that glistened like a pool of dusky blue oil. It would sit beautifully on Rani's collarbone, while the earrings would become Sumbul even better than silk. 'How much for both?'

'For you,' declared Hero, 'only three thousand rupees.'

'You know how much I have.'

'We will reach a fair price. But first, I want to show you something else. Something that will delight you.' He pulled him toward the shop's rear. The carpets on the wall were in fact curtains, and there was no wall. Hero pulled back the lower corner of one rug, careful not to snap a peacock feather, and they entered another room. 'Call if we get customers,' he ordered the boys.

It took Salaamat an instant to adjust to the odd light. When he did, he saw two men on stools shining guns. They were both fair-skinned and decked in finely embroidered vests. Smoke from oil lamps rose in the air and the flames shivered, throwing into relief the firearms displayed on the walls.

'Tea for my friend,' said Hero.

In the shadows Salaamat distinguished a figure hunkered over a small burner. A sweet smell began to rise. Two more stools were arranged next to the men in vests who grunted at Salaamat. A cup was handed to him. The dark room was cool and Salaamat thirsty. He sipped gratefully. Peering around, he then noticed the two men who walked along the walls, examining the firearms.

One of them, short and with a jutting, rectangular jaw took a gun down and brought it over to where they sat. 'There are more than one hundred thousand of these Tokarev pistols in the country yet your price has not come down. The bullets are cheap. Parts easy to repair. You cheat us.'

Hero yawned. 'Then why do you come back?'

The man swiveled and spoke rapidly in another tongue to

his partner. Salaamat's heart pounded. He understood them.

'*This Pathan son-of-an-owl knows he has the best collection in this Godforsaken nuthouse.*'

'*We should crack his skull.*'

'*We can get the bullets lodged inside it.*'

'*We'll feed them to his sister while we fuck her.*'

He turned back to Hero. 'We want a case of the Tokarevs. And our Chief wants another one of those Rugers.' He pointed to the pistol being shined by one of the vests.

Hero bowed in mock servitude. 'As you wish. The Chief likes the best. Those Amreekans make first-class pistols and this is the most popular one in the world: .22 caliber with a detachable ten-shot magazine. See this button? Push and the cartridge slides in. That's a unique feature. But,' he chewed his tongue, 'the best is never cheap.'

'*How many sisters does he have?*' the partner hissed from the back.

'Karim,' said Hero. 'Let our faithful client hold the Ruger.' Karim thrust his cloth one last time into the pistol's barrel, twisting it inside like a pipe cleaner. Then he offered it to the customer. 'Feel it,' Hero smiled beatifically. 'The stock is made of Amreekan akhrot. The rest is stainless steel. I will gift you the case and an extra magazine.'

'They always come with that,' Jutting Jaw snapped. 'You don't fool us.'

Salaamat was beginning to feel an odd tickle in his throat. It was as if Karim had thrust the cloth down him instead of the barrel and was jiggling it.

The Sindhis spoke his tongue and this was soothing, yet they were not like the people in his village. He didn't know if they'd want him to understand them, and what they'd do if they didn't. He was an insider, but still on the fringe. And yet, the longer he listened, the more desperate he grew for them to know him. It was as though he was riding in his bus and had only this one chance to stand on the leopard-skin seats, lean out the tinted windows, and utter a scream long silenced, 'Here! It's me!' He took another sip of the tea.

Jutting Jaw weighed the pistol in his hand and grinned. *'The Chief will reward us well for this.'*

'Nadir, bring out more Amreekan ones,' commanded Hero. The other vest went to the back of the room, toward the burner. He opened a trunk and returned with three different kinds of guns. He began to recite, 'Every strong man's favorite shotgun is the Remington, favorite rifle is the Colt and favorite machine gun is the Ingram. Every common man has the Kalashnikov – you ought to have something different.'

'Show the Winchester,' Hero yawned again. Nadir retrieved the rifle and handed it over. 'This is our most prized addition. It's an antique. Look at the floral carving at the base of the barrel. Who can resist it?'

The partner came forward. He was taller than Jutting Jaw and wrapped in an ajrak. *'The bastard knows he has us now.'* He ran his fingers along the engraving. *'It's finer than a Turkish scabbard. Maybe the Chief will even let us use it.'*

He looked up and noticed Salaamat. 'Who's this?' He pointed the muzzle at him.

Hero continued smiling magnanimously. 'He ought to be one of you. Instead, he's suddenly feeling very shy. Must be the tea.' The vests snickered. 'He's understood everything you've said. Every filthy compliment you've paid me.' He laughed.

Something crawled inside Salaamat's forehead, just above the bridge of his nose. He laid a hand there and held his breath. Both men were dark like him but without his pale blue eyes.

The one in an ajrak insisted, *'Speak.'*

Salaamat gulped the last of the sweet tea. It left a cool,

menthol shiver on his tongue. He said, '*Your words are music to my ears. I hate this man.*'

The men looked at each other and burst into laughter. Then the Pathans switched to their tongue and laughed too. This made the Sindhis guffaw. More tea was made. More stools brought. The buyers sat down. '*Shake hands,*' they said to Salaamat.

He shook the muzzle of the Winchester. '*My name's Salaamat. Not Ajnabi like this jackass.*'

'*Fatah,*' said Jutting Jaw, gripping the rifle's other end. '*Second Commander. Not a cheat like this rat.*'

'*Muhammad Shah,*' said the other, slapping his hand on the stock. '*First Lieutenant and tea advisor. Next time, don't drink it. You'll wake up puking acid.*'

Salaamat's fingers curled around the slender barrel as he continued shaking it. He swayed, feeling increasingly queasy.

Hero offered him the butt of a Kalashnikov. When Salaamat took it, Hero said in a mocking child's voice, 'We make more than two thousand rupees.' And to the others, 'How many of these?'

The vests stood up and began wrapping the supplies. Fatah counted rupees. Salaamat learned there were thirty bullets in the magazine of an AK-47, and that each bullet cost a mere ten rupees. The machine gun itself was four thousand, the Winchester, sixty-five. Others, sold by the case, cost anywhere in between. These men had more cash than even a bus-owner.

He felt Fatah slipping something into his shirt pocket. He wasn't sure what. His vision was blurry and he thought he might vomit. But he clung to the machine gun's cylinder. It was as smooth as the slim neck of the frosted blue vase outside. It was cold, fragile. If he let go it would snap and little blue splinters would pierce his skin.

'It's a small world,' said Muhammad Shah, in Urdu again. 'From Amreeka to the Soviets, we all meet here.'

'From the mountains to the sea, where black fish like you breed,' said Hero.

If there was a fight, Salaamat missed it. While losing consciousness, he crumpled to the floor, believing he dived down the neck of a vase, into a vast blue bowl.

4

The Fire

When he came to, Salaamat's head was an inferno. He touched it: his fingers came away sticky. Squinting, he saw he lay in the middle of a street in flames. Tires burned. A mob threw stones. He crawled onto the pavement behind him, seeking a door to duck inside. But there was only broken glass, burning carts, people scrambling, and the sound of shotguns. Shops had their shutters securely down. Those that didn't were being smashed. He tried to stand up. Stumbling down the street, he vaguely recalled a different world of glass.

The stench of charred rubber mingled with singed hair, food and plastic, and his stomach heaved. A dismembered car stood deserted in the middle of the road, the holes where doors had been yawning, screaming. He remembered the maze. And the tea. He reached into his shirt pocket: the bills were gone. In their place was a scrap of paper. When he opened it, a pair of silver earrings inlaid with blue lapis lazuli fell into his hand. The ones he'd wanted. The paper had a phone number. He remembered the two dark faces who spoke his tongue. And the three pale men on stools. And the one he'd never seen at the back, making the tea. Which had stolen his first earnings?

Three years of drudgery, three with no home or family, three listening to Handsome's men jeer him. And now this. Hadn't God thrown enough humiliation his way? He turned back. But then he paused: to get to Hero's shop, he'd have to pass the mob.

When a man ran by him, he grabbed his arm and demanded, 'What's happening?' His face was seared and oily. He must look like that.

'You should be heading that way,' the man said, pointing away from the building with Hero's shop. He pulled away.

Slowly, Salaamat followed. *I'll be back*, he swore.

When the next shot rang he found himself wondering which kind of gun had fired it. He'd never known each could be so different. Some shapes were finer than others, and the finish varied greatly, just like in bus-body-making. But when instead of a single shot, he heard a burst of several dozen in succession, he remembered the machine guns. Salaamat began to run.

5

Ashes

An old man's face shone an eerie green in the last glare of the fire that consumed the bus.

'It was a nice one,' muttered a youth beside him. 'New. Not even two weeks old. There was a big ant there,' he pointed at the fender.

Salaamat knew before he'd even reached it. Maybe because of the purple strip a child kicked all the way down the street – the only part that survived. Or maybe he'd simply heard death in the smoke that swished toward him. It smelled different this time, different from all the burned rubber he'd walked past to get to the bus stop. Maybe it was the smell of premonition. His entire life had been pointing to this moment. He was a fool not to see it before. He was always meant to stand here, at this junction.

There was no turtle now. The paint, metal, and pictures were all singed and furled. Only one wooden plank still burned. Orange flames rose around it half-heartedly. They'd bored into the iron, shattered the disco lights, stripped the plastic seats, gorged the tinted windows, blackened the silver steering wheel.

Salaamat walked around his bus. *His*. His months of barely any sleep; his runny eyes; his hands sliced by steel; his glittery fish; his Rani; his chronology. His first income, also gone. He kicked the front tires. Smoke permeated every cell in his body. He shut his eyes, overcome by an exhaustion that was absolute. There was not one thing around him that suggested the order he'd slogged to construct since the day he'd left his village. No, before that: since the trawlers and his attack. His father's cowardice. His mother's silent humiliation. Her death. Or maybe even earlier. Maybe the lines on his hands, if he could read them, told that it had all gone wrong at his birth. That was the real mistake.

There were no beautiful things to focus on in this life. He had to begin another. And he knew now which road would take him there. The scrap of paper in his pocket pressed into his chest. He tossed it in the cinders. But first, he memorized the number.

6

Brother and Sister

APRIL 1987

Salaamat visited the farm often after that. Sometimes he rode on buses with torn red seats and sometimes he stood. He noticed little about any of them. He spoke to no commuters. And he paid no attention to the daily strikes or the burgeoning body count.

'I won't be seeing you for a while,' he said to Sumbul one morning in mid-April. She sat under a mulberry tree, feeding her second child.

The last time he'd been held like a baby was the day his grandmother found him drifting in the sea. She'd rocked him after his uncles pumped his chest. And she'd sung, just like Sumbul sang now.

She buttoned up her shirt but he glimpsed a nipple twice the size of a Fanta bottle cap. She was only fifteen. She, who'd been flat as a coastline and lithe as a fish. A strand of hair strayed loose from her braid. He gently arranged it behind her ear, grazing her earlobe, where a thin ring hung. 'Remember how you screamed when Dadi put those in?'

'I thought she'd pierced my heart and I'd bleed to death! If I'd known then what God still had planned for me, I'd have screamed a thousand times louder.' She laughed.

He reached into his pocket. 'These are for you.' He placed the lapis earrings on the baby's cheek. He'd been saving them for this last visit before he joined Fatah and his men. He'd gotten his money back too, and much more besides.

Sumbul gasped, holding the earrings up for inspection. 'Where did you get them?'

Salaamat carefully removed the old circles from her ears. 'Do you like them?'

'Of course,' she laughed. 'They're beautiful. And they must have cost a fortune.'

'Shake your head.' She did. 'They were made for you,' he smiled, admiring how her creamy brown neck offset the smooth dark stones. 'You need a mirror.'

She leaned forward and kissed his cheek. 'I can see my pretty gift in your pretty eyes and need no mirror.'

They sat quietly awhile. Around him rose other trees planted soon after his family had come to the farm. It was they who'd sowed the seedlings, watered and pruned them, stood guard outside, and helped raise the caterpillars in the shed opposite from where he now sat. Sumbul would go from feeding the baby to feeding the silkworms. But he never went inside the shed. The white wriggling bodies reminded him of the shrimp his mother had spent her last years peeling.

'Are you happy here?' He turned to Sumbul.

She cuffed him lightly. 'You always ask me that. I always tell you yes. They are good people.'

'But you work with *grub*,' he snarled.

'There's nothing wrong with that. It's honest work. And Aba's treated kindly at the house. Their daughter's really taken to him.'

Trying to appear casual, Salaamat asked, 'Is she here today?'

'My poor lovesick brother,' Sumbul pinched his cheek. The baby lay in the crook of her crossed knee. Wiping the girl's chin with the folds of her shalwar, she continued, 'Instead of asking after rich girls, you should ask after your ageing father.'

'Don't start on that.'

'Forgive him, Salaamat Bhai. Just let it go. He was weak. We all have our weaknesses. If Ama forgave him, you should do the same.'

'What kind of man would loll in bed while his wife slaved in a stinking factory?'

'The kind I too have married. Only I'm on a farm and it doesn't stink.' She glanced at his waist. Strapped to it was a pistol. 'Are you going to tell me what kind it is?' she asked sarcastically. 'I see it's different from the German one you had last time. That was, let's see, half pistol and half Kalashnikov. You got it at a subsidized rate, if I'm not mistaken. All thanks to the bountiful General.'

'Do you think I'd be any safer without it?' he retorted.

'You'd be safer if you stayed away from people who used it,' she rejoined.

'And do what, spend my life feeding maggots?'

Her lips trembled. She picked up the child and as her head tilted to the side, a tear rolled down to her ear and on to the blue lapis. He sighed, wiping it off.

She leaned into his shoulder, whispering, 'I love you. I don't want to lose more of us.' And then she talked, as she so often did, of their family's last year at the village, and how she'd ached for him, her favorite brother.

Much as this pained him, it was so delightful. He stared proudly at the stones and let her ramble, sensing it would be a long time before anyone would speak of love again.

Sumbul arranged her dupatta on the ground and rested the baby there. Then she took Salaamat in both her arms and twirled his coils with her fingers. 'I always wanted hair like yours.'

'Yours is much more beautiful.'

'Then at least give me your strange blue eyes. Just like Dadi's.'

'But I love looking into yours. Round and cinnamon-colored.'

'You hear everything I say.'

'Yes. All of it.'

'Then you aren't deaf any more.'

'Sometimes I am. But somehow, never with you.'

She laughed, 'One of those is a lie.'

He promised, 'When I come back, I'll buy you many more jewels. I'll have so much money you won't even have to work here.'

'And if I want to, will you still give me money?' she teased.

He grinned. 'I'll always give you half. And we can send that stupid husband of yours to a land of permanent rest.'

'Shh. Children listen in their sleep.'

'Good. She should know there aren't only men like her father. There are men like her mamu.' Then he pushed Sumbul gently away. 'I must say goodbye to Chachoo now. Don't worry about me.' He kissed first her forehead, then the baby's. 'I will return.'

Sumbul pledged to always adore and defend him, at any cost.

7

The Witness

Salaamat passed his brothers standing guard at the farm's gate. He embraced them quickly and with a minimum of words. They'd not missed him when he'd left the village; he owed them little in return.

He walked the half-kilometer to Makli Hill, where his father's brother was the guardian of the tombs. The man had decided not to work at Mr Mansoor's farm or his house, and Salaamat respected him for it. Whenever he came to see Sumbul, he visited Chachoo as well.

Little was left of the tombs besides broken walls and chipped tile. But one in particular still offered a glimpse of its six-hundred-year-old self, and it was outside it that his uncle usually paced, as he did today.

Salaamat kissed the man's grizzled cheek. He was tall like himself, and stronger of build than Salaamat's own father. He'd been a good fisherman. Now he wandered here alone all day, staring at the deathbeds of kings and queens.

The iron gate leading into the tomb's courtyard was unlocked. This was rare. 'Visitors?' Salaamat asked.

Chachoo paused. 'You could call them that.'

'Let's go in as well.'

The old man paused again. 'Perhaps we shouldn't disturb them.'

'And why not?' He stepped inside. Reluctantly, the old man followed. 'I like coming here,' Salaamat said over his shoulder, climbing the narrow, decrepit staircase to a verandah that wrapped around a second chamber. 'I prefer it to the farm Sumbul loves.'

He moved carefully, stopping to finger the cool blue mosaic tiles of the brittle terrace. He wondered about the hands that had made the delicate pattern, or fired the clay, or glazed it, and for an instant, wondered if he'd miss his work at the workshop. After all, he'd been good at it.

He turned to his uncle. 'What did you do today, Chachoo?'

The old man shrugged. 'What I always do. I walked off my age. And watched these mirrors dance on the rock.' The sun bounced off his cap and tiny yellow diamonds flickered on the sandstone. He pointed to this. But when Salaamat reached another staircase, this one leading to the crypt, he placed a firm hand on his shoulder. 'I must speak plainly. I've been paid today to keep others away from here.'

Salaamat was about to ask him why, when he realized he could hear a rippling murmur. Voices. Despite the old man's repeated warnings, he pushed Chachoo aside and began descending the stairs, eventually arriving in the dim chamber housing the crypt.

Above him rose a richly carved dome supported by four pillars. Several hundred bats swung from the ceiling, gazing down from their nests of chiseled vine. Their invasion gave the design, already in relief, an even more three-dimensional appearance. Mid-way up the canopy's length and spanning its breadth hung a net. It kept the tittering aerialists at bay.

The mesh was ideal for snaring insects: the bats were like spiders in a web they didn't even have to weave. Every time Salaamat came here the colony appeared to have doubled. Now, as he approached the first pillar, one creature shot down like a trapeze artist toward him, only to bounce back up at the net.

But today he and his uncle were not the only ones the bats struck at. There was someone else behind the next pillar. Chachoo frowned but Salaamat kept advancing.

In the dusky tomb he gleaned two figures. Surely one was Mrs Mansoor? Yes, that was her, exactly as she'd been that time in the garden, sitting beside a table laid for tea. Except now she stood. They'd never met on his visits to the farm, but he recognized the straight, boyish physique and short, masculine hair. She hadn't changed. Salaamat leaned forward, but Mrs Mansoor obstructed the other figure from his view. He listened. Her voice, and a man's. Why would husband and wife pay Chachoo to keep their meeting quiet?

The old man caught up with him.

'Who is he?' Salaamat whispered.

Chachoo shook his head.

There was a movement behind the pillar now. The man reached for her but she pulled away. In this way, he came into view. It was not Mr Mansoor. Their voices rose.

'You should not have asked to see me,' she was saying.

'I have a right to stay in touch.'

A moment later, two bats plunged toward them and all four figures ducked.

'Oh what a place to meet!' the woman cried.

Outside, before Salaamat left him, Chachoo cautioned, 'Today you are a witness. But you are also deaf, dumb and blind.'

ANU

I

The Doctor Looking In

JULY 1992

Anu said goodbye to a friend who'd come to condole, and offered her afternoon prayers. Then she entered the television lounge where Daanish was reading the paper. He sat where the doctor had always sat while doing the same. But first, the doctor would set breadcrumbs out in a small saucer for the birds. He'd then settle in that chair, which granted the best view of them feeding, and smack his thighs when the sparrows fought each other. Daanish would run in from the kitchen where she was giving him breakfast and if any other kinds of birds – parakeets, bayas or babblers – visited, father and son would talk at length.

Daanish continued reading without noticing her.

She'd kept her part of the agreement. Daanish had agreed to see Nissrine on the condition that Anu would not pressure him into a commitment. That was nearly two weeks ago. Though yearning for their engagement, she remained silent, with the occasional, 'That Nissrine is so slim and educated. Just the type for young boys your age.' Most of their conversations, whether about dinner or rain, began that way. It was just a suggestion. Not pressure.

She stood beside Daanish, the lawn outside conspicuously without birds and crumbs. The sky was overcast, soporific. The room, even with the fan above her head, a sauna. Perhaps July would bring rain. But then the roof would leak. More plaster would crumble onto the frayed carpets. It had been an ongoing fight between them: she wanting to spend on the house, the doctor on his travels. She save, he surprise. The worn carpets were visible again since the white sheets for the Quran readings were removed. She'd preferred the sheets.

Today was the fifty-first day after his death.

She was waiting for his presence to diminish. Waiting to stop counting the days. But she knew tomorrow, upon awakening, she'd think: fifty-two. Sitting up on her right side of the bed, she'd smooth the sheets carefully, afraid that her hand might stray over to his side, and touch, not emptiness, but him. And she'd rest her head on her knees and try not to hear his last words to her, spoken from the space her hand dared not venture. But she'd hear it, louder tomorrow than even today: *There's one gift you still haven't found. But then, neither have I.* She'd resolve not to let it haunt her. And all day, it would.

Anu sat down with a heavy sigh. 'That Nissrine is so slim and educated . . .'

From behind the newspaper, Daanish cut in, 'Just the type for young boys my age.'

She pursed her lips. 'You're enjoying keeping me in suspense.'

'I admit I'm fascinated by your self-control. It would be interesting to see how long it lasts.'

She clicked her tongue. 'You sound just like your father. He was always studying things. A man should not study his mother.'

'Then what should he do with her?'

'He should,' she said emphatically, 'listen to her every wish.'

'When have I not listened to you?' He smiled, putting the paper down.

'I'm a very lucky mother,' she said. 'My son always listens to me.' Then she added, 'And always will.'

He laughed. 'Unless his happiness is at stake.'

'I think only of your happiness.'

'But,' he started to say, then hesitated. 'I know you do, Anu.'

She was pleased. 'Well, she *is* slim and educated.'

'Do I detect you beginning to give in?'

'You can at least tell me what you thought of her.'

'I thought we'd already established that. She's slim and educated.'

'Did you *like* her?'

'Her? Oh yes.'

Anu's face lit up. 'I *knew* you would. Well, I'm not going to, you know, put pressure.' She stood up and walked over to his chair again. 'You keep thinking that way,' she patted him.

'All right.' He returned to the paper.

Protest March, it said. Anu peered closer, but the print began to swim. She was distracted. Snippets of the conversation she'd had with Nissrine's mother the day after the tea returned to her.

'Who was that *horrible* girl?' she'd asked. 'I'm so surprised someone as *sensible* as your daughter would be friends with, with *that*. And that's twice now she's spoiled it for her.'

'You're *absolutely* correct,' Tasleem had answered. 'She's a terrible influence on my child and always has been. That's what I've *always* said. And when Nissrine told me she'd actually invited her, I just couldn't *believe* it. I mean, after that disgraceful episode in front of everyone. That be-shar'm has *always* made my daughter look bad. She has no sense of, of *form*. No social grooming What So Ever.'

'What's her family name?'

'Dia Mansoor. Whoever heard such a silly name? What can you expect, given who the mother is . . .'

Her child.

She looked out again at the spot where the doctor would put the saucer. He was standing there, a touch blue in the arms and face, clad in the dirty white hospital gown he'd died in. When alive, he'd sat in the sofa and looked out. Now he looked in, as if she and Daanish were the sparrows his hand fed. After fifty-one days, he was still in charge. She panicked, growing increasingly desperate for Daanish to answer her.

She cleared her throat. 'What are you reading? Anything interesting?'

'Just sobering.'

'Why don't you read it to me?'

He looked up skeptically, then quickly summarized the article. 'The office of an English-language daily has been raided. The five men in khaki claimed the paper had been making "anti-Pakistan" statements. So they confiscated its printing press. This was the two hundred and thirty-third attack on a newspaper office in the past six years. Journalists are protesting.'

Anu tried to read but the newsprint again flew in her face. Instead, she saw Daanish in Tasleem's drawing room, twiddling his thumbs nonchalantly. He'd barely even looked at Nissrine.

She began combing his thick hair with her fingers. 'This is,' she said. 'I mean this must be very interesting for you. Since you're studying journalism.'

'Yes,' he pouted reflectively. 'It is.'

In Nissrine's drawing room, he'd turned to the girl with the bent nose. Riffat's nose. Not much more resemblance. Her messy hair, for instance, was not like the mother's. That woman had nothing better to do than trim and set hers daily.

268

Her son had smiled at her. She knew that smile.

Now Daanish was saying, 'Aba never wanted me to be a journalist. He said I'd spend my life fighting, not just for the right to speak but to live. Poor Dada, who wallowed alone in jail all those years.'

His knees had been inches from the girl shamelessly pulling closer to him. Just like her mother. It was all in the blood, wasn't it? And Nissrine's blood was pure as the mountain air her ancestors had breathed centuries ago. Anu's ancestors too. That's why her flesh was so fair, her walk so measured, her eyes so lowered. But *that* one – shamelessly throwing her head back, cooing, 'Really? What? Amazing!'

He did not even notice poor Nissrine offer the tea. Did not watch her pour the milk, mix the sugar. It sat on the table, cold, untouched. And all the while, the dark girl blinked flirtatiously, and he swiveled, and swiveled.

'And yet,' continued Daanish, 'Dada was my hero. And so are these men and women,' he pointed to the newspaper. 'They live for a cause. What else is there to live for? They make me proud. There was no protest march by American journalists when a few came forward and confessed how they'd been silenced during the Gulf War. They admitted that if they'd spoken, they'd have lost their jobs. Speaking up at all was brave, but journalists here risk much more.'

What did he see in her?

'But I wonder sometimes, Anu, am I as tough as them? It would have been easier if I were just like all the other Pakistani boys in the States, studying engineering or business. I'd come home fat and bouncy, like Khurram.'

Perhaps he liked them slightly boyish. Like that short, brown one in the photograph. She wore a cap that said Fully Food. An apron too. She didn't appear to be wearing anything else. But there was hardly anything to see.

'And then I read how the US insists we sign the non-proliferation treaty and I know I have to write. Never mind that not one member of the UN Security Council has signed. Never mind that all five permanent members began the arms race. Never mind that the weapons on our streets came from them, or that US arms exports continue to escalate. The Cold War has ended, and we're no longer useful against the Soviets, so we're the enemy.'

No, he liked them buxom too. That blonde one, well, she could have been lactating.

'Yesterday, the paper printed a statement issued by US Intelligence. Know what it said? It said the risk of missile attacks against the US was on the rise, so America must increase defense spending. Can you believe it? While poor countries are punished for defending themselves, the strongest military power in the world comes up with excuses to keep building its weaponry.'

He talked, looked and behaved just like his father.

Daanish folded up the paper irritably. 'The problem is that we require aid at all. Beggars, that's what we are. We can either join the bullies or stay the beggars. Those are our two choices.'

She stroked his cheek. He shrugged her off. 'You haven't been listening at all, have you Anu? You're not interested.'

'Oh, don't be that way,' she pulled him.

But he stood up and walked up to his room, adding over his shoulder, 'Aba would have listened.'

She glowered at the doctor still looking in.

2

The Clue

She had stood beside him, fanning his forehead.

He grasped her wrist and said, 'I must talk.'

She was terrified of what he would say next. Why should she listen? She'd heard enough.

'Haven't you ever sinned? Done anything reprehensible, disgusting, vile?' He shook her wrist.

She begged to be released.

'No. I want you to listen.' He began stroking her hair with his other hand, tenderly kissing its tips. 'I've tried to always stand by you. Even though, sometimes, I failed.'

'It's too late for this,' she sobbed. How dare he ask for her forgiveness now, when she'd lost the appetite for it! Why was it her job to absolve him of guilt? He'd had an easy life. And of her he now demanded an easy death.

'No,' she pulled her hand away. 'I won't hear it.'

'You will,' he laughed. 'And you will know there's one gift you never found. But then, neither did I.'

She climbed the stairs to Daanish's room, hearing him call

and cough. She began removing her boy's things and never saw the doctor open his living eyes again.

Fifty-two days later she woke up thinking: fifty-two. She had to find the gift.

She wondered what clues he might have left, and where they'd be hidden. It was cruel indeed: during his life she'd never played along. But now she was consumed. Would he leave any hints in the house? Perhaps. Most of his gifts to her somehow related to food and drink. She started in the kitchen, emptying cabinets, poking through drawers and under the stovetop. Once he'd left a camel bone fan for her on a blade of the ceiling fan, and it had shot into the window when she pulled the switch. Nothing up there now.

When the kitchen was thoroughly searched, she dug around her plants. These were also his favorite haunts. Nothing. Nor in the television room, not even near his sofa. She couldn't find it.

Daanish passed her on his way out. He was going somewhere with Khurram again. He kissed her goodbye. She watched him leave – the strong arms, long limbs. It could have been the doctor, twenty-three years ago. Before he began balding and his midriff started to sag. Before she became the shadow in the cave.

She stepped out into the lawn, watching Daanish recede down the street to Khurram's house. Then she held her clammy face up to whatever breeze blew. She didn't want to go back inside. What she wanted was to stand here till the compulsion to play the doctor's game left her. She looked around her small garden, where the plumbago bush was a spring of blue stars, and each anthurium blossom a pink palm with a white middle finger rising. The doctor had always said it was the most obscene thing he'd ever seen. He'd had such a one-track mind. Still did. She wanted to forget him and enjoy the flowers, simply because they were hers to enjoy.

She wanted to let the sluggish day pour into her. She wanted to touch what was hers before she'd married him.

Leaves rustled. A stray cat had given birth to four kittens that huddled beneath a banana palm. One kitten, black with a white spot on its tail, pounced on the others and swatted the air. His mother growled softly.

Before her ovaries were removed, what gift had the doctor given?

She couldn't stop. She was his sparrow yet. Sighing, Anu went inside to start cooking.

Entering the kitchen it hit her. Of course: the doctor's first gift was their son. The last gift would be connected. She'd found the clue. It was Daanish.

But what next?

She stood at the sink, cleaning a chicken, feeling his presence still. She would learn to accept this too. She'd adjust, wrap up the guipure and spread the tea. Throw out the tea and make it fresh if he wanted. It was like lying still beneath him when he awoke in the middle of the night, no doubt dreaming of *her*, and, without caring whether she slept or not, entered Anu roughly in the dark. He'd never die; even this could become routine.

Leaving the chicken to simmer on the stove, she consulted her watch: just after noon. Daanish was coming home later each time.

3

The Doctor Looking Out

The child was leaving again.

'Where do you keep going?' she pleaded.

'I go to have fun, Anu,' Daanish answered, exasperated. 'Why don't you get together with your friends?'

'But,' her voice trembled. 'Maybe I could come with you. Khurram's such a nice boy. I'm sure he wouldn't mind.'

He stood in tattered shorts and a T-shirt, gaping at her from under a cap. 'I've been trying my best to stick around you, but I need time away too.'

He made it sound like a favor. As if her company was penance. Just like the doctor. 'I won't be getting in your way,' she whimpered. But he was stubborn and pulled free.

She spent the day pacing from one window to the next, frequently moving outside to prune her hibiscus bushes bare. Several times, she walked up to Daanish's bedroom, believing the door had miraculously unlocked. Foolishly, she'd forgotten to remove the key from the knob before his arrival. If

Daanish was the clue, perhaps the gift was in his room. Should she get a locksmith?

Every time he returned from these outings, his clothes were matted with sand. Rivulets of salt hung in the dense hair of his legs and his lashes were like a dusty paintbrush. Once, she was sure of it, his upper lip was cut. Just where it curved, under his right nostril. He tried to hide the smear of blood by pointing his chin away from her, sucking it in, keeping the cap on all day. But the shadow of its bill had not fooled her. The thin nip was prominent. There was little doubt in her mind that he went with Khurram to the cove. Probably, he'd fallen on rocks, though why only that centimeter of upper lip was struck was a mystery. And why the secrecy? He'd loved her to go with him as a child.

She started on the bougainvillea. Unlike the uppity wives of the doctor's friends, she'd never relied on domestic help to get her work done for her. The gardener came once a week to mow the lawn – most of the watering and pruning she managed on her own. She required no help with the cooking. They had no driver or chawkidaar. Then again, she sighed, why hire someone to guard property in obvious decay? The house's exterior should have been repainted years ago, and the cracks filled. Perhaps that would be her next project. She'd have to wait though: the money spent on refurbishing Daanish's room had come out of selling the pearl necklace and other gifts, and she didn't have many left to sell.

Clipping the thorny bougainvillea stems, she gazed up at the muted sky. It was the color of the pearls. She mopped her forehead. Humidity was in the nineties but still not a drizzle. Barely even a breeze today. Her modest garden lay in a stifled haze. She walked barefoot on the prickly grass with browning roots. The doctor had given her a monthly allowance enough to purchase only one tank of water per week. Not enough for the lawn. Those wives he flirted with bought American grass seeds, and their lawns were

soft as pillows. And *hers*, that horrible Mansoor woman
with the horrible daughter, hers had won every horticul-
tural award since Anu first learned there even was such a
thing. She pictured it: green like the jade box the doctor
once hid for Daanish. The child had of course found it the
same day. How did they communicate so flawlessly with
each other?

She'd left something for Daanish to find too. But he'd said
nothing about the picture in the lacquer box. For twenty-three
years that face had followed her: wind-blown curls framing
a smooth high forehead, nose a touch pink, lips parted in a
jubilant smile. Shoulders pressing into his. His scarf grazing
her cheek. Both laughing as though unable to believe they
could be so happy.

She'd wanted Daanish to know how the image taunted her.
But he'd said nothing.

The clouds sailed sluggishly by, occasionally yawning, letting her peer inside a charcoal gray window. Sometimes the
picture on the other side was blue. At others, impenetrably
black. Then the window swallowed itself and opened somewhere else.

Would God forgive her wrath? She wanted only to be sure
of one thing, and that was her son. The doctor had stripped
her clean of all pleasures but that one. He'd never touch it,
though even in death, he kept trying. That's why he'd left the
gift with Daanish. If she could find and destroy it, at last,
Daanish would be hers alone.

She sighed: she'd over-pruned the bush.

It was just after one o'clock. He'd left three hours ago. If
he'd let her accompany him, she could be sitting with him
on the shoulder-boulder, and together they'd look out at the
roiling sea, under the roiling clouds, and perhaps the first
monsoon of the season would fall on them. The thick plump
drops would strike their teacups and they'd sip the rainy brew
down, watching the drops bounce in the same way over the

vast sea. She'd wear her blue shawl, and they could hunker beneath it.

Anu clipped her way over to the plumbago bush, the fantasy so vivid she could smell the rain. It occurred to her that since she knew where her son went every few days, she could follow him. She could ask her brother to take her, or perhaps one of the neighbors. The boy had always liked the doctor's surprises; why wouldn't he like hers?

The top of her head was like a hot plate. She'd been outside far too long. Her fair skin would burn. Gathering the trimmed branches and mound of fallen leaves into a plastic bag, she opened the front gate. She was about to drop the bag in the basket by the mailbox when she paused: it was Monday, the load would not be picked up till Friday. She decided to walk to the empty lot at the end of the street, where everyone left their trash.

Plastic bags flapped in the branches of the tree sprouting in the center of the dump. Beneath it was a pit stuffed with rotten food, plastic containers and ash from numerous trash-fires. Waving the flies away, she tossed her bag inside, disturbing the fiery red ants crawling in feces. This was where she'd thrown Daanish's photographs the day of his arrival, and before that, while the doctor lay dying, where she'd dropped many of his smaller things. Like his shells.

It hadn't been easy but she was glad she'd done it. The doctor had sent him to Amreeka but Daanish didn't need those pictures. The doctor had chosen the colors of Daanish's room but then he'd died. Wouldn't the poor boy miss him more if she hadn't repainted it? Ditto with the shells. The doctor had given them but Daanish wouldn't want them any more. By throwing the doctor's things away, she was only helping ease Daanish's pain.

Anu turned back. Passing Khurram's house on her right, she squinted up at the enormous concoction of green marble columns, pink tile and brass fixtures. Voices approached. The gate opened. A car reversed onto the road. She moved aside, glancing within. It was the doctor, off to attend a meeting in a dark gray suit and striped tie. He threw her an admonishing look: *Go back to your silly household things.*

Blinking, she saw it was in fact Khurram, talking into a cell phone.

Spotting her, Khurram gaped with as much astonishment as she did. She read him thus: realizing he was supposed to be with her son, he ducked to escape her attention, felt foolish for already being noticed, sat up again, hesitated, and as the car drove away, decided to wave.

DIA

I

Turmoil and Bliss

As humidity levels rose, Dia suffered intense mood swings. The only place to be was the cove, with Daanish, despite Salaamat's still, ominous presence. So why wasn't she always there?

Her time was spent listening for the phone to ring (how could she ever have cursed man's greatest invention?), and when it did, she rushed to answer the gnawing bell that now was dulcet melody. If it was him, she practically pirouetted.

If not, sometimes she called, at others she told herself it was his turn. Then she gazed from the phone to the gray sky, and then to the calendar hanging on the kitchen door. June slipped into July and July into its third week, but this barely registered. Nor did Inam Gul, who trailed her open-mouthed. All that mattered was her next meeting with Daanish.

But within moments, she chided herself for wasting her days in this disgusting expectant haze. How girlish. How *typical*.

Next she'd worry. On average, he called twice daily. Did this mean he wasn't thinking of her in between?

And finally, her heart raced as she repeated every word Daanish had last spoken, beginning with his passionate insistence through the tiny holes in the plastic headset: 'I must see you. Not tomorrow. Today. Now.' The memory so excited her she'd freeze, oblivious to where she sat or stood, ate or read, said or had been thinking of doing. It was more essential that she imagine where he stood or sat, what he ate or read, said or had been thinking of doing. She saw the muscle on the inside of his thigh, just above the knee – had it clenched when he leaned to speak into the phone? And the long scratchy neck, the hairless spot on each forearm – when could she circle them again with her nose? Until then, the hours were on hold.

The long drive to the farm was just what was needed: an ideal pretense for nonstop dreaming. She filled the thirsty plains outside her car window with her longings, barely even noticing the guards flanking her. Whether they ogled or shifted too close, she was with Daanish, lolling in the sand between massive boulders, relishing his fresh scent. Listening to the waves crash into their fort of rocks, foam occasionally spilling over, onto their nest. Wiping the salt from his eyes, while he promised, 'When I'm here next, in the winter holidays, the sea will be perfect for teaching you to swim.' He refused to accept her fear of water. She refused to accept that in less than a month his college would reopen and he'd be gone. While the car raced through the scorched riverbed, she floated with him, limbs entwined, and always would.

At the farm, yet another cycle had begun. The breeder moths' seed was scrupulously analyzed for disease and the stainless eggs kept in incubation for ten days. The first to be stored had already hatched into tiny, baby caterpillars that wanted nothing but to eat.

Their greed was like hers.

Today, Dia stood before the trays that held the half-inch-long, newborn larvae. Her thoughts drifted from Daanish to the exam results printed in the paper that morning. She'd failed the retake, obviously. It meant she'd have to repeat the class. All those who'd cheated had passed.

Angrily, she shook the leaves in a tray. The larvae twitched, then champed again. The ones dropped down Nini's shirt had been several days older. She missed her friend. Never again would she love another woman with such ease. Their trust, impervious for nine years, was gone for ever. It had splintered; she was left examining the sores. Possibly, Nini did the same. Dia considered it her second-greatest loss, after her father. Only this time, contrary to what Daanish insisted, she was responsible.

Or was she?

Since college was out for the summer, neither had run into the other. After the tea, days had passed before Nini finally called. Her abusive rampage had only made it easier for Dia to continue with Daanish. But then a week later, Nini had visited.

She'd looked terrible – bags under her beautiful bright eyes, complexion wan, gait uncertain. How had Dia appeared to her? Glowing?

They sat opposite each other on Dia's bed, each determined to let the other begin. After ten minutes of steely silence, Nini left without a word. Dia whispered: *Run. Rush into her arms and beg to be forgiven, you fool.* But she sat still. Daanish's reasoning echoed in her head: There'd been nothing between Nini and him. They weren't married or engaged or even friends. There was nothing but an interest on their mothers' part. Nini had become a stranger before Dia had even met Daanish. She let Nini recede down the corridor.

Sara, Inam Gul's niece, was talking. Dia blinked. 'Hmm?'

'I said you look a little tired,' Sara repeated.

'I suppose I feel it a bit. Did these hatch today?' She pointed to the tray being replenished with fresh leaves.

'Yes. This is the third time I've fed them since the morning. Six more to go.'

Dia felt silly gliding along the table in her self-absorbed daze while the women around her toiled. How many around her had time to daydream? Sara looked as though she'd long since stopped trying.

Without greeting the other employees, an agitated Dia left the lab and walked toward the adjoining shack. On her way she met Sumbul, rubbing her fourth baby's nappy under the tap outside. The child was suffering from diarrhea and Sumbul washed his clothes almost hourly. She squatted, hair in her eyes, worry on her face. The fifth child was beginning to show.

Dia hunkered, nauseated by the sight and smell of the boy's watery shit. 'Hopefully by tomorrow this will end,' she consoled. 'The medicine will start to work.'

'Hopefully,' Sumbul forced a smile. She wrung the cloth and rose, leaving it on a branch to dry.

They entered the shack together. The baby slept on a well-worn sofa, a cushion on his free side preventing him from falling. Sumbul adjusted it and settled beside him. The telephone was in the other room. Dia didn't want to talk to Daanish in front of Sumbul. Salaamat had obviously been reporting their trysts because Sumbul was growing increasingly inquisitive. She'd even begun insinuating that if Dia's mother advised staying away from Daanish's family, she should. As if it was her business!

Pretending to busy herself, Dia picked the top off the pot on the burner – the staff's lunch. 'Smells good,' she muttered foolishly. On the couch, Sumbul wound her hair up and started humming.

Then: 'Are you going to see him again today?'

Dia blurted, 'Salaamat at the cove, you here, Inam Gul and

my family at the house. Even the guards. There's no privacy in this country. Only secrecy. We're not doing anything wrong. In fact, what could be more right? Yet, *I'm* the transgressor. I've become the gunnah gaar.'

Sumbul looked up, hurt. 'We're just all worried about you, Dia Baji.'

Couldn't she see the irony? Sumbul, at exactly Dia's age, was bogged down by four children, an ill-tempered husband, and a fifth pregnancy. Yet it was Dia, the one in love, whom everyone worried about.

She marched into the next room and shut the door. Sumbul could listen at the keyhole if she wanted. She dialed Daanish's number.

'Hi. It's Dia.'

'Khurram! What a surprise!'

'Oh, no. You too? Who's there, your mother?'

'Yes, yes.'

'Well call me back, will you? I'm at the farm.'

'That's a great idea. I'll come over right away.'

Falling back on the bed, she inhaled deeply. *That was rewarding.*

While waiting for his call, she breathed his crisp, ruddy scent. It had lodged deep in her pores. A quiver swept across her cheek and down her neck.

She thought of the other men in her life – brothers, both virtual strangers; the eternal Inam Gul; a father till age fourteen. Then there was romantic love – crushes on gangly boys met at desperate parties. Kisses in strangers' toilets. Little else. No nudity. No sex. Daanish had made it clear he desired both. Did she trust him? She remembered her own warning to Nini: *He'll have fun with foreign women but marry a local one to please his mother.*

So where did she fit in?

Dia turned on her side. Pride prevented her from asking how many others there'd been. Or still were. Yet the thought irked her. One moment she flushed at the mere futility of it, the next she concluded it wasn't futile. It might help determine whether she could trust him. After all, if a man were more experienced than a woman, wouldn't she always feel like a child? Wasn't that part of his thrill?

The phone rang. 'Yes?'

'Sorry,' he sounded more relaxed. 'Anu's become insufferable.'

'What happened?'

'She's figured out Khurram doesn't have incisors like yours.'

Dia gasped. 'She actually asked how it happened?'

'No. She saw him on the street when he and I were really at the cove, necking.' Over the receiver, Daanish slobbered and drooled.

Someone was chuckling in the background. 'Is that him?' she giggled.

'Yup. He says this is the most fun he's had since shopping in Amreeka.'

She laughed again. 'So now what?'

'Now,' answered Daanish, 'I might as well use our rickety car. I'll just drive away on my own and if she asks where I'm going – which she will – I'll think of something else.'

'No Salaamat,' she felt a rush of relief.

'No. Just you and me and *a lot* of space to do as we please.' He paused. It was the most calculated silence in the world. And the most exciting. Then, 'Can I pick you up tomorrow?'

They decided on the fast-food joint to rendezvous at. Then he blew her a kiss and they hung up.

When Dia walked back out Sumbul eyed her disapprovingly.

She'd moved to the floor, where it was easier to change the whimpering baby. The dirty linen – a piece of an old kameez of Dia's – lay bunched beside the boy and the room began to stink. Sumbul gave him more medicine. 'One more drop. Shabash, how brave you are!'

She could help Sumbul tend him. But Dia did not want to. And Sumbul wouldn't speak to her again that day. Her mother, her best friend, and now even her favorite employee; because of Daanish, she was losing all three.

2

Rain

In the car, Dia's tension grew threefold. She hated deceiving Riffat, feared the rioters, and panicked at the thought of losing herself to a man she wasn't even sure she knew.

The day before, yet another strike had been called. Streets were desolate and shops closed. Were they mad to be out alone? Both knew that if stopped, they could be in serious danger. Dia half-missed Salaamat. He looked like he could protect her. Daanish didn't.

Daanish held her hand, steering with his other. 'You're very quiet.'

She squeezed his hand. 'The city looks so sinister. Like a vacated bombsite.'

He nodded. 'I was thinking the same.'

A bus passed them, flashing messages of love, belching gallons of carbon monoxide. The back featured kohl-rimmed eyes that teased, *Dekh Magar Pyar Se*. Look, But With Love. Swarming around the eyes were pink parrots with heart-shaped flowers in their beaks and limbs of passengers trying desperately to stay on board.

'Everything's so complicated.' Dia rolled up her window against the fumes. 'What was it like in America, having the freedom to see whomever, whenever?' She balked at her own nerve.

He was silent, she felt, for two heartbeats too many. Finally, 'It certainly made things simpler.'

Too casual. *What things?* She let it go.

They heard a slight rumble: lightning further west. 'Perhaps it'll rain,' Daanish mused.

They said little else till the cove, although Daanish never released her hand, even when the road narrowed and steering required both, even when a tanker pushed in front of them and nearly ended everything right there.

At the cove, she bit her lip, recalling reports of beach huts being raided and women raped. This hideout didn't even offer a hut to duck into. Dia's mind swam with newspaper accounts of women being killed by their uncles and brothers for doing less than she already had. She looked around with trepidation, she, the product of a country where self-consciousness was basic survival. Where a woman's reputation was the currency that measured her worth.

Would being discovered here be the end of her? What would her brother Hassan turn into? She barely knew him after all. And did she know her mother? In their last argument, Riffat had toed the party line. She'd told Dia that she too would have to think about these things someday. *You've no idea how hostile society gets if you challenge it.* She'd pledged loyalty to Dia and yet, at the last, imposed her own will on her. Nini's plaint – *my parents' image is my headache* – tormented Dia now. What if Riffat was the same?

But Daanish began massaging the knot that had been building inside her ever since their first tryst. The pain of lying to those she loved, doubts about Daanish, terror of becoming the thing Khurram or Salaamat chuckled over with their friends – some of that slowly left her. It was like shedding half her skin. The old half looked quickly around, wondering if they were being watched. She didn't think she could ever completely slough this layer off.

Or maybe she could. Daanish's fingers probed expertly. She was twenty years old and ready to be something more than the repository of her family's honor. She was twenty years old and ready to be loved.

The sea was swollen and raw, rising above her waist as they headed for the sandy enclosure between the boulders. Jellyfish lined their path. They dodged them while scurrying, occasionally spotting other life blown to land: a baby sting ray, its tail wagging in the surf, and any number of shells.

The cove was as sublime as it was worrisome, she thought, leaning into Daanish as he leaned into the rock. The sky was a solid slab of gray. It growled, very softly, as though her head rested on its hungry belly. 'You'd think others would have discovered this place by now.'

'I keep fearing that,' he answered, wrapping his arms around her from behind. 'People attract people. The minute a crowd passes through, I'll lose my childhood paradise.'

She kissed him lightly on the neck. 'Green apples,' she whispered. 'That's what you're made of.' Her arms rested on his. His the color of ochre, hers a shade lighter. Copper. His carpeted with hair. She smiled, recalling how this had elicited minus-points the first time she'd examined him. Brushing his lower lip over her lanuginous upper one, he said she wasn't exactly hairless herself.

He wore shorts, and this made reclining against him all the more intimate. She ran her hands over his long, lissome legs: shaggy, even along his inner thighs, and wonderful to tug. She tasted his collarbone, where the necklace hung. The shells were salty and damp. Her nose rested against a small one he

called a Venus Clam. It was milky white with thorny black
v-shapes sprawled across its front. The back was smooth, as
bone ought to be.

'Any idea why it's called that? Venus Clam? After all, you
have others more beautiful.' With anyone else, she wouldn't
have asked. But Daanish was as intrigued by the origins of
things as she was. It was what had united them. They'd begun
with a beginning, as she liked to think of it.

'No idea. Guess away.'

'Well, she's said to be born in a scallop. So I'm wondering
if the scallop's cousin, the clam, got the name by mistake?'

'That's weak.' He licked the bend of her ear.

'You know Venus, or Aphrodite, wore a girdle that smelled
so bloody good even land-locked gods found a way to get to
her. That much I know. It's why we call intoxicating scents
aphrodisiacs.'

'Um,' he bit the other ear, hard, 'in the case of this particular goddess, the magic appears to be right here, in this peculiar
organ on the left side of her head.' He pulled her closer to his
chest, breathing loudly.

She was getting that feeling on the soft flesh of her cheeks.
It was sweeping down to the cups of her breasts. She wanted,
more than anything, for him to touch her there. But she pulled
free. 'Come on, Daanish. Humor me. Tell me more about
your shells.'

He looked at her. Then he tilted his head toward the ocean,
as if to say, *Look at where we are, and how alone we are, and
how rare this is. We can talk any time, but we can't always
do this.*

She hung her head, ashamed.

But then he rubbed his thumb against her cheek and asked,
'Do I make you nervous?'

And all she could do was nod.

So he pulled her back against him and talked. He spoke of
the link between mollusks and mythology. Venus was not the

only god or goddess to have shells named after her. There was the New England Neptune. Triton's Trumpet . . .

She loved his voice. The medley of accents, the American slang interspersed with proper English. *Mere* and *come about* one minute, *whoa* and *bucks* the next.

'Hindus also value a particular shell. It's said the Vedas were stolen by a demon that hid them in a left-handed chank. Vishnu dove deep into the sea and salvaged them. These days, a left-handed one can fetch a hefty price. Couple thousand bucks I'm told. By the way, I used to have a right-handed chank. No idea where it went.' He went on.

Remembering Sumbul's warning, she loved him all the more fiercely and cut in, 'Take your shirt off.'

Again, that quizzical look. But he pulled the T-shirt over his head. 'Anything else?'

'No.' She rested against his bare chest now. 'Continue.' She pierced the flesh under his necklace with her teeth and rubbed his taut, spherical shoulders, thinking, These are the first I ever kissed. And with each caress, she repeated it: the first earlobe, the first cleft of a chest, the first slope of a stomach.

He started to remove her kameez, but she bit him, hard, on the scant bulge of a love handle, and pushed his hands away. 'Don't touch me till I allow it.' She licked around his silken nipple, flat and swirling, her tongue a needle reading a minute musical record. The tiny crater in the album's center rose, and the tune was the shudder running down his gut. She was a microscopic particle caught in the spin and it didn't matter if she eventually blew away. She moved to his thighs, where his smell was strongest, and touched him through his shorts. It thrilled her that he'd stiffened even before their first kiss.

He was on precious shells now, uttering names like the Glory of the Seas, like Junonia, between gulps and pants. 'The Glory was so rare . . .'

She tapped the cold metal button of his shorts, and released it.

They met every other day, always following the same pattern – a tense, silent drive followed by giddy love at the cove. Even when lying under him, she found a way to peer out at the needlelike rocks rising on the opposite end of the beach, waiting for a shadow, a gun, a pirate flag flapping on the horizon. The more she loved, the more paranoid she became. She held Daanish the way she'd held herself when her brothers had forced her to shower alone in the dark.

At the farm, Sumbul hammered her with questions. Dia found she didn't even enjoy the silkworms any more. She neglected her graphs. She couldn't read. Inam Gul was in the way. So was her family. Alone at night, she felt his palm on her stomach sliding slowly down. He marveled at her softness and said the scent of her dampness on his fingers would linger. It was what helped him survive the hours they weren't together. She asked him to describe it. He brought his hand up first to his nose, and then hers. 'I want to say like mushrooms simmering, only that doesn't sound as good as it is. But I love mushrooms, you know.'

She slept in a cloud of heat and green apples. And in her dreams, admitted: I don't know him.

The thought plagued her once in daylight, while they lay together in the sand. He was nuzzling her armpit, she watching his slick penis sway, discreetly testing the air, searching. She gently pulled away.

Rubbing the back of his neck, she said, 'Daanish, you never speak of your life in the US.'

He looked up and frowned. Then: 'I appreciate that you don't ask me to.'

'Why?'

'It's just too much to think of. Specially,' he sniffed her hair, 'when I'm so peaceful with you.'

'Can we walk?' She sat up and dressed.

He sighed, but pulled his shorts on.

Neither had the courage to amble naked down to the surf. Though they never said it, the cove's insulation made them even more nervous when they left its only mooring – the boulders. They both looked anxiously around as though still naked.

The gray clouds drooped even lower than in past weeks. There was lightning to the west and the thunder clapped nearer than ever. They hopped over bluebottles, examining the creatures washed ashore. There was a foot-long deep-sea fish without eyes, and even, to Dia's dismay, a porpoise. She paused, moved by the beauty of its sleek snout, the rings of its closed eyes, and the smile, kind and forgiving, even in death. 'Water kills,' she murmured.

'No. It brims with life.' He kissed her forehead.

She told him then about failing her exam.

'I'm sorry,' he said. Nothing else.

She watched him pluck cowries and walk into the waves to rinse them. He'd gone to another place. He could do that – simply squeeze into a knot and shelve the wad away. It was why, after nearly a month, she had to admit – *Oh Sumbul, why are you haunting me!* – she didn't know him. And in another month, he'd go completely to that other place.

'Daanish, I want you to share more of your other life with me.'

His face closed.

'You know everything about the only one I have.'

'I know only what you choose to tell, and the rest is all right.'

He walked one step ahead of her. His spine was a dark, sinewy ladder. She lifted a finger to touch each bow of muscle, but changed her mind. He raced on, two paces ahead now.

Finally, she said, 'This isn't turning into a very good day.'
When he turned back his eyes were stern, chiding almost.
'You look so angry!' she cried.

'Fine. What do you want to know? How can I satisfy some warped, magical notion you have of this other life of mine? How about the fact that it's where you learn to be despised, absolutely? Sound like fun?'

'I don't know what you mean, Daanish. What have I said?'

'Well then think before you speak.' He was shouting. 'Dammit, don't be all pathetic like my mother.'

Turning away, she walked quickly back up to the boulders. Tears streaked her cheeks and she started to run. She was still running while collecting her sandals and purse, as if stopping would be the end of her. When he caught up she started running toward the rocks on the far side, over which lay the road. He pulled her arm and she screamed, 'Drive me back. Now.'

'Stop a minute.'

'Now.'

'I'm sorry,' he tightened his grip. 'Sorry.'

'I want to go back home.'

'Just let me explain something. Please.'

They were standing at the mouth of the cave. The tide dashed up her legs. She'd worn her kameez backwards but wasn't going to take it off in front of him again.

He released her. 'Dia. Let's go back to the other end. Please. Five minutes. Then if you still want me to, I'll drive you back.'

She didn't like standing here, with the sea crashing into the cave and the walls bellowing like a furious monster awakening. *Thud! Ewow!* The mild terror she always felt when the ocean wrapped around her was all the more acute now, with the fiendish cave on one side, and a fiendish lover on the other. She knew which one to walk away from.

He squatted in the sand between the boulders and patted the space beside him. She sat on her haunches. 'Dia, how can I put this? Being with you helps ground me. Yes, it's as simple as that. May I?' He sneaked closer, winding an arm around her shoulders. She sat still.

He said that ever since leaving his country, three years ago, a tiny rent had formed in the center of him. 'Right here,' he put her finger in his navel. 'Like a zip unfastening. I wasn't even aware of it till I came back. And now I realize the zipper has fallen so low, I'm sort of, well, divided. I think that's what happened to my father. These days, I look in the mirror and see him.'

It was the first time he'd mentioned him, outside the context of the doctor's quarrels with his wife. Dia could never bring herself to speak of her own father. She leaned into his shoulder.

'You're lucky you've never left home,' he continued. 'And I guess I don't want you to. When I speak of America, I take you there. But I want you to stay here. Put crudely,' he kissed her forehead again, 'you zip me up.'

She considered this, but didn't like it. Was this another way of saying she was only good to him if kept ignorant?

'You speak of the cheating at your exam,' he pressed on. 'There's cheating there too, you know. Everyone thinks *there* is different. It isn't. The deceit is more covert. The shell is more beautiful. But the interior is just the same.'

When she still said nothing, he added, 'Do you think we can forget my outburst?'

He spoke more, as on their first time alone. This made her love him again: he'd learned his voice soothed her, just as he'd learned how to touch her. He described a town with gray-stone buildings in fields of rolling green. His campus had no gates; the windows bore no grills. She let her head slide into the crook of his arm, imagining turrets and buttresses, concocting sharper smells in a climate with four seasons and little dust. He wasn't making his other life sound like this one at all.

She thought of the rooms in her college: airless and dingy, with wooden benches women had to fight over to make room for themselves. The stench always made her head reel, but all that was nothing compared to the books and the instructors, who tested students on how well they regurgitated passages, word for word. No discussions. No questions. When the teacher got tired she asked one of her 'pets' to read, and more than once, Dia had seen a teacher lay her head down and sleep.

No, she didn't believe Daanish. He, who had the opportunity to see more of the world than most, was cruel to deny her even the option of hoping it held more than a room in an attic, with women squeezed into each other, a teacher snoring on her desk, and no questions asked.

His heart pounded under her cheek. She asked, 'Could we do this there, Daanish?'

'Hmm?'

'Could we hold each other, just because we wanted to, and not have to hide it? Because if so, how can you say it's just the same?'

He traced her jaw with his thumb and tightened his hold.

She reached up to stroke the point where his side parting met the back of his head, but the first raindrop of the season touched him first. It was loud and fat, and Daanish shook his hair and laughed. The rain quickened, drumming in a steady stream, while the sand whipped around and layered them. When she kissed the back of his neck, she tasted rain and grit and bit sinew and watched the prints her teeth left behind in the moist sand.

3

The Blending of the Ways

Normally, the monsoons were Dia's favorite time of year.

Before daytime storms turned to week-long affairs, before gutters spilled, electricity was cut off, telephone lines burned, cars stalled, and grief afflicted thousands of flood victims, there were crepuscular days lulled by pattering on rooftops, rich smells, bright hues, and a steady, puissant breeze. Best was when the rainfall softened to cool drizzle, driving the tiny, furtive creatures she loved out into the open. The torpid snail emerged, leaning far out of its shell, creeping up walls and staircases like an errant knight. Earthworms slithered, dragging fallen leaves back down to their burrows. Ants swarmed, mating in the moist air. The leggy cranefly sipped moisture from grass.

She'd step cautiously along her brilliant green lawn, absorbing it all: a residual raindrop on a single leaf, causing it to shudder like a hiccup; hoverflies swilling mist; bulbuls diving for dancing gnats. She'd feel things so poignantly it was as if the flaccid sky had sunk into her bones, teaching her to see life up close, closer than anyone else. When a thin, flaxen light cut through the clouds – the clouds that were *in* her – she could hear earthworms die, and aphids sweat honeydew. When the sun descended and the air turned tawny, bulbuls sang more vibrantly, as if the rain had cleansed their vocal cords. At nightfall, she'd slip into the deliciously chilled, damp sheets that smelled of rain, and think, as she so often did at the farm: God is here; God is detail.

But this year the before period never came. The first storm continued for three days, and Dia felt a reality devoid of meaning press against her. On the drive back from their last meeting at the cove, Daanish's car had stalled several times and she'd had to flag a taxi. Slick with mud, she'd passed Inam Gul on her way up to her room. She hadn't wanted to get into a Sumbulesque discussion, so insisted she'd been at Kings and Queens. He was silent, tentative – not the Inam Gul she knew.

Since then, Daanish had called to say his car had still not been repaired. None of the mechanics were picking up their phones and he couldn't go out looking since all the roads around him were knee-high in putrid waste. They wouldn't be able to meet again for days. He was leaving in less than three weeks.

Her own neighborhood was cloaked in a darkness only earthworms would celebrate: for the last twenty hours they'd had no electricity, and in the refrigerator, food was beginning to rot. Mosquitoes invaded, as did the drone of generators.

On the fourth day, she squatted on the muddy doorstep, looking helplessly around her. The rain fell like a sheet of armor. It had a point to make, and would continue making it as obstinately as it damn well pleased.

The creatures that thrived on its fury taunted her, for they were free to court each other, while she and Daanish alone were not. A bright emerald frog hopped by her damp feet, croaking with gusto. Its throat ballooned to three times the size of its head and it blinked with lust. Slugs wrapped frilly feet around each other in wild abandon. She thought, Daanish would love to see this. Perhaps he did, at that very moment, in his own house. So why weren't they together?

She began to see her world from his eyes, as if the rain had pulled her into the sea, and all the land dwellers had changed to their earlier, watery state. Insects like the leather jacket suddenly looked more like a cuttlefish, tentacles rippling as it slid along the wet ground. A spider hanging nearby carried an egg cocoon in her arms, reminding Dia of the argonaut Daanish had spoken of. Sopping ivy was seaweed. How she longed to hear him speak of such things in his lilting voice! But the rain beat down, building a wall inside her garden wall.

In that other place of his, which he said was just the same, did weather get in the way of love? She was beginning to think like that. In her mind, phrases were increasingly punctuated with in *this* country, or, in *other* countries. She'd never done that before. This had always been the only place she knew, loved, and wanted to be immersed in. It was Nini who'd dreamed of that *other*. Not her.

But she was getting entangled in aspects of that faraway world Daanish reluctantly shared with her. To get to his classes, he had to cross a sloping wooden bridge above a stream that in winter rang with icicles and in spring, teemed with carp. She'd never known ice. Rain, yes, but not a bank of singing frost. In fine weather, he said students walked the campus barefooted, and discussed assignments with professors under the shade of towering oaks. It all sounded wonderfully intimate and fabulous to her. And though he claimed otherwise, she could read his eyes well enough to know there was magic there for him too. And so she was beginning to understand what he meant when he said he was divided.

The thought of him leaving filled her with more anguish than she'd ever known. It had come to this: in less than a month she'd allowed him to tear most of her old skin off. When they weren't together, she wanted it all back. And there was no one – no Nini any more – to cry to.

Two days ago, she finally phoned to tell him this. She was amazed at his response: 'Going away will be easier for me because we'll always be together, won't we? I'll be back in the winter and you'll be here, waiting, and nothing will change. Now my life has direction, Dia.'

Out on the doorstep, under cover of the seaweed-crawling roof, Dia shivered. The wind picked up. Rain fell at a slant and her clothes were soaked through. She'd been in drenched clothes a lot lately. Lightning ripped the sky, and the rain crashing on the ground sounded like a herd of camels, racing toward her.

You zip me up, he'd said.

She held herself tight, cold and miserable. The opposite was happening to her.

4

Darkness

Days later, it still rained. The electricity returned then shut off again. Riffat, exhausted from nights of blistering sleeplessness and days of surviving drivers whose aggression feasted on bad weather, stayed home. With no power at his office, her brother, the computer engineer, did too. The household was inebriated with stale air and even Inam Gul was more juvenile than usual. Their company was driving Dia mad.

Candles were lit in every room, casting shadows over walls and floors. 'I feel a mysterious presence!' the cook said, pop-eyed.

Dia clicked her tongue in irritation. 'It's the KESC. And there's nothing at all mysterious about them.'

He waved skinny, veined hands. 'No. It's the unseen.'

Dia nodded, 'The KESC.'

From Riffat's room sounded a snort. Hassan's. Dia could hear desperate gusts of wind blow as he waved a paper fan. The fan flashed white in the light from the candle on Riffat's bedside table. 'The thing I hate the most about power breakdowns is how *useless* they make me feel,' he offered uselessly.

Riffat said, 'It's cozy. In a sweltering sort of way.'

Dia listened to the chatter by default. Around her, shadows caressed paintings of nudes, and Riffat's art books slipped in and out of sight, as though jostled by unseen hands. The rugs and cushions smelled of mildew. Inam Gul continued to look around him like a child in a haunted house. Sleepless nights were catching up with them all.

On the roof, the rain continued to pound. Once, it had been sweet music to her ears. Now only the telephone was. It hadn't rung for her today. Possibly, Anu was swamping Daanish. Bitterly, Dia remembered how she herself had warned Nini: the woman was recently widowed and had only one child, that too a son.

Riffat too was a widow. She too had suffered, and Dia did not ever want to be the cause of more suffering. As her mother's sweet, sleepy chit-chat blew in the dark rooms Dia's stomach clenched. Both she and Daanish betrayed their mothers.

She wondered if, like her, this bothered Daanish more because his father was dead. And whether he'd give anything, even his time with Dia, to have him back again. Just once. Would she?

Riffat said, 'I'm hungry.'

'Well,' replied Hassan, 'we can always avail ourselves of the scrumptious food in the refrigerator. The *functioning* refrigerator.'

Dia exhaled loudly, enough to let him know he was a pompous beast.

'It's sort of like sleeping over at the farm,' Riffat continued. 'We could have a picnic. Sandwiches and lemonade . . .'

'Warm lemonade,' Hassan interjected.

'. . . It's been so long since we had a picnic.'

'Eating in the house you've lived in all your life,' declared Dia, 'isn't exactly a picnic. Lights or no lights.'

Inam Gul drifted by again, still spooked. The soles of his rubber slippers squeaked and he spun around, spooking himself. He tried to settle quietly beside Dia on the damp rug but quickly jerked up again, ready for battle.

Dia clicked her tongue once more. 'What's the matter with you, Inam Gul?'

'What irks *you*, darling?' Riffat called from inside her room. 'You've been rather sullen lately. Is it still Nini?'

Dia blinked back tears. She rose, took a candle from the shelf, and without answering, walked into the dining room. She stared at the telephone, the one that had transmitted her first conversation with Nini about Daanish. She moved quickly to the bathroom and locked herself in.

Setting the candle down near the soap dish on the sink, Dia unhooked her shalwar. She didn't really need to go – these days most of it was sweated out. But she lingered on the toilet seat, glad for a quiet moment alone. The yellow tiles of the wall were dotted with moisture, and a tiny mushroom spore was beginning to form. It held her attention for several minutes before she forced herself back out.

In the kitchen, Inam Gul was squeezing two lemons while Riffat opened a tin of cheese. She sliced and arranged it between pieces of bread. Hassan had already begun on a sandwich. Between great mouthfuls, he reported how dry they were. Then his chatter turned to politics, over which he and Riffat always disagreed.

There was talk that the President would depose the Prime Minister again. 'The army should do it,' he proclaimed. 'It should just take over.' Inam Gul handed him lemonade.

Riffat, her back to him, said, 'Will we ever have a civilian government for more than two years? Generals and presidents have to let elected leaders run their course.'

'You can hardly call them leaders,' he chewed. 'And who knows if they were really elected.'

'Ditto for the generals.'

'They might bring more peace at least. Fewer strikes and riots. God knows Karachi needs a break from that.'

'Imposed peace is not peace. People will only simmer more.'

'Simmer,' Hassan nodded, 'but at least not boil.'

'If elected leaders could complete their term,' Riffat insisted, 'the anger would boil away.'

'Eventually, maybe. But after how much more bloodshed?'

'You forget,' said Riffat testily, 'the bloodshed began when a general ruled.'

Such references were the closest Riffat ever came to discussing her husband's murder. Hassan understood this. So did Dia, standing in the darkened doorway.

'That was,' Riffat continued, 'during the third military rule. How many more do we need to understand our mistakes?'

Hassan, though mouthy, was by temperament skittish. He shrugged, and attempted to get out of the question by teasing Riffat. 'You just want to see our poor, martyred, "daughter of the east" back again, don't you, Ama? You're Sindhi to the core.'

Riffat, exasperated, answered, 'I just want to leave politics to the politicians. God knows from whom you inherited your coup mentality!' She sat down, adding, 'There's biscuits.'

Dia entered the kitchen.

'There you are,' Riffat looked up.

'We're having a gala time.' Hassan champed on a second sandwich, speaking with moist cheese on his tongue. 'I know someone who said you submitted your exam blank.'

'Oh?' Dia pulled out a chair. 'Did that someone tell you she cheated?'

'It was a he. And no, his sister did not tell him she cheated. Not all sisters do.'

She glared at him. 'What's that supposed to mean?'

'You're right, Ama. She's very cranky lately.'

'I didn't say cranky,' Riffat gently interceded. 'I just think something's bothering her.'

'Do I have to be referred to in the third person when I'm at the same table?'

'You see,' Hassan nodded.

Inam Gul coughed in the dark. He ate alone in a corner, listening.

'Well, the last time I addressed you,' Riffat said, 'you walked away. So I didn't want to chase you out again.' She watched closely while nibbling cheese.

Dia tried to eat.

Riffat pursued, 'What happened at the exam? I saw you studying. Was it hard?'

Dia peeled off a slice of the bread. There was too much butter and Hassan smelled bad. 'I just didn't want to be there,' she replied. 'Everyone was making me feel ill.'

'Oh, poor baby,' cooed Hassan.

'You didn't have to focus on them.' Riffat's tone was neutral. Not accusing, but not sympathetic either.

'I don't want to talk about this.' Dia stood up.

As she left the kitchen she heard Riffat call, 'You're going to have to some time, Dia. Because I want to know why a brilliant girl like you . . .'

She drifted back through the room where the telephone beckoned, hesitated, then wound around to the front door. Here her father's portrait met her. The portrait she hated. The one that did not capture what she'd known of him: the soft jowls shaking with laughter as she read to him; the tattered, cotton banyaans and coconut oil; the heavy, ungainly walk in contrast to Riffat's vixen trot; the tree-climber. Her fat, agile father was turned into a still life in a suit with a gilt frame holding him in, forcing those eyes to stare in horror at the future looming close.

Holding a candle up to his face, Dia peered, as she had so many times before, for something familiar. But the only thing that was common to both the person and the portrait was that she couldn't see a trace of herself in it. Where did her large, amber eyes come from? The deep dip between her nose and upper lip? Dark complexion?

She blew out the candle and pressed deep into the portrait. In the dark, she could believe he was as he'd been when she'd read to him almost every night from her Book of World Fables. They carried pillows up the mulberry tree, a light (it had to be electric, dias were too flammable), and in the still, dry months, paper fans. While she read, he enjoyed the pictures. His breath smelled vaguely of brown sugar, and his arms of milk bread. She did not know it at the time but the crafty pages of the book were trapping his scents, blending them with their own old, ligneous sigh, so she was left less with the stories, and more with his vapor. She had to work hard to conjure up solid memories of him, but Dia *felt* her father everywhere.

To have more than this, to have him back even once, could she really give Daanish up? To go back to the night before his death, before Riffat huddled with her children, muttering, *I shouldn't have told him.* To have a different branch of the river flow into the sea, not the one that had swept her alongside Daanish. To be, instead, sitting with her family in the kitchen, watching a mother and father who were strangers, not lovers, yet loving them both. And back even further, to whatever it was her mother shouldn't have told him. Before, before, when she was just a tiny mulberry knot, slipping howling into the world. Before the lines on her palm were even scratched. Before she must choose who she wanted to be.

DAANISH

I

News

AUGUST 1992

Anu was the only one delighted with the intensity of the rains. It didn't matter that the electricity was out for seven or eight hours at a time, that she was stuck in a sweltering kitchen without even a pedestal fan, or that the house she spent so much time complaining about aged considerably with every storm. Inclement weather meant her son stayed home. Their barely functional, twelve-year-old excuse for a Datsun was entirely nonfunctional now. The day Daanish turned the ignition and it clicked dead, she'd beamed.

If he hated her for smothering him, the next minute he grew so guilty he loved her more. If he loved her more he spent less time shut in his room and more time shut in her love. But that made him hate her more. He remembered her often as she'd been the day he arrived from the airport: standing at the front door with arms open wide, firmly positioned between him and his aunts, his things, his past. She rolled comfort and isolation into one soft embrace. The fact was, he wanted both.

When not with Dia, lethargy steeped him. He woke in a stupor, gazing out at Karachi with narcotic dullness. The air was a whirlwind of opium-thick grime and smog – it latched on to his collar and screamed: Stop! Rest! Do nothing at all! And when he tried to fight, he only sank deeper in inertia.

He'd sit with a pencil and pad in his room and try to order his disorder the way he'd once classified his shells:

1. Aba's absence
2. Anu's presence
3. Heat/humidity
4. Noise. Always noise. Construction, neighbors, children on the street, generators, loudspeakers. Never a moment of natural silence, the kind in the sunken garden. Or the cove.
5. Dia

He'd throw the piece of paper away. All he'd written was trivial. That was the problem. His problems were not tangible monsters. They were tiny invisible bacteria. The monsters were the strikes in the city, journalists killed, burgeoning beggars. Recently, a devoted social worker had fled because his life was being threatened. No one had ever threatened Daanish's life. Shantytowns were mushrooming. He had a house. In that house, the closer life pressed against him, the more he could think only in headlines. And in a city of eleven million, life pressed very, very close.

There were roaches bending backwards in the shower drain. Crickets chirping under the no-longer-pristine white rug. Dia had told him an interesting fact about crickets: not all of them could sing, and the ones that did sang with wings. They rubbed these together in a dance and the dance sang. Crickets with no rhythm pretended otherwise. They hung around the dancers and when the latter drew mates, they sidled up to female crickets and said: 'Hey baby, I'm the singer in this band!' Some singers never got a girl, and some liars did. And some crickets amplified their song by dancing in a burrow. The hole became a trumpet, like loudspeakers in little underground mosques. Daanish entertained himself for hours picturing maulvi sahibs rubbing wings together in a dark tunnel. It was either that, or the big picture: toppling governments, ethnic hatred, foreign aid, sanctions on Iraq, eighty per cent of the world's wealth in the hands of fifteen per cent of its people.

What could he possibly do about any of that?

Was he to become a journalist in America, a country that taught students of journalism *not* to unearth the big picture, only to come back here and find he too needed a cleaner, less overwhelming truth?

Was that *his* filthy truth?

There were ants on his toothbrush. So the ad had lied. The product did have sugar. The toilet paper plugged the toilet. The tanker did not show so there was no water to flush the toilet with anyway. And when the rain fell and the power shut off, there was no fan to air out the stench in the toilet. It drifted all the way down the hall. It crept under his door and under the rug where the dancing crickets sang. Could crickets smell human shit?

If Daanish had a filthy truth, he hoped Dia could save him from it.

One day when there was a break in the rain the postman rode his bicycle through the flooded street, dropping a bundle of mail in a puddle by the defunct Datsun. In that bundle there was a letter from Liam. It was on top of a pile of bills and didn't get too badly soaked.

Dear Daanish,

It's been two months since you left, but no news. Didn't I tell you not to be a stranger? So what's up, man?

I'm at Iris's house for the week. Her folks are real cool. They're building this house in the woods in N. Vermont, real close to the Canadian border. It's just about complete. There's pine trees and elms, and days are in the mid-60s. Not another house for miles but we do have visitors: bears! It's like living like Grizzly Adams, man (and Grizzly Iris, no doubt). We've been eating more blueberry pie than we know what to do with, and Iris even tried making blueberry ice cream. Du-ude! Maple syrup flows like water around here. Iris' mom makes bitching pancakes. I must have put on ten, twelve pounds. Although maybe not: I walk and swim and chop wood.

Her dad did a lot of the building on the house himself. He's tight-mouthed and tough like a bull, but I think he's finally warming up to me. Yesterday, when I was helping him lay tiles in the bathroom, he told me this joke and I think we really bonded. Then all five of us (Iris' mom and sister too) went for a dip in a nearby lake. As her dad said, it was cold as a witch's tit.

Iris is still my queen. She played again at a church and again had everyone in awe. We go into town alone sometimes. Catch a matinee, hear some tunes. Have lunch at this diner where she's going to work for the next month before college reopens. And I'm going to have to go home to D.C. next week. But then she'll visit some weekend.

Hey, I heard about the chaos in Karachi. What's going on there, man? The television made it seem like a damn civil war? Give me your news, okay?

Stay alive,

Liam.

P.S. Iris' dad's joke: An 80-year-old man starts going out with a 20-year-old woman. The doctor tells him to be careful. It might not be good for the heart. The man shrugs, 'Well, if she dies, she dies.'

2

Ancestry

MAY–OCTOBER 1991

In the weeks following the success of Operation Desert Storm and the television broadcast of the biggest ticker-tape parade in history, Daanish stopped writing in his journal. A silent terror seized him, leaving him incapable of articulating anything any more. He finally felt what he'd been meant to feel since the first air strikes: nothing. He really didn't know if anything had happened after all.

Only once did something speak to him. He clutched it in his hands, words by Vonnegut about a previous conflict: *The war was such an extravaganza that there was scarcely a robot anywhere who didn't have a part to play.*

He recited them while rinsing pots at Fully Food. There was Robot Wang who scraped ranch dressing and beef and rolls into trash bags that Robot Ron tied and heaved onto his back like Dick Whittington off to seek his fortune in a great city. Robot Nancy had simply quit. She was going to take part-time classes in a community college and work a real job. 'Not like here,' she said, 'in the united fucking colors of Benetton.'

At the bus station, he gave her a robot kind of kiss and the next day, a robot from Trinidad replaced her. Daanish never bothered introducing himself, nor did anyone else.

It continued like that into the fall. He barely even wrote to his parents. Sometimes the phone rang in the hall and he heard a student pick it up and say, Who? *Day-nish?* He knew it was his father but didn't answer when the messenger knocked on his door. He'd always remember that: he hadn't answered all his father's calls. The following year, he'd be dead.

Most of all, Daanish avoided Liam. The two had hardly spoken since their argument outside Hallmark, even though he'd gone to Iris' recital. The notes had scraped his nerves and from the way Liam clenched his jaw Daanish knew he couldn't concentrate either. Afterwards, they both congratulated Iris excessively and then Daanish took a taxi back to his dorm. It had cost everything he had, but he wasn't going to wait for Liam to offer a ride.

Increasingly, Daanish retreated to his sunken garden to watch the season change. And to reflect on his friend. Looking up at an old oak, he remembered climbing it last fall, while Liam photographed him from below. He'd almost fallen off when Liam hollered, 'Why do women have vaginas?'

'No idea.'

'So men will talk to them.'

Daanish snorted: 'Not in my country.'

Liam guffawed. 'You're living in the wrong place, man! Here's another one: why do women take so long to orgasm?'

'Who cares?'

'Oh, you knew it already!'

And in the winter, the two had come here often to enjoy the chilling silence, occasionally puncturing it with chatter. But they never discussed the war.

Eventually, alone in the garden, Daanish slowly began to feel his pulse again. The nuthatches were preparing for winter.

So were the honeybees, circling around him less with each day. Petals curled and dried, and the color came early to the leaves. A tiny leg of sensation kicked inside him. After many months, he found himself compelled to again make sense of what had been effaced.

He enrolled in a journalism class with a different professor. But like Wayne, she steered discussion toward consumer happiness. If the public wasn't getting the story it wanted, it was being exploited. She called the right story 'soft news' and showed videos of anchor personalities that made the softness the softest. Unlike Wayne, she asked for no journals.

Daanish never interrupted her but still continued his search in the library.

In a medical journal one day, he found a letter written by a conscientious objector, a Marine who'd spoken at protests throughout the war before turning himself in.

Daanish read the letter.

Gandhi and Martin Luther King Jr are heroes but my greatest hero is Mohammad Ali. No politician or activist can understand the shame of being asked to serve your country but refusing. A man on a hunger strike feels cleansed. Maybe he sees God. But a man who says no to an oath feels like a coward. He feels like a wuss. Like no God could ever love him. He hangs his head and wonders if he's a man or a sick nothing. Ali knows. And now look: people in every corner of the world are crazy for him.

I grew up the fifth child of a white laborer from Indiana. A hod carrier whose every second was taken up by water and sand. What were the right proportions? That's what my old man cared about most. Mortar and stone. He liked to say that stone was the oldest construction material in the world. Before wood, before brick. He was carrying on a tradition left behind by people who must have looked very different from him. The Druids. The Pharaohs. He was poor but he was no fool. He had respect for those who came before him. And he wanted me to keep building too, but differently. None of his kids became hod carriers.

I joined the army at seventeen and it sent me to college and gave me health insurance. I was nineteen when training for the Gulf War began. Most of the faces around me were not white. They had been lured, like me, by the promise of security. But most of them started wondering why they were fighting for a country that didn't give a shit about them. Yeah, they had the right to vote now and they could own land – a step up from many Americans who fought in World War II. But they came from neighborhoods racked by crime and illness and they knew they were only going to see more of it. From being the victims of despair, they knew they'd become its agent. They asked why the wealthier kids weren't willing to fight for their country. They are the ones who ought to have enlisted. They are the ones who ought to say thank you.

The numbers refusing to go to Saudi Arabia started rising. This was not reported in the media. We were only shown kissing our girlfriends goodbye. That's good business, and that's what corporate America is all about. The best brand. We have the most famous in the world: Coca-Cola, McDonald's, Nike, Kodak. And now another: Desert Storm. They want you to buy it, today.

Daanish made a photocopy and put the journal away. Then he tried to picture the Marine, the son of a hod carrier. What exactly had pushed him to take this stand? Was it a moment, a face, a nightmare, a prayer? A combination of things more abstract? He'd wondered the same many times about his own grandfather.

Daanish kept digging, finding the most detailed analyses of the war and its outcome in other medical journals and in the European and Asian press. The library carried these

– it was just a matter of finding them. Maybe the doctor's game had given Daanish good practice.

He learned that earlier in the year, an International War Crimes Tribunal had been held, astonishingly, in New York City. The tribunal, presided over by judges from many different nations, had found the US guilty of breaking nineteen international laws. The American media did not report this but many foreign papers did.

Daanish's heart raced: In New York City! Wasn't it something that a country would host a council that condemned it? It proved freedom of a kind that perhaps no other nation enjoyed did exist here. Yet the media wouldn't make use of it.

A few days later, he saw Liam. It was a bright blue afternoon in October, with benign cushiony clouds and a wisp of a breeze that was sometimes warm, then suddenly cold. Liam was leaning into the wall of a building, buttoning up a flannel shirt, books on the grass.

'Hey,' Daanish said.

'Hey,' answered Liam, forelock in his eyes.

'What's up?'

Liam shrugged. 'Nothing much.'

They walked and eventually Daanish asked him if he'd heard of the tribunal.

Liam shot back, 'No. Educate me.'

Daanish stopped walking. 'Why are you so defensive all the time?'

Liam moved on, but then turned back. 'There's something I've been wanting to ask you. If you don't like it here, why don't you leave?'

Daanish laughed. 'I don't believe I'm hearing this from you! Are you saying I can only stay if I'm silent?'

'This college is giving you aid.'

'So I'm a beggar? And beggars can't choose? Has it

occurred to you that by asking questions, I'm living up to your country's ideals better than you are?'

Now Liam laughed. 'You know nothing about this country. Let me tell you the first thing you should know. All Americans have experienced prejudice. That's why our ancestors had to leave their homes in the first place, and come here.'

Daanish took a deep breath. 'That may be true. But whatever it was your parents or grandparents had to put up with, the fact is that you never did. Now you're not the persecuted any more, so don't turn to that every time your country screws another. People who fled here to escape being dumped on are now doing the dumping. Still you think of yourself as the victim.'

'I didn't say I do. I just said that Americans know what it's like.'

'And I'm saying you don't. *You* don't. Even if your forefathers did. Yet you want the kind of news that says you do. You want to hear about being wronged. Not about who you're wronging. A bombing raid kills hundreds in Panama or Iraq, it's not even on the news. But an American is harassed anywhere outside the States and it's the lead story on every network.'

Liam flicked his hair back. 'I've got class.'

'That's why you care nothing about breaking international laws or the effects of the sanctions. They hate you, remember? So it's okay to kill them.'

He walked away.

Seven months later, when Daanish's father died, Liam insisted on dropping him off at the bus station. Daanish wondered how he'd found out, but didn't ask. He liked to think that in the months of estrangement, indirectly, Liam had still enquired after him.

As he mounted the bus, Daanish knew Liam was trying to catch his eye.

'I'm really sorry, man,' he said.

Several thousand deaths couldn't make him remorseful, yet Daanish's father's death could. Still, he was glad to have his friendship again, though he never told him that.

3

Rooms

AUGUST 1992

None of his old friends were in Karachi any more. They were in the US, either doing summer internships or pretending to. Anything so they didn't have to come back. Literally, anything. Two friends in New York City toiled in the subway, one in a mezzanine news-stand, the other as a ticket-seller. It was risky work, sometimes worse than a taxi-driver's. Anyone attempting it was an immigrant, or an immigrant-aspirant. Either way, an alien. Was that better than this? Better than knowing the house at least was yours and the meal waiting? Was the future here even more uncertain than in the NYC underground?

Outside, the house under construction stood sopping and unattended. The workers had stopped coming since it began to rain. He'd seen Salaamat walk around the skeletal foundation once during the downpour, perhaps missing the cups of tea he'd shared with the old worker in the late afternoons. He'd not come back, yet Daanish still looked out for him, feeling he was there, and maybe even wishing it. That was how little there was to do.

Each time he saw Anu, she reminded him that their savings would last eight, maybe nine years. But then she'd kiss and bless him, saying her son was her insurance.

Some insurance: he was a sack of useless bones. The doctor was right. He'd chosen the wrong profession. *You will spend your life fighting others then come back here only to fight your own. Think!* He had the statistics for murdered reporters. And for those jailed. And for presses destroyed. When he shared these with Anu he knew she hadn't listened. She watched her own crickets: she plotted his marriage. He remained supremely indifferent to her antics, as if the plot revolved around someone else. Someone he used to be, but no one she knew. And no one his father would ever know.

He sat with the lacquer box on the dirty white rug. The crickets hopped aside as he stretched his legs. Once again when he looked inside his father looked back. He was perhaps his age. No sign of balding, no sign of anything really except happiness. Daanish squinted, wondering at the building in the background. The photo probably dated from his father's student days in London. Not a doctor yet. Not a groom yet. Something about the way the scarf fluttered and the nose reddened made him smell the crisp autumn air of Massachusetts. Even the brownstone tower, the neatness of the green grounds sweeping to the right of the frame – it could have been downtown Southampton or Springfield in not England but New England. It could have been him and Nancy, or Becky.

While examining the photograph, Daanish remembered the ones of his parents on their wedding day. Where were those black and white prints that used to be on the table near the doctor's chair? There'd been the groom in a pavilion strewn with rose petals. Beside him, his shriveled father, still devoted to Pakistan's first English-language newspaper. The doctor's long-suffering mother pressed against her sixteen-year-old daughter-in-law, whom she offered a cup of milk. Four on a couch with a curtain of roses around them. A groom with an MD from London! Dr Shafqat, the rising, dashing star. The photographers clicked and clicked.

In another, the doctor drank from the cup his mother presented him, exactly where Anu's lipstick mark must have been. The photo didn't show the mark but that was their first kiss: on a china cup. Wasn't it worth savoring? Apparently Anu didn't think so. Yet, though she turned her back on that day, she wanted to duplicate it for her son so now she could hold the china cup.

Shaking his head, Daanish put the box away.

It was only drizzling softly now. When he returned to the window, a man walked through the cavities of the unfinished house. He was creeping forward like a chambered nautilus, sealing the smaller spaces, carving larger ones with each stride. A man with hands clasped behind him and a cloth around his head. The wind licked his kameez as his shadow stretched from one concrete division to the next.

Maybe it was the worker who wanted the visa. No, he was too short. It must be Salaamat. He was glad the last few times with Dia they'd not used him: he'd seen too much already. It was not simply infuriating but humiliating. How dare he look at her – he who probably never had a woman unless he paid for it! His presence put Daanish in the same league. If his eyes tainted Dia, they completely soiled him.

It had been days since he and Dia last met. Though he wanted her, he could wait. She wasn't going anywhere. It was pleasant to think of that. She'd be pacing the spaces of her own mansion, hands behind her back, thinking of him. It seemed she kept an ear out for the phone to ring. When he called, she almost always answered, with a delightful pant, as though she'd run to him. He was beginning to like the fact that his time with her was infrequent. It was hard to get, hence more intense when he got it. And when, such as these days, he couldn't, it was all he had to look forward to. So did she. There were no other distractions. No catching matinees, or tunes at a club. She waited for him. She counted the minutes. She ran to the phone. She wasn't running into boys on her way to the laundromat. She was always indoors. And even within, her space was heavily guarded. If he had to enter her world with caution, well, so did everyone else. It left him feeling exquisitely secure.

The reclusive shadow did not reveal itself and Daanish turned to the drawer where his shells used to be. There was nothing there now except the silk thread. He picked it up. A few particles of sand remained from the time he'd taken it to the cove to show Dia. Maybe he'd call her later today. Maybe he wouldn't.

4

Thirst

Two days later, when the rain finally halted, a lean sunlight gradually commenced soaking up the runoff gutter water in his street. Daanish decided to do something for Anu. He'd go to the Housing Society water office and bring home a tanker. It would get him out of the house, please Anu, and even make a good bit of news. He could finally tell Liam what he was doing here.

But it struck him that he'd absolutely no notion how to go about the business. He had, in fact, no notion how the house ran at all. Who paid the bills and where? How much did a tanker even cost?

When he asked Anu, she said he was a dear for wanting to help her and handed him a hundred rupees plus a file the office would need. Then she told him to be careful. 'It seems everyone is getting kidnapped these days. It's even worse than before you left. You've no idea!'

He especially hated it when she declared he had 'no idea' because the doctor had 'sent him away'. He blew her a quick kiss.

The car was still dead so he began walking to the main road for a taxi. There were tiny islands of dry concrete between slimy puddles as thick as the soup in airplane toilets. The air was entirely saturated, enveloping him in a dense funnel. The sun warmed this moisture-funnel and he began to sweat, all the while hopping from one dry patch to the next. He passed Khurram's house, looking up at the hideous glazed domes and brass balcony. Throughout the rains, the lights circling the verandah were the only ones to be seen on the dark, putrid street. He wondered again what Khurram's father did. Khurram refused to say. All three cars were gone. Salaamat was nowhere in sight.

He covered his nose when passing the large patch of land where the neighborhood dumped its trash. Polythene bags hung on tree limbs and telephone wires, plugged open gutters, tumbled along driveways. He turned onto a side street, wanting really to head back to his room. His powerlessness overwhelmed him. How could he even think clearly when his body struggled at the most basic level: for water, electricity, clean streets? What could he begin to do here? And yet, somehow, millions survived. Was it survival or immunity? Was there a difference?

He hit an intersection. Into his moisture-funnel swirled car-exhaust. The horns drained him further. Drivers flickered lights even at daytime. There was no sidewalk, no zebra crossing, and there might as well have been no traffic lights. A lame beggar sat on a plank with wheels in the center of the road. While Daanish dodged two Toyotas, the beggar chased him, dashing like a contestant in a luge-race, wheeling himself forward with his hands. Catching up with Daanish, he reached out and grabbed his shirtsleeve. Daanish ran faster, inadvertently wheeling the man along.

A taxi stopped. Daanish leaped inside, panting, 'The water office.'

Days after the pre-rain strikes, many shops were still closed and hardly any fruit-stalls had been set up. The driver said, 'First I missed work because of strikes, then because of rain. *Allah malik hay*.'

Still collecting himself, Daanish said nothing.

'How are they supposed to get here?' the driver continued. 'When all the buses are burning and there's curfew in the streets, how are they to lead normal lives?'

In the rear-view mirror Daanish saw he was a wiry man with eyes heavily rimmed with kohl. The mirror was bedecked with a prayer the Prophet had read when traveling, a photograph of the Kabbah, beads and a scented pine. The dashboard was sprinkled with blue and yellow stickers in the shape of flowers and hearts and the steering wheel was upholstered in a shaggy red rug. The car reeked of sweat-soaked lavenders.

In the mirror, the driver's eyes scrutinized Daanish too. 'You don't look like you know much about curfews.'

'No,' Daanish confessed. 'Just about water on the streets and none in taps. I'm going to get a tanker.'

'Ah!' The driver chuckled. 'See how there's no one around? They're all trying to get a tanker!'

What if he knew Daanish had recently returned from Amreeka? He'd laugh them both off the road.

'You should have brought your sisters along,' the driver pursued. 'You know they always let women through first.' When Daanish said nothing he added, 'I see documents. Good. You should at least be carrying documents.'

'I'm glad you approve,' Daanish muttered.

The car stopped outside a building and Daanish paid. The man drove away, bemoaning, 'What is normal any more?'

When Daanish walked inside the gate he saw it was not a building but a wide expanse of dirt, on each side of which stood a desk. Both desks were surrounded by a mob. Daanish chose the desk further from the gate; it looked a little less swamped. He stood at the back, attempting to get in line, knowing he was an idiot for trying. As soon as two people tried to stand in series, the one at the back stuck his head forward, which led to the first nudging the second back in line by popping out himself. While the two danced sideways, newcomers simply cut ahead. Eventually, Daanish began doing the same.

But he couldn't get too far. Standing on his toes, he tried to steal a glimpse of the official hidden behind the mob, but he only heard angry customers shouting at the man, and then at each other. The voices rose and a full-blown stampede appeared imminent. And all for water. It was that tail-biting frenzy he'd felt in his uncles. That inbreeding of disappointment, as if they were all stranded on an island in a long-forgotten sea.

Returning to the back, Daanish was immediately met by a man so emaciated his gray polyester trousers flapped around his hips and legs like a skirt on a scarecrow. To Daanish and a handful of recent arrivals, he declared, 'How will our nation prosper if we can't even make a line!'

One of the newcomers was a stocky woman with a dupatta around her head. She cut straight to the front. The men reluctantly let her through, grumbling that women who grumbled about how hard they had it ought to have it harder.

'Like in the West!' Scarecrow said. 'No one respects women there. These are the sound traditions of our country. Reverence of the female!' He turned to Daanish. 'I was a student at the University but it is closing for weeks. Everywhere you looking students joining politics. Almost everyone in engineering has gun.'

Daanish wondered why everyone cried to him. Anu, the taxi-driver, now this man. Then there was the worker who insisted Daanish could get him a visa. What was he, a healer's son? Yes! He grew miracles on his fingertips!

Like Khurram, this one was just as keen on practicing

his English. He said, 'Parents are checking their children's things when they no look. You know how many unlicensed guns were buying last year, and most by teenager?' His head jiggled on a stalk-thin neck.

Daanish decided it was time to swim into the sea breaking over the official's desk. He drilled forward, hands out, head lowered, hips smacking sideways, arriving no further than the third ring around the desk. The ground was wet here. Those who exited bore signs of a stiff price: their clothes were caked in mud. But in their hands was a chit of white paper, and this put an immense smile on their ruffled faces.

Daanish was about to ask the young man beside him what the chit meant when the wave parted again, allowing yet another woman through. A young man fumed, 'That's not in Islam!'

The man who'd been in front of him, but due to the adjustment for the woman, now found himself pushed to the third ring, said, 'Yes, the Quran does not say I am to sacrifice my place for a woman.'

'How would you know, my love?' replied the one who'd snatched the gap. 'You can't even read!'

Daanish and a couple others made use of the diversion by sliding up. He asked another man, 'What does the chit say?'

This man wore blue shades. He said, 'It's the NOC.'

'What's the NOC?'

He didn't answer. Here was the opposite problem: Daanish wanting to talk but bumping into a wall. Or rather, blue shades. He turned to his left and repeated the inquiry.

A paunchy elderly man replied, 'The No Objection Certificate.'

Daanish laughed. 'That's a good one. What is it really?'

The paunchy man was equally confused. He dug under his kameez to scratch his stomach. 'The NOC: No Objection Certificate. If they have no objection with you, they'll give the NOC, and then you can deposit the chit and get a tanker.'

'But how do they decide if they have an objection or not?'

The man tapped Daanish's folder. 'They check your documents.'

For the first time that day, Daanish looked inside the binder Anu had given him. There were bank statements, income tax returns, property tax forms, and a host of other signed and stamped papers. 'But do we have to show these every time?'

The man gave him a look that said, *You fool.*

He was getting a terrible feeling about this. Most of those exiting did not bear the all-powerful chit. He'd left the house before eleven. It was now one-twenty. The office, the paunchy man disclosed, shut at two.

At a quarter to two, Daanish inched into the first ring. Crashing into a puddle, he at last saw the desk, chock-full of files. The man behind it consulted his watch every other minute, while a desperate father of four kept urging him to look a little harder for the file that would match the one he'd brought. 'Maybe it's under that pile.' He pointed to one that was as much a pile as they were a line. Pages fluttered out as the tower collapsed, and the man behind the desk again studied the fake Omega. Five minutes to two. The father waved his documents under the man's nose. 'I'm sure you have a record of this somewhere here,' he pleaded hysterically. 'If you'll just look.'

The watch struck two. The official slapped his hands on the desk. Daanish was pitched into the desperate father as the wave parted again and another woman appeared. She was quite young, quite pretty, and for a moment there was palpable hesitation. But lunch beckoned. The man rose. The crowd erupted in fury, 'I've been coming here every day this week!' 'We've not even had drinking water!'

'My mother is ill!' 'How much? How much to make you stay?'

The official trotted toward the gate, meeting his colleague from the other desk along the way.

The desperate father shook his head. 'Who has more sense: thieves like them or honest men like us?'

5

The Authorities

Daanish returned the next day. He couldn't even squeeze into the second ring. So he stood at the back with Scarecrow, who'd lost count of how many days he'd been awaiting his turn. It was as if, more than even water, he wanted a place to speak his mind. He'd made the water office his venue.

'Three million,' he said. 'Last year three million unlicensed guns were buying in country. The Afghan War ending three years ago, but guns keep coming. The Amreekans were arming and training us to fight the Communists but now we are left to fight ourselves.' He shook his head. His entire body seemed to sway. 'They just left, those Amreekans. They didn't care what they leaving behind.' Then he stared at Daanish. 'You are going in Amreeka, I think?'

Daanish bolted. But it was too late: his two selves were squabbling. The Amreekan one argued that he had a right to act on his own interests, so stop complaining. The smaller replied that the other was powerful, rich, and in the habit of dropping old friends to whom he exported arms and torture equipment that made him even richer.

He squeezed into the fourth ring, and then the third, where the desperate father of four was on the cusp of madness. At two o'clock, Daanish once more returned home.

It had been five days since either he or Anu had showered or even washed. An uncle had twice brought them drinking water from his house. It was 36C° and humidity was ninety per cent. When he wiped off the sweat dripping down his face and neck he smeared gray filth over his body as though it were soap. Then he sat flicking the dirt out from between burgeoning fingernails. Should he cut them? It was too exhausting. Anyway, they'd only grow again. He began to chew them off, swallowing the slime wedged inside. Some particles he spat onto the increasingly soiled rug. Since he kept his door shut, the room was never swept. He'd rather live in filth than have his things disturbed further.

The next day, he wrestled the mob and staunchly stood at the desk before the lunch hour. He handed over his documents. The official frowned at each. He wore a dirty bush shirt and his hair, Daanish was amused to see, was no less greasy than his own. The air around him reeked of mustard and cheap cologne. The desperate father stood behind Daanish, with more documents, just as he'd been ordered. Daanish wished he had it in him to offer his place. But he did not. He had finally gotten a hearing. He deserved it. If others were denied what they also deserved, it had nothing to do with him.

The man searched through the clutter on the desk, shaking his head. He couldn't find Dr Shafqat's file. 'We have no record of him.'

Daanish's knees began to quake. 'But I do. You have just gone through my file. All of them are stamped, official papers. All our bills are paid.' He was astonished to find his voice cracking.

Scarecrow called from behind, 'Give the Amreekan a break!'

The men around Daanish stirred. They examined his rumpled shirt, his jeans caked in dirt from all the days he'd worn them here. There was no sign of glittery Amreekan-ness. He looked as tattered as they, if not more.

'If you're from Amreeka,' Omega said, 'why have you come here?'

The others nodded, oblivious that the wily official was making time fly.

'I am not from Amreeka,' Daanish snapped. 'And I'm here because I have no water, just like all the others around me who've been waiting for days for you to issue the No Objection Certificate. I object to all this waiting!'

Omega grinned. His teeth and gums were stained with paan and the long hand of his watch inched closer to the hour. When he laughed, so did some of the others he was putting off.

Daanish's face flushed. 'I continue to wait.'

'Gently, gently,' the man cooed. 'All in good time.' He sat back. 'I was once given very good cigarettes by an Amreekan like yourself . . .'

'I don't smoke.'

'. . . Let me see, what were they called?'

'You're wasting these good people's time.'

This finally triggered something in the others. 'I want my turn before you go for lunch!' one declared. More began protesting.

Omega sighed, sitting upright again. 'Really, you do not look much like an Amreekan. Next.'

'But you haven't finished with me,' Daanish yelled.

'You will come back tomorrow and I will see where your file is.'

'Tomorrow is Friday!' He wanted to weep.

Panic broke. He was pushed and shoved as the men realized

in another ten minutes the office would close for the next sixty-seven hours. He found himself beside Scarecrow again. The student slapped his back as though they'd become soul mates. 'It is not like this in Amreeka, no? You are finding lines in offices and water in tapses?'

Anu was sitting in the TV lounge when a taxi dropped him home. He seemed to have lost his sense of smell. She too hadn't washed but he noticed nothing different in her appearance or odor. She pushed back greasy hair from his sweaty forehead and kissed him. He never repulsed her.

'I don't know how you've done it all your life,' he said, 'shuttling back and forth for something this basic.'

'They let me get in front,' she replied. 'But I have been sent home many times when they can't find our file. You poor thing. I'll go on Sunday.' She wiped his sweat away with her dupatta, taking some of the dirt on his flesh with her.

The electricity had gone again. He looked at the ceiling fan, waiting for the miracle rattle.

In Anu's lap was a bowl of lentils, soaking in less water than she liked to use. He sat quietly beside her as she washed them, remembering a day like this twelve, maybe thirteen years ago. The doctor and he were watching a television show about a prospector. He tried to remember the year. Somewhere in the late seventies. The doctor was handsome, trim. A torrential spirit full of stories to share. So it was not a day like this. There were hardly any houses on the street – Khurram's had definitely not been there. The Soviets hadn't yet, or maybe just, invaded Afghanistan. Pakistan was a useful US ally. Aid had somersaulted into his country as rapidly as guns did now.

The prospector had held a pan with chunks of black rock. He spent his life waiting for the odd nugget, reminding Daanish of his grandfather: shriveled and somewhat bad-tempered, but unflinchingly determined. Willing to put up with rubbish for the rare bit of truth. Writing and fighting, yet never speaking of his own pain. Stubborn as lichen. Did he not have a drop of that feisty man's blood in his own veins?

Had the doctor too been thinking of his father as he sat beside his son, watching the crotchety prospector? Did he wish he were more like him, as he flew from place to place, bringing back gifts for Daanish and a wife who'd rather he spent on the house?

Anu probably had no recollection of that day. She'd been in the kitchen. She hardly ever watched television with them. Yes, it definitely wasn't a day like this.

He rose to turn on the TV, forgetting there was no electricity. Anu went into the kitchen. He could hear her put the lentils on the stove. She returned with two oranges and a salt shaker. She peeled the first orange, sprinkled each wedge with salt to cut the tartness, and offered the pieces to him. 'It's been in the fridge. Still cold.'

He smiled. The fresh, cool citrus after his ordeal at the water office was unspeakably delightful. He sat with both hands by his side, doing nothing besides parting his lips and piercing the skin of the orange lightly with his teeth.

Seeing how it revived him, Anu peeled the second one. 'You mustn't let yourself get dehydrated. The salt is also good for you.' Then she told him her brother would pick them up in the evening so they could go to his house and get cleaned up. 'A shower after all these days will do wonders for your appetite.'

There was a rattle, and then a click. The fan started turning and the TV lit up: Pakistan vs Australia. Daanish sank into the couch, relishing the gust of air on his face; the sweet tangerine; the leisurely pace of cricket.

After losing two wickets in succession, Australia finally smashed a six. Australian fans cheered. In amongst the bouncing crowd were two women in skimpy T-shirts. The screen quickly switched to a cigarette ad.

Daanish laughed, 'Smoking is better than skin!'

Anu pursed her lips.

'I bet the Censor Board had a good look.'

She slapped his leg. 'Just what your father would have said.'

'The men are too busy ogling to notice the slogan is highly inappropriate.' The slogan read: *For the taste alone.*

'You were so innocent once!'

It was too bad, really, because one of them had had boobs like Becky's. Anu had probably seen those boobs in the photos she'd stolen. He could embarrass her by asking whose were bigger. They'd play their own little censorship game: she hiding Becky, he hiding his liaison with her. She hiding that she'd hidden Becky, he hiding his knowledge of it all.

It was just a matter of time before she started on Nissrine. First she'd be of genteel birth, what with all that Ghaznavid blood coursing through her veins. (Just how many distant cousins of this regal clan did he have? Daanish couldn't remember any.) Then she'd be just his type: slim and educated. Finally, he got to say he liked her, without having to name *her*.

The game came on again but the cameraman was still focused on the women so it was back to Gold Leaf.

'I wonder if the water office and Censor Board are run by the same people? They both get paid to object.'

She looked at him. Ah, there was the preparatory look! The pleading eyes, tilting head, the words clustering on the tip of her tongue. Marry Nissrine . . . Marry Nissrine . . . the girl with the fair, fresh complexion. Just like her grandchildren should have.

Before she could say it, Wasim and Waqar were back in action, baffling the batsmen with reverse swing. 'We might win the series, don't you think? A nice follow-up to our World Cup victory.'

She bit her tongue. Not yet.

But when the game was over, and when they'd returned home after a rejuvenating wash at his uncle's, with five pots full of water to last, hopefully, till Sunday, she did say it. And once again, he implied he had no objection.

6

Open-ended

He called her at last after a week. 'When can I see you?'

'Where have you been?' She was panting, but her voice was different.

He felt a constriction around his neck. 'I've been trying to get a tanker to the house. Long story. When . . .'

'I've called so many times,' she pressed.

He paused. 'I'm sorry. When I'm home Anu's around me a lot.'

'Well, you could have at least tried.'

His irritation mounted. Finally: 'Let's figure out how to meet. My car's still broken . . .'

'I'm going to have to call you back. I don't like you right now.' She hung up.

What was he going to do with himself now?

Anu's brother had taken her to the water office. He had the whole house to himself but Dia had to make a fuss.

He walked out into the lawn and onto the street, winding

around the unfinished house. Had the contractor been fired? Work still hadn't resumed.

He thought of the choices he could offer her, when she eventually called. He could find a mechanic. But the thought itself was draining. It would take days before a mechanic kept his promise and came to the house, and in any case, the car would only break down again. He couldn't bring himself to chase both a tanker and a mechanic, even though Anu chased the former now.

Dia's car, like Khurram's, only came with the driver so that was out.

They couldn't take a bus because the cove was outside its range.

They could take a taxi, though that too wouldn't go all the way. It would involve walking the distance, in this heat, as Dia had had to do the day his car broke down. It had meant more men like Salaamat leering at Dia.

So what was left?

As he walked through the partitions, he wondered, Right here? It might be quite cozy, cuddling in one of these half-built chambers. He could simply tell Anu he was going to find a mechanic. It was too obvious to suspect.

The only problem he foresaw was Salaamat, if it was he who occasionally lurked in the crevices. But when no other options arose, he suggested the house when she finally called.

Days later, in a cavity furthest from the street, she sulked, 'Oh what a place to meet!'

'But aren't you glad to see me? This is probably going to be a guest bedroom or something. We're the first guests!'

'This is absurd. There are puddles everywhere. We're barely out of the sun, and most of all, we're sandwiched between your mother's house and Khurram's house, where Salaamat knows us too! It's like we're having to create our own village just to be together, only the village is in their lap.'

He sat her down. 'Let's talk about your lap.' He tried to rest his head in it.

But she remained aloof, looking about the empty room with the half-raised, unpainted walls, and above them, a gray and bloated sky. The ground was muddy and uneven. The arm he touched soon covered in sweat.

'This is no good. I can't hunker like this with you, Daanish. I miss the cove, even though it frightened me. But we belong in someplace beautiful. There's not even a tree around us.'

He had to admit: it wasn't cozy. He sat up. 'Well, where else?'

Instead of suggesting something, she kept complaining. 'This place makes me feel like I'm doing something wrong. I'm not.'

He checked himself for getting impatient with her, and touched her smooth, clean-cut jaw. It curved beautifully at the chin. He traced her lips, his thumb wiping the sweat gathering on her upper lip, where a thin line of hair grew. Her large eyes were so sincere, and just now, so sad. He sighed. 'Was it hard to get away?'

She slid a hand in his. 'Very. Inam Gul said, "Where do you keep going, beti? Why do you not speak plainly with me?" I hate upsetting him. Plus, I'm afraid he's going to squeal.'

'If I were some other guy, would your mother still object?'

'No, that's what hurts. She's probably the only mother who wouldn't. Yet why should I feel guilty? We're doing nothing wrong.' She said it with great conviction, snapping herself out of her despair, and at last kissed him.

They lay in each other's arms in the guestroom-to-be, blowing the sweat dry on each other's skin. She whispered, 'You leave for America soon.'

It was true. In less than two weeks, he'd be on the plane again. 'We can meet here often.'

She said nothing for a while but then both of them pulled slowly away. It was too hot, too sticky, and they felt too keenly how constrained they were. Their love needed room. Here it was so capped, so smothered, how could it possibly grow?

Dia said, 'Last summer, a black rain fell. People said it was because of the bombed oilfields in Iraq. For months, soot covered the world and fell like ink. Ama said the rain destroyed our mulberry trees, but she'd no way of confirming that. We ran short of food for the silkworms.' Her voice was breathy and detached.

He rolled onto his side. 'Dia, this isn't perfect, but let's try to make the most of it?'

They tried.

The next time, Daanish brought a thermos of ice water and they sprinkled it on each other, kissing early, before the balm withered and they were too clammy to embrace. He told her they had plenty of water now – Anu had prevailed, but she wondered why he never came home with a mechanic.

Sometimes Dia spoke of Sumbul and Inam Gul, of how their queries were increasingly intrusive. But mostly, the two exchanged stories. It was what they had to count on. Tales of beginnings, and of eternity.

One day she leveled the ground with her palm, stretched her legs and leaned into a dividing wall. She told him how the mulberry fruit got its red color. 'I'd tell the story to my father at bedtime and he'd repeat it on the drive to the farm. It got so that each time, we had to come up with a different ending. But this is how it starts.

'There were once two young lovers, say Raeesa and Faraz. Raeesa was lean and dark, with sparkling eyes, rich black hair and lips like fuchsia petals.'

Daanish laughed. 'How can poor Faraz match up to that?'

'He doesn't,' she smiled. 'He was short and lumpy-nosed, but what he had was zip. More than a honeybee's.'

'I see, zest makes up for the fact that he's a *bonga*.'

She tweaked his arm. 'He was sweet, not a *bonga*. Anyway, their parents forbade the children from even looking at each other. But Faraz had to pass her house on the way to the field where he worked, so many opportunities arose for Raeesa to watch him coyly from behind her thick curtain of hair.' Daanish combed Dia's tresses with his fingers, arranging them over her eyes. She obliged him by peering out mischievously.

'Faraz would linger feverishly when he spied her lithe, eel-like presence, hopping from foot to foot, terribly nervous about being caught. But he'd brave anything for a look of his beloved.

'At night, on his way back from the field, he'd stand beside the wall of her house. There was a small crevice there no one besides the lovers knew of. While the household slept, they'd speak softly to each other through it. Her voice was kind and seductive. His lips drew nearer to drink the delectable aroma.'

Dia stalled, and Daanish gently rubbed her back. 'Why did you stop?'

Her brows were furrowed, and she looked away before answering him. 'I just remembered something.' She paused again. 'My father would always describe it as Faraz wanting to drown himself in Raeesa's breath. It's nothing. Just that it's cruel, the way words twist around, take on unwanted meanings. It was a perfectly good metaphor. Now I'll never use it.'

Daanish kept stroking her back, and it was then that Dia came to tell him of her father's murder. 'Technically,' she said, 'he didn't really drown. I mean the coroner said he was dead before being dumped in the river. Still, his body wouldn't have looked the way it did if he hadn't been steeping for days.' He held her then, struck by how her anger was still so fresh. She shed no tears but her eyes were haunted. She said she still wondered daily who'd killed him, what she'd do if she ever found out, and most of all, feared it would have to be nothing.

*   *   *

It wasn't till their next meeting that she resumed the tale.

'Nightly, Faraz was drawn to the crevice in the mud wall, a moth assembling around his eager mate – let's use that metaphor. His fingers scratched the crack hungrily as he imagined her on the other side, where Raeesa too was tortured, where she too scraped her delicate fingers, hoping for just one caress from her love. Her fingers grew bloody, and she kissed the wounds later, while falling asleep, imagining they were his. Her sleep was a series of dreams of him. Some sweet, others so terrible she woke up keening.

'Finally one night, able to stand it no longer, they arranged a meeting. Faraz said he knew just the place. It was under an old mulberry tree on the banks of a river, two kilometers out from the wheat fields. "Meet me there tomorrow night," he whispered through the hole. "It will be a new moon and we won't be seen."

'Raeesa listened, twirling her hair absently. She longed for a look of reassurance from her beloved. She'd never walked alone in the dark before. How far was two kilometers? What would her parents say if they found out? She didn't want to betray them. After all, she loved them too. Suddenly, she wished to be a child again. Children knew nothing about needing to choose. That was their innocence. She was about to give up hers. Where should she go: in the arms of passion or trust? What did she want more: a new beginning or old certainty?

'For the first time since their hidden affair, she wondered about Faraz. Was he the one for her?'

Dia looked at Daanish long and hard.

He'd been combing her hair with his fingers again and now he didn't know whether to remove his hand or let it linger. He decided on the latter, but the hiatus gave him away. He brought both hands up to his face, deciding to make them useful by mopping up his damp cheeks. He couldn't return her look. He didn't know what he felt.

He wished he could tell her that: I don't know what I feel any more. About anything. Love. War. Death. Home. All mere headlines. He couldn't touch or string them together. That was what she'd been doing for him. Was she going to stop?

He sighed, and his breath was a touch sour. Nothing crisp and ruddy about his scent here, in this gnat-ridden corner of the unfinished house. In truth, they were mad to tolerate this hovel. Humidity must be approaching one hundred per cent. They were both slick with it. She didn't smell good either.

She wiped her face with the hem of her kameez, in the process revealing part of her soft, flat stomach. If his timing were better, he could circle her naked waist, or lift her shirt up further. But he just wasn't moved to do anything at all. Guiltily, he thought he'd rather be in his room, where at least he could quench his thirst and cool off under the fan.

She continued, her voice giving away none of what had passed between them in the silence. 'Raeesa searched the crevice for a sign from him, but it was too small to reveal anything besides the darkness on his side.

'He asked her again, "Will you meet me under the mulberry?"

'"Yes!" she cried hurriedly. "I'll be there."

'So the next night, when her family had fallen asleep, Raeesa packed a small bundle of clothes and slipped out of the house. It was indeed a new moon. Every time she looked up, more stars appeared. They seemed to shine for her and she talked back to them while crossing a field. In this way, Raeesa resisted the urge to turn back.

'At last she heard the river. And she saw the silhouette of the tree. It hunkered over the water like a curved band of ageing men, arms askew, leaves flapping. The sky began to pale. But where was Faraz?

'Unknown to Raeesa, Faraz had started out for the river much earlier that day. Unable to contain his excitement, he'd not worked in the field. He could focus on nothing but the prospect of at last embracing his love. But that was still so many hours away! After waiting so long, these final hours were excruciating. He wandered away from the river, thinking, then sauntering back. He paced in circles.

'What he wanted was to declare his love openly, in broad daylight, so he could wear it proudly. He wanted to face her family, and his. Deceit would taint the beauty of what they'd have that night. They were above that.

'He came up with another plan. He stood outside her house and told himself: If she loves me, she'll know I'm here and come out. If she doesn't, I'll know her love is not true.

'But Raeesa, counting on tonight, did not step out all day. She suffered indoors, in silence, tormented by the enormous gamble she'd committed herself to.

'And so Faraz left. What she loved best about him – his enthusiasm, his childlike earnestness – would be their undoing.'

Daanish pouted. 'You're losing me: Faraz just created this problem for himself when he could finally have what he wanted?'

'Yes. He was misguided. Mind you, I'm coming to the part that could go many ways, and you can tell me your version. Let me finish my father's.

'So as the sun rose the next day, Raeesa sat between the roots of the mulberry tree in disbelief. Had she made the wrong choice? Or had something happened to her beloved? Should she get help? Indecision and fear paralyzed her.

'And Faraz, heartbroken by his own folly, roamed the village in stupefied horror, convinced it was he who'd been wronged. He was observed in this state by an old woman who counseled him thus: "Go where you agreed to go before you lose sight of where you are." She walked away, leaving Faraz to reflect on her words.

'Under the tree, Raeesa suddenly noticed a tiger lurking

nearby. He'd come to drink at the river, licking his lips dry of gazelle blood as he sipped. When she saw the beast, Raeesa, delirious with despair, assumed the blood on his whiskers was her beloved's. She fell before the tiger. The great cat snapped her neck, slurping an unexpected second course. Her blood sprouted up like a fountain, toward the bone-like branches caressing her, rinsing the white berries burgundy. And that's how they got their color.'

'I almost forgot that's what this was about,' Daanish frowned. Then he added, 'I don't like it.'

'Well, change it then. I said it was open-ended.'

He considered this. 'What happened to Faraz?'

'The saddest thing is that he'd been making his way back to her. And when he finally arrived, and saw Raeesa's carcass, he too let the cat have him. Once my father told it another way. Faraz had been excited, yes, but instead of wandering to her house, expecting her to come out, he'd simply parked himself on the banks of the river. He'd never met the old woman at the village, and he hadn't worked the fields either. He just sat under the tree from morning till night, so when the tiger with the bloody mustache came to drink, it was Faraz who thought Raeesa had been eaten, not the other way around. And then he too dropped before the beast, so it was Faraz's blood that turned the fruit red, and it was Raeesa who found the carcass.'

'But either way, the tiger gets them?'

'Yes. Another time, my father said there was a double metamorphosis. Not only did the fruit change color, but the lovers change too. They turn into tigers, and roam free through the forest, with no predators to hinder them.'

Daanish pulled her into his arms. 'Well, let me think of another ending.'

She smiled, waiting. But his attention wandered. Would it rain again? There was lightning in the distance, and the power must have gone because a generator droned. He wished she'd be the way he liked her best: the warm, soft Dia who freed him from chaos because she knew nothing about it. He wanted her to always be that way. Not like this, slyly nudging him.

She said, 'My father would often look over to my mother riding beside him in the car, silently requesting her input, but she never gave it. Nor did my brothers. It was just the two of us talking. After his death, I changed the story again: it isn't a tiger that lurks around Raeesa while Faraz pities himself all day. It's a band of dacoits. They carry pistols, shotguns, machine guns. They torment her for hours. Then they toss her in the river, where she floats beneath the stars that had been so kind on her lonely journey across the wheat field.'

Dia twisted off the cup of the thermos, saying the mugginess was making her faint. But there was no more water. 'Oh well,' she sighed. 'You tell me something now.'

And then they looked at each other. Was it her story or did a shadow really flicker between them? They froze. Daanish still hadn't told her Salaamat sometimes came here.

Cautiously, the two peeked outside. There was no one there.

SALAAMAT

I

Schoolboys

MAY 1987

'How can you be a freedom fighter if you'd rather stare at the river?' Fatah chided, settling beside Salaamat on the beach.

Salaamat grinned. It had been years since he'd felt like this. He said, 'Every evening after closing her teashop, my grandmother would stare at the sea till she was in a trance. She was tossing her worries out, letting the waves carry them away. Now here I am, on the water again, and I feel like her. Down the Indus flows, taking the worst of me with it. You can call that freedom.'

'Pah! What nonsense you speak!' answered Fatah. 'And don't let the Commander hear you talking such crap. He'll let the waves carry *you* away.'

The sun was rising behind them. On the opposite bank the sandstone cliffs glowed a pale peach and a cormorant stretched its wings. The other men were slowly emerging from their tents, buttoning shirts, combing the hair from their eyes with bare and blotched fingers. Murmuring greetings they stumbled to the river's edge to perform the morning ablution.

Fatah said in the coming months, when the rain fell, the color of the Indus would change. But for now, it was clear and blue like Hero's glass, with a pink dawn rising from its depths.

With glistening faces, the other men joined Fatah and Salaamat in waiting for the Commander. At twenty, Salaamat felt he was at last attending school. He was the new boy, the one who'd have to prove he'd assimilated. Soon he'd go south to the National Highway to do just that.

'Here he comes,' Fatah whistled. The men spun around so their backs were to the river, and their faces to the sun. The Commander liked to say that anyone who claimed crime was chaos had never committed a gruesome enough one. Crime was discipline. Sunburn and teary eyes were part of the discipline. So the men squinted up into the rising star while the Commander stood glowering in the shade of a sisky tree because there was nothing to smile about, given the qaumi halat, the state of the country.

'Anyone who smiles has never looked at the sun,' whispered Fatah. The man next to him snorted.

The Commander began, 'What has the nation done for you? You are illiterate, homeless, and hungry. You have been cut from your mothers too early, ripped from her womb like the slimy yellow fish eggs in a maha sher's gut! See how they drift in the river? That is you. Filthy, ugly, destined to drift from current to current. God cannot even grant you the mercy of camouflage. You can see those sons-of-owl fish eggs from the tallest cliffs on the banks!'

Salaamat and the others shifted. The Commander had never climbed a dune, let alone a cliff. He had the job because the Chief was his brother-in-law. Salaamat looked up at the sandstone towering around them. The sun was gradually creeping over to the ledge where every morning, around this time, a fish eagle fed her nest. Fatah and Salaamat had climbed these cliffs; they'd almost seen the nest. They'd also seen the fish eggs from all the way up there. And the Commander was right: they were an eye-sore.

The Commander paced in front of them with a keekar stick in one hand, the antique Winchester in the other. Much to Fatàh's disgust, the Chief had presented the gift to his brother-in-law. The eddying design on the stock glistened, because while the men trained, the Commander oiled. The keekar was his toothbrush. He probed his mouth with it, then spat. 'So what do you do? One word: dislocation. They cut you off, now you cut them off. We will achieve our goal through discipline. Mental discipline.'

The eagle soared into view, and then she must have landed on the faraway ledge because the chicks' greeting echoed in the gorge.

The Commander smacked his toothbrush against his thighs as his voice thundered, 'You have to temper your longings, to stop answering to this environment. You have to shut down, and then you have to shrink. You have to will yourself into a tiny steel nugget. You have to concentrate and learn to target this nugget. You will not simply use rounds. You will become them. In this camp, there are exactly twenty-seven Bullets.'

When he was finished, half the men retired to a stretch of beach reserved for combat practice. While they primed their bodies, the others, led by First Lieutenant Muhammad Shah, headed south to the highway. Their victims were taken to the Chief's bungalow, many miles inland.

The training varied in intensity, depending on, Salaamat realized, nothing at all. It was haphazard, random. It could involve assembling and disassembling Kalashnikovs more deftly than lacing boots, pitching tents one-handed (while the Commander, shining the Winchester, timed them with a stopwatch), or firing pistols at a mark in the center of a slab of sandstone. The last was what he thought he'd enjoy most, except the acoustics in the gorge were wreaking havoc with his left eardrum. If his hearing had fluctuated before coming here, now he heard too much. His eardrum was a golden whistle and the slightest sound was augmented by several decibels. He learned to shoot little but with expert precision, and became better than most who'd trained longer. He used the cheap Tokarev .22 – slept with it, ate with it, never leaving it in the tent even when others appeared to be resting. Tempers flared quickly here.

Then there were sit-ups, push-ups, jogs along the length of the beach in the blazing heat with weighted backpacks. Or the men wrestled – half scuffling, half kicking. Or scaled the steepest reaches of the cliffs while the Commander frowned deeply behind the little stopwatch. This was Fatah's forte. He was like a well-fed goat – sure-footed and taut around the gut. Compact, but strong. Salaamat had control but Fatah agility, and Salaamat let himself be lured into betting away most of his cigarettes because he loved watching Fatah leap past him as eagerly as the children swimming out to the anchor line in his village had done. Fatah would turn and smile back in the same way: *Look. I did it.*

When they weren't training, the men slept, played cards, argued, or disappeared in twos and threes behind rocks. Salaamat and Fatah explored the gorge like boys on a field trip. The floor was carpeted with soft pine needles and pigeon shit. Some of the bluffs resembled white volcanic ash, too soft to climb but pitted into chimney shapes so that from the shore, the tiers were like an army of ghosts presiding over them.

Fatah liked to hop up the cones and peer through the natural windows. He'd strut like the Commander. 'So. Let us not forget why we are here!'

If Salaamat didn't play along he'd smack the back of his head and strut some more till Salaamat, taking pity on him, squealed, 'Why are we here, sir!'

'Why, you fool. To fight for a separate Sindhi homeland!' Then he'd pretend to brush his teeth.

He was two years younger than Salaamat but had already killed three men.

Today they climbed nimbly up the pass for a better view of the eagle's nest. Fatah spoke of the last raid he'd been in. Two men on a motorcycle were rounding a bend off the highway when Fatah and three others opened fire. One man had two thousand rupees on him. The other had nothing but a photograph in his wallet. They were shot in the limbs and then Muhammad Shah wanted to try the stun belt recently acquired from Amreeka. So they took the men to the cell farther inland but on the way one bled to death. The other was still in the cell, alive.

A sheer wall blocked their path so they retraced their steps and looked for another way up. Fatah explained that though the Commander was a chichra, he was right about a few things. They really could never forget where they were. 'Who we are and how we end up depends entirely on gigraphy.'

Salaamat said nothing. Fatah liked to talk about geography as much as he liked to win bets. And Salaamat rarely interrupted because Fatah was awesome. He'd gone to school. Real school. He had books he could read. He'd even attended a few months of university. He was not from an old village like Salaamat. He grew up in Karachi and had a kind of worldly air about him that was foolish to refute. While Salaamat had wasted his time painting buses, Fatah had been scanning the highways. He knew more. And he thought more too. He had a clear philosophy, while Salaamat simply drifted.

Fatah reminded him that he too would have to kill one day soon. Salaamat walked faster, losing sight of the ledge completely.

They paused on an outcrop. The river looked immensely blue from here. In a few months, when it rained, the glaciers of the north would melt and pour into it, hurling gray debris.

What would he have done by then?

He liked to shoot, it was true, but he didn't know about

changing his target. He didn't want to be pinned down to that. Maybe he'd do it, maybe not, but it was wrong to judge him on that alone.

The truth was he wished sometimes that the camp weren't in such a beautiful place. It should have been in a filthy burning city street. In the charred backseat of an overturned bus. The stinking hole Handsome's workers shat in. Instead it was here, in an isolated patch in the far north of the province. Fatah said most camps were further south, where the banks were heavily forested. Maybe that would have been better. More confining. Dark. These capacious rocks spoke to him. He'd joined the camp thinking it would be his way to at last shrivel up and die, but if anything, the opposite had happened. Salaamat was beginning to like his world again.

The sand beneath his toes, the scent of the river, the way his hair blew out of the twine of grass binding it, the sky free of dust and haze, the feathery sisky leaves – all refreshed him. Though a strong fighter and accurate shot, he fulfilled his duties with a minimum of interest and his spirit wandered. Instead of distancing himself from the land, he was entering it. And he grew unconvinced that the answer to all his troubles was a separate state. If anything, this land the others wanted to split was showing him how to glue back his splintered pieces.

But Fatah was awesome and he was scratching a map of Pakistan on the powdery outcrop. He knew the country's contours from memory. He could draw several countries freehand. He said the map of the world was in his hands. Now he rubbed and fine-tuned the lines, and said, 'Pakistan is easy – an arm extending from China into the Arabian Sea, with the thumb and little finger sticking out sideways like that.' He crouched on his haunches and pulled the hem of Salaamat's ratty trousers, forcing him down too. 'Sindh is the thumb. Notice none of the countries that affect us most have any shape to speak of. Afghanistan is a shapeless glob.

What is Russia? Amreeka? Big like Anjuman but with none of her curves. A bump here, a finger there. Granted, India has some shape. But look at Sulawesi! She has arms, legs, even a braid!'

Fatah also kept meticulous track of what each country exported to theirs, as Salaamat had witnessed in Hero's shop. He said those claiming that Sindh couldn't stand on its own were wrong – they had only to learn to make the equipment and then sell it to others even worse off. 'Maybe the people of Sulawesi!'

Salaamat nodded yet his spirit walked away. There was no way to get any closer to the eagle's nest from here. They should turn around and start again. But the spot was well shaded, and a pleasing wind wafted in from the river sweeping placidly below.

Fatah went on, 'So, about this thumb. We are what we are because we've lived on it for thousands of years. Once it had pride. Now it has a cuff around it. It's been bent and beaten and the blood's been shut off. It dangles impotently. To stand erect, it has to break free.'

Salaamat knew by blood, Fatah meant the Indus. He'd spoken many times of the dams in the Punjab that were choking off the supply. That province teemed with life from five opulent rivers but it had to have more. 'More is what the Punjab is all about,' he'd say. 'More food, more water, more wealth, more hideously fat men like that Handsome you speak of.' In much of Sindh, the Indus had dwindled to a trickle.

Salaamat's village too had teemed with talk of this. There were fishermen who depended on fish that in turn depended on the mangroves that once flourished in the estuaries. With the fresh water cut off, the trees were withering, and the fish dying. Many of these villagers too had had to leave, and, like Salaamat, bow to those who displaced them. He'd tell Fatah of his nights of rage at Handsome's, and how ridiculous it was that Handsome's workers complained of those that displaced them. Fatah would seethe: They're all bastards. All of them. That's why we're here.

The first thing the Bullets did when they captured someone was cuff his thumbs and the last, dispose of the body in the river.

Salaamat took a deep breath of the stream of pure air floating around him. The day he'd watched his bus burn, he'd thought he could never find beauty again. He wished he'd been right. He wished God hadn't lodged that something in him which stubbornly refused to shut down. He wished he didn't feel God when he heard the eagle's chicks greet her. He could will himself into a steel nugget, yes, better, in fact, than anyone here. But it was a superficial nugget, as easily rejected as summoned. Beneath the skin, he was as vulnerable as he ever had been.

Fatah began descending the cliff. 'We're not getting any-where with those birds.' Salaamat followed.

They were dropping fast, to a familiar expanse of wild flowers. In amongst the rug of mulch, well hidden by the brittle grass, was a tin can. The other men also hid their supplies here. Fatah's was a can of liquor, bought from the Mohanas who lived further up the river. Salaamat took a swig and passed it back to Fatah. It was made from oranges and tasted like jackal piss, but he liked it anyway.

When the can was half consumed Fatah returned to mimicking the Commander. '*You can see those sons-of-owl fish eggs from the tallest cliffs on the banks*. Hey, there we are, slimy yellow fish eggs! You *can* see us from up here.'

'No you can't,' Salaamat punched him lightly. 'Give me the can.' After two hefty gulps he said, 'My God you're right!' They laughed so hard their sides ached, and when they shrieked the valley answered back. This made them laugh even harder.

Suddenly Fatah asked, 'What's the best sex you ever had?'

Again, peals of laughter.

Salaamat faced his friend. 'You know, you're a total rectangle.'

'Get lost. You came out of your mother feet first.'

'Your head is rectangular, your hands are rectangular, even your smile is rectangular.' He squinted. Yes, Fatah was shaped like a tree-trunk, with a mop of stiff hair for leaves. He took another mouthful of the tangerine torture. 'Your teeth too. Rectangular.'

'Give me that,' Fatah snatched the can. 'It's frying your brain.'

'In a rectangle.'

They exploded again.

Fatah smacked Salaamat's cheek and wheezed. 'So, who was your best fuck?'

The sun was dipping behind the cliffs on the opposite shore. It must have been about four o'clock. The men would be coming back from the highway, and from the Chief's. He remembered the women Chikna would sometimes take him to. Oily-skinned, with mascara-clogged eyes. In tight kameezes they'd little to flaunt besides rolls of stomach fat. Never like Rani. But he'd undressed each while thinking of her, so his knees didn't bruise from thrusting into a whore on a plank of wood covered by a filthy cloth stained with blood and semen. He didn't taste grime or smell the sweet cakey odor of her make-up as it blended with her sweat. Air didn't pass through her broken teeth as she snarled, 'Enough!' No, he had her positioned in front of a waterfall, just like the one in Dia's house. Standing, and with the sunlight falling directly on the outer bend of her slightly fuller, left breast.

He whispered, 'The best was in a cascade.'

'Ah!' Fatah admired. 'Now that's something I never did.'

'I wanted her stripped to the waist only. Then I took her shoulders and turned her first to the left, then the right. That way the fountain hit each breast exactly at the point where it swelled like a cup, just around the nipple. That's the best part of a woman's body.'

'Her neck was long and white,' Fatah nodded dreamily.

'Her eyes so innocent, so afraid.'

'But what about *below*?' Fatah frowned.

'That too,' Salaamat smiled mysteriously. 'After an hour or so. She was wearing a green silk petticoat. It was soaked through.'

'Yes. I can see it. Her long hair is drenched. One thick strand clings to a breast. Water drips around and around her smooth cool nipple. You smell her flowery shampoo as you taste the teat.'

'That's when I unhook the petticoat.'

'It's too wet to fall down itself. You help. Your fingers slide over the silk around her bottom.'

'The biggest, roundest, most generous bottom God ever made.'

'You cannot wait. You push the slip up instead of down.'

'Her thighs are cold but inside, she is a soft, warm blanket.'

On the grass they lay perfectly still, their shoulders touching. Salaamat only now realized they were touching. Fatah barely breathed. Slowly, Salaamat turned his head and looked at him. A total rectangle. Eyes still shut. Thick dark lips parted slightly and twitching. Jaw heavy, forehead furrowed. Pictures still fluttering beneath those squeezed eyelids. Muscles contorting as he struggled to maintain his concentration. A mud-colored shalwar in whose side pocket bulged a pistol – a Ruger. Men could upgrade from Soviet to American firearms after they'd killed someone. Yes. In the center of Fatah's body was another bulge. Like his lips, also twitching.

Salaamat plucked a stalk of yellow grass. He saw movement to the left of his vision – probably a squirrel. He whispered, 'And when we're done I lay her down behind the fountain, and we look out at the curtain of drops. I dry her like this.'

He twirled the flower on Fatah's nose. 'And like this.' Very gently, he kissed his lips.

Fatah did not immediately respond, nor open his eyes. Salaamat kissed his forehead, then the gray pits beneath his eyes. He brushed his dark leathery cheeks with the flower and kissed the lips harder.

This time hands came up. They grabbed Salaamat's locks, yanking him close. Teeth struck his mouth. A tongue sought his with a hunger that made him choke.

'I bet even your navel's a rectangle,' Salaamat whispered, helping Fatah undress. He bent down as though, at twenty, to finally give thanks.

2

Discipline

JUNE 1987

His first test came the following month.

He got into the back of an open jeep where six men already waited. Fatah draped an arm around him.

After driving south a few kilometers, the driver turned into a dirt track heading east. One of the men put a blindfold around Salaamat.

'You can trust him,' Fatah grumbled.

'Those are the rules,' the man replied flatly, 'till the Chief says otherwise.'

Salaamat was not surprised Fatah raised no further objection. He worshipped the Chief. Still, he'd have liked Fatah to throw more allegiance his way. Of the eight men in the jeep, he was the only one they blindfolded. He thought: I am to be the blind, deaf and dumb witness again.

The jeep stalled several times and he heard men get out to heave rocks from its path. Sometimes Fatah would leave too. Once, another man settled back beside him, resting an elbow on Salaamat's thigh. When he spoke Salaamat recognized the heavyset man everyone called Gharyaal Bhai, because he boasted of being able to wrestle a crocodile with one arm tied behind him.

Behind the cloth, Salaamat's eyelids flickered, alert to the land they couldn't see. There was a creek flowing – he caught the gentle music as it tumbled by. Woodpeckers knocked at towering gates. Jackals hid in caves, panting softly as the jeep's tires groaned past their lair. The ravine echoed with bullets fired by the group back at the camp. The noise bounced from cliff to cliff, weaving a web around him. Branches brushed him; threads caught in his hair.

The Chief, the others said, had a bulletproof vest made of spider silk, just like Genghis Khan did. Salaamat thought of Sumbul back on the farm, enmeshed in a different silk. She told him once what Dia had told her: tiny creatures spit the strongest materials on the planet. Bigger creatures stole them to pretend they were strong.

So here he was now, on his way to the biggest creature of all. That's what Fatah called him: bigger than Russia and Amreeka put together (but still no curves).

The trees thinned and his head burned. Sweat poured down his back. The creek was gone. The jeep accelerated. The jackals ran away.

When next the vehicle halted, his blindfold was torn off. His head throbbed. He'd never before seen such glare. The clearing was drenched in it. It pierced his eyes and seared his brain. When they led him to the house his eyes were only half-open.

'Ha ha!' the others laughed. 'What you're about to see will make you open them all the way!'

Fatah smacked his back. 'You're going to make me proud.'

There were two buildings: one the Chief's, the other for purposes. If he fulfilled his purpose well, he could meet the Chief.

Muhammad Shah came out of the Chief's bungalow with keys to the second building. He unbolted a door and they all stepped into solid darkness. After a few moments, with the aid of the glare flooding in from the open door, Salaamat could make out a man tied to a chair. He was blindfolded and gagged. He was naked.

More men from the Chief's bungalow followed them inside. When they untied the man he did not change his position, did not even stretch an arm or shrug loose knots from his shoulders. When they pulled off the blindfold his eyes remained shut. Salaamat thought: he can't stand the light. And when they ungagged him and he did not open his mouth, Salaamat wondered if the captive was even alive.

The men spoke in his tongue but Salaamat said nothing to them. He was back to talking to himself. He was afraid. The room smelled of shit. It was smaller than his cell at Handsome's. He saw no bedroll. How long had the man been here? Was he the one Fatah had spoken of weeks ago – the one with the two thousand rupees or the picture?

The door shut. Flashlights came on. Muhammad Shah passed one to him. Addressing all of them, the First Lieutenant said, 'This man has mastered the art of shrinking. He does not see, does not eat or drink, listen or even feel. Let me show you.' The butt of his machine gun struck the back of the man's neck. He leaned three inches forward and hung still.

'See?' Muhammad Shah puckered his lips, impressed. 'This is discipline. He has willed himself into a tiny steel nugget. Sadly, that's no fun for us, is it?' He grinned, kicking the man's shin.

Salaamat barely even saw it. The back of his neck throbbed as though a frog were lodged there. There was one on each side of his neck too. And one at each temple. Every time they belched, his ears rang.

The other men closed in on the seated man, the perfect

bullet. 'I can crack him,' someone said. He lifted an eyelid and shone his torch.

Ri-bit, the frogs replied, pulsing under Salaamat's skin.

Fatah pulled him close. 'You haven't switched your flashlight on, stupid.'

Salaamat flipped the smooth tip under his thumb.

'See those thumb cuffs?' Salaamat looked. 'From Germany.' The circle of iron enclosing each thumb was banded in flesh. Fatah shone his light there like a surgeon at an operating table. Salaamat peered down. 'It took many days for the cuff to saw through the bone. First it just slipped around, tearing skin, and the wound was only pink. Now look.' It was turning green. Even the decoration police had never done that to him. Salaamat pressed the side of his neck. A lump moved between his fingers.

Fatah continued, 'Gharyaal Bhai bets another week before the thumb falls off. I say just two more days. What do you think? If you're right we'll tell the Chief.' Then he grew distracted by Muhammad Shah.

Salaamat did not follow him. He'd at last found the courage to look at the man, really look at him. He was wearing leg irons. The legs were so badly cut it was as if a hairbrush made of blades had been run across them. The hair grew in sticky patches. The knees were swollen. Above them, the thighs too were studded with cuts and bruises. Thighs like a plucked chicken's, with barely any flesh at all. And what about *there*, Salaamat flashed his torch higher up the thighs. What had they done to *that*?

He couldn't look.

Yes he could.

Up, up, there in the center, just below another straggly, sticky bush matted with something brown, and something white.

He could not look.

367

He switched his light off.

He was the one being violated. Angrily, he turned to demand of Fatah: Who did everyone think he was? A damn puppet?

But Fatah was still with Muhammad Shah, who was handing him something like a wheel. In his own hands, Muhammad Shah held a knot of wires. A third man fiddled with a switch.

'He looked! He looked!' Another squealed. It was the one who'd shone the torch in the captive's eyes. 'He opened them! I swear he did!' Then he frowned, 'You did, you bastard, admit it!' He began kicking him.

'Shut up, mouse. If you keep on we'll wire this all wrong and what good will that do our friend?' They laughed.

The man by the switch said, 'Try it now.'

Muhammad Shah pressed a button. Everyone cheered. 'All right, strap it on.'

There was resistance now. Hands with broken thumbs fought men that slipped the ring around the head. The head that Salaamat now saw closely. The narrow dome with scars and bald patches, finally opening its eyes. Red eyes, with an expression he'd never known in a human face. Like burning metal. Yes, if his bus had had eyes, it would have looked out at the world like that. It would have looked left at the torch lighting the pictures of the glittery golden fish. 'Don't touch!' it would scream. 'That's mine!' It would look right at the forest of lofty trees, where the preening parrots were set ablaze. It would look out of a ring-of-fire and keep looking till the eyes had burned. But before that, it would look at him.

Salaamat flinched. A moan moved up from his guts and pealed through the darkness. It was not a moan, it was vomit, and it was stuck in his nose. A drunk man was punching his stomach while another struck his head.

He dropped to his knees. Three feet away, a turtle was done laying her eggs. He was being dragged to the sea. He was vomiting oyster-white albumen, blood, and something green.

In the room flickering with torchlight, the stun belt was now firmly around the captive who'd shut his eyes again. Salaamat saw the laughter; he didn't hear it. It was as if the room had sunk underwater. When men moved, they moved slowly. When they talked, he heard waves. Muhammad Shah pressed a switch on a square slab of black plastic. A current shot through the captive's sides and his head and torso jerked. The hands flew. The legs in iron danced. If the shackles jingled he didn't hear them. He was swimming away. He tasted salt and then he felt a shell. The captive was in his arms.

Ride, ride, Salaamat said to him.

Ri-bit came the reply.

The room stank and the men held their noses. They passed the switch around like a tube of oxygen. Soon it was his turn to take a hit. He held it but did nothing. The man still convulsed.

Why do you twitch when I have not yet shocked you? he asked.

Ri-bit.

Well then, if I do shock you what is the difference?

The man was still thrusting.

Should I try?

Ri-bit.

He moved the switch just barely, pretending to strike it.

The man jerked even more furiously, writhing in his own shit.

Pretend. Jerk. Pretend. Jerk.

The men were laughing soundlessly. Clapping too. Splashing him from head to toe. Smacking his back. Only the

369

thumps never landed, because you could never thump someone underwater. Pretend. Jerk.

He passed the button to the next man, who silently
congratulated him on fulfilling his purpose. Nobody knew
he hadn't done a thing. Not even the captive.

3

Fate

'You know I run faster than you,' called Fatah. 'Stop trying to outdo me.' He caught up with Salaamat, who turned and ducked into a cramped bed of pine needles. 'I thought the Chief gave you fair marks but you're failing the after-test.' He plunked down, squeezing beside him.

Salaamat sucked on a cigarette and passed it to Fatah who smoked, like the Chief, by pulling on his fist. A kingfisher perched in the fissure of a rock, then dived out of sight, into the river. He surfaced again, his wings a span of jet black and brilliant white. The tuft around his forehead fanned out in the wind, like a lily.

It was good Fatah came after him but he wished to be alone.

'You didn't even look at me at practice this morning,' Fatah complained. 'And why didn't you wait before coming up here?'

He said nothing.

'Oh my Rani.' Fatah tickled him. 'What blue, blue eyes you have!'

Salaamat slid free, pressing deeper into the rocks cupping them.

'You're very boring today,' he frowned. 'Acha listen, answer my riddle. What's the best sex the Commander ever had?'

Salaamat lit another cigarette and exhaled in a slow tunnel.

'When he brushed his wife's teeth with keekar!' He plucked a pine needle from the floor and rolled over Salaamat, prying his mouth open, forcing the stick inside.

Salaamat threw him off. 'Stop it!'

Fatah's temper rose. 'You're a bitch, you know that? A good-for-nothing cowardly bitch.'

'Why do you make fun of the Commander when you're just the same?' Salaamat snapped suddenly.

'Me? *I* would do a much better job.'

'So that's it. You want to be the one who gets to stand in the shade, shining the Winchester?'

Fatah reached for his kurta collar but before he could strike, Salaamat leaped over the rock. In the chase, Salaamat found he'd finally become the swifter one. He raced up massive boulders without needing any footholds, running through thorns fearlessly. He felt exhilarated.

'See?' Fatah yelled from below. 'You're running away. Just like a coward. Come down and fight!'

Salaamat panted. There were no trees at this height. The sun blazed down and he felt a sting under his right ear. Touching it, he saw blood. But he was on top of the world. They'd never been this far up before. He called down, 'If you were commander, what would you say to your men every morning?'

There was no answer. The barbed mesquite blocked his view. Maybe Fatah was drawing closer. He pushed on.

Then he heard: 'I'd tell them if it weren't for the Chief they'd be nothing. That we can be anything we want, and

get anything we want, all because of him. And I'm telling you you've got a second test coming up so don't be
stupid.'

Salaamat paused again, barely even able to remember his
meeting with the Chief afterwards. He'd felt none of Fatah's
wonder in the presence of the nondescript man seated on a
takht, leaning on satin pillows. Half a dozen men surrounded
him with fans and refreshments. All carried machine guns.
A young boy, perhaps twelve, hunkered at the Chief's feet,
pressing his calves. Another stood behind the takht massaging
his shoulders. There was a trial underway. A quarrel in a
village. He hadn't listened to the details, but there was a
woman sobbing, and an elderly man pleading for protection
and justice. He presented a gift, which Salaamat remembered
well: a rocket-launching missile wreathed in a garland of pink
flowers.

'So this is your group's best shot?' The Chief pointed at
Salaamat when he was introduced.

'It is indeed,' Fatah bowed. 'Kneel!' he hissed at Salaamat.
He knelt.

While details of the torture were graphically presented, the
Chief examined Salaamat. There were sounds from another
room. Plates banging. Women talking. The boy at the Chief's
feet lit an imported cigarette and passed it to him. He cupped
his fist, inhaling loudly.

Salaamat remembered little after that. Just that his eyes
went from the sad, tattered old man to the gift to the Chief
and the sickness he'd felt in the cell transformed to hate,
especially when the Chief concluded, 'Well done,' and swiftly
dismissed them.

And when blindfolded again in the jeep, he'd been grateful
for the chance to shut his eyes. That's all he wanted to do:
shut his eyes. Sleep for days.

Now he looked about him. The river appeared motionless
from here, a sheet of blue tranquility, with yellow glitter

bubbling down. The air smelled wholesome. They'd eat carp for dinner. This was all good.

He called out to Fatah, 'And what if I don't want to take it?'

The answer was swift and came from nearer. 'Who says you have a choice?'

'I thought we could get anything we wanted?'

'Depends on who's giving it.'

Still higher. There were green dots on the shore and black specks rolling in and out of them like peppercorns. He felt he could scoop them all into a jar and toss the lot into the Indus.

He said, 'What if I don't need anyone to give me anything?'

'You'd be killed.'

Salaamat stopped. 'Is that a threat?'

'It's the rule.'

Fatah was too close now. 'And no one changes the rules?'

'You've learned well. No one but the Chief.'

He could see him now, behind a dense bush. His thick, bristly hair was a mess and he cursed while trying to leap across the thorns. Salaamat lowered his voice. 'How long had that man been locked up?'

Fatah looked up, plucking thistles from his sleeve. 'I don't remember. Who can recognize any of them after the first week? There were many cells you know, all of them occupied, so relax.'

He could tell Fatah's humor had changed. He let him catch up with him. Three feet away, he bent at the waist, breathing like he'd just climbed Rakaposhi. It was his turn to say nothing; he was exhausted.

'What's happened to you?' Salaamat snarled. 'The Commander could climb faster. I should have placed a bet. Won back all my cigarettes.' He lit another one. Then: 'When you see those men, don't you wonder what it would be like to live in your own shit?'

Fatah had collapsed on a rock. When he got his breath back he shook his head. 'I wish I'd known how stupid you were before I climbed all the way up here. Live in my own shit? I have lived in my own shit. And as long as I give my land to everyone else, I'll continue living in it.'

'You live in it because you talk shit,' Salaamat spat.

Fatah threw his head back and laughed. 'This country is a sister-fucking urinal, my foolish friend. Who hasn't pissed in it? Have you gone to the mountains? Those fools are so cocky because they think they're descended from Alexander! They're proud his army raped their women because now they have white skin and eyes even bluer than yours. And what about the British? The Afghans? How much do we have to share with those bloody Pathans because of their war? How many of us will the General keep sending, so we don't see who we really have to fight? Even the Gulf Arabs fart here. Taking our children, taking our workforce. You know what my brother did when he went there? They told him he could work on their jets, but what did he do? He cleaned air toilets! And the Amreekans, why should we work for them? Why do our leaders wag their fat bottoms in their face, begging, Pat me! Rub your slime all over me! Pah! Everyone in this country is a lapdog of someone who isn't from here.'

'You're a lapdog too.'

'I'm the lapdog of someone who represents my land. You can either be faithful, or you can be a traitor. There is no other way.'

Salaamat folded his arms. His gaze drifted down Fatah's long broad nose, always a little oily. When he was worked up, especially during target practice, he'd wipe the grease with the back of his right thumb and smear it on his chest. He did that now.

Salaamat sighed. 'You can belong to the land, instead of forcing it to belong to you . . .' He was beginning to sound stupid even to himself.

Fatah spat another laugh. It sounded like, Chuff! Then he did it again. Chuff! 'You're just a no-good dreamer. The Koreans took your sea, but you learned nothing. The Punjabis took your sweat, still you learned nothing. The Urdu-speakers burned your bus: nothing. The Pathans took your first pay: nothing again. It's not just land and sea they all want. They want the air we breathe. And what does this country do? It begs them to take it. It says, please, please, stick millions of dollars into our fat bottoms and own us all! Just let me keep my car, my house, my job. But I promise I won't let those who've lived here for thousands of years have any of it!' Fatah jabbed the air with his rectangular chin and pronounced, 'No. If you don't control them, they control you.'

Salaamat looked away. 'That man yesterday was controlling no one. Not even himself.' He wondered for the millionth time: was anyone else in there only pretending to push the button?

'If we'd let him go he'd be part of the system that controls us.'

'If you'd let him go you'd never even see him again.'

'You're wrong. He'd be the one to take my car, house, and job. He'd be in my space and I would see him everywhere. With every man I kill, I make a little more room for my people. For us.'

They stared at each other. Fatah's sunken eyes were not angry now. They were cold and set. If Salaamat weren't on his side, he'd also be in his way.

But he wanted neither. He just wanted to be here, at the top of the world.

Fatah continued, 'He's nearing the end, anyway. If we don't destroy him, someone or something else will. And if it's not him, it's someone else. See? The Commander is wrong. We don't have to target the bullet. No, we have to let it fly. Fate takes care of the rest. I wouldn't be a freedom fighter if I weren't meant to be. That man wouldn't be in our cell if he weren't meant to be. See? There's a bigger force on our side. Everything is clear and simple.'

'One day it'll fly at you.'

'I know. And I'll embrace it proudly.' He tossed his head. 'If I were commander, *that's* what I'd tell my men every morning.'

Salaamat shook his head. 'I'm wasting my time talking to you. Leave me now.'

'Your time? Your time belongs to us.' Then he looked around him. 'I bet no one down there's ever climbed so high. Look at them! Smaller than rabbit dung!'

The peppercorn-men still mulled around on the shore and now there were two bread loaves whirring through the sand. Jeeps. The men had returned from the Chief's. They'd speak of him later tonight, as they ate by the campfire. Maybe they'd brought supplies. They were running low on cigarettes and sugar.

He shut his eyes: the burning metal eyes of yesterday's captive now lived behind his own. They said: the fat, drunk poacher with the woman waiting in the hut, the one who'd nearly killed him years ago in his village, Salaamat had become him.

What if he could erase yesterday? What were a few hours in an entire lifetime? That's all they were: a few hours. Efface them! Be gone!

Pretend. Jerk. Pretend. Jerk.

He cringed.

Did the man even have a mind somewhere inside that convulsing body? Could he have had a single thought left in him?

And what would his last thought have been?

He couldn't know, but he could see it. It would look like Handsome's favorite dish: brain. He cursed his own for bringing the picture to him. Little slimy noodles in a wet pulp. That was what sat in the writhing man's skull. The button was a benign black circle, soft to the touch. And each time it went down, those little slimy noodles flared out, out, out, a sea anemone yawning. Slow, graceful undulations. Soft, powdery hues. Out, out, out, only there was nowhere to go so they started moving down, and around, and soon there were knots, and the knots were angry because there was no space, and then they just shot off. One by one, each noodle burst out into nothingness, and there was a terrific fight between the remaining knots because they each saw now what would happen to them, and even when it didn't happen, it did. So off they went. Panic in the sea. Mayhem in the seat. One little noodle left screaming, Oh please God, help me. Just wipe off my shit.

He turned around and began to scramble down, on the other side. Why was he torturing himself? Why wasn't Fatah?

Fatah followed him down a precipice. 'Leave me,' Salaamat pleaded.

'I will not.' Fatah had got his old speed back and skipped beside him, whistling. Then he broke into song, '*On your red lips, if only once, my name would fall . . .*'

Salaamat shut it out. He never knew love could surge with a hatred this fierce.

The rocks were gashed in places by deep gullies that pitched dangerously. Salaamat carefully maneuvered the ridges, feeling deftly for notches, and even Fatah held his breath. But eventually, the slopes flattened closer to the angle of the riverbank. Salaamat hurried on, stepping at last into a leafy path. Then, all of a sudden, a few feet below, he spotted a small field of a flowering crop.

'Well imagine this!' Fatah halted. 'There must be an underground spring nearby. Let's go see.' They jumped down the last incline and were level with the shore. Fatah turned into the field, tearing a handful of blossoms. 'Smell. Sweet as honey!' He slid the bouquet into Salaamat's hand.

Salaamat took it sadly.

Fatah stopped, astonished. 'I know where we are! This is the closest Mohana village to us. Who knew it could be accessed from here? Takes for ever by road. Look,' he pointed to a row of orange trees. 'I bet we can fill up on tangerine torture!'

There was a small thatched hut and in the distance, the kind of Mohana boathouse sometimes seen drifting down the river past their campsite: flat-bottomed with a high prow and a canopy of reeds. The boats were big, often with two or three families in residence. This one was about ten feet long – nothing resembling the smaller, canoe-shaped boats of his village. Fatah was right about the spring: an ox turned the wheels of a water pump.

Salaamat was wondering how they'd got the huge animal all the way here when Fatah gently tugged his sleeve. 'Sit with me a while before we go any further. Here, in this beautiful bower.' He pulled him into the shade of an orange tree, and reclined his head on Salaamat's shoulder. He was the shorter one so when they lay with feet together, his hair brushed Salaamat's ear. He kissed it loudly. The ear started ringing.

Fatah said, 'If it weren't for the Chief, I'd go to Sulawesi.'

Salaamat folded his arms. His Sulawesi was down there, with the Mohana fishermen.

'You're supposed to say, "What's in Sulawesi?"' When Salaamat still wouldn't answer, he sang, '*I've nursed you like the beat of my heart. I've snatched you from the hands of fate.*'

'I'm going across.' Salaamat pulled away. He stood up and began walking.

Fatah followed. 'All right. I'll buy the drink if you stop being so foolish.'

Children were running along the bank, calling out to two women washing clothes in the river. They held strings in their hands, though Salaamat couldn't see what was tied to the ends. Not kites, something much smaller. One woman looked up and saw him approach. She sent a child into the hut, probably to call the men. Salaamat now saw what the boy had on the end of his string: a dragonfly, beating violet wings as the child twirled the line around and around.

4

The Highway

Salaamat was roused early in the tent he shared with five others. 'Get up!' A man shoved him with the barrel of his gun. 'Time to go.' He peered out from under a grimy sheet, grabbing the man's arm with one hand, his pistol with the other. It was Gharyaal Bhai, and his watch showed just after three o'clock.

'We have a long journey,' the man grinned. He prodded him once more, gently this time. Salaamat stumbled out with him.

Fatah had already washed himself. Under the stars his mop of hair shone like a cannonball, dripping over a beaming face. He thumped Salaamat's shoulder. 'Ready for test number two, meri jaan?'

Salaamat dunked his head in the dark river. He shook it dry, spraying Fatah. 'What's the hurry? There's going to be no one on the highway to rob at this hour.'

'We don't rob. We clean. And you'll be surprised how many cars we'll find, especially around Thatta.'

Salaamat stared at him. Fatah knew his family worked on a farm near there. Why had he planned it this way? 'Why do we have to go that far south? It will take hours.'

Fatah smiled mysteriously. 'We have hours. We might even make it back in time for a quick walk up the gorge, just you and me.' He winked, walking away.

One minute Salaamat loved him, the next Fatah was everything he despised. Everything. Anger welled inside him as he joined the half a dozen others awake now too. He helped collect sticks for the fire, his mind racing. What was he, the wife in this marriage?

Gharyaal Bhai made the tea. The jeep hadn't brought supplies yesterday. They were down to drinking hot water with only enough leaves and milk powder for color. There was no sugar. Rusks were in short supply. No one betted away cigarettes. The Commander said it was all part of the discipline. No one argued. He was the Chief's brother-in-law.

But in private, the men said the Commander had hidden sugar packets under his tent, which was why he never allowed his to be assembled and disassembled during morning drill. They swore they'd seen him digging up sacks in the middle of the night, shoveling crystals down his throat like a lunatic.

Fatah took the first cup Gharyaal Bhai poured. The men let him. He was, Salaamat had only recently discovered, First Lieutenant Muhammad Shah's brother-in-law. Salaamat scowled: if everyone around him was related to the Chief in some way, wasn't he the outsider again?

The other men too were growing increasingly sullen. They were losing weight. Only a visit to the Chief's lair or an expedition to the highway animated them. They seemed to be thinking of this while sipping the hot water daubed with token Lipton leaves. In silence, they prayed together for parathas, chat, halwa puri, fresh milk. When no miracle hand served them, they talked about Thatta. 'We can always get rewri there,' someone said, and the others cheered up.

From across the fire Fatah called out to him, 'Oh Rani, the Chief said if you pass this test too all of us can get as many dishes of rewri as we want.'

A few men snickered. Though he didn't like Fatah mocking him this way in public, Salaamat knew many of the others had paired up, some even in his tent. There was plenty of fire to throw around.

After the measly breakfast, they headed for the jeep. This time no one blindfolded him. He sat, as on the trip to the Chief's, beside Fatah. The vehicle wove through dense thickets, sometimes paralleling the river, at others cutting perpendicular to it. A lank sunrise slowly crept around them, bringing the flutter of birds and the silence of crickets.

Gharyaal Bhai reached over and pinched Salaamat's cheek. 'You'd better pass because I'm getting very hungry.' Conversation returned to food. Men exchanged notes on the best dessert ever made by their mothers. As excitement escalated, each man praised his own mother at the expense of another's. Abuse flailed. Fatah, disgusted, growled, 'Conserve your strength.' He forbade anyone to speak of sweets till they were actually being eaten. A sullen silence descended again.

Further south, the level of the Indus began to drop. Fatah's jaw muscles twitched. 'They've stolen our Sindhu.' The others nodded, urging him to continue. He did. 'Once we called it the life of the lower valley. What valley? This is a desert. What life? We're being buried alive.' He recited the famous lines: '*With homes on the river bank, those who die of thirst, die of their own making.*'

There was consensual muttering, '. . . *Of their own making.*'

Salaamat watched his friend, feeling the performance was delivered partly to show him what a fine commander he'd make.

The jeep took a short cut through the dry riverbed, kicking up dust. It was June but the monsoons gave no hint of calling.

383

The sun rode beside them, stealing up from the parched land, roasting everything in sight. To preserve his saliva, even Fatah talked less.

Finally, they turned onto the National Highway. Salaamat again thought of his family. They were getting too close to the farm where his sister worked. He looked around him. Judging from the height of the sun, it was close to seven o'clock. They were near Keenjhar Lake; the farm was perhaps an hour away. Sumbul wouldn't have arrived yet. He wished she had. What if their jeep intercepted her bus? He tried to remember which bus she took in from her husband's house in the city, and what time it got to the farm. He realized he'd never asked her these basic questions. Now his mind swarmed with many others: if the men conducted raids this far south, who was to say she was safe, ever, not just today? And what about his brothers, Shan and Hamid, whom he always brushed by carelessly at the gate? And his father? Salaamat sighed with relief. The old man did not commute to the farm. He was safe.

It was the first time he'd thought of the old man with anything but disdain. What was happening to him? His stomach felt woozy. Liquid was floating in there. He squeezed his rectum and pressed a hand to his gut to stop the pain.

His thoughts returned to Sumbul. He saw her again with a baby suckling her Fanta-cap nipple. She looked beautifully up at him, the deep blue lapis lazuli stones as dazzling as her smile. He swallowed: what did the men do to the women and children on board the buses?

Fatah was still scowling at the naked riverbed. 'It looks obscene,' he declared.

'What kind of vehicles get stopped?' Salaamat tried.

'Nice ones,' Gharyaal Bhai flashed his teeth.

'Not buses then?'

Someone else volunteered, 'Depends.'

Fatah looked him full in the face. 'You'll do whatever's expected.'

And then they turned west and Thatta flew by. They weren't stopping. The arches of Shah Jehan's Mosque receded like a massive ribcage: white bone after bone after bone.

But then there was a bus. It was heading toward them. They headed toward the bus.

Neither stopped.

Salaamat grew teary with relief.

They passed the farm. Inside, perhaps his brothers had already taken their place at the gate. He turned, but saw nothing – no shadows, no movement. Months later, when he saw it again, there'd be armed guards stationed there. But not today. Now they were entering the strip where his family commuted daily: between Makli Hill and Karachi. He could see the dome of the bat-infested tomb. Not long ago, he'd been witness to a secret tryst there. He carried that secret with him, down the National Highway, and the terror of intercepting Sumbul's bus rose again. If anyone so much as laid a finger on her beautiful smile, he'd disembowel him.

He wanted to freeze time. Or maybe it was only in retrospect that he wished he'd wanted to. Later, he'd need to know if Fatah was right: who you are depends on where you are. So he observed the men the way he should have then. He went back to the jeep racing along at 110 kilometers an hour. He gave each man the attention he wished he'd given his brothers, sister, nephew, nieces, cousins, parents, grandparents, great-grandparents. He was never able to forget a single line on their faces.

Dil Haseen: the doolha with the deep, impassive voice, who joined the camp soon after his wedding. The men said he was too deadpan to consummate his marriage. No, he himself had said that.

Next to him was the baby-faced Gharyaal Bhai, always the first to volunteer for any expedition. Salaamat could see him with teeth bared, meeting a crocodile's fangs with his own. Those teeth were going to stay far, far away from his family.

Ali, the malakhras wrestler. He still oiled himself every morning. He shared Salaamat's tent and Gharyaal Bhai shared him.

Mirchi, small and eager to please. He hailed from Kunri, which gave the world more red chilies than any other place on earth.

Those were the four sitting opposite him. On his side, other than Fatah and himself, sat Yawar. Though zealous as Fatah, Fatah did not like Yawar because Yawar was the most educated man in the camp. He insisted Yawar was really a Muhajir spy in Sindhi skin.

And finally, the soldierly Amar. Broad-shouldered and sinewy like Salaamat, and just as quiet.

Ten, maybe twelve kilometers went by. They were approaching a village. Wheat and millet sprang around them and the trickle of irrigation canals was heavenly.

'Let's stop here,' Ali suggested. 'We can get a drink.'

'No,' Fatah shook his head. 'We're nearly there.'

At last the jeep came to a halt. 'Park around the corner there,' Fatah told the driver. 'Come on,' he said to Salaamat, and hopped outside.

They walked on the highway, eight men with two firearms each. Fatah positioned Salaamat in front of a wire fence enclosing a field of wheat dotted with egrets. 'Right here?' Salaamat protested. 'In broad daylight?'

Dil Haseen extended a hand as if testing for raindrops. 'Sun's up.'

'What do you mean in broad daylight?' Fatah snarled. 'It's daytime isn't it?'

'Maybe he's missing his blindfold,' Yawar suggested.

'Stay there,' Fatah ordered. 'The first vehicle you see, you stop.' The other men crossed the street, leaving Salaamat alone to face oncoming traffic.

He had no watch, but it must have been after eight o'clock. His throat was so dry he could have sucked on a shoot of grass. In the distance, he saw farmers wandering about, and thought he even heard a goat bleat. Was he beginning to hallucinate? More than four hours without a drink, and with nothing in his stomach but a cup of feeble tea. The seven others stood across from him, maybe twenty feet away. They were haggard, humorless. They wanted nothing more than a cold shower, a hot meal and a soft bed. That ought to have been home. Instead, here they were, fighting for it on a sizzling day in June.

He began to see double. There were fourteen men across the street. There were two streets and there were four drops of sweat sliding all the way down his nose. When one drop struck his lips it was saltier than the godforsaken sea. He was ready to jump the fence and suck on anything, goat dung if he had to.

He heard a whistle. Someone waved from across both streets. It was Fatah, and he was excited. Salaamat knew why but he could not bring himself to look. Fatah whistled again, as if he had a bleating goat stuck inside him, the bastard. It was a dark car. Not a bus. Perhaps this wouldn't be so bad after all. He couldn't see the driver but the driver had seen them. About one hundred feet away the car stopped and began turning around.

'Shoot!' Fatah shouted.

Salaamat stared as the black car screeched and swiveled. The men had aimed their weapons and the driver panicked. He reversed into a ditch.

'Shoot!' Now the others were yelling too.

The engine roared. Tires pealed. The car was on the road again. In a few seconds, it would escape. Salaamat jogged towards it, holding up a pistol but doing nothing else.

'Chootar,' Fatah ran forward. 'Fire!'

The air exploded in gunshots. At first Salaamat thought the shots had somehow turned to little flecks of light and the highway had shrunk into one of Hero's magic vases. The glow was delicate, astral. Entirely at odds with the bellowing bullets. But then he saw it came from inside the car, or rather, around it. It was the windshield and the windows, and it sprayed the road in a light rain. Within seconds, the highway glittered like a forest of diamonds. When the men ran forward they crushed the diamonds to powder.

Fatah skidded up to the driver's shattered window, dragging Salaamat with him. He kicked Salaamat's shin. He tugged his locks. Salaamat fell in the powder laughing, 'It's not her bus!'

'Stand up, cunt.' Fatah kicked him again. 'What do you think you're trying to prove?' Hauling him up, he kicked a third time. 'When I say shoot, you shoot.' This time he shoved him so hard Salaamat lunged forward, head and torso blasting into the broken window, hands flying up to break the momentum with the driver's shoulders.

When he saw the man time did freeze. 'Oh God.'

'Are you going to shoot him now?' he heard Fatah say. The voice was hollow, lifeless. It drifted far into the dusty haze.

Mr Mansoor gaped out from the car. Glass studded his fat cheeks as though he'd made a mess of a meal. A wound in his flabby arm bled like a faucet. He wheezed, trying to contain the bleeding with the other hand. Blood oozed out from between the pudgy fingers. It turned into a cricket ball and the wounded arm became his daughter Dia. She was running toward him from the top of a hill, in a yellow dress. Barely thirteen. Flushed, leaping with joy. 'Out!' she screamed, and her brother at the bottom of the hill in front of their house threw down his bat and sulked into their twelve-foot-tall gate. But her father the umpire waited to embrace her. He judged it a fair ball: her brother was out.

Salaamat's hand shook as he tried to hold the gun to Mr Mansoor's temple. Over his shoulder he said to Fatah, 'Look at the car. Let's take it and leave him.'

A barrel stabbed his spine. 'Shoot. Next time I won't say it, I'll do it. To you.'

Salaamat pulled the trigger but aimed a few inches down, and to his right. Another red ball exploded, this time above the left knee. Mr Mansoor screamed. His free hand came away from the wounded arm and squeezed the fresh wound.

'Bad shot,' said Gharyaal Bhai. 'Not like you.' He stuck his hand into the window and grabbed the wounded arm. Then he snapped the right thumb loose. 'You're going to do the left one. Today. Now. To hell with the cuffs.'

Between deafening screams, Mr Mansoor pleaded with Salaamat, 'Tell them to stop. Help me.'

Had he recognized him then?

Salaamat did not want the men to know he knew him. Fatah was too unpredictable. If he learned the man was his family's employer, he might do anything. They'd pass the farm again on the way back. Maybe he'd want to stop there.

'Shut up!' Salaamat waved his gun in the diamond-raked face. He held Mr Mansoor's left fingers with one hand, caught his elbow with the other. It was like the first time he'd jumped in the sea: he had to do it quickly, without thinking. He caught the thumb and pulled it forward, in one swift motion, like he'd seen men rev the motor of a scooter. He heard the bone crack. Mr Mansoor put his forehead on the steering wheel and began to sob.

Yawar settled in the backseat with Gharyaal Bhai. 'Let's take him to the Chief.'

Gharyaal Bhai nodded. 'But first we stop at Thatta, for rewri.'

Salaamat got in with them. The others followed in the jeep.

Yawar punched the back of Mr Mansoor's head and hissed, 'Drive.'

389

A hand with a slack thumb started the engine and tried to steer. All eight fingers were used to change gears. The wound in the knee bled lavishly. He swallowed hiccups. In the rear-view mirror, Salaamat saw his eyes still stream with tears. Then they met his own.

Why did dying men and burning buses always look at him?

The lips trembled but Mr Mansoor uttered nothing more. Perhaps, as his wounds bled and his mind shrank, he didn't even know Salaamat any more. Maybe, when he'd asked for help, he hadn't recognized him. Or maybe he chose not to reveal that they knew each other. Possibly, he was thinking the same: the farm was coming up, and his wife and children might be arriving soon. Perhaps, to look for him.

Salaamat thought now of the Muhajir student who'd crossed the street at the wrong time on the wrong day. If only there'd been a sign: Trespassers will be prosecuted. He said to those small wet eyes in the mirror: *Why here, when there were so many other places you could be?*

But Mr Mansoor never spoke again. Not when the men stopped for rewri, and spooned some into his quivering lips. And not when he was taken to the cell from which a corpse was taken out.

5

Remains

AUGUST 1992

They sat under the same tree where he'd given her the earrings. The leaves were turning crisp. Sumbul said Riffat Mansoor's farm was in the throes of a water crisis.

'The level in the wells has risen but it needs to rain much more,' she explained. 'Poor Bibi. She says when it rains life stops. But when it doesn't, the spirit just shrivels up and dies, slowly, slowly, curling with exhaustion.'

After a pause, she added that for the first time in all the years Riffat had devoted to the farm, she was beginning to wonder if it had been a mistake. It had taken so much of her life. Perhaps she should have stuck to imported threads and dyes. 'I told her, "No, Bibi. You made your dream come true, how can you say it hasn't been worth it?" She looked so frail, suddenly, and even a little old. She said, lately, she'd begun missing her husband dreadfully again. It would have been nice to simply grow old with him.'

Salaamat played with a strand of Sumbul's hair. He hadn't told her what happened on the highway. He hadn't told a soul.

But he'd shared what was heard in the governor's tomb, after leaving her with the earrings years ago. He knew it was about this she wanted to speak.

She'd sold the earrings soon after her third child was born. Now in her lap nestled a fourth, brittle-boned, unable to retain food. The child was shriveling; dehydrated as the land they lived on. Yet Sumbul refused to accept it. Even with a fifth child in her womb, the fourth evoked as much love in her as the first. She offered him milk. Her breast sagged like a stuffed sock: stout at the bottom, flat at the top. Nipples still Fanta-cap sized but ragged now. She was just twenty: his age that day on the highway.

The boy rejected the milk. Sumbul buttoned her shirt up. Salaamat kissed the child's feverish forehead. He said, 'Why do you care so much about your Bibi's troubles?'

She rocked the child, desperate to get a reaction from him. His thighs, slender as her wrists, bent closer to a tiny, sunken chest. He was moving backwards in time, back to the little foetus in her womb, back to the egg that swam free. Her eyes welled with tears but she blinked them back impatiently before answering him. 'Bibi has been like a mother to me. She too has suffered great losses.'

Salaamat rolled on to his back in the dirt, gazing up at the top of the thirsty tree. 'How touching. Aba has been like a father to Bibi's daughter Dia, and Bibi has been like a mother to you.'

Sumbul turned her head away, whispering, 'Be gentle with me today.'

He quickly repented. Taking her free hand in his, he asked for forgiveness.

But when she turned to look at him again he saw the shine in her eyes. 'What do you know about being like a parent, when you won't accept your real father? You haven't even returned to our village once since Ama died. Dadi wants nothing more than to see you again before she dies too.'

'She sent me away.'

'She had to! We're much better off now. What would we be doing over there? Serving tea to the jobless for the rest of our lives? There's no fishing for the men any more. You would have felt as useless as Aba did before we finally left.'

He raised his hands, drawing a partition between them. 'I would never have become like him.'

'Pah! You men are all the same. Pining about the past while we think of what's to come.' She looked down at the child again.

He pursed his lips, holding back anger. He knew she knew that by leaving everything he'd once had, he was left with nothing besides her. Sumbul was mother, father, and home. He was terrified of invoking her wrath. What if she stopped loving him? The wench: his fear allowed her to manipulate him.

'You ask why I care about Bibi,' she continued. 'Do you know the day after her husband was found, she got straight out of bed and came to the farm? Yes. She didn't lick her wounds. She didn't cry to the world. And because of that, the world has done nothing but speak ill of her.'

'She did not love him,' Salaamat said, before he could help it.

'How dare you! Just because of what you heard long ago? It takes courage to go on after a husband's death. Even more when his corpse is found in the river, with gruesome injuries. Whether you loved him or not.'

Now it was Salaamat's turn to look away.

Once they'd pledged to always love each other, at any cost. By confessing, he'd force her to break the promise. Even if he shared how he'd practically kissed the ground when it hadn't been her on the highway, she'd stop loving him.

She was saying, 'Men have extorted more and more protection money from her ever since. They're worse than the authorities at the body shop, the ones that bothered you about decoration tax.'

'How would you know, my innocent one?' Salaamat replied, wondering why he couldn't simply let her ramble on. 'They never smashed your limbs.'

She tossed him another look, but let it pass. 'So it pains me to know Bibi has even more troubles. And this time, from someone she'd never suspect. Someone I also care about. And someone you do too,' she looked up, smiling mischievously. And then she couldn't help it. 'Exactly what have you seen Dia Baji and the Amreekan boy do?'

Ah! Power to manipulate back! He lay down again, pretending to fall asleep.

'Oh, you're evil!' she cried. 'But I see through you. You're dying to tell me!'

He snored.

She clicked her tongue. 'I've tried to ask her but she won't tell. I've even listened at the door when she calls him up but half the time they speak in English. Has it gone very far?' She giggled, then covered her mouth in horror. 'Oh but it would be so, so . . .' She tried to shake the thought.

He watched with eyes half open. She was more entertaining than anything on television.

'Aba's been trying also,' she went on. 'But, for once, even he can't get anything out of her.'

'Just like a father,' Salaamat muttered.

She smacked him, hard. 'Oh this is awful, we can't make light of it. It's serious. *Serious*. It would be bad enough, but knowing what we do, *if* it's true.' Again she shook her head, as if sneezing. 'It would be almost like . . . me and you!' The hand came up again and her face was the picture of shame.

'Not exactly,' Salaamat shrugged, feigning indifference. 'Anyway, from what I heard, they never knew for sure.'

'Well, if they're *not*, then I suppose it's not that wrong to, well, imagine what they *do*.'

394

He snored again.

'Oh what do you know, anyway,' she huffed. 'You need a wife to teach you.'

He couldn't help but laugh at the absurdity.

'And you'd better marry quickly or no woman will even want to teach you.' She raised a brow provocatively.

'Don't you think I've at least twenty more years of good looks ahead of me?'

'No. Five, maximum.'

'Well then, I'd better enjoy myself before I lose them. Then I'll get married.'

But again he found he'd upset her. She was so sensitive, this sister of his, who'd been married to a forty-year-old at fourteen. Kissing her hand, he said, 'Forget this silly chatter.'

But she wouldn't. 'One of us needs to talk to Bibi. Either you, me, or Aba.'

His fingers turned clammy. 'How can it be me? I've barely spoken to her before.'

'Well, you're the one who saw her that day. And you're the one who's seen Dia Baji with the boy. You can tell her everything you know.'

'Are you crazy?' He was shouting now. 'Why would she believe me? You're the one she'd listen to.' *Everything you know!*

'Calm down.' She looked surprised. 'Just listen. If I tell her what you've told me, she'll still want to hear it from you. The same if Aba tells her. You're the witness.'

He stood up. 'That's always been my curse. But no more. I won't get involved. No more!'

She clutched his hand. 'Sit down at least.'

'Only if you won't bring it up again.'

'Fine!'

He sat down.

She put the baby in his arms. 'Hold him while I fix you a sherbat. Unless you want to come inside?'

He shook his head. He refused to take shelter under Mr Mansoor's roof. It was bad enough coming to the farm, but a tree at least, in the grand scheme of things, belonged to no one.

The child opened his eyes, aware of an alien scent. If it repulsed him, he was too spent to protest. The lids fell over eyes like tiny specks of ink, and then went back to flickering.

Sumbul returned with a glass of mango squash. Salaamat hesitated. He drank *his* drink, in *his* glass. Still, it was a hot day, and Sumbul had made it especially for him.

6

Fatah's Law

Outside the farm, Salaamat stood a while on the highway before walking over to his uncle on Makli Hill.

After Mr Mansoor's body was found, Sumbul had told him Dia wondered often if silk had been the culprit. She needed desperately to find a reason. Business? Rivalry? The dye company that had lost its contract? Middlemen who no longer supplied cocoons? Other factory owners who paled next to Riffat Mansoor? Though they gossiped about her, rich women would pay anything to boast, at parties, that they wore Riffat's silk. Was it competition, and if so, was it the woman who ought to have been killed?

He'd listen to Sumbul's reports in silence. If there was a reason, he didn't know it. Maybe it had to do with Fatah's law. If there were any other reason, maybe someone else knew what it was. Maybe Riffat Mansoor herself could do some explaining.

Salaamat peered down the highway. The tarmac shimmered in the heat, shooting up into fog. Somewhere beyond the tombs in the mist was the village with the millet and wheat fields. Somewhere in the fields chimed the irrigation canals that, five years ago, had slaked his ears. Perhaps those fields had exhausted their water supply as well. A little deeper into the fog would be the fenced wheat field outside which he'd stood. Egrets had flecked the pasture. They could fly in and out of any fence, but not he. He'd stood watching seven men with guns on the other side of the street turn to fourteen. And then Fatah had whistled and he'd seen the dark car try to backtrack. As if that could ever be done.

They'd stopped for over an hour to eat rewri while Mr Mansoor bled. 'If those bastards don't hurry up,' said Yawar, 'the Chief will never get a look at him.'

Finally, the men returned with a dozen dishes for each vehicle, and again they were on their way. Mr Mansoor's breathing grew increasingly uneven and he began muttering incoherently to himself. The car swerved unsteadily.

'This will keep him conscious,' said Ali, spooning the sweet into Mr Mansoor's mouth. If he refused it, Gharyaal Bhai wrung the wounded arm and Ali dug into the other with a knife. He'd vomited twice on himself when the car pulled up outside the Chief's house.

But before that, Salaamat memorized the route. The men had not blindfolded him. He stared outside absorbing every turn, stamping each detail in his mind: left at the spear-shaped rock, right at the flat one. How could he tell them apart? That one had a branch falling mid-way over it. And so on. Twice he got out to piss and mark the spot with stones. His vision was like a telescope. He ceased noting events inside the car. He was going to get on the other side of the fence even if it killed him.

That's what he told Fatah as Mr Mansoor was thrown into the torture cell. He grabbed his collar and took him around the back. If they were seen, no one interfered. After all, Fatah was First Lieutenant Muhammad Shah's brother-in-law.

'You coward,' Fatah whispered, enraged. 'You're going to let others sell you. You'll become their whore.'

'I'm already a whore,' Salaamat choked. 'Yours.'

And then, for the first time since leaving his village, he began to sob. His shoulders jerked in a spasm of its own momentum, independent of the scream in his nose. He'd never lost control so utterly. He, the best shot, the tightest bullet. And the shame of it all was that Fatah saw him unravel. The dam he'd learned to contain fanned out of him; the water swirling in his gut rushed out. He loosened his shalwar and crapped a stream of rewri three feet from Fatah.

His friend did nothing. He didn't kick or punch him in his filthy, exposed behind. He held his nose and looked away.

Outside the room from which Mr Mansoor would never escape, the dregs of the love Salaamat once had for Fatah surfaced again. He felt a rush of gratitude: he was not despised. Fatah loved him still.

When Salaamat stopped crying and dressed again, Fatah put a slip of paper in his shirt pocket, just as he'd done on their first meeting. 'If you run the men will hunt you down, especially now that you know the route to the Chief's. There's only one way out for you. Go to the Mohana village we found. Have Hameed Bhai take you downriver. The boathouse will hide you well. When you get to Karachi, find him,' he pointed to the slip of paper.

'But who is he? And how can he protect me?' Salaamat sniffled, staring vacantly at the chit of paper.

'His company supplies our equipment. He always needs drivers and has used dissidents before. Everyone knows that. You're running from one chief to the other.'

He went into the cell and that was the last Salaamat ever saw of him.

7

A Visitor

His job with Khurram's family was simple. He drove a van to the designated place where the clearance agent waited. The fake bill of lading was handed over, the consignment of goods transferred to his van, and the agent paid anywhere between 20,000 to 50,000 rupees, depending on the size of the shipment, and the number and needs of other officials. Sometimes Salaamat met him along the coast of the Balochistan border. At other times, off the National Highway, close enough to the scene of the abduction. He asked no questions, though he did sometimes wonder how the goods came in – at one of the dark bays of Balochistan's cavernous coast or via the porous Afghan border, like the heroin and firearms? Probably neither. There were more ways to cross borders illegally than legally.

Behind the wheel, Salaamat consoled himself that if he carried a load of torture equipment, it was better than being the one tortured. And he resolved never to belong to anyone again. It made no sense: Fatah's men got guns from the

Pathans and these supplies from a Punjabi, who in turn imported from Amreeka and the Angrez. And Mr Mansoor had been Sindhi. What about Fatah's talk of protecting his own people?

Never again. He worked only for himself, and occasionally, Sumbul. Nothing else mattered. Something that had come alive again in the gorge had finally shut down for good. God had gone and shrunk everything in His wake. Life was trivial now.

So he'd concluded the day he stumbled down to the Mohana village, after a night spent escaping the Chief's den.

The stars were still bright when he reached the camp. The men who'd stayed back were asleep. He tiptoed past them and began lumbering up to the top of the world. Just before dawn the next day, he curled under an orange tree outside the thatched hut. The Mohanas nursed him with patience, asking for nothing in return. Some folks were as fine as that. Others weren't. It made no sense.

The eldest boatman, Hameed Bhai, sat beside him every morning as he drank the reviving broth, echoing Salaamat's thoughts. He spoke of how his people had built their lives around the river for thousands of years, but now were forced to find other means. It was always the same story. Always the same fight. And it was just so trivial. Every night, he fell asleep to the tune of Hameed Bhai's lament. The next day, he woke to the women washing clothes, the children twirling dragonflies, and some of the older boys teaching cormorants to dive for fish. He watched as if from a great distance. None of it touched him any more.

On the long voyage down the river, he recalled his grandmother telling him that the last journey – the one that carried the soul to heaven – was in a quiet boat. All he wanted was for this to be that last journey.

He gulped tangerine torture while Hameed Bhai rowed

like he was in the prime of his youth, pointing places out to him. 'The river would feed that lake over there. But the Mohanas who live on it weep now. The lake has grown salty. It is stagnant, filthy. Dead are the freshwater fish: kurero, morakho, thelhi. And what are the people to drink? We were born to water. We drown on land.'

The boatman's woes drifted in and out of Salaamat's tangerine stupor, in and out of the river's song, in and out of the faces of the men who'd been with him on the highway. He imagined how they'd acted in the cell, invented their dialogue, and even pushed the button when they did. The next moment, when the oar dipped into the river, it pulled up a weed-entangled Mr Mansoor.

The phantom Mr Mansoor had hung there all the way down to the bank where Hameed Bhai eventually let him off.

Khurram's father was loud and stout, like the son. He returned Salaamat's greeting every morning with a hearty, 'Waalai-kum-asalaam, Salaamat.' Peace be upon you too, Peace. He never kicked or jeered him. He paid 4,000 rupees a month – twice what Salaamat made after toiling three years under Handsome. He had two daughters, both married, who came often to the house with their children. His ailing wife kept to herself. He had three cars – a Mercedes, Land Cruiser, and Honda Civic. The first for the evenings, the second for Khurram, and the third for the day. A second driver transported him to work. A third was hired for Khurram when Salaamat delivered shipments to the warehouse.

Salaamat's quarter was at the back of the three-story house. It was twice the size of his cell at Handsome's and he'd even been given a tape-recorder and a twelve-inch television. When not busy with a consignment, the day was his. He listened to pop songs, watched television, walked over to the nearest video shop, visited his sister or the workers down the street, or, if the daughters called in, played cricket and pugan pugaai with their children. Sometimes he ran small errands for Khurram. If, for instance, there was no ice cream in the house, he fetched it. He also ran errands for Khurram's friends, such as taking the Amreekan to the cove.

One thing he liked to do was share a cup of tea with the old construction worker down the street. It was a little like being back in his grandmother's teahouse. The unfinished house, without a roof and doors, was strangely soothing, and as he sat there, he was a little closer to being in a cottage by the sea. He couldn't explain why. But since the rains, the workers had gone away so he mostly stayed in his room.

This afternoon he lay on a charpoy and pressed *play* on the tape-recorder. It was the sound track to a movie he'd seen snippets of at the video shop. A luscious woman in a choli ghagra pranced around a mountaintop while her lover chased her. Her breasts were peaks in their own right, bulging through her blouse like cones re-routing traffic. She jingled and jiggled, pouted and fell flat on her back, writhing over the pasture while her man tumbled onto her. He belted out: *'You and me, what mischief, what magic!'* She screeched: *'Open yourself to me . . .'* He kissed her lips and peaks rolled down peaks.

Sumbul would say he was like his father in this respect too. 'Aba spends all day glued to the television, imagining he's Dilip Kumar. Who do you think you are?'

He never told her that if anyone had got him on to love-songs, it was Fatah.

He didn't ache for him as much now. He could remember, without longing, a tender Fatah in the grass, nuzzling his neck, piping, *'White, white is your body, made of electricity. 440 volts!'*

'But I'm black as tar,' Salaamat would say.

'Silly, close your eyes. We can pretend, can't we?'

He didn't want that any more. He belonged to no one.

On the charpoy, Salaamat turned up the volume of the

song when Khurram's old chawkidaar shuffled into his room. 'There's a woman asking for you at the gate,' he said.

'What sort of woman?' Salaamat sat up.

'How should I know?' The man went back to his work.

At the gate stood a short and rather dowdy woman, clad in rubber slippers. The only thing going for her was a very fair complexion. He recognized her immediately: the Amreekan's mother. She sometimes walked past them to throw litter in the empty plot. Once, while rummaging through a pile she'd left, he'd found the most enticing pictures imaginable, such as the one of the blonde woman in a skintight sleeveless top, with breasts like cones. Oh yes, she'd prance for him and sing, *Open yourself to me*. There was another with bare legs, sitting on the Amreekan's lap. Salaamat had kept them all. The next time the video shopkeeper threw him out after he'd seen only one dance number, Salaamat had shown him a photograph. He'd been allowed to stay till the end of the film. On the next visit, he'd shown more. By now the shopkeeper and his friends had seen the pictures at least a dozen times but the bribe still worked.

When she saw him, the woman cleared her throat. Then she seemed astounded by her own audacity, and for several seconds, stood speechless. Finally, 'Is my son here?'

'No.'

Now she was astounded by his audacity. Well, he wasn't going to address her by a title just because she expected it. The only man he called sahib was Khurram's father and the only woman who was begum sahib to him was Khurram's mother.

She cleared her throat again. 'Well, it seems he'd been coming here a lot and you'd been taking him somewhere. Is this correct?'

'Yes.'

'Where?'

Salaamat leaned into the tall gate. It was happening again:

he was being sucked into another world. Didn't they all see how trivial it was? He chewed the inside of his cheeks.

Suddenly, she handed him fifty rupees. 'Please tell me.'

He took it. 'To a beach, far away.'

She nodded, as if expecting this. Then: 'With whom?'

Again he chewed his cheeks. She came out with another fifty. 'With the Mansoor child, Dia.'

She sighed but he saw she wasn't surprised about this either. 'And have they gone there again?'

He shook his head.

'Do you know where they are?'

Of course he did. He often saw the girl getting dropped at his end of the street, then walking down to the teahouse. She chose this side so she'd not be seen walking past the Amreekan's house. It was a silly plan, made by a silly girl, to get together with a silly boy. He frowned. She repeated the question, this time with twice the money.

He shrugged. 'Yes, I know.'

'We can take a taxi,' she pleaded.

Maybe saving Dia from further disgrace would have been Mr Mansoor's own last wish. Who could say? Sumbul had wanted him to talk to the girl's mother. Now here was the boy's mother.

He shrugged again. 'We don't need a taxi.'

RIFFAT

I

A Usual Day

Riffat Mansoor walked briskly, as always. Leaning over the trays of caterpillars she exchanged a few words with her employees, examined the mulberry stock, drafted notes on her clipboard, and exhaled so vigorously the curls on her forehead fluttered like down feathers. She was exhausted. Every few weeks a team of men arrived with a long list of reasons why they needed to be paid. Otherwise, they threatened to burn her farm, or simply cut off the water supply. She was tired of ringing her lawyer, who'd increased his charges. She'd been forced to hire engineers to tell her if the current water crisis had more to do with the Mafia than the drought. They said, 'It could be,' and sent a team of experts who complained about the heat and vanished. She'd hired someone else who sent a different set of experts. They dug around her land, shook their heads, demanded tea. If she lost her temper she was called a fool for breeding silkworms in Sindh. When reminded that she'd succeeded thus far, they waited for her to lose her temper. And this was a very small part of her day.

Another worry was that for the past few years, the trouble in the province made it hard for her workers to get to work. Transport was infrequent and unsafe. Besides, with the exception of the gardeners and guards, the staff was all women, and this meant family came first. There were days when husbands and in-laws threw tantrums or children fell ill. All this meant the caterpillars weren't fed, and since there were as many as two hundred thousand to feed, it meant she or Dia spent the entire day chopping a ton of leaves. Once she'd even asked an armed guard to pitch in, and had had to laugh when he said it would get his Kalashnikov dirty. 'Set it aside,' she'd argued, certain that no woman had ever asked him to mince anything before. He grudgingly complied, wrinkling his nose at the foliage as though it were a used nappy.

Then there was the factory. After Mansoor's death, she'd refused to let his family take over her silk line, but this meant she'd also retained the stress of managing it. Her weavers came from Orangi Town, a neighborhood that was plumb in the center of the arson and strikes, and many had suffered tragedies in their own families. They'd say, 'Bibi, if a rich man like your husband could be a victim of crime, what hope is there for people like us?'

To combat power breakdowns she'd finally installed a high-power generator, but every time the engine revved and black smog lifted into the air she winced. It made no sense: this use of fuel to sustain an industry she'd taken pains to start cleaning by introducing natural dyes. But it pained just as much not to use the generator when the weavers did show up and the power shut down – it was the choice between a waste of human or natural resources, even as she worked hard to prove the two were the same. But there was no arguing around it, especially when she conceded that fuel was depleted in another way too: by commuting between her house in K.D.A, the farm near Thatta, and the factory near the dead Lyari River. It was the choice between working and sitting at home. Both produced their own waste.

And somewhere in the equation lapped her children – fatherless atoms orbiting worlds increasingly hidden from her. What could she do about Hassan's arrogance? About her older son who'd given up on his homeland? The grandchild she hardly knew? And Dia – where was she these days? She'd never known her to look so distraught, not since Mansoor's death. Had Nissrine's desire to marry unleashed some dread about her own future? Well, with good reason. Dia was doing miserably at college, Riffat knew, because she wasn't being taught the things that mattered to her – entomology, zoology, mythology. She'd heard they offered degrees in just about everything now, in the new colonial power many parents were sending their children to. More even than England had offered when her generation went abroad to study.

Riffat tapped on her clipboard, unhappy with the turn her thoughts were taking. She didn't like to think of her London days. Not because of her classes – those had enriched her. She shook her head. Her attention returned to Dia. The child didn't want to leave home, but was it coming to that? Wouldn't it be better to send her away than watch her feel ineffectual here? Would it?

What kind of reception would her daughter get in a country where people applauded their government for waging a war no less ruthless than in Vietnam? She'd been a part of the rallies in the '60s, in London – so her thoughts were taking her back there after all. She'd been witness to the outrage. But many who'd protested then would remain silent during the Gulf War. If 'peace' and the 'people's movement' had been popular causes when Riffat was a student in London, the murder of hundreds of thousands of innocent Muslim civilians had nothing to do with either.

She straightened her back. Her neck and shoulders were heavy with the tension building inside her. She pressed a finger deep into the muscle just below her shoulder blade. Her scapula. She'd known someone once who liked to name her parts as he kissed them. No! She could not dwell on that.

Sighing, Riffat remembered a relative had called last night, and she'd promised to phone back but hadn't. It was a miracle anyone still tried to reach her. She'd made too many angry too many times with all the phone calls never returned, weddings unattended, deaths only hastily condoled. The truth was brides and corpses made her cry – not crocodile tears but real ones.

When Dia had told her of his death, after snapping at the poor child she'd slipped into the bathroom and wept as if it were 1968 again. Wept more, she knew, than his wife would. It should never have ended this way. Two youths who'd fallen in love in another land ought to have returned to their own to cement that love. Love knows no boundaries. No geographic, man-made perimeters. That's how she'd tell it if she ever had to. Make a story of it. Pretend it happened to someone else. Let Dia jot it down, slip it into her Book of World Fables along with all her other tales of beginnings. Read it up in the mulberry tree, adding her own twists, so it metamorphosed into something other than what it was: the story of Dia's own beginning.

Riffat Mansoor was exhausted when Sumbul met her by the silkworm trays, took her hand, led her into the shack, made her a cup of green tea and offered painkillers for her ulcers. Riffat thanked her, adding that the business would have completely dissolved if it weren't for Sumbul's family. She, her cousins, her father – what comfort hadn't they provided, especially in the years following Mansoor's death?

Sumbul smiled, waiting till Riffat had drunk the soothing leaves. Then she said she'd something urgent to confess.

2

Awakening

APRIL–MAY 1968

She'd been sipping coffee from a flask under the eaves of an old brick café, waiting for her bus, when she first noticed him: a tall, dapper man in a maroon scarf, with a smile that could fracture clouds. The scarf matched his large, amber eyes beautifully. One didn't have to attend design school to notice, as the other women throwing covert glances his way confirmed.

The smile was for her, as he stepped aside to let Riffat on the bus first. All day she sketched impatiently, chewing her pencil stub, shading a poster for dog biscuits in hurried, clumsy strokes. Her professor snapped, 'No self-respecting terrier would eat that!'

In the following days, the elegant man repeated the moves – the bow, the beam, the arm extending to usher her on without once brushing her jacket. At last she touched her curls and tossed him a sassy, we'll-see-about-that look, and then they both laughed while the bus slid away.

He invited her to eat with him in his tiny hostel room.

Lunch was arranged on a rickety desk full of medical books he picked up and placed carefully on the already cluttered floor. An old towel functioned as the tablecloth. He was entirely unembarrassed by his modest means and this moved her.

The daal tingled with heaps of tamarind brought from home. 'Hyderabadi style,' he said. 'The way my mother made it.' There was rice, a small salad, and a slab of Cadbury's milk chocolate for dessert. And throughout, his easy, cheerful manner and boundless hospitality as he spooned most of the meal onto her plate because if she ate well he'd cooked well. No man from her household had ever offered a woman his share, let alone prepared it. She'd not thought Pakistani men did that.

In the musty room lit by wavering candlelight, he watched her eat and said, 'We wouldn't have met if we hadn't been waiting at the same stop.' He touched her wrist under the cuff of her right shirtsleeve. Then he touched her chin, sliding his thumb along her jaw. He said she had the loveliest bones imaginable and that her curls enhanced them. Twisting a coil around his index finger he brought it forward, so it fell on the smooth shelf of her right cheekbone, just above the deep dip of her cheek. 'This is called the zygomatic bone,' he said. 'If I ever have to remember that, I've only to think of you.'

In her lap, her fingers twitched. She thought herself too thin to be lovely and had always fought her mother to keep the hair short. 'Hair could make up for the body you lack,' her mother would argue.

Now here she was, fed by such a handsome man. And so tender too.

When at last she found the nerve to look up at him, she wanted it to be in the same sassy way she'd found earlier. No tears of gratitude. No violins. She wasn't going to turn into the girl her mother wanted her to be. She stared him in the face and said, 'I'll leave you now. But the next meal is at my place.'

'Let me walk you home.'

She was the wealthier of the two. Her father had land in Sindh and a flat in London, in the West End. They held hands and nobody looked. It wasn't a shameful thing to do though her family would have said otherwise, even as they watched Shammi Kapoor plant famished kisses down Saira Bano's zygomatic bone.

They walked to her flat via Goodge Street, for the names it rang with: Woolf, Orwell. He spoke of the irony of their schooling. He, the son of a rowdy journalist whose pen had fought the colonialists, was learning through them how to treat the wounded. His father said benefiting in this way was just. But he wasn't sure. Was it equilibrium or a step back? Or could he really find a way to take it forward?

'I understand the conflict,' Riffat replied, speaking at length of studying textiles in a land that had stripped hers of the very plants she hoped to one day reintroduce, like indigo and catechu. 'Yet it's in these libraries that I'm learning what we've lost.'

How could they create peace from paradox?

She'd ask herself this often in the following years, particularly when training weavers descended from those whose thumbs the British had chopped off because they'd been too adept at turning fiber to tissue.

And particularly when marrying Mansoor.

In the following weeks, Riffat and Shafqat rendezvoused between rows of fiction in Foyle's, nibbled Greek take-out in Russell Square, vowed never to let go of each other all the way from Bloomsbury to Soho. Dangerously enraptured, they began weaving a world around themselves, legs looped, breath knotting tighter with each moment. They'd grow as one or not at all. That was the pledge. It had to do with gravity. It was the only natural way to mature.

Between curling up together in her one-bedroom flat, study-ing, attending classes and walking the city, they steeped themselves in the student movement pumping the streets. Riffat's awakening in London was not merely of her own self, but of her place in a world eager to decide its future for itself. In Iran, the democratically elected Prime Minister had been ousted and the Shah affixed like a plug; in Guatemala, the CIA had engineered a similar coup and tried again in Cuba. And US-backed Israel occupied the West Bank and Gaza. *Let the people choose!* Che Guevara placards bobbed around Riffat as she held Shafqat's hand and listened to speakers from around the world. A Pakistani journalist who'd sneaked into Hanoi and later given accounts of American atrocities at a War Crimes Tribunal, addressed them: 'Until we own our own resources, we'll never be free. And as long as the West keeps stealing the forests and minerals of the South and the East, we will fight!' He spoke of the swindling of Congo's wealth, of attempts to sink ever deeper into the Middle East. 'See how the CIA overthrew Kassem in Iraq? It's because he nationalized oil. They will always seek to depose any ruler who wants Iraq's assets to stay in Iraq.'

She and Shafqat left these rallies resolving to return home and together make a better world. They scoured the paper for news of events in their own country, fuming about press-censorship, delighted that back in Karachi, Shafqat's father was at the center of anti-martial law protests. Holding her, marching down to the American Embassy in Grosvenor Square, Shafqat would excitedly proclaim, 'That general is sitting on top of us because of the same power that sits on Vietnam. But things are changing. I can feel new wheels in motion.' And he'd tell her how the notion of fate enraged him. History was a question of conscious, free will. Not of helplessly succumbing to choices made by others.

3

Her Job, His Fight

JUNE 1968

For many years she held on to the fossilized shark tooth he'd hidden in her flat one night.

'It's something very womanly,' he teased.

'So it has to do with my period?'

'You might say that.'

She fished in amongst sanitary napkins. Nothing there, nor in her make-up kit. She padded back into her bedroom and threw underwear out from a drawer, exasperated.

'You were closer in the bathroom,' he grinned.

She finally saw it in the bristles of her toothbrush – two crusty inches sticking out like a siphon in a bed of white kelp. 'What on earth is *this*? And what does it have to do with my monthly flow?'

'People once believed shark teeth had magical powers. If you left one with a woman, you'd win her heart. And, she'd get good and fertile.'

'Oh, so you'd have sex and offspring, all thanks to a three-hundred-million-year-old jaw?'

'Let's see.' He wound his arms around her, loosened her blouse, buried his scabrous chin between her small breasts.

Happier than ever before, she was also miserable: she lived under her father's roof, ate his bread, earned her degree with his pounds. Yet the best part of all – Shafqat – her family could not know.

Her mother hadn't wanted her to come here. Girls didn't go abroad alone. Otherwise, who'd propose to them? But her father trusted Riffat, the youngest of five daughters. And in return, Riffat brought Shafqat to the apartment. She could just see her mother's delight: See? I told you.

Even in her most private hours she couldn't get away from feeling dirty. Boundaries existed even here, in this vocal city, after all. She vowed then to never make her daughter, if she had one, feel this way. She'd never cause her to steal furtively in corners for fear of incurring her mother's wrath. She'd never tell her who to love and who not to. Instead, she'd tell her to choose independently and to hold her head up high when she did.

That night she toyed with the tooth in her palm, feeling the coarse rock against her smooth thumb. It was a frosty June, but the days were long and they slept late. Sprawled on the carpet of the living room-kitchenette, their conversation turned, as it often did, to Shafqat's father. He re-read her bits of the man's letter on the anti-Ayub agitation.

Her head was propped against the couch, her one foot in a gray sock on his bare foot. She was tugging his thick hair with her woolen toes. The floor was strewn with her sketches and his diagrams. Suddenly, she said, 'Your poor mother.'

He looked up, 'Poor?'

'Well, she hardly ever sees her husband.'

'My mother's brave,' he replied. 'A woman doesn't know what resources she has till she's put to the test.'

'All right for you to say,' Riffat looked at him.

'Yes it is,' he looked back. 'She's my mother.'

'But there are things she might not share with you, so you won't worry. That doesn't mean she ought to keep being put to the test.'

'I'm not saying she should be. All I'm saying is that she's proud to have a husband who fights for a freer environment. He speaks for all of us. Including her.'

'But what if she preferred to speak for herself?'

'What do you mean?'

'I mean: would he live up to the test?'

Shafqat stared as if he'd turned to stone.

She sat up, crossed her legs. 'I mean, would he be the one to stay at home with the children, to feed and nurse them, to attend to her phone calls, arrange her meetings, swallow his terror every time she was arrested and the family stood to become motherless?'

He folded the letter. 'These are my parents you're hypothesizing about.'

'Well, why not? I think it's a perfectly fair hypothesis.'

He stood up. 'It's getting late. I think I'll go.'

'Am I not *allowed* to ask you that? So much for a freer environment!'

'What's the matter with you today? One minute we're having a cozy time on the rug, the next you're leaping at my throat.'

'Leaping at your throat!'

He picked up his jacket. Then he smiled as if nothing at all had happened. 'I'll meet you tomorrow at the bus stop?'

Riffat took two deep breaths as he walked away. Her voice was icy but calm. 'Answer the question Shafqat, or this day will end very badly. I'm asking because I need to know what you'd do in your father's position if your mother chose his.'

He laughed, without even turning back to look at her. 'No one can hold me hostage. I speak willingly or I don't speak at all.'

She was shouting then, words she couldn't enunciate. They

stuck to her teeth, glued with spit, and all the time he kept walking, turning the lock, sliding free the chain. And then he was gone.

She stared at the rug he'd stepped across. At the knob, the blond wood of the door. She clutched her waist and started rocking because really, she was teetering, coasting through an open sky, and might crash. Below awaited her mother: See? I told you. Below, placards flew: *Let the people choose!* A speaker waved his fist, packing her with courage, 'Until we own our own resources, we'll never be free.' All the speakers were men. This hadn't even dawned on her before. She only saw it now, as she teetered above. There were other faces waiting below. Her four sisters, who didn't go abroad, her father, who wished he'd listened to his wife, and a nation that wagged one thick finger and yelled, After all you were given. What a selfish, spoilt, ungrateful girl!

Falling back in her flat, she wept on the carpet littered with his books.

He was waiting at the bus stop with a bouquet of yellow roses and his neck in the maroon scarf she loved on him. His cloud-fracturing smile too was back. She was terrified of how happy it made her to see him. When they hugged, she kissed his long, sturdy neck, imbibing what she'd lost of him last night.

In her flat, when next he undressed her, something new loomed over them: the conversation he'd walked away from. She wondered if he felt it too. It didn't appear so. What made him so confident? Confidence came with experience. But she'd not stoop to ask whether she was his first. He made her feel good, and not just physically. He overflowed with assurances: she wasn't too flat, or too skinny. On the contrary, he loved her alert, athletic build. Busty women couldn't walk like her, could they? Nor could fat thighs and a sweaty ass be limber in bed. (Did this mean he *had* done it with fat thighs and a sweaty ass?) She had the grace of a heron, poised and regal, and he'd take that over anything else. She was his queen. No, even more than that: she was an empress. An empress in bell-bottom jeans with smart curls, a breezy run, and an easy laugh. She was a stately casual, with crayon smudges on her nose and silk tops in her drawer. He'd breathe his faith into her bones while sliding his tongue across her clavicle, nibbling his way down to the pit of her sternum while she moaned, only half listening when he got to the bit about the silk tops. The truth was he made her feel good enough to forget that others would want her to feel bad for feeling good, even as the topic he'd forbidden her from touching towered ever higher.

He started growing mercurial about her work. Sometimes, her design samples delighted him. Silk-screen or batik, embroidery or paint, he went through her portfolio meticulously, commenting on the materials, colors and patterns, encouraging her to set up her own shop when they went home and got married. He listened for hours as she spoke of the dyes and astringents, of the madder-dyed cloths found in the ancient site of Moenjodaro, so near Karachi. She wanted to revive all that. He said she must. Her heart raced as she wondered how, and whether he would really want her to. Then, just as she convinced herself he would, his mood changed. He stopped listening, stood up, suggested a stroll, or else admonished her for being too ambitious.

'Too ambitious for whom?'

But he'd take her hand and laugh it off, leaving her to yearn increasingly for an answer.

It happened at last many weeks later, as they sat on the pavement outside a kebab shop. It was still chilly but the clouds had lifted. Sweaters and stockings came off. Cafés with outdoor seating bustled. Riffat rolled a cigarillo-slim kebab between a hot, sesame-sprinkled naan and bit in. She scooped the grease off her chin and sighed. 'When we're back in Karachi, I want you to take me to all those roadside cafés my family insists women should be protected from.'

The upper corner of his lip twitched. For the briefest instant, a dark flint cut his sparkling amber eyes. He took a sip of lassi and said nothing but his face closed. She wondered if he'd looked like this that day he walked out the door, without showing her his face.

She took another bite. 'This is our cuisine, after all. A shame half our population can't enjoy it like this.'

He pushed his plate back. 'You sound so immature when you talk that way.'

'Immature?'

'Irrational then. It's not done, Riffat. You can't transport something that exists here to another place.'

She blinked, genuinely confused. 'Something? Like what?'

'Like another system. You know perfectly well it doesn't look good for a woman to eat in those cafés. Men ogle. And if she's with a man, they want to know why he can't shield her from their lust. He looks even worse.'

She put down her sandwich. It was slowly making sense. 'Democracy, health care, and education can come from within our system?'

'Of course.'

'But when women appear in public as frequently and comfortably as men, that's an import? An evil outside influence?'

He shrugged. 'Some things will take longer.'

'Because some people want them to? Could it be the same people who speak so eloquently of new wheels turning?'

He raised a brow and looked around. The couple at the next table was laughing and had noticed nothing. A few others lingered on the pavement, waiting for a table to clear. 'Maybe we should hurry up so they can sit down.'

She grabbed his hand. 'No. This time you're going to answer me. You want efficiency, hygiene, and a free press

– but not that modernity should benefit women. You want one you can keep putting to the test, just like your mother?'

He snatched his hand away. 'Don't start on my parents again.'

'Are you speaking for me? Do you even know how like our very own general you sound?'

He walked away but she came to his hostel later in the evening, and they argued more. She hounded him for days, hating what she was becoming, she, whose strength was grace and elegance, who was regal as an empress. She was driven to teary stridency, begging him to give her what should have been hers, forced to sink to the degradation of demanding it. At last, he snapped: No, he wouldn't be the one to stay home with the children, or attend to her phone calls or arrange her meetings. Never. That was her job. His was to fight for freedom.

4

Parting

Her mother said she'd found the perfect match: Mr Mansoor owned a textile mill and would be open to suggestions from a designer like her. Furthermore, he would let her establish her own silk line if she so desired.

Riffat did not want to meet him or see his photographs. She wanted to remain a petrified shark tooth. Meeting the groom-to-be or even knowing what he looked like might prompt her to live again. She was just the kind of smooth granite that later made her break down when she saw other brides.

But she held on to one dream. As a wedding gift, her father gave her several acres of land outside Karachi. She'd do something with this land, something for herself, something that allowed her to sow all the turmoil and bliss of her London days. She was going to revive what had lain latent for thousands of years. She'd watch it grow into something soft and durable, so that when she, a tiny speck in time, vanished, it would still be there. Somewhere between the mulberry seeds and the yarns of indigo-washed silk, Riffat Mansoor learned to find her place in the universe again. She stepped outside the cocoon of the marble-bride and moved on.

But first, she had children. And before that, she looked at her groom.

He was everything Shafqat wasn't: fair-skinned, slouch-shouldered, tire-necked, short. How long does it take a woman to get accustomed to a man who repulses her? That's what she asked herself while lying under Mansoor, barely breathing while he pushed inside her on their wedding night. She somersaulted like a little top, a tiny feather in the mattress torn by springs. How long?

She knew well that another man would have left her the morning after, when the sheets weren't stained. But he said nothing. He seldom did. He had none of Shafqat's eclectic knowledge. He didn't get her laconic humor and offered none of his own. He played no delightful games, hated to walk, over-ate, and had absolutely no flair for conversation. When he spoke it was to grunt something about food, funds, and fabrics. About the latter, she joined in heartily, and throughout their nineteen years of marriage, he remained in awe of the confidence with which she did. He was one of the few who never discouraged her mulberry scheme. He was, from the day they married till the day before his death, deferring and suspicious. When he touched her he remained, as on the first night, so clumsy she developed a second skin, something that would molt and drop off after he fell asleep. In the finer, bottom layers dwelt the farm. And, underneath it all, Shafqat.

He tiptoed down the staircase of her sleep, stealing into keyholes, wriggling under cracks, helping himself to her rooms. She sealed these off, but then he'd slink into another, stretch out, flash his grin. She felt her insides had been completely and utterly violated and was left with no choice but to move into the gaping holes. The loneliness that engulfed her then was the worst agony ever known.

He came to her their fourth year apart. She had two children, he one. She welcomed him as she'd done in London after their first fight, when he'd brought the yellow roses. And then she threw him out for ever.

5

What Sumbul Says

AUGUST 1992

Riffat looked at Sumbul's child staunchly refusing to die. He whimpered and wheezed, and Sumbul told Riffat she wished the end would come quickly now. Riffat was about to tell her again that she could take a few days off, but she knew why Sumbul came to the farm. Home meant a mother-in-law working her from dawn till midnight, a belligerent husband who sometimes beat her, three other children, countless neighbors pouring in for gossip and meals bought with her money, an open sewer outside the kitchen, and absolutely nowhere for her to sit quietly for two minutes and sip her very own cup of tea. If she tried, the other women would snap, 'We never had such luxuries at your age.'

Yet, Sumbul found it in her to care for Riffat, though surely in Sumbul's eyes she lived like an empress. The contrast pained more because it highlighted the limits of each. What would it take to make Sumbul cross over to Riffat's? What would it have taken for Riffat to cross over to Shafqat's, or for him to leap past his own confines? He, who'd traveled

427

and ruminated more than anyone she knew, could never overcome them.

They both knew that. She could see it when they met for the last time at the tomb. He was sagging, in body and spirit, as far as possible from the youth who'd run from protest march to student meeting. He was waiting, like everyone else, for a meteor to shatter the walls. Like so many political liberals of the time, he turned out privately orthodox. As if a thin membrane snagged his beliefs each time he stepped inside his home and he could do nothing but surrender because change was only in God's hands. That was the principle he'd despised, but the one his life had followed. So he came to her, hoping for miracles. This one would be Dia.

'I know she's my child,' he began.

They stood behind a pillar underneath a dome clustered with bats. Riffat shuddered. 'You have no way of knowing.'

'She has something of me. I do know. My eyes. My curiosity . . .'

'Oh, and her mother can't give her that?'

'One simple test. As a doctor, I can arrange for it to be strictly confidential.'

'You fool,' she trembled. 'You're at your wits' end for something to fill your vacuum. You didn't let me in, you won't let your wife in, obviously your son's not enough. And your wife is barren. So now you want to disturb the peace I've built from ashes.'

'If she's my child I've a right to know,' he retorted. 'You can insult me all you want.' He stepped forward, causing her to stumble back. 'I have a right to stay in touch with her.'

She shut her eyes against the threat. He'd been watching Dia then. Stalking her in school? She didn't want to know. And she didn't want any more of the noise in the dome. The bats chittered as if in mockery, swinging above them like soothsayers. Riffat looked up at the net that had been strung across the dome's breadth. She thought back to the day she'd learned of Shafqat's marriage, and how, in her anger, she'd let her mother pick her groom. She'd regret that, always, and to make up for it, warned Dia often of the pernicious fatalism the nation was increasingly trapped in. It was a deadly cycle. Dia had to understand that in her own small but tenacious way, she could break it.

Shafqat stood a foot in front of her, less defiant than pathetic. She told him she'd slept with her husband the same night.

'At your initiation? Because you suspected?'

She asked what he planned on doing if a test proved him right. Take a child away from the father she'd known all her life? 'You think at fourteen, she's going to jump into your arms? You haven't seen Mansoor with her. They adore each other.'

He repeated, 'If she's my child, I should know it. I'll fight for her if I have to.'

'And of course, what she feels will have nothing to do with your decision?'

'Not if she's been brainwashed by you.'

'Not if you can't see past your own selfish needs.'

They argued till he said he'd kidnap Dia and draw the blood test whether she acquiesced or not, and that if he was right, he'd contest Mansoor in court.

She went home and wrestled with herself for weeks.

The period was already marred by anonymous phone calls in the middle of the night, presumably the work of the rejected dye-company, or some other severed thread in a business that was increasingly self-reliant. Between these anonymous calls were Shafqat's. Riffat was high-strung, Mansoor irritable and confused; the boys fought, Dia cried to the cook Inam Gul.

At last Riffat decided to tell her husband everything.

He was almost three hundred pounds then, and it was as if

she'd stuck a thorn into the mass. Whistling softly, he started to deflate.

His tiny black eyes seemed to look back over the last two decades of his life, dwelling especially on all he'd never said to her, from their first night together to this, their last. Or so she thought. Why had they never learned more of each other? They'd been married nineteen years while she and Shafqat had lived together barely four months. Yet, as Mansoor swore and wept, she could not go to him. She did not know what there was to go to.

Hours later, he stepped outside and climbed up the mulberry tree planted when Dia was born. While the neighbors gathered at the foot of the tree, he cried like a demented ape, and someone even rang the press. Riffat gathered her children to her and murmured, 'I shouldn't have told him.'

A frightened Dia asked to go to him.

'No.' She tightened her grip on the child, terrified of what Mansoor might say. The two had spent hours up in that tree, with pillows and sandalwood fans, where Dia transformed him from a mass of sedentary blubber to a tree-climbing, storytelling sprite. What would he tell Dia now?

She packed the children off to bed and the next morning, Mansoor was not in the house, and not in the tree. The car was gone. A chawkidaar in the neighborhood said he saw him driving off early in the morning.

'Any idea where he went?' she'd asked.

Nobody knew.

When he turned up dead at a village near the mouth of the Indus many days later, Shafqat left her alone. He said he'd continue to be tortured by this gift he'd never found, but he didn't want to cause Riffat any more pain by claiming it. And he kept his word.

But what Sumbul had come to tell her was that he couldn't keep away someone else.

Riffat sat up with a jolt. 'Good God, how do you know about Shafqat?'

Sumbul bowed her head and admitted that Salaamat had seen them at the tomb, years ago.

An enraged Riffat demanded, 'Can't we have a moment to ourselves in this country? Does anyone do anything besides snoop around?'

Without meeting Riffat's eye, Sumbul fanned her son with the edge of her dupatta.

Riffat shut her eyes. Her wrath was always misfired: at her husband, her daughter, and now her sweetest employee. Touching Sumbul's hand, she muttered an apology.

Sumbul cleared her throat. 'I've been wondering whether to tell you this. I think I should. It's not just that Salaamat saw you with him. It's that he's been seeing Dia with someone else. Someone you wouldn't want her to be with. His son.'

While Sumbul provided details, Riffat sat stunned. Then she whispered, 'I cannot think. Please leave me.'

After Sumbul shut the door behind her, Riffat crawled into the bedroom where she and Mansoor had slept when the family spent weekends at the farm. She received solitude like a perfume rarely permitted, lavishing it on her skin till her temples gradually stilled. She looked up at the ceiling fan, at the tiny ring of metal in the center, and saw Dia cowering in the corner of a grimy open plot with Daanish. Fearing censure as she'd once feared it too, but also relishing his assurances, his touch. Did the boy have the father's cloud-fracturing smile and his own delightful stories? Did he have strong limbs and a full-blooded scent? Did he give her what was hers to have without asking or did he keep that only for himself?

Riffat lay flat on the bed, arms akimbo. She stayed that way a long, long time.

DIA

I

Fourth Life

Dia sat on the grass, her back against the mulberry tree where her father had sheltered the night before his death. In her lap was the book with the tales and pictures he'd loved. Around her drooped a leaden sky, nuzzling the gate where the armed guard paced.

There'd been no rain since the downpour last month. The sultry, torpid air was a thick compress holding the torrent back. Perspiration dotted the thin fuzz of her upper lip and the hair around her temples crimped like her mother's.

A few days ago, she'd begun writing her own account of the Empress Hsi-Ling-Shih, the founder of sericulture. *At one time the cloth was as valuable as oil and men went to equally grotesque lengths to acquire it.*

But now Dia decided to scratch the sentence out. She wasn't meant to stop the clock at the tortured Greek, Bengali or Benarsi weavers, nor pause over the Caspian Sea two thousand years ago, to watch Roman soldiers fleeing the Parthians. The Parthians waved banners of silk, and the Romans ran because something so fine could only be the work of sorcery. She might reconstruct that some other time.

Now she went forward, clenching the hour hand before it could race to the present. It was a blustery day in spring and the clock struck 4.00 p.m. She wrote:

The Empress stepped out of a bus with a portfolio tucked under her arm and went to meet the Emperor outside a brick café. She put a maroon silk scarf around his neck. She'd designed it, choosing the color because it matched his eyes. He said the pale red selvage of embroidery was a bit effeminate.

'Are you rejecting my gift? After all the ones you've sent me on wild-goose chases for?'

'But you enjoyed each chase, didn't you?' He kissed her, swiftly adding that he loved the scarf and would wear it even in Karachi in mid-summer.

They sat in a corner of the café. Under the table, she slipped her feet out of her sandals and over his boots. He told her she'd always be his. That was the only thing that wouldn't change. Otherwise, he could taste a difference in the air. Around the globe, people were taking risks to speak their minds, and they spoke with such conviction, such humanity. His father was part of that, wasn't he?

She nodded. The blood rushed to her cheeks as he traced her bones. They talked until twilight of her farm-to-be, the children they'd have, the home they'd build.

And then they did a little dance, wriggling right there on the floor of the coffee shop. There was a rip, a tearing of hide, a circuit of the earth, and Riffat became Dia loving Daanish in the cove.

'The next time I'm here,' he clasped her in his arms, 'I'll teach you to swim.' While he described the magnificent creatures of the sea, the wind tossed his fresh scent with the fecund fragrance of her groin. 'Like mushrooms simmering in the salt air,' he said.

The sand was a pumice stone. It chafed her back and rent a chasm down her spine. Another creature wormed its way out, and when it was free, Nini stood before them.

'I want a change,' she said, carrying a tea tray. The Emperor's son took his cup and ate a chicken patty. The halwa she'd made herself. Because it was just right, he slid a ring around her finger.

'She comes from good blood,' his mother said.

'Have another cup of tea,' she said.

'Lucky Nini,' the sisters giggled, dreaming of their turn.

Dia stopped.

She tore the page out and breathed heavily. This wasn't working.

She hadn't eaten in days. Severely dehydrated, she felt woozy and her head ached. Her clothes were drenched in sweat. They were the same she'd worn for days, as she sat here each morning, trying to synthesize what she felt. Inam Gul kept calling but she ignored him. Her mother also called but she wanted no more of her. At least not yet. She looked up. Daanish's flight had left that morning. Perhaps at this very moment, he was crossing the Atlantic. That's where she was, and she had to find her way back. No more detours.

She remembered their last meeting.

They'd sat in the unfinished house, in the section he called the guestroom, when the shadow appeared again.

'This time you go see who it is,' she whispered. 'I'm staying here.' Daanish stood up, and then they saw two shapes approach, one distinctly larger than the other. He took a few brave strides, leaving Dia concealed behind a wall. She peered out and gasped: it was Anu. Behind her, Salaamat.

'What are you doing here?' Daanish's voice was surprisingly meek.

'I should ask you the same,' she replied. 'But I know the answer. Where is she?'

Dia stepped out, scowling at Salaamat. He'd told. She forced herself to look at Anu, who was scrutinizing her.

'The gift,' Anu muttered. 'Could it be? But the nose is not his. Nor the mouth. You are short, he wasn't.'

'Anu,' Daanish interrupted. 'This is Dia. Dia, my mom.'

Dia turned to him, exasperated. 'We've already met. Remember?' To Anu she uttered a futile greeting.

Anu did not return it. She was saying, 'Hair too straight, but complexion nearly his.'

Daanish looked helplessly over his shoulder at Dia. 'This is way harder on her than it ought to be.'

Why don't you tell her that, Dia thought. And while you're at it, ask her what she's talking about. She rubbed her forehead uneasily as Anu's ghastly inspection continued.

At last her gaze drifted up. Gouging Dia's eyes, she nodded, 'His.'

'I'll call you later,' Daanish hurriedly declared. 'Let's go,' he pulled Anu away.

Dia was left alone with Salaamat. 'What are you waiting for?' she wheezed. 'You've spoiled it all. You have none of your father's goodness!'

Storming by him, she wished she had it in her to kick his shin, or strike his cheek. Anything to make him repent, to shatter that stony composure. But she didn't.

It was in the days when Dia waited for Daanish to call that Riffat told her about Shafqat. Dia would not speak except to tell Riffat she'd only ever have the one father she'd known. It was her mother there were two of.

She retreated then, just like her father had done.

Riffat followed, pleading, 'Anything you want, Dia. Please say it. Anything.'

Anything?

And then Daanish called.

They said nothing for a while, each listening to the soft breath of the other through the receiver. She wondered if, like her, he was recalling her every feature, puzzling over which they shared, and which they didn't. Anu had stopped at the eyes. But Dia's were a different shape from Daanish's – hers were rounder, his longer. Or was she already rewriting him?

At last she whispered, 'Now I know why I've collected stories of origins all my life. I'll never know my own.' She fell silent. Her own voice was alien to her. Then, 'What can we do?'

She thought she heard a gulp. After several more seconds, she asked, 'Are you there?'

He sighed. 'I don't know what to do. Maybe Khurram's right. I should do what everyone wants. Marrying Nissrine would make so many people happy.'

Dia was in the dining room, the same place she'd stood when discussing Daanish with Nini. Was that just a few months ago? She'd felt revolted then; only now did she realize what revulsion was: a pressure in the pit of her stomach, rising in a scream like a tea-kettle's: 'What the hell are you talking about?'

Daanish's answer was terse, his voice hard. Good – she should not be the only one enraged. He said, 'Listen before you judge.'

'Talk then,' she spat.

'This has been hard for Anu. Try to understand that you're not the only one affected. If I can make up for all Anu's suffered, why shouldn't I?' His voice trailed. 'Maybe just a simple engagement now. I don't know. I haven't decided. The wedding could come much later, if I'm still inclined.'

Dia wrapped an arm around her gut, trying to shake the picture of Nini marrying the man on the other end of the line. The one with the comforting, lilting voice. Yes, even now, she could hear that lilt. And feel the smooth stomach strung with muscle and just barely, a little hump to each side. She'd always thought she wouldn't mind if those love handles grew, if that was what was imminent. She could smell him too. And she could lean into him, even as he pushed her away. Even as history pushed him away. She insisted, 'But you said she was nothing to you! Think about that if nothing else!'

'Dia,' he replied, 'what do you want? Don't pretend things haven't changed . . .'

There it was again: *What do you want?* She cut in, 'Pulling Nini back into the equation is not what I want. I'll tell you what I do want. Answers. Tell me – would this have happened anyway? Even if our parents never knew each other? And tell me this: do you need another zipper now? Or are you just going to leave yours open all the time?'

'Screw you!' he shot back. 'You're just mad because for the first time in your pretty, sheltered life, you're up against a wall.' He was panting, hurling incomplete sentences at her: 'That's why you're attacking me!' She could hang up. She could just hang up. 'Well I've been up against more walls than you could ever imagine . . .'

'I *don't* want your self-pity.'

'Aba's dead. I never knew him. He cheated on my mother . . .'

'Almost ditto for me,' she interrupted.

'Don't butt in again,' he snarled. 'I have to support my mom,' he took a deep breath, 'and the best way is to work in a country that bombs others but lets me in. They could just as easily let *them* in and bomb *me*. I have to find a place in that puzzle.'

Dia chewed her cuticles till she tasted blood. 'Have you finished?'

'All yours.'

'Do you have any idea how completely humiliated you have made me feel? How naked I felt when your mother walked in on us? I'm still feeling filthy. And you said nothing to her in my defense. They were blaming me, not you. That's something you'll never have to understand.' She crouched on the carpet.

Daanish was silent. 'Perhaps I should go,' he murmured at last. 'We're only making things harder for each other.'

If they hung up now, neither would call again. Riffat had said this would be their last conversation, and Anu had not wanted it at all. The clock ticked.

His voice was gentler when he added, 'This might be a strange thing to say but I can't help wondering about your mother. I admit I have blamed her. But I'll try to look beyond that. I have a picture of them, you know. They made each other happy.'

She let the tears flow now. Then, 'You were right. I should go.'

'Right. Good luck, Dia.'

She snorted, 'Luck!'

'Well, this is hard, you know. So, don't be a stranger.'

'*What?*' she choked.

He'd hung up.

Outside in the garden, Dia wiped the sweat off her face with the edge of her kameez. She stared at the page on her lap. Today, finally, she'd fill it. Then she'd go inside and look closely at herself in the mirror, the way she'd been doing for days. The face was changing; there was less and less of Daanish in it.

She adjusted her position on the plush grass and shut her eyes. Her mother had her farm. Daanish had Amreeka. Nini, possibly, had Daanish. Everyone had a plan but her. Maybe there was something that needed to be done before she could find one. But she didn't know what, and she didn't know who to ask.

She picked up her pen again. Maybe she did know.

Nini and Daanish retreated into the past. The Emperor and Empress molted a fourth time.

He was enormous, nearly ninety kilos, with slouching shoulders and a thick neck. She was slender and poised, even after bearing two sons. The boys were sleeping in the shack next to the shed where the silkworms would be housed. The couple watched their children sleep. Then they tiptoed out into the clear night. They were naked and held hands.

It had rained the day before, a light, steady patter that polished the stars and stirred the earth, so the creatures dreaming in its bowels stretched and tasted something brisk. The irrigation canals gurgled a salient song. Mansoor told his love there was plenty of groundwater in this land she'd been gifted, which she wanted transformed into a silkworm farm. He said he was proud of her, that he was the luckiest man in the world: two boys asleep in the cottage, a beautiful wife by his side, a second business on the way.

A sliver of a moon hung before them. It cast a soft, lambent light on her cheeks and her brown curls shone like copper. Fireflies orbited her navel. He touched her there. 'If we have a third child,' he said, 'I hope it's a girl.' And then he planted a kiss in the small cool pit, and she laughed. The glowworms dispersed, fluttering like saffron ribbons, leaving them in a trail of gold dust.

They ambled between the mulberry seedlings only recently sowed. The ground was wet, their footsteps muffled as a cat's. A nightjar called her mate. Bats brushed their ears. Riffat said it was both beautiful and frightening at this late hour, with not a soul about and a graveyard just up the road.

'Kings and queens lie there,' he said. 'They rest side by side, just like I want us to.' When she shuddered, he added, 'In the meantime, you should squeeze into me.'

She wrapped her arms around his globe of a stomach and they came to a clearing. 'This is where I want to plant the lost dyes of this soil. The colors are faster than synthetic ones and they smell good. Plus, it'll help me feel that I'm at one end of a cord that leads back thousands of years. The cord is here,' she said, pointing to her navel. He kissed it again, and again she laughed. In the clearing, husband and wife made love as easily as shedding skin.

Afterwards, he sat behind her and she leaned into his chest. From the highway came the sound of a car. They listened as the engine pitched into the next day. He twirled the curls at her temples and asked, 'What if you had the chance to do this all over – from our wedding, to our sons, to this moment right now, and whatever lies ahead. Would you marry me again?'

She looked up at his chin, touched it. His flesh was scabrous and left hers tingling. 'Yes,' she smiled. 'Of course I would.'

EPILOGUE

Birth

'Don't go near the huts along the shore,' his uncle warns.

The boy rests against a dune, far from the huts. He wants to please his mamu. He wants his seekh-kebab locks, his cigarettes, his job that puts him in the driver's seat of a long and beautiful van. So he won't even look at those huts.

His mother is in her grandmother's teahouse. The old woman died today. She was more than a hundred. The women bathe her so her soul ascends to heaven in a quiet boat. Then the men can bury her outside the shrine of the great martyr. In the old days, when a fisherman drowned at sea, he became a hero and got a shrine all his own. But now there are more martyrs than land, and anyway, the men don't drown while fishing, they drown while swimming up to the great ship and peeping inside the portholes.

His uncle points to it. 'You see that anchor line?'

The child nods.

'When I was your age, we'd dare each other to swim out and touch it. Even in the summer months, when the sea was a ferocious brute, sucking you in with long, slimy tentacles.'

The boy squeals.

'When we reached the line, we'd bounce up and wave to the others waiting on the beach. Want to try?'

The boy hesitates. He grew up in the city and does not know how to swim. The best he can do is suck on a hookah like his great-grandmother did, before she died.

'Come on,' coaxes his uncle. 'It's the winter now. The sea is calm. She isn't hungry. She'll spit you up even if you try to slip into her bowels.'

'Why don't you do it?' the boy blurts out.

His uncle laughs. 'That's a child's game!' His ringlets blow in the breeze and smoke twists out from his nostrils. His van waits on the road. He has returned to his village for the first time since he left, many years ago. He'd told the boy he did so only for fear of Sumbul. 'Your mother is far, far more vicious than any sea,' he'd winked.

The boy now asks, 'Where do you go in your van?'

'Oh,' he slides into the dune, his thick black feet sinking into the cool sand, 'I pick up boxes full of very heavy things and deliver them to a shop. That's my work.'

'Can I come with you?'

Again he laughs. 'Listen. If you swim out to the anchor line, I'll take you with me next time.'

The boy hangs his head in shame. He can't do it. Not even for the honor of riding beside his mother's magnificent brother. He stares at the pale expanse of beach stretching around him.

'Okay, I'll go,' his uncle sits up. 'You stand right here like a lighthouse. When you see me surface, blink your lights. Like this.' He waved his arms. 'Agreed?'

The boy nods but is still too ashamed to look up. He takes his place, watching the older man saunter to the water's edge, take off his kameez and slink into a swell.

While he waits, something distracts him. Tiny mounds of grain erupt first beside one foot, then the other. A little boat trundles out, replete with oars and even a rudder.

'What's this?' he says to the air.

No one answers.

Something tells him they are the turtles he has heard about. Baby ones. 'Come back!' he calls his mamu. 'Look at this!' He beckons the distant cluster of aunts and uncles around the teahouse. But no one hears; they are all busy. He is alone, and yet the beach is a flurry of lumbering saucers the size of his palm, bursting out from under him, all heading for the sea.

His instinct warns of danger: gulls soar overhead, dogs pad overland. He follows the migration, waving both arms, scanning the water for his uncle. But the anchor line alone cuts the glassy sea.

Then he hears his mother call. 'Lunch is ready! And bring your mamu too!'

The child frowns. He is busy but his mother would say he is too young to be busy. Kneeling, he picks up a hatchling and turns it upside down. The creature's feet wriggle imploringly and the boy giggles.

His mother calls once more. 'Hurry up!'

He frowns again. When his uncle surfaced, he would expect him to be here, blinking like a lighthouse. He can't leave. But why hadn't Mamu appeared yet?

In his hand, the baby turtle continues to squirm. Some of its siblings have reached the surf. 'All right,' he says to the one in his grasp. 'Time for you to go too.' He puts it down. When his mother calls a third time, angry now, he casts an anxious look out at the sea then hurries to his great-grandmother's teahouse.

Halfway there he looks back. Still no sign of Mamu. More turtles melt into the waves breaking on the shore. A few remain tentatively where he'd last seen them. Then he observes one – perhaps the one he'd lifted – making for the huts. You should be going the other way, he thinks. He decides to tell it.

Jogging over to the hatchling, he picks it up and turns it around. The little creature's legs again wave in the air. The child squats and gently releases it. Touching ground, the turtle immediately bursts forward, this time toward the sea, as though its course had never changed.

ACKNOWLEDGMENTS

I am grateful to the outstanding, independent-minded writers and journalists whose efforts formed the basis of my research on the Gulf War. While space does not permit them all to be named, I do want to single out one book: *The Fire This Time* (Thunder's Mouth Press, 1992), by former US Attorney General Ramsey Clark. This finely documented analysis, which the author presents simply, with compassion and outrage, is strongly recommended to anyone seeking a view of the war that challenges the one presented by the US Government, with the cooperation of the mainstream media.

I am also grateful to Dave, for being my most insightful critic, for giving me the time and space to complete this book, and most of all, for our love; V.K. Karthika, for opening the envelope and discovering my first novel; Laura Susijn and Philip Gwyn Jones, for launching me farther than I ever dreamed I could go; and my parents, for their continued love and support, prayers and generosity of spirit.